A THREAT OF SHADOWS

THE KEEPER CHRONICLES BOOK 1, EXPANDED 2ND EDITION

JA ANDREWS

A Threat of Shadows, The Keeper Chronicles Book 1

Expanded 2nd edition

Website: www.jaandrews.com

SECOND EDITION

Ebook ISBN: 978-0-9976144-6-6

Paperback ISBN: 978-0-9976144-7-3

For my husband.
This story has always been for you.

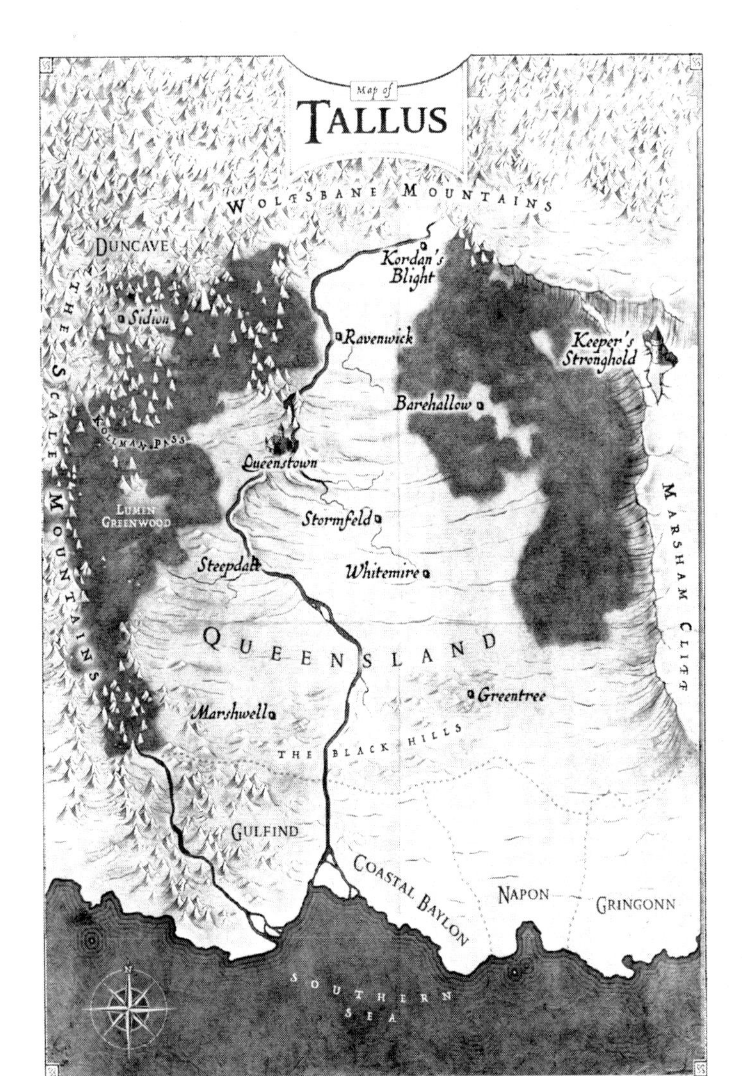

Map of
TALLUS
WOLFSBANE MOUNTAINS
DUNCAVE
THE SCALE MOUNTAINS
Sidion
Kordan's Blight
Ravenwick
Keeper's Stronghold
Barehallow
KOLLMAN PASS
Queenstown
LUMIN GREENWOOD
Stormfeld
Steepdale
Whitemire
MARSHAM CLIFF
QUEENSLAND
Greentree
Marshwell
THE BLACK HILLS
GULFIND
COASTAL BAYLON
NAPON
GRINGONN
SOUTHERN SEA
N

CHAPTER ONE

THE DEEPER ALARIC rode into the woods, the more something felt... off. This forest had always fit like a well-worn cloak. But tonight, the way the forest wrapped around felt familiar, but not quite comfortable, as though it remembered wrapping around a slightly different shape.

"This path used to be easier to follow," Alaric said to his horse, Beast, as they paused between patches of late spring moonlight. Alaric peered ahead, looking for the trail leading to the Stronghold. He found it running like a scratch through the low brush to the right. "If the Keepers weren't too meek to hold grudges, I'd think the old men were hiding it from me."

All the usual smells of pine and moss and dirt wove through the air, the usual sounds of little animals going about their lives, but Alaric kept catching a hint of something different. Something more complicated than he wanted to deal with.

Around the next turn, the trail ran straight into a wide tree trunk. Alaric leaned as far to the side as he could, but he couldn't see around it. "I could be wrong about the Keepers holding grudges."

Well, if they didn't want him at the Stronghold, that was too bad. He didn't need a warm welcome. He just needed to find one book with one antidote. With a little luck, the book would be easy to find and he could leave quickly. With a lot of luck, he'd get in and out without having to answer anyone's questions about what he'd been doing for the past year.

Beast circled the tree and found the path again, snaking out the other side. As his hooves thudded down on it, a howl echoed through the woods.

The horse froze, and Alaric grabbed the pouch hanging around his neck, protecting it against his chest. He closed his eyes, casting out past the nearest trees and through the woods, searching for the blazing energy of the wolf. He sensed nothing beyond the tranquil glow of the trees and the dashing flashes of frightened rabbits.

"That's new." Alaric opened his eyes and peered into the darkness.

A louder howl broke through the night. Beast shuddered.

"It's all right." Alaric patted Beast's neck as he cast farther out. The life energy of an animal as large as a wolf would be like a bonfire among the trees, but there was nothing near them. "It's not wolves. Just disembodied howls." He kept his voice soothing, hoping to calm the animal.

"That didn't sound as reassuring as I meant it to. But a real wolf pack wouldn't keep howling as they got closer. If we were being tracked by wolves, we wouldn't know it."

Beast's ears flicked back and forth, alert for another howl.

"Okay, that wasn't reassuring, either." Alaric nudged him forward. "C'mon we're almost to the Wall."

A third howl tore out of the darkness right beside them.

Beast reared back, whinnying in terror. Alaric grabbed for the saddle and swore. He pressed his hand to Beast's neck.

"Paxa," he said, focusing energy through his hand and into Beast. A shock of pain raced across Alaric's palm where it touched the horse, as the energy rushed through.

Mid-snort, Beast settled and stood still.

Alaric shook out his hand and looked thoughtfully into the woods. This wasn't about a grudge, or at least the howls weren't directed at him. Any Keeper would know there were no wolves. Even one as inadequate as he would know there was no energy, no *vitalle,* behind the sounds. So what was the purpose of it? The path had never been like this before.

With Beast calm, Alaric set him back into a steady walk. Two more howls rang out from the woods, but Beast ambled along, unruffled. Alaric rubbed his still-tingling palm.

Beast paused again as the trail ran into another wide tree.

Alaric growled in frustration. The path to the Keepers' Stronghold shouldn't be this troublesome for a Keeper.

Unless it no longer recognized him as one. That was a sobering thought.

As they skirted around the tree, a white face thrust itself out of the trunk. Alaric jerked away as the hazy form of a man leaned out toward him. When the figure didn't move, Alaric reined in Beast and forced himself to study it. It held no life energy, it was just an illusion—like the wolves.

The figure was a young man. He had faded yellow hair and milky white skin. Once the initial shock wore off, the man was not particularly frightening.

"What are you supposed be? A friendly ghost?" Alaric asked.

It hung silent on the tree. Alaric leaned forward and backward, but the ghost remained still, staring off into the woods.

"The howls were more frightening than you." Alaric set Beast to walking again.

"You are lost," the ghost whispered as he passed.

Alaric gave a short laugh. "I've been lost many times in my life, but this isn't one of them. And if it's your job to scare people off, you should consider saying something more chilling and less...depressing."

Beast kept walking, and Alaric turned to watch the ghost fade into the darkness behind them.

A rasp pulled his attention forward. Another white form slid out of the tree they were approaching. This one was a young woman. She was rather pretty, for a ghost.

"Hello." Alaric gave her a polite nod.

"You have failed," she whispered. "You have failed everyone."

Alaric scowled. The words rang uncomfortably true.

Alaric stopped Beast in front of the ghost. Behind the woman's face, Alaric saw thin, silver runes carved on the bark. He couldn't read them through the ghost, but he didn't need to. Narrowing his focus, he cast out ahead of them along the trail, brushing against the trunks with his senses. Now that he knew what he was looking for, he felt the subtle humming runes dotting the trees ahead.

Alaric sat back in the saddle. This wasn't what he expected from the Keepers. The old men protected their privacy like paranoid hermits, but they'd never tried to scare people away before. Of course, these ghosts weren't frightening. If the Keepers were going to make ghosts, these are the kind they would make.

Years ago, during his "Defeat by Demoralization" lesson, Keeper Gerone had declared, "Control the emotions, control the man!" Gerone was probably responsible for the depressing ghosts.

The ghost runes were on almost every tree now, faces appearing every few steps.

"Your powers are worthless," the next whispered and Alaric flinched.

"It's your fault," another rasped. "All your fault."

Alaric clenched his jaw and stared ahead as the whispers surrounded him.

When he passed close to one large tree, a ghost thrust out close to him. Alaric turned toward it and saw his own face looking back at him. A pale, wasted version of himself. His black hair was faded to a lifeless grey, and his skin, far from being tanned from traveling, was bleached a wrinkly bone white. Only his eyes had stayed dark, sinking from a healthy brown to deep, black pits.

Alaric stared, repulsed, at the withered apparition of himself—it was decades older than his forty years. The ghost looked tired, a deep crease furrowed between its brows. Alaric reached up and rubbed his own forehead.

The ghost leaned closer.

"She's dead," it whispered.

Guilt stabbed into him, deep and familiar. He shuddered, grabbing the pouch at his neck, his mind flooded with the image of Evangeline's sunken face.

Alaric slammed his palm against the rune on the trunk.

"*Uro*!" Pain raced through his hand again. He poured

energy into the tree, willing it to burn. The bark smoked as he seared the rune off.

Out of the corner of his eye, pulses of white light appeared along the path ahead of them. He glanced at them, but the distraction had consequences, and the pain flared, arcing up each finger. He gasped and narrowed his focus back to the energy flowing through his palm. The pain receded slightly. The ghost stared a moment longer, then faded away. Alaric dropped his arm, leaving a hand-shaped scorch mark on the trunk where the rune had been.

"She's dead."

Alaric's head snapped forward.

The trees ahead of him were full of ghosts, each a washed-out version of himself.

"Dead… She's dead… Dead." The words filled the air.

Alaric clutched the pouch at his neck until he felt the rough stone inside.

A ghost reached toward him. "She's dead…" Its voice rattled in a long sigh.

Alaric spurred Beast into a gallop, trusting the horse to follow the trail. The whispers clung to them as they ran. Alaric shrank down, hunching his shoulders, wresting his mind away from the memory of his wife's tired eyes, her pale skin.

The trees ended, and they raced out into a silent swath of grass, running up to the base of an immense cliff. Alaric pulled Beast to a stop, both of them breathing hard. Gripping the saddle, Alaric looked back into the trees. The forest was dark and quiet.

"I take it back," he said, catching his breath, "the ghosts were worse than the wolves." He sat in the saddle, pushing back the dread that was enveloping him. She wasn't dead.

The ghosts were just illusions. He'd get the antidote tonight. She'd be fine.

When his heart finally slowed, he gave Beast an exhausted pat on the neck.

"This path used to be a *lot* easier to follow."

CHAPTER TWO

ALARIC TURNED AWAY from the forest. Before him stood a short section of stone wall twice his height. The unusual thing about the Wall was that, instead of enclosing anything, it sat flush against the base of the Marsham Cliffs.

Ignoring the looming presence of the forest behind him, Alaric cast out toward the Wall until he sensed the stone with the vibrating runes. His left hand ached from the last two spells, but there was no point in having both hands sore. This time, he gathered some *vitalle* from the grass around him. With a grim smile, he pulled some from the nearest ghost-trees as well and lifted his hand toward the Wall.

"*Aperi.*" Pain burst through his hand like fire. He let out a groan as the stones shifted. An arch opened, revealing a dark tunnel boring deep into the cliff.

Alaric walked Beast inside and turned to look back at the trees. He caught sight of a milky white face, and his stomach clenched.

Alaric thrust his hand toward the entrance. "*Cluda.*"

This time, the shock raced all the way up to his elbow.

Alaric gasped and clutched his arm to his chest as the opening of the tunnel sealed itself off, leaving them in blackness. He clenched his jaw until the pain faded. He should have used the other hand for that last one.

Alaric started Beast toward the bright moonlight at the far end of the tunnel, wishing he could use the *paxa* spell to calm himself.

In the calmness of the tunnel, the memory of Evangeline's hollowed face flooded his mind again, followed by the familiar anguish.

He pushed that image away and drew out the memory of the night they had walked together along the edge of the Greenwood. She had peered into the woods hoping to catch a glimpse of an elf. He had explained that no one caught sight of an elf by chance, but she had ignored him, jumping at every flash of a bird or a squirrel.

He held that idea for a long moment. The way she had looked. The way she had been. The way she would be again.

He tucked the memory away and refocused on tonight. All he needed was to slip into the library and find one book. It should be easy.

Of course, the path should have been easy, too. The wolves and ghosts made no sense. Alaric had lived at the Stronghold for two decades and had traveled that path countless times. It had never given him trouble. It had never needed to. The Wall was more than enough defense for the Stronghold.

To anyone but a Keeper, the Wall would appear to be just an odd bit of wall sitting right against a cliff face. None but a Keeper knew how to open the tunnel, and the tunnel was the only entrance to the valley holding the Keepers' Stronghold.

The obvious question was whether the Keepers had

changed the path in the year since Alaric had stormed out, or whether Alaric had changed, and this was how the path had always treated strangers.

Beast nickered as the tunnel spilled out into a grassy field in a narrow valley. Ahead of them a tower rose, its white stones shining in the moonlight. The smells of the day lingered in the valley, bread and smoke and drying herbs, but this late at night, everything was quiet.

A glitter of light from the very top of the tower beckoned him. The Wellstone.

It tempted him to go up, to dive into the pool of Keeper memories that it held. It was the other option besides the book, the quicker option. He needed knowledge from Kordan, and Kordan had been a Keeper. He would have stored his memories in the Wellstone, just like every other Keeper for the last two hundred years. Certainly, the information Alaric needed would be there.

But the price to use the Wellstone was too high. Evangeline was safe for now. The reference Alaric had found about Kordan had mentioned a book, so he was here for a book. *Please let the antidote be in the book.*

Alaric crossed the grass to the wooden front doors of the tower, bleached to grey in the moonlight and flung wide open as always. Alaric stepped through them into the heavy stillness of the entry hall. He ignored the lanterns sitting on the shelf next to the door, reluctant to disturb the darkness. Hopefully, he could find the book and leave without having to explain himself, or his long absence, to anyone.

On his left, the wall was dark with cloaks. Reaching out, he brushed his hand along the soft fabric. True Keepers' robes, managing to be both substantial and light, might be the thing he missed the most.

Before he left, he would take one. He'd leave this thin, worn cloak behind, the one that wasn't quite black and wasn't quite right, and take a real Keeper's robe with him.

He walked out the end of the hall, through the open center of the tower to the entrance of the library.

He paused near the door, hanging back in the shadows. The library was lit by glowing golden orbs tucked into nooks between the bookshelves. He could hear the scratching of a pen as a Keeper wrote somewhere deep in the library, but there was no one to be seen. He stepped up to the wooden railing in front of him and looked out into an immense circular room. Four stories below him lay a tiled floor with patterns swirling like eddies in a stream. Three stories above him, a glass ceiling showed the starry sky. A narrow walkway stretched around the room alongside age-darkened bookshelves.

If the Keepers could be relied on for anything, it was to record things. And then cross-reference that knowledge. Repeatedly. Alaric wasn't sure where Kordan's book would be shelved, but all of his works should be recorded in the Keeper's Registry.

Alaric walked to the winding ramp spiraling along the inside of the railing, connecting each floor to the next, grateful for the thick rugs that muffled his steps. He climbed up two floors, still seeing no one, and made his way to the thick black tome that recorded the life's work of each Keeper.

A puff of air breezed past him as he opened the Registry, as though the book was crammed with more knowledge than it could hold. It had always felt strange to hold this book, knowing that one day, there would be an entry in it under his own name.

Alaric flipped to the index. No listing for Kordan. He tried alternate spellings, but found nothing. He growled in frustration.

"That has got to be the most boring book in the library," a voice said from behind him.

Alaric's heart skipped a beat at the sound of the Shield's voice. Silently cursing the thick step-muffling rugs, he turned to face the leader of the Keepers.

"You've been gone over a year, Alaric. Please tell me you didn't come back just to browse the Registry."

The tiny form of the Shield stood behind him smiling, his bald head barely above Alaric's elbow. His clear eyes peered up at Alaric from below wooly white eyebrows. Alaric braced for questions, but the Shield just smiled benignly, displaying none of the accusation that Alaric expected.

"How did you know I was here?"

The Shield shrugged. "I'm so old that at this point, I'm bordering on omniscient."

Alaric let out a short laugh, his tension releasing with it.

The Shield glanced down at the book in Alaric's hand. "As any omniscient would ask, what are you looking for? And can I help you find it?"

Alaric almost said no, but though the Shield was not omniscient, the amount of knowledge contained behind those fluffy brows was astounding. He could save Alaric hours of research.

Alaric offered the book to him. "I'm looking for information on a Keeper named Kordan. He lived about a hundred years ago."

The Shield weighed the words for a moment, and Alaric knew he was making connections and filling in blanks until he understood far more than Alaric had said. The old man waved away the Registry and turned toward the shelves. "You're looking in the wrong book. Kordan was a Keeper, but after dabbling in some darker magic, he left the Stronghold and requested to be removed from the ranks of Keepers. He'll be recorded over here." He pulled another book off the shelf, *Histories and Works of the Gifted.* "Specifically, he'll be under the *Magic-Capable, Affiliation-Unknown* section since he never aligned himself with any other group. He's under Kordan the Harvester."

Magic-Capable, Affiliation-Unknown. Alaric sighed. *I'm right there with you, Kordan.*

"He has a town named after him," the Shield continued. "Kordan's Blight. It's up near the foot of the Wolfsbane Mountains."

"Kordan's Blight? That sounds... ominous." Alaric slid the Registry back into place on the shelf.

"Mmm," the Shield agreed, flipping pages. "There wasn't much of a town when he lived there, just a few homesteads. Kordan lived there for some time doing experiments. I'm sure you can guess that his time there didn't end well. You know how local legends are. The memory of him stuck, and when a town did grow there, it inherited the name. Ahh, here it is." The Shield set his finger on a paragraph then looked up at Alaric with a searching look.

"So... you came back looking for information on a Keeper, and you decided to come down here. To the library..."

Alaric didn't answer the unspoken question.

"...when we have a Wellstone upstairs which holds all of Kordan's memories."

"I'm not using it," Alaric said flatly. He wouldn't pay the Wellstone's fee. He wouldn't share with it all his memories since the last time he used it. The memories of meeting Evangeline, of when she was poisoned, of the things he had done to save her and the dark days since. "My memories are my own. I'm not interested in sharing them with the Wellstone so they can be studied and analyzed." His voice came out sharper than he had intended.

The Shield considered him for a long moment. "Then it is safe to assume you don't intend to stay."

Alaric let his eyes run over the books in front of him. Shelves and shelves of annals, a running history of Queensland kept by the Keepers for hundreds of years.

"But I need you back at court," the Shield said when Alaric didn't answer. "The queen needs you back."

"I can't."

"Queen Saren needs a Keeper to advise her."

"Send someone else."

"Who?" The calmness in the Shield's voice cracked. "Who here has the strength to travel two days to the palace, then keep up with the pressure of life at court?"

The answer to that was obvious. There was only one other Keeper young enough to travel. "Send Will."

"Will never came back from the Greenwood. It's been over a year, and we've received no word."

Alaric looked sharply at the Shield. Will should have only been gone a couple of months. He was in his thirties, barely younger than Alaric. He'd been like a brother to Alaric since they had joined the Keepers twenty years ago.

"Well, let someone else read some books and take over," Alaric snapped.

"If all Saren needed was books, I'd send her books. But I don't even have another Keeper who can piece together history and politics and answers the way you can. No one else who can draw out the important parts of history and make it useful."

Alaric shook his head. He couldn't go back to court. Not right now.

The Shield's voice grew quieter. "How is Evangeline?"

Alaric felt the familiar stab of guilt. He took a deep breath. The library air smelled of paper and ink and knowledge. He'd missed that smell. He took another breath. That was all he seemed to do these days, take deep breaths.

The Shield let the question drop. "What are you looking for from Kordan?"

Another hard question. It wasn't that he didn't want to tell the Shield, exactly, but it was hard to say out loud. The hope was too fragile, like the new skin of ice over a pond. Just the effort of shaping it into words could shatter it.

But that fear was irrational. He looked down into the Shield's face. "I'm looking for the antidote to rock snake venom."

The old man's eyebrows shot up in surprise. "I wouldn't have thought to look in Kordan's work."

Under other circumstances, Alaric would be pleased that he'd told the Shield something he didn't already know.

The Shield turned back to the book, and his surprise turned into a scowl. "This lists one reference in the library from Kordan, a scroll. But it's not in the medicinal section." He glanced up at Alaric. "It's on the restricted shelves."

The restricted shelves? Alaric felt the hope he'd been carrying so carefully crack.

The Shield gave Alaric a long, measured look. "I hope you find the answers you need, Alaric." He turned to go.

"There were ghosts outside the Wall," Alaric said quietly.

The Shield paused and turned back. "There are always

ghosts on the path back home. They must have never had anything to say to you before."

Alaric looked at the old man in surprise. "You see them?"

The Shield gave a short, bitter laugh. "Every time. The sentinels may be the reason that so few of the older Keepers ever leave. They're too afraid to take the path back. You live long enough, Alaric, and you build up quite a few ghosts." The smile he gave Alaric now was tinged with sadness. "I meant what I told you before you left. No one is defined by a single choice. All of us have ghosts. And regrets. If you ever see a road back to us, I will be glad of it."

Alaric felt a momentary swell of gratitude. But the Shield didn't know what Alaric had done, the places he'd gone, the things he'd been a part of. He didn't know how many lines Alaric had crossed trying to save Evangeline, only to fail again and again. He tried to return the old man's parting smile, but he couldn't quite force one out before the Shield was too far away to see it.

CHAPTER THREE

ALARIC WATCHED the Shield leave the library before he moved. Then he went to the ramp and headed to the lowest floor. Two levels down, he almost ran into another Keeper walking with his nose in a book.

The man looked up with an apologetic smile. When he saw Alaric's face, his smile withered. Alaric held in a sigh.

"Mikal," Alaric said, nodding his head slightly. Of course it had to be Mikal.

Mikal narrowed his eyes. "Back so soon?"

Alaric felt a pang of regret at the Keeper's reaction. But here, at least, was the welcome Alaric had expected. "I'm not really back at all."

Mikal gave a little snort, his eyes running down Alaric's worn cloak. "Never thought you would be." He stepped around Alaric and disappeared up the ramp.

Alaric stood still for a moment. It was surprisingly depressing to realize he was living up to Mikal's expectations, not the Shield's.

Alaric descended quickly all the way to the deepest floor

of the library where the oldest books were stored. Their spines, even with the meticulous preservation of the Keepers, were flaking off, leaving a fine dust along the front of the shelves. There were books on this level written in runes so ancient that none but a Keeper could read them.

He crossed the floor to a bookshelf covered by a wooden gate. When Alaric touched the wood, red words flared into existence.

Herein lie words of darkness and death.

A year ago when he'd touched this gate, he'd been looking for a way to save Evangeline's life among these restricted books. A way that was different from all the ways a Keeper would try. A way that might work. Most of these writings were from Sidion, works the Shade Seekers had written. They spoke of dark magic that the Keepers would not consider using. When the red warning had sprung up that time, Alaric had almost walked away.

Almost. He hadn't heeded the words. He thought he had found new paths of life. He had been wrong.

"Darkness and death," he agreed quietly.

He opened the gate and began to look carefully through the first shelf that held scrolls. At one end of it, he found one ruined, crumpled red scroll. Alaric winced in guilt and skipped down to the lower shelves. On the very bottom sat the unassuming brown scroll labeled, *Death and Life of a Seed* by Kordan the Harvester.

He pulled the parchment from its place and moved to a nearby desk positioned between the shelves. The cheerful glow of the golden orb above it felt out of place.

He unrolled the thin, crinkling paper.

Herein, I write the final record of my work. I cannot bear to write any more. I will store all of my memories in the Wellstone, and bury my treasure beneath a young oak. Then I am finished with it all.

It is only now that I see the darkness in what I have been studying.

I realized, as every farmer does, it is only in dying that a seed creates a new plant. I remembered that the Shade Seekers have a way of manipulating the energy of a creature at the moment of its death. If I could use that power with a seed, I might grow a plant greater than expected. I failed many times before I finally succeeded. I was elated when a sunflower sprouted and grew to an enormous height overnight.

I was coming to understand the exact nature of the seeds, the exact way in which they died, the exact moment in which to impart my magic. I began to see that I could control death, even stop it and replace it with life. Far from frightening me, I was thrilled by this new power.

Everything went perfectly for a quarter of a year.

Then came the day when Peros, the farmer's son, was bitten by a rock snake. Roused by the commotion, I ran outside and saw his parents holding him in despair. A man had killed the snake, but too late. Blackness was seeping up the boy's leg. There was nothing to do. No way to stop it.

Sometimes, I try to justify myself by remembering that I had been cooped up for months, focused exclusively on my seeds. But I know that does not excuse me.

When I saw the boy dying, it was as though he were a seed. I could see the life in him and knew how it would leave. I knew the moment of action. The despair of his parents drove any thought from my head, and I raced to the boy, cradling his head in my hands, whispering the words of death and life. Through his pain, he looked up at me, and I know that at the last moment, he understood what I did. Oh, worthless man! To have that moment back and watch the life fade from his eyes!

The boy did not die. A seed, when it is 'reborn', splits open and a new life springs from within it. But a boy is not a seed—Peros had nothing inside him to grow. There was nothing but the snake's venom and death.

The fear that he would split open paralyzed me for a moment, but he did not. He writhed and screamed in agony, an agony far worse than the bite. His parents tried to calm him, but everyone else drew back in terror. What came out of him was his energy, the essence of him. I can still hear the scream he let out as a green glow radiated from every part of his body. This glow swirled and pulled away from him, causing him terrible pain. It coalesced into a green focus of light as the last tendrils were torn from him.

The screaming stopped, and he collapsed to the ground. His eyes were glazed and empty, but he breathed. An enormous rough emerald dropped onto his chest, the solid form of the green light, the solid form of the boy's vitalle. His father cast the gem off the boy and clung to him. He spoke his son's name, but there was no response. The boy's eyes stared vacantly. He was alive, but hollow.

Eventually, they stood him up and led him away. He followed their every command, but lifelessly. They had never trusted my powers, but now they looked at me in horror as they left.

I picked up the emerald. It was warm and pulsed with a swirling green light. The Shade Seekers call it a Reservoir Stone. I almost took it to his family, but I did not. I do not know what I hoped to learn from it. Maybe it was a sort of punishment to keep it with me and remember what I had done. I did nothing with the gem but look at it and weep.

Although the boy felt no more pain, the venom continued to eat away at him.

The light in the emerald dimmed through the night. When the boy died near dawn, the gem grew dark and cold.

It wasn't until days later that I realized that I have an antidote to the snakebite. It had never occurred to me. Perhaps this is the danger the Keepers warned me of. Not that my experiments were evil, but that they focused on death to the extent that I stopped looking for life.

Tonight, I end the record of my experiments. I have not the heart to work even with the seeds again. I will return to the Stronghold one last time. I know they will accept this scroll, even if they no longer can accept me. After what I have done, I can no longer call myself a Keeper. There are decisions that can't be unmade, paths that cannot be unchosen, choices that change us too much for us to ever change back.

The emerald sits next to me now, dark and empty.

I will leave here and give the villagers their peace.

Tomorrow, I deliver this scroll to the Stronghold. May it serve as a warning.

Alaric stared at the page in horror. His hand reached for the pouch around his neck. Trembling, he yanked it open, dropping its contents into his hand.

Out fell a huge, rough, uncut ruby filled with swirls of blood-red light.

Alaric rested his forehead against the warm gem, shutting his eyes against the red light. The same red light that had glowed while Evangeline had screamed in agony as he'd slowly drained her of her life energy to form the Reservoir Stone.

He opened his eyes and watched the eddies move through the ruby, the light scattering between the irregular faces of the gem. The energy was still there, still moving, just as it had for the last year. The crystal he had placed around her body to preserve it was working. She lived, and would until he removed the crystal. But that wouldn't matter, not if he couldn't find the antidote.

Alaric set the ruby off to the side and picked up Kordan's scroll and scanned it again, desperation rising. Kordan must have written something more. He had an antidote to rock snake venom. He must have recorded it somewhere.

With a growl of frustration, he flung the scroll away.

I will store all of my memories in the Wellstone.

Alaric dropped his head onto the table with a thud. How hard would it have been to write out one antidote?

He turned his head to look at the ruby again, letting the swirls of light calm him.

A sliver of darkness spun past the surface.

Alaric grabbed the ruby. He watched it closely. The currents flowed around each other until the black line appeared again, no wider than a blade of grass, wrapped around and through one of the streams of light.

Alaric's hand clenched the stone.

When the boy died near dawn, the gem grew dark and cold.

Alaric held the ruby with shaking hands. The bit of blackness continued to swirl in with the red. When had the darkness appeared? He studied it for a long time, but the black line didn't change. How long did he have before the ruby went dark?

He needed the antidote. Soon. If Kordan had put it in the Wellstone, then Alaric would use the Wellstone.

Alaric put the ruby back into the pouch at his neck. A tight ball of anger began to grow in his gut at the thought of sharing with the Keepers the things he had done during the last year. Once they knew, Alaric would never be welcomed back here. They wouldn't be able to look past it.

But he needed the antidote, so he would use the Wellstone, and then he would leave before they had to ask him to. He would get the antidote and go back to Evangeline.

Alaric stood up and placed Kordan's scroll back where it belonged. The warning gate closed on the bookshelf with a click.

He left the library quickly. The center of the Stronghold tower was open to the ceiling, its white walls rising up a half-dozen stories, drawing closer together as the diameter of the tower shrank. Along the wall, a ramp led upward. Dotted with arched doorways, it spiraled up until it passed through the ceiling. Through that opening, he could see flashes of light from the Wellstone.

Alaric began to climb the ramp. He passed his favorite study, the one with the deep fireplace and deep chair that always smelled like bread from the kitchen below.

Up near the top of the tower, Alaric passed his old room. It was thickly rugged, the walls blanketed by shelves of books, scrolls, and jars. All the things he used to value sat patiently, waiting for him to come back.

He moved on, climbing upward until the ramp led up through the opening in the ceiling and out into the night. The room at the top of the tower was walled almost entirely with open windows. The warm breeze swirled through, tucking dried leaves and dirt deeper into the corners.

The Wellstone, more valuable than everything else the Keepers owned, sat on a small silver pedestal in the center of a table.

It was a round, multifaceted crystal the size of a small

melon. Colors flashed erratically through each of its facets, a few of them shining brilliantly.

The Wellstone served as a vessel, storing both energy and memories. The Keepers had been sharing their memories with it for centuries, helping to keep the things they recorded as close to fact as possible.

A chair sat next to the table, and Alaric sank into it. He touched the Wellstone, the edges cold and sharp beneath his fingers.

It would be here, all the knowledge Kordan had shared with the Wellstone when he had come to the Stronghold to deliver his book.

I might have an antidote to the snakebite.

Alaric took a deep breath and steeled himself for what was about to happen. Forcing himself not to consider it any longer, he reached out and cupped his hands around the Wellstone.

Connecting his mind to the crystal was like stepping into a raging storm. Images and sounds battered against him, not because it was trying to push him out, but because Alaric was too insignificant for the Wellstone to notice. He fought for a place in the chaos, fought to be stronger, louder.

When the Wellstone finally noticed him, it drew him in hungrily, the chaos shifting to swirl around him. He stayed still in the center of it all, still reluctant to release his memories. It tugged on his mind. With a groan, Alaric let go.

CHAPTER FOUR

THE CHAOS FADED, and the Wellstone swept him along through his own memories. The first images were from court, flashes of the queen, the beginning of his trip to investigate troubling rumors from countries to the south.

Then two eyes, somewhere between green and brown, caught his attention. Alaric grabbed at the stream of memories, slowing them, watching them unfold.

The eyes peered out of a window at him, curious and amused.

Alaric froze, tottering on an upturned bucket, reaching his arm up as high as he could toward one specific apple high on the tree. He laughed self-consciously. With the break in his concentration, his spell faltered and the apple hanging far above him stopped quivering.

"Hello," the woman said politely.

"Hello," he answered, smoothing out his black robe and stepping off the bucket.

The woman raised her eyebrows and looked up at the tree laden with apples.

"Would you like a boost up?"

"No, thank you," Alaric said. "There's something undignified about a grown man climbing to the top of an apple tree for an apple when there are perfectly good ones within arm's reach."

"Was dignified the look you were going for?"

Alaric laughed again. He looked back up at the apple high on the tree and sighed in resignation. "I'd love a boost up."

The woman came outside and looked up at the tree. She was almost as tall as Alaric, with golden hair that was trying valiantly to escape from a long braid. Her face, while not striking, was open and happy.

"That particular apple is worth this much work?" She gestured to his robe with a grin. "Not to mention the destruction of your reputation as a respectable Keeper?"

Alaric considered the apple for a moment, knowing it seemed odd. "It's worth at least that much."

She offered her hands as a step, and between the two of them, Alaric was able to scramble up onto the first branch of the apple tree. Several minutes later, Alaric dropped back down out of the tree, holding his apple victoriously.

"I hate to tell you this," the woman said, "but your prize apple has been nibbled on."

Alaric turned the apple around to look at the bites taken from the side of the fruit.

"I know," he said. "That's why I wanted it."

"You're a very strange man," she said.

"This apple was bitten by a green-breasted robin," Alaric explained. "The saliva of a green-breasted robin is very rare and has some unusual qualities. It's very exciting to find this apple."

"Thrilling."

Alaric grinned and gave the woman a bow. "I'm Alaric. You have the thanks of the Keepers for your assistance in my quest. If there is any way the Keepers or I can repay you, we are in your debt."

She laughed and curtsied. "Well, Keeper Alaric, I am Evangeline, and this is my inn. If you would honor me with your patronage and some Keeper-storytelling for my customers, I would feel overpaid."

Alaric agreed to the storytelling and followed Evangeline into the inn. The walls were rough grey stone. The wooden planks of the floor were worn smooth by years of traffic. The hearth held a cheery fire, and smells of dinner and comfort wafted out of the kitchen. It was everything an inn should be. Alaric found himself relaxing, wanting nothing more than to prop his feet up on the hearth and enjoy a meal.

The common room was full for mid-afternoon. Workers wandered in and out for quick drinks, and a gaggle of old women played a noisy game of cards at a corner table. Three equally old men sat nearby, heckling the card players. Evangeline walked Alaric to a table near the fire.

"I bring you all a treat today," Evangeline announced to the room, handing Alaric a mug of cider. "A storyteller!"

A cheer went up from the room, and there was a scuffle of chairs as people rearranged themselves to take advantage of the new entertainment.

Alaric rubbed his hands together. "Are there any requests?"

Several suggestions were shouted from different parts of the room.

"Tomkin and the Dragon," Evangeline said.

A round of hollers agreed with the choice and Alaric nodded. It was a good choice. He took a deep drink of cider, pulled his hood up over his head, and looked down at the floor, letting the room fall into silence. From beneath his hood, he glanced at Evangeline and saw her leaning on the bar, her face set in a look of anticipation. Pleased by her interest, he began.

Images flashed by, of him and Evangeline traveling south. How nervous she had been to meet with the king of Napon.

His memories reached the evening on the sea cliffs.

Did the Wellstone know that some of these memories were more worn than others? Pulled out more often and clung to?

The moon sat low over the ocean, embodying every bit of poetry ever written about such a moment. Evangeline held his hands while the local holy man spoke the wedding pledges.

The image shifted.

The two of them pulled the unwieldy rowboat up onto the lakeshore and collapsed on the sand, half laughing, half groaning. Alaric could barely move his arms, and his back ached. The wind that had risen, making the water so choppy, blew across the beach, cooling him off so quickly he began to shiver.

"That is the worst rowboat ever made," she said, panting.

"With the world's smallest oars," he added. So much for a relaxing afternoon of fishing.

"If we find that obnoxious woman who was yelling, 'Row! Row!' from the shore, can you turn her into a rock?"

Alaric laughed. "I'm not good at messing with the boundary between the living and the non-living."

"A frog, then?"

"A frog is a possibility."

Alaric loosened his grip, letting images flow past faster, like water through his fingers. Images of walking a forested road with Evangeline, talking about everything and nothing. Sitting around a bonfire, watching village children dance. Scenes of easy happiness.

But then he caught a glimpse of the Lumen Greenwood in the distance, and a small village. The village that had been terrorized by an enormous fire lizard, which had been preying on their flocks and killed a child.

Alaric's heart faltered, and he grabbed at the flow of memories to stop them, but the Wellstone pulled him on.

Alaric set out with the three villagers to find and kill the fire lizard. Evangeline hadn't wanted to stay behind, but he'd gotten her to agree at last.

The dull orange lizard attacked them when they were barely out of the village.

Alaric drew vitalle *out from it, slowing the lizard, but it was still so fast. The men shot arrows at it, most of them missing wildly as the creature darted around them, spitting burning liquid, raking the men with its claws.*

The beast was finally brought down, its body prickling with black-fletched arrows. Alaric stumbled over to the men strewn on the ground. Not one had survived.

There was a noise behind him, and he spun around. Evangeline staggered toward him, a black-fletched arrow lodged in her thigh. His heart faltered.

"No," he cried, catching her as she fell. "I thought you were in the village."

She clutched at him, her face white with pain.

Alaric set her down gently. The arrow wasn't deep. A simple, clean wound like this would heal relatively quickly.

He gave her a moment to brace for the pain before he pulled it out.

She screamed.

Alaric clawed at the memories, frantically trying to stop them, to change them, to block the arrow, to change the story.

The wound had been simple, but it had not been clean. Of course the villagers had poisoned the arrows. But in their terror, they had poisoned them with things they didn't even have an antidote for.

Alaric climbed the stone steps of the small mountain keep, carrying her in his arms. Her breath came in shallow gasps. Her face was gaunt and pale.

The blanket he had wrapped her in slid off her black, swollen leg. Lines of dark red snaked up her thigh, tracing the poison's path. He tried to carry her gently, but she shuddered in pain with each step.

Alaric reeled away from the memory, but the Wellstone dragged him relentlessly on.

Alaric stood in the Stronghold council chamber trying not to crush the red scroll in his fist. Sixteen Keepers in black robes were seated at the long, map-strewn table, looking at him with troubled faces.

The Shield smiled warmly. "Brother Alaric, you have a request for the council?"

Alaric held the red scroll from Sidion securely in his hand, feeling the rich thrum of power it held. A power with more fire than the Keepers' books held. "I would like to travel to Sidion."

Most of the faces remained impassive. Keeper Gerone sighed, and Keeper Mikal huffed in disapproval.

"For what purpose?" the Shield asked.

They already knew the answer, but Alaric forced the words out, anyway.

"All my attempts have failed. Evangeline is at rest in a holding trance, but I cannot completely stop the progression of the rock snake venom. Our skills cannot save her. I need a way to extract it from her body without killing her."

Several men murmured in disapproval.

"And you think this is wise?"

"I think my wife is too young to die," Alaric snapped. "It's arrogant to think we have all the answers. There are references"—he waved the red scroll at them, causing little bits to crumble off—"of magic beyond what we practice. The Shade Seekers can sever the vitalle *from the body—"*

"Sever!" cried out Keeper Mikal above the muttering that filled the room. "The body is nothing without vitalle. *The life energy and the body are intertwined—"*

"Peace, brother," the Shield broke in. The room fell silent. "Alaric knows all these things. His learning has never been deficient."

"Any man can become a fool," muttered Mikal.

"Yes, and any man can stop being a fool and become something better," the Shield answered. "I, myself, have done both—more than once." He turned to Alaric. "You knew that we wouldn't approve this, and you knew why."

Alaric thought of Evangeline, the blackness of the venom twisting through her body. "Your reasons aren't as compelling as they used to be."

The Shield sighed. "No, I don't suppose they are."

"This is why Keepers don't waste time marrying," Mikal said. "It divides loyalties."

Alaric's anger flared, but he refused to look at Mikal, refused to have this fight again. "Will you give me leave to go?"

"No." The Shield's answer was simple. More sad than angry.

"Then you sentence my wife to death." Alaric flung the word across the table.

The Shield did not flinch. "I would save her, and you, from something worse."

"You sit here in your tower," Alaric said, biting off each word, "isolated from the world, judging and recording only part of it. You disregard and forbid things you are ignorant of."

"It is not from ignorance that we have banned the practices of Sidion."

"You've been there? You've studied their arts?" Alaric shot at the Shield.

"Yes."

Several heads turned sharply toward their leader.

"One of those choices that made me more of a fool."

Alaric paused at that. But then her face came back to him. Her desperate eyes, her hollowed cheeks.

"I must go."

"Then you will no longer be a Keeper." Mikal shoved his chair back as he stood.

"No one is discussing casting Alaric out," the Shield said firmly.

Mikal glared at Alaric before slamming back down into his chair.

The Shield looked around the room. "We do not cast men out for a single choice because no man is defined by a single choice. With each day, we decide anew who we are, what we will grow toward. Alaric has chosen to be a Keeper a thousand times in a thousand ways. No one is discussing his place here, only his request to travel to Sidion." He turned back to Alaric. "We cannot give you leave to go. It is forbidden."

Alaric stood, looking down the table at the frail old man. "I asked as a courtesy. I don't need your permission."

"We will not stop you, of course, and you will be welcomed back when you return." The Shield met Alaric's gaze. "But I beg you to reconsider. This is not what you want. Shade Seekers do not value the things we do. Please do not go. For her sake."

Alaric stared hard at the man. "I will not sit by and watch her die," Alaric said, crushing the scroll in his hand. Keeper Gerone's face grew white, and he stretched his hand toward the ruined red parchment.

Alaric would not be swayed.

He would not lose her.

The Wellstone continued to pull him on. Alaric was at Sidion, reading dark, heartless books. Then he was standing over Evangeline, drawing the red light out from her, apologizing over and over while she screamed in pain. Finally, the ruby solidified, swirling with red light.

Alaric let the memories flow, letting the Wellstone pull them out as quickly as it wanted. When Alaric reached the Death Caves of the southern blood doctors in Napon, the memories slowed. Alaric tried to push them faster, but the Stone recognized that here was a place no Keeper had ever been before. It spent too long absorbing the horrors of that place. Watching healthy people, even women and young children, poisoned. Their symptoms, responses to antidotes, and deaths recorded meticulously. There was so much blood and sickness in those caves you could taste it in the air.

The Wellstone sifted through every memory as Alaric

stood by, watching the doctors perform experiment after experiment with the rock snake venom he had brought. They didn't have rock snakes this far south. He hadn't known what they would do when he brought it to them. He hadn't known how many people they would kill trying to develop an antidote. How many people Alaric would have to watch die, unable to stop them.

And even the blood doctors found no antidote.

The Wellstone's pull on him lessened as the pool of unshared memories shrank. It settled finally on an image of the small keep where Evangeline lay, pale and still. Moonlight fell through the balcony doors onto her thin face, her limp hair. It glinted off the crystal surrounding her, keeping her body alive.

With a moan, Alaric pulled his hands off the Wellstone.

CHAPTER FIVE

ALARIC LEANED his head on the table and closed his eyes, clasping his hands together to stop their shaking. He wanted to run, to run and forget the fact that those memories were shared now, held permanently in the Wellstone to be studied by Keepers whenever they wished.

Alaric shook out his hands. He shoved the thoughts of what he had just done away. It was done, and with it, his time as a Keeper. He would find Kordan's antidote, and then he would leave. He thought of the swirl of darkness in the ruby and felt a wave of anguish. How long did he have before that darkness spread? How long did Evangeline have left?

But the Wellstone demanded focus, and it was a long time before he was calm enough to try. Finally, he set his hands on it and concentrated on the entry he had read in Kordan's journal. The boy, the snake, the emerald.

It was a process, looking for information in the seemingly bottomless pool of memories in the Wellstone. Slowly, painstakingly, he nudged the chaos toward the memories Kordan had left. When he finally found them, he found the boy, writhing in pain while a green glow radiated from his body.

The emerald formed, and the boy was led away by his parents. If Alaric could see where Kordan kept his notes, he could sift back through memories until he found the Keeper writing the antidote. But Kordan's home was bare. There was only one book, the small brown journal Alaric had already read. Where did Kordan record his work?

Kordan pulled the emerald out of his pocket, watching the light swirl. He picked up a box from the mantle, a sprawling oak tree carved into the lid. Gently, he wrapped the emerald in a red handkerchief and placed it in the box.

Then he dropped into a chair. On the table next to him, sitting on a silver, three-pronged stand, was a small crystal with irregular surfaces, but each facet flashed with color.

Kordan had a Wellstone.

Alaric tried to see more, tried to draw out more memories from Kordan. But all he could see was Kordan looking into his own Wellstone.

Alaric's stomach dropped. Wellstones must not record memories recorded in other Wellstones. No matter what he tried, he found no more of Kordan's life.

He let his hands fall off the crystal.

He was looking in the wrong place. Kordan had kept all of his knowledge in his own Wellstone. This one was useless.

He sank back into the chair, dropping his face into his hands. His dismay was so great that he could hardly breath.

He had just used the wrong Wellstone. There was no antidote here.

Alaric had just shared all his memories with the Keepers for nothing.

I will store all of my memories in the Wellstone, and bury my treasure here beneath a young oak, Kordan had written.

Alaric thought of Kordan's sparse home. The Keeper had had no treasure besides the Wellstone. One even as small and irregular as his would be worth a fortune.

Somewhere in Kordan's Blight, under what must now be a hundred-year-old oak, the antidote Alaric needed was buried.

He stood up, refusing to look at the useless Wellstone, refusing to think about the memories he'd just shared. The Shield would come see them soon enough and realize that Alaric wasn't really a Keeper any longer. Kordan was right. There were choices that changed a person too much.

Alaric strode back down the ramp into the dark tower. When he reached the council chamber, he stopped to check a map, slipping in and closing the door behind him before lighting a lantern.

The council table was spread with woefully incomplete maps of the Lumen Greenwood, the forest of the elves.

For eight years, the Keepers had been trying to find out what had happened the day Mallon, a ruthless Shade Seeker with seemingly limitless power, had disappeared. He had bent the country to his will, leading an army of nomadic warriors right to the walls of the capital. Neither Queen Saren nor the Keepers had had any real hope of stopping Mallon. But then he had turned his attention toward the elves and disappeared into their woods.

That day, half of the Greenwood had burned and Mallon had disappeared along with every trace of his power. The thousands under his control had been released, and his nomadic army had drained back through the Scale Mountains.

But the elves had disappeared as well. It was challenging to find the elves in the best of times, but since Mallon, it had been impossible.

Alaric pulled maps off a shelf, tossing aside assorted maps of Queensland, the Dwarves' capital of Duncave, and other miscellaneous maps until he found one showing Kordan's Blight. It was far north, the last village before the Wolfsbane Mountains began.

He took a moment to memorize the map, then blew out the lantern and went quickly downstairs.

When he reached the ground floor, he could hear the thwump-thwumping of Keeper Gerone kneading the morning bread. It must be close to dawn. Alaric walked over to the kitchen door and saw the Keeper's bent back as he steadily worked the dough. Alaric breathed in the smell of home and belonging.

He opened his mouth to greet Gerone, eyeing a kitchen chair he could drop into and spill his troubles out to the old man. In the quiet, while it was still dark, had always been a good time to talk to the brilliant man, looking for new perspectives or connections or answers.

But Alaric couldn't bring himself to tell Gerone what he had done. He'd see the memories in the Wellstone soon enough.

Gerone began to turn around and Alaric ducked quickly past the door.

He paused for just a moment at the Keepers' robes on the way out. He let his fingers run across the fabric again. He could leave the worn-out one he was wearing and put on a proper robe. The robes were made to look common, giving Keepers a measure of anonymity when they traveled. But they weren't common. They were perfect. The perfect weight, the perfect warmth, the perfect black. The first time he had worn one was the first time he had really believed he was a Keeper.

Alaric let his hand drop. Leaving the robes on their hooks, he left.

The woods allowed Alaric to leave without being visited by ghosts or wolves, and by the time the sun had fully risen, he was on the King's Highway heading north. When dusk came, he stopped for the night at a small tavern in a small town. It had been before lunchtime when he had passed the last thing that could be called a city. From here north, it was just scattered homesteads and the occasional village.

In the tavern, even though he was exhausted from not sleeping the night before, he settled into the commotion and camaraderie of the dining room. He was reluctant to call himself a Keeper tonight, so he introduced himself as a royal historian tasked with recording local histories. Several men joined him at a table and talked over each other to tell a legend of a crazy miller woman who haunted Dead Man's Hollow.

When the sun set, Alaric continued recording stories by candlelight. The room was alive with laughter and folktales. For the first time in a long time, his enjoyment of the world around him drowned out his own worry and guilt.

The tavern brightened slightly as the front door opened.

A hush fell over the room. Alaric glanced up to see where the extra light was coming from.

It took a moment to understand what he was seeing.

Standing in the doorway was a group of travelers. A young man, an old man, a stocky dwarf, and glittering like her own candle flame, was an elf.

CHAPTER SIX

THE PEOPLE around Alaric sat perfectly still, staring unabashedly at what was surely the only elf they had ever seen. Alaric stared along with them. He had forgotten how luminous they were.

"Good evening," she said, gracing them with a smile that spread through the room like a wave of warm water. Alaric smiled back at her. She was so very elfish—like a sparkle of sunlight. Her simple white dress reached down to her knees and was belted by a ring of purple flowers. The waves of her hair, and maybe even her skin, shimmered with specks of gold.

The sounds of the rest of the room faded—she lit up like a beacon of light in a dull world. Like a beacon of pure, stunning, mesmerizing brilliance.

Alaric realized he was gazing oafishly at her and blinked. He shook off the unfocused feeling creeping across his mind and studied her. She was pretty, but not nearly as lovely as he had thought. Or maybe she was. She was mesmerizing.

Alaric tore his gaze away from her. Scowling, he braced

his mind against her, willfully choosing to focus on his own hands, the bread on the table, the smell of onions and roasting meat. He took control of his own thoughts, leaving no room for any outside influence. His mind cleared, and the room settled back into perspective.

That was disconcerting.

Elves could sense more about living creatures than humans could. They could see emotions and the general state of well-being that a person had just by looking at them. But this elf was doing more than that. Alaric glanced around the enthralled tavern. It sure looked like this elf wasn't just reading emotions. She was controlling them.

"Are you done?" the dwarf asked the elf as he jostled past her. "I'm hungry."

She let out a tinkle of laughter, and everyone blinked and moved again, leaning toward their neighbors and whispering.

The man next to Alaric tore his gaze away from the elf and continued his story. Alaric gave enough attention to him to write it down, but like everyone else, he mostly watched this new group. Now that his mind was clearer, he realized the full impact of what he was seeing.

The elf by herself would be astonishing enough, but she had settled into a chair right next to the dwarf. Alaric had never heard of an elf and a dwarf interacting. As far as he knew, there had never even been a meeting between the two peoples. If a dwarf happened to be in the capital during the short time an elf had visited, the two avoided each other.

But these two seemed perfectly at ease with each other.

When the barmaid took drinks to the table, the dwarf lifted his glass. "To the richest family in Kordan's Blight."

Alaric's quill stuttered. Kordan's Blight?

He wrapped up the story with the man, crossed the room to where the group was sitting, and introduced himself.

"A royal historian?" the dwarf asked, glancing down at Alaric's worn cloak. "So you're a cheaper version of those Keepers you humans like so much?"

Alaric forced a smile at the dwarf. "Precisely."

"You'll have to excuse Douglon," the young man said, shooting the dwarf a disapproving look. He had an open face topped by a tousle of indistinct brown hair. "He's hungry. Please, have a seat. I'm Brandson."

Alaric took the seat. "I must say, you are the most interesting group that I have ever come across in my travels."

"You have no idea," the elf said, smiling at him. Then she peered at him as though working out a puzzle. "Is this place calming your soul?" she asked curiously.

"It is," Alaric admitted.

"Wonderful," she said, bathing him with a radiant smile. "A soul with burdens such as yours needs some calming."

Her smile sank into him, sending tendrils of comfort deep into his chest.

Alaric liked elves. They kept you on your toes. He firmed up the focus of his mind so that she couldn't influence his thoughts. It was stimulating to be around a people who had such casual intuition. She wouldn't care enough about a human to wonder what his burdens were, but she'd see that he carried them as easily as she'd see his brown hair.

The dwarf rolled his eyes. "Good evening," he grunted. "I don't care about your soul."

Alaric laughed. "And I don't care about yours, master dwarf." Douglon was exactly what Alaric expected from a dwarf, with the darkened leather armor and his long copper beard, beaded and tucked into his belt alongside his scarred battle-axe.

Douglon flicked his hand toward the elf. "The annoyingly cheerful elf is Ayda."

"And I," the old man proclaimed in a nasal voice, "am Wizendorenfurderfur the Wondrous." He wiggled his fingers through the air. "Holder of Secrets, Caster of Spells, and Spinner of Dreams!" He wore a long, dark blue robe, embroidered with stars, moons, and swirls of lighter blue thread. Matched, of course, by his pointy hat.

Brandson bit his lip to keep from smiling, and Douglon snorted in annoyance.

It was rare to run across someone with a talent for magic. Not as rare as elves, but if the man was telling the truth, this group just kept getting more interesting. "Wizendorenfurderfur," Alaric repeated.

"Close enough," the old man replied with a dismissive wave of his hand. "I don't expect common folk to be able to pronounce my name. I allow these people to call me Gustav."

"Naturally," answered Alaric, keeping his face serious while he gave the wizard a slight bow.

Alaric looked back at Douglon and Ayda. "I've never heard of an elf and a dwarf traveling together."

"You still haven't," Douglon said, grumbling but not moving away from her. "I travel with Brandson. Ayda just shows up sometimes, and Brandson is too kind to send her away. No one would choose to travel with an elf."

Ayda smiled sweetly at the dwarf.

Alaric glanced around the table as the tavern keeper brought them all some dinner. Taken together, they were an odd collection, but when he looked at them individually, they each embodied their own people perfectly. The elf was flighty, the dwarf was gruff, the young man was friendly, and the wizard wore a pointy hat. Alaric smiled at them all. He couldn't have put together a more entertaining group if he had tried.

"I heard you mention Kordan's Blight," Alaric said. "That is one of the towns I'm planning on visiting."

Brandson nodded. "That's where we live. We're headed home from the market at Queenstown."

"Brandson is the town blacksmith," Douglon said.

"A town with the name Kordan's Blight promises some interesting local legends," Alaric said.

"I can tell you how the town was named!" said Gustav. He took a dramatic pause, then shot an impatient look at Alaric. "Aren't you going to write this down, historian?"

"Um, of course," Alaric said. He pulled out his book and quill, receiving an approving nod from the old man.

Gustav narrowed his eyes and began in a hushed voice. "Long ago, the evil wizard Kordan dwelt in the town. He tyrannized the people, stealing their crops and murdering their cattle. Then one day, he took an innocent boy and turned him into a demon! The people were terrified until my great-great-grandfather, Meisterfoltergast, cast the wizard out and killed the demon. Meisterfoltergast spent days cleansing the town of Kordan's evil. He restored their crops and blessed their cattle but renamed the town Kordan's Blight as a warning to the people to remember what evil is."

Gustav fixed Alaric with a glare and whispered, "People always forget that there is evil nearby. Always."

The old man picked up a piece of chicken and tore off a bite.

Silence reigned for a moment while everyone stared at the wizard.

"I'd bet my beard there's not a lick of truth to that," Douglon said to Ayda.

Gustav huffed and glared at the dwarf.

Brandson shrugged. "I've lived there most of my life, and that's essentially the tale I've always heard. Although until I met Gustav, I hadn't known the part about Meisterfoltergast." He gave Gustav a small smile.

Alaric looked back at his paper and kept writing. The tale of Kordan these people knew was warped, but he was definitely the same Keeper that Alaric was interested in.

"Is there anything left of Kordan? A monument? Signs of destruction? His home?" Alaric kept his eyes on his work. "Any of his valuables the town kept?"

When no one answered, Alaric glanced up. Brandson, Douglon, and Gustav were focusing intently on their food. Ayda was smirking at them.

"It was a very long time ago," Gustav pointed out.

"Of course," Alaric said, letting the question drop. "It would be strange to keep mementos of an evil wizard."

Alaric didn't glance up at the group, but the tension in the men was palpable. Alaric blotted the page he had written and turned to Gustav.

"You seem quite knowledgeable. I'd be honored if you shared some of your stories with me."

"I suppose I could do that." Gustav sniffed. "I'll have to select the best. We don't have time tonight for all of them."

"You could come along with us tomorrow if you are going to Kordan's Blight," Brandson said, causing Douglon and Gustav to scowl.

Alaric gave the blacksmith a warm smile. "I would love to."

Ayda cocked her head and looked at Alaric. "What are you looking for there?" She sparkled captivatingly.

Alaric pulled his eyes away, focusing on the concrete things around him, the feel of his quill, the sounds of the tavern. "Just looking for old stories, wives tales, histories."

She narrowed her eyes.

"Any local knowledge I can find, really. Recipes for local dishes, remedies for sicknesses, anything people can tell me." The remedies part was true, and it seemed best to throw in a little truth when talking to an elf.

She nodded slowly. "And the queen cares about all of this?"

"The queen cares about all of her subjects." That, at least, was completely true. "I'd love to hear some stories from you as well. The world has been asking a lot of questions about the elves since Mallon disappeared."

Ayda's smile froze, and her eyes flashed with an anger so deep that Alaric drew back. "The elves are fine." She bit off each word.

Her gaze pinned him to his seat. He forced himself not to shift in discomfort.

Brandson, Douglon, and Gustav looked anywhere but at Ayda.

"Good," Alaric answered, forcing a smile. "The queen will be glad to hear it."

Ayda nodded curtly.

"So, Alaric," Brandson broke in, "have you come across many interesting stories?"

Alaric turned toward the smith and grabbed for the change of subject. With more enthusiasm than was probably necessary, he launched into a legend from a southern town about their haunted chicken coop.

The next time he glanced at Ayda, she had relaxed back into her chair, smiling and laughing with the others. He braced his mind against her again, but he couldn't quite shake the fuzziness that had been on him since she walked through the door. It was going to be a long trip with her if the elf made him feel like this the whole way.

Alaric set aside the question of the elves. Maybe once he got to know her better she would give him at least some hints. Whatever had happened with the elves, they obviously weren't fine.

CHAPTER SEVEN

ALARIC LED Beast alongside the interesting group the next morning as they headed north along the King's Highway. Brandson drove a slow horse cart loaded down with assorted blades, horseshoes, and wagon parts from his smithy. Gustav and Douglon walked while Ayda traveled through the edge of the woods along the road, placing her hand on trunks as she passed in the elfish way of listening to the trees.

It had been a year since Alaric had traveled with anyone, a year since he'd wanted to. But there was such an easy camaraderie about this group that he found himself enjoying it.

"Oh, look at that oak tree!" Ayda cried out.

Alaric glanced at the oak. It was one of a dozen he could see around them. Hopefully, there weren't this many oaks in Kordan's Blight, or it was going to be hard to figure out which one Kordan had used as a marker for his buried treasure.

"Which tree?" Douglon asked. "The boring one right there?"

Alaric tried not to laugh. It wasn't exactly boring, but there was nothing unusual about it.

Ignoring the dwarf, Ayda stepped over to the oak, slipping in under the heavy branches.

"I think it's a nice tree," Brandson said.

"It's a tree," Douglon said. "Like that one and that one and that one."

Ayda came back weaving a chain of leaves together. Alaric watched her hands closely. It almost looked like she was creating new leaves as she walked, but that was impossible.

"Here you are, noble dwarf," Ayda said, holding out the chain. "A gift from Harwood."

"Harwood?" asked Alaric.

"Probably the stupid tree's name," explained Douglon, backing away as Ayda tried to put the chain around his neck.

"It is his name," Ayda said. "And stand still, dwarf, or I'll enchant this so that you can never remove it."

Douglon paused, and Ayda took the opportunity to fling the necklace of leaves around his neck. They fell over his shoulders, the bright green leaves lying across the front of his red beard. Douglon stopped and glared at her.

"Come now," she said, patting his bearded cheek.

Alaric was caught between admiration for her bravery and concern for her safety. He certainly wouldn't have patted a dwarf wearing that expression.

"Wear it a bit for old Harwood," Ayda said. "At least until he's out of sight. It makes you look ferocious."

The dwarf growled and leaned toward her menacingly. Ayda laughed. "See?"

Douglon's hand went to the chain of leaves, but he didn't pull it off.

"You can write this down, historian," Gustav said in a nasal voice from beside the cart where he had been walking. "In ancient times, the leaves of the oak tree were used to form crowns for the victors of war. I myself have formed weapons out of oak leaves, using spells to harden them and hurl them at my enemies!"

Alaric forced an interested look onto his face. "I'll add that to my notes tonight." The part about the crowns was true, but hardening leaves into projectiles seemed like a waste of energy. If you needed to hurl something hard, just pick up a rock.

"Not the dreaded leaf attack," Douglon muttered. He began to peel the green blade off each leaf, leaving only a wiry chain of stems around his neck.

"That sounds impressive," said Brandson to Gustav, giving the old man a smile. "I hope we'll never be in a position to need that useful trick."

"Surely we will, my boy," Gustav said. "Surely we will. Danger is always close at hand." With those ominous words, the wizard moved ahead of them down the road, peering into the underbrush.

Brandson glanced at Alaric and shrugged.

Alaric still couldn't completely shake the unfocused feeling that he'd had since the group walked in the door of the tavern last night. He couldn't sense Ayda actually trying to influence his mind, but he also couldn't quite shake the feeling that his mind wasn't completely his own.

But in spite of that fuzziness, part of his mind felt more alert. It required a vigilance that he hadn't needed in a very long time to make sure Ayda wasn't influencing him. Nothing about her was particularly threatening, but he wasn't going to be able to relax until they reached Kordan's Blight and he could put some distance between himself and the elf.

Alaric let the wizard, the dwarf, and the elf pull ahead of Brandson and his slow cart. The young smith would be the easiest person to start a conversation with about Kordan's Blight.

Brandson hadn't been any more forthcoming than the others last night when Alaric had asked them if anything of Kordan's was left in Kordan's Blight. Would the young man need encouragement to talk? The Keepers wouldn't approve, because they didn't use magic to manipulate people. But the spell wouldn't really change Brandson, just make him a little more…whatever he already was. Brandson was already a trusting sort, so it would encourage that a little. Still, it was a morally hazy area.

Last night, when Alaric had pulled the ruby out of its pouch, the inky line had seemed darker. It had still been the only dark line in a sea of red, but each time it had swirled across one of the faces of the Reservoir Stone, it had felt more ominous. The thought pushed away any remaining guilt about using his magic. A little information up front could save Alaric a lot of time searching for Kordan's Well-stone. Alaric wrapped his hand around the reins to hide any tremor and made sure the rest of the group was far enough away to not be affected by the magic.

"*Augmenta,*" he whispered. He fisted his hand against the pain as the energy was released.

"You have a unique family," Alaric said to Brandson.

"Yes," Brandson agreed. He continued in a confiding whisper, "You may be surprised to learn that we are not blood relatives."

Alaric laughed. "Astonishing."

"We are all orphans of one sort or another and have thrown our lots in together. I am an orphan of the sort that is actually an orphan. My parents died from one of the outbreaks of the yellow plague during the Riving of the north."

Alaric made a sympathetic noise. The people of the north were spread out into such small villages and towns that Mallon, when he had come here, hadn't bothered bringing an army. Instead, he had sent a sickness. The yellow plague had been especially deadly to healthy men. In many parts of the north, not a single man between fifteen and fifty survived. Most of Brandson's generation were fatherless.

"When I was fifteen, the blacksmith in Kordan's Blight took me in and taught me his trade. He died five years ago and I have been the town blacksmith ever since."

Ahead of them, Gustav stalked along the road by himself, muttering.

Brandson smiled after the wizard. "Wizendorenfurderfur appeared half dead on my doorstep during a blizzard late last winter. I dragged him in and thawed him out. The story of his life before that is so... complex... that I can't follow it. But I don't think he has any family. He's hung around ever since. We haven't seen much of his dazzling magical powers, but he's a good cook, and my stomach is glad of his company."

"Is he really a wizard?" Alaric asked, his voice pitched low so Gustav couldn't hear.

"I think so." Brandson wrinkled his brow. "At least he

tells an awful lot of stories about his magical skills. I have seen him start a fire with just a word."

Manipulating energy to light a fire wasn't difficult. The old man might have some minimal talent. Maybe a touch more than the average street magician who could often sense energy without being able to manipulate it.

"And those two?" Alaric asked, looking at the dwarf and the elf who were haggling over the color of a blackberry.

"Black," Douglon said, "it's a blackberry."

"The berry is purple. And there is a hint of gold," Ayda said.

"Gold? Let me see."

Smiling triumphantly, she handed it to him.

Douglon popped the berry in his mouth. "Tastes black."

Ayda glared at his mouth for a moment as though she might reach in and get the berry back. Then she shrugged. "I'll find more. I wonder if they will all have gold in them?"

Brandson let out a laugh. "I found Ayda when I was hunting not long after the snow melted. She was wandering through the forest chatting with trees. I had never seen an elf before, so I invited her to my home for a meal. She agreed, which surprised me. I didn't think elves bothered with humans."

Alaric watched Ayda scampering along the bushes next to the road. "They usually don't. I'm not only surprised she came to your home, I'm surprised that she would travel with you on a trip as long as this. She isn't anxious to get home?"

Brandson shook his head. "No. And it's not just this trip. Ayda's been staying at my smithy for almost three months. She does leave every once in a while, but then she shows back up again."

Three months? Elves that had come to the capital to meet

with Saren were unhappy if they were out of the Greenwood for three days.

Brandson watched Ayda for a moment. "I think she left her family, but I don't know why. As far as I know, that is unusual for an elf."

It wasn't unusual. It was unheard of. The elves shared a communal life force. If something were urgent enough, an elf would leave the Greenwood, but they always hurried back. Some Keepers went as far as to believe that isolating an elf would lead to its death.

"She's been with you that long? Elves never form attachments to anyone but other elves."

Brandson shrugged. "She's become friends with us."

Alaric looked closely at the elf, wondering if Brandson was bestowing her feelings with a name they didn't deserve.

"I met Douglon that same day. Ayda and I discovered him in the woods on our way back home. He was standing in a clearing, poring over a map. He hid it as soon as he noticed me. I approached him first, in case he was hostile, but he was nice enough. Especially when he saw my hunting knife."

Alaric glanced down at the knife on Brandson's belt. He looked closer. "Is that dwarf-made?"

"No, I made it, but I modeled it after the dwarfish blades. Douglon was intrigued. I invited him to my forge to see my work, and he accepted. But when Ayda stepped out of the trees, he almost left. Said his beard would fall out if he had to listen to the prattling of an elf for an entire meal.

"It was the most serious I'd seen Ayda all day. She told him he was in need of a bath. It turns out Douglon is proud of his hygiene. Her words almost sent him into a frenzy.

"I managed to calm the two and remind them that as my

guests they would do well to respect my friends. They agreed, but it was a tense walk back. Part way through dinner, though, we had a breakthrough. Douglon, who'd had several pints of ale, confided to us that he possessed a treasure map. But he'd gotten himself stuck since he was unable to interpret the runes on the map."

Alaric was part fascinated, part alarmed. His *augmenta* spell might have worked too well. He had only wanted the blacksmith to feel comfortable, but if Brandson started spilling secrets, he might grow suspicious as to why. Alaric cast about for a moment, but could think of no way to end the spell.

"Gustav, as you will soon learn," Brandson continued, "has enormous amounts of knowledge of all things, including runes, and offered to interpret them. After some haggling, we decided that between Gustav's knowledge, my familiarity with the region, Ayda's ability to talk to the trees, and Douglon's map, we might be able to find this treasure. Gustav, when he had interpreted the map, claimed he had heard of it. His great-great-grand uncle or some such person had passed down information about it."

Brandson sighed. "But that was months ago, and we still have found nothing. Not for lack of trying. We've dug in dozens of places, but we haven't found—"

He stopped and looked at Alaric in dismay. "I shouldn't be telling you this. We swore an oath of secrecy to each other."

Alaric worked hard to keep his face bland. "That's the way of the road, isn't it? Talking to strangers. I've had no one but Beast to talk to for a long time. By now, he knows all my history." He patted Beast's neck. "He's probably thrilled to hear someone else's for once."

Brandson paused and Alaric waited, trying to look unconcerned. Finally, he sighed. "It's actually something you might be interested in writing about. The treasure supposedly belonged to the wizard Kordan. It's some sort of enormous gem that might have magical powers. Kordan buried it before he was driven from town."

Alaric's hand clenched on the reins, and he whipped his head around toward Brandson so quickly that the blacksmith drew back.

Ayda stepped into view around the carthorse, her hands overflowing with blackberries.

Alaric focused on her quickly, an inept cover up for showing the surprise he had to Brandson. But that was another mistake. As soon as he focused on Ayda, he realized the fuzziness had crept across his mind again. Pulling his eyes away from her, he fixed his eyes resolutely on the berries while she laid them out on the seat next to Brandson. Being with these people was like being caught in a mental whirlwind. He took a deep breath, trying to calm his mind and to school his features into a more reasonable level of surprise.

Ayda beamed at Alaric and offered him a berry. "You look like you've seen a ghost."

He managed a weak smile. "Not since yesterday."

She cocked her head at him, her expression bemused. "Well, there's nothing like a juicy berry to remind you you're still among the living." With a grin, she walked off ahead of them.

Alaric stuck the berry into his mouth to give himself an extra moment to recover. It burst with juices, the tartness clearing his head. He grabbed another one before even trying to think straight.

These people were searching for Kordan's Wellstone? The same Wellstone that he had learned existed only yesterday? He shoved against that fuzzy feeling in his mind again. What was he missing here?

"That's quite a treasure," Alaric said finally. "And it is exactly the sort of thing I would love to write about."

Brandson nodded slowly.

"It does seem strange that Gustav happened to have information about a treasure Douglon was looking for," Alaric said, attempting to move the focus of the conversation off himself.

"That's what Douglon thinks, too," Brandson said. "He doesn't believe Gustav knows anything. Thinks he's just along to steal the treasure. It doesn't help that Gustav's clue is too cryptic to make sense of. *'The stone lies beneath the oatry,'* whatever that means."

Alaric reached for some more berries and forced his face to stay neutral even though his mind spun.

The stone lies beneath the oak tree.

How exactly had the dimwitted wizard discovered that piece of information?

CHAPTER EIGHT

"YOU TOLD HIM WHAT?" Douglon hurled a stick into the fire that evening and glared from Brandson to Alaric.

Alaric toyed with the idea of using *augmenta* again to bring Brandson more firmly onto his side. But with everyone this close, it would influence everyone. Gustav and Douglon would become angrier. It probably wouldn't affect an elf, but it wouldn't stop Ayda from watching him with that odd look, either.

"You told him all that without him influencing you in any way?" she asked Brandson, eyeing Alaric.

"Of course," Brandson said. "I told him because I trust him."

"I'm honored that Brandson entrusted me with your secret," Alaric said, stepping back from her. "And to prove my goodwill, I will help you find your treasure."

"We don't need help," Douglon said. "Or anyone else to split it with."

"What help could you offer?" Brandson asked, talking over Douglon.

Alaric was tempted for a moment to tell them he was a Keeper. For Brandson and Gustav, that would put him in a position of authority. But it wouldn't convince Douglon. All Douglon would see was that he was still a human, and dwarves were unimpressed with humans. Mostly, though, he was reluctant to claim the title.

"I have found a decent amount of treasure myself," Alaric said instead. "And I have a good sense of an object's worth."

"We can figure out how much it's worth," the dwarf said.

"Probably," agreed Alaric, "but I do bring one more thing. A buyer."

Brandson looked curious, but Douglon scowled.

"If the gem is as large as you think it is, the queen would be interested in it. I'd imagine she would pay you generously for it." It wasn't exactly a lie. "If this stone is even a quarter as grand as you say it is, I will talk to Saren about buying it." The Keepers would pay any price for a Wellstone. And Saren would help.

The group exchanged wary glances.

"And *Saren* will just do as you say?" Gustav asked.

"*Queen Saren,*" Alaric corrected, berating himself for being so careless, "likes gemstones. She buys them at a generous price from miners. I'm sure she would do the same for yours."

Douglon and Gustav were watching Alaric with distrust. This wasn't going all that well.

"If you decide you don't want to sell it, the queen will have to be satisfied with that, of course," Alaric said. "But a gem doesn't split four ways. A pile of gold does."

"That's a good point," Ayda said. She sat a little off to the side, thoroughly entertained by the discussion.

"If you tell your queen about it, she's likely to take it from us by force," Douglon said.

Alaric let out a laugh. "You don't know much about Queen Saren, do you?"

"Queen Saren is known for her fairness and generosity," Brandson said. "She wouldn't take it by force."

"That doesn't mean a lot coming from you." Douglon shot a glare at Brandson and gestured toward Alaric. "You trust people a little too easily, don't you think?"

Brandson scowled.

"It seems to me that you've benefitted from that trust a bit," Ayda pointed out to the dwarf.

Douglon included her in his general glare, then turned to Gustav. "Is it true what they say about the queen?"

"You could probably convince her to pay you more than it's worth," Gustav said. "She's never been particularly strong."

Alaric bristled, but clamped his mouth shut.

"How generous would she be?" Douglon asked, his expression calculating.

"Very generous," Alaric said. "I've seen her pay almost twice what a gem was worth if she thought it was beautiful." Not to mention powerful and magical.

Douglon stroked his beard absently.

Brandson cleared his throat. "I vote to let Alaric join us."

"Me, too!" Ayda burst out, as though she'd been waiting for the chance.

Alaric didn't meet her eyes. It would be nice to keep his wits clear right now.

He looked at Gustav and was surprised to be greeted by a shrewd look. When Alaric met his eyes, though, the old man's gaze faltered and dropped to the fire. "Fine with me," he muttered.

Douglon stood and approached Alaric. The dwarf extended his hand. "Your word that the treasure is ours unless we agree to sell it?"

Alaric didn't need to own the Wellstone, just get his hands on it for a few minutes. He stood and shook the dwarf's hand.

Hours later, the talk of treasure dwindled and all parties settled down to sleep. Alaric leaned against a tree at the edge of the firelight, surrounded by the lingering warmth of the day. The only sounds were the chirps of the forest bugs and the crackle of the fire.

It was odd that he had run into this group. More than odd. To find people searching for Kordan's buried treasure? It was impossible to think that was coincidence. If it was something else, though, Alaric didn't have any idea what it was.

"Are you going to try to influence me?" Ayda's voice slipped out of the darkness next to Alaric's ear, causing him to start.

"Of course not," he answered. It wasn't worth pretending he hadn't used *augmenta* on Brandson. Ayda probably knew he had. "You seem to be an expert at influencing people. Even for an elf."

Ayda laughed, stepping out of the darkness and settling herself beside him on the grass.

"Influencing is such a vague idea, isn't it? It comes in all different forms. Am I still influencing people if they just like me?" She cocked her head to the side, looking at Alaric. "But I don't know that I could affect you, at least not without some actual effort. That is unusual, you know."

Alaric snorted. "You don't actually believe that."

He couldn't quite pull his eyes away from her. There was something fascinating about Ayda. Something shimmery around the edges, something warm radiating out, something troubling tucked in the background. Elves had a sort of intensity about them that humans and dwarves lacked, but Alaric had never met one whose intensity was so… visible. So glittery.

"Why are you such a challenge, I wonder?" She rose up and walked to the fire.

He focused on the skin of her arm, trying to catch what sparkled.

She knelt and stretched her hand straight into the fire. Alaric gasped and started forward, but she pulled her hand back out, pinching off one small flickering flame between her unharmed fingers. There was no kindling or fuel, just a single flame. She gazed at it with a pleased expression while Alaric stared at her open-mouthed. Lifting it close to her mouth, she blew on it. Starting from the bottom, the flame grew still and hardened, forming a smooth crystal.

She walked back to Alaric, pulling up a piece of long grass on her way. Stretching it between her fingers, she set the end of it against the side of the crystal and pushed. The blade of grass pierced it, leaving the orange flame dangling like a gem on a chain.

"There you are," she said. She knelt down next to him and tied the necklace around his neck.

Alaric sat, too stunned to move.

"You are better suited to fire than leaves," she added, motioning to Douglon who still wore his chain of oak leaf stems.

Alaric reached up to touch the necklace. It felt like a piece of glass slightly warmed from the sun. The gem was the exact likeness of the flame.

It would have taken Alaric weeks to theorize a way to do that, and even then, he probably would have only ended up with burnt fingers. Elves' magic was elemental, but this was different. They talked to trees and helped flowers grow, but he had never heard of an elf manipulating fire like that. Fire couldn't be changed to stone. The two things were too different. What she had done should be impossible.

He raised his eyes to hers warily. She showed no sign of pain. It was as though she paid no price for the magic.

"Why are you such a challenge?" she repeated. Even though her smile remained pleasant, her gaze pierced into his mind.

He tried to wrench his gaze away, but he was pinned.

He couldn't even blink.

She stepped into his thoughts and began to look around. He shoved against her presence, but it was like shoving a mountain. Disregarding him completely, she stood still in his mind and peered around as though she were in an interesting room.

Alaric focused his entire mind on her face, filling his consciousness with her eyes and smile, dragging all of his thoughts and emotions together. He felt his other thoughts strangled out by this single image.

After a moment, she blinked and was once again merely sitting in front of him, looking at him with eyes that were the soul of innocence.

"That was more interesting than I expected," she said.

Alaric stared at her, his mind staggering, furious.

"I saw the woman in the crystal box."

Alaric grabbed the pouch at his neck, the image of Evangeline lying still beneath the crystal flooding his mind.

"She's the answer, you know."

"What?" His mind was grasping about, trying to understand what had just happened.

"The answer to why you're such a challenge. What is her name? Evangeline?"

Alaric's gut clenched.

"A man who loves a woman that fiercely isn't easily influenced by another." She smirked at him. "Even by an expert influencer like me."

Again, Alaric tensed.

"Don't worry," she said, her eyes still bright. "I'll keep your secret. Interesting, though. Very interesting. I'm glad to meet you… Keeper."

Alaric darted glances at the others, but they were asleep.

Ayda looked at him questioningly. "Do all Keepers have minds as distracted and fuzzy as yours?"

Alaric stared at her, incredulous. "What is wrong with you?"

She let out a peal of laughter. "I feel fuzzy sometimes, too. It's so hard to keep our minds to ourselves, isn't it? Evangeline looks kind. I like her."

She faded into the darkness, leaving Alaric breathing fast, his fist clenched around the ruby at his neck.

CHAPTER NINE

Alaric sat up for a long time, his eyes and ears straining for any sign of Ayda. He couldn't remember the last time he had felt this vulnerable.

Even though they knew how, Keepers did not invade each other's minds and few others had the ability to do so. Alaric hadn't practiced protecting his mind since eight years ago when Mallon had spread terror across Queensland, stepping into men's minds and ripping out their wills. It was clearly time to brush up on that skill again.

Regardless, it shouldn't have been hard to push Ayda out. He knew his Keeper skills were rusty, but this was more than that. Entering someone else's mind wasn't like walking into a library and opening a book. Each mind was a layered labyrinth, the darkest secrets hidden so deeply they were impossible to find. The only thing evident when entering another's mind was what they were most focused on. But Ayda had stepped in and seen Alaric's most protected thoughts with ease. And despite his efforts, he was certain she had left only because she wanted to.

And he still couldn't completely shake the haziness she caused in his mind.

The stars had traveled a good distance across the sky before the vulnerable feeling faded and he could assess the situation he was in.

He had found a group looking for the exact same gem he was. Even though they didn't know who Alaric was or that the gem was a Wellstone, it was still too much of a coincidence to ignore.

Far from being troubling, the thought was invigorating. It had been a long time since he had anything to focus on besides looking for the antidote. And here, right in the direction he needed to go, sat the tantalizing prickle of a new, unsolved mystery.

Besides, this group, whoever they were, had a map—an actual map—to where Kordan had buried his Wellstone. They could be a group of Mallon's personal Shade Seekers whose entire purpose was to lure Alaric to his death, and he would still go along with them.

It was almost fun.

"We should be home by dinner," Brandson told Alaric after several hours of walking the next morning. Alaric led Beast alongside Brandson's cart like he had the day before. The smith called ahead, "With any luck, Douglon, by tomorrow night, I'll have that axe head finished for you."

The dwarf turned and waited for them to catch up.

"Brandson is pretty handy in the smithy," Douglon said to Alaric. "He makes blades that look dwarfish, and they're strong, but they're also light."

"When he says 'light' he doesn't really mean light," Brandson said. "I'd have a hard time swinging it. But it is lighter than the axe he carries now."

Douglon rubbed his hands together in anticipation. "It's light. And the blade holds an edge. My cousin will finally be jealous of my axe."

"Are you usually jealous of his?" Alaric asked.

"Hardly," Douglon said, "but he thinks everyone is. You should see him strutting around with that purple-shafted axe on his hip."

"Purple?"

"Exactly. Patlon is a good warrior and has proved it often enough, but he drives us all crazy with his stupid axe. He insisted on wearing it in the presence of the High Dwarf so he would be able to describe it to the royal blacksmith when he wants a replica." Douglon threw his arms into the air. "It's purple!"

"Why?"

"Some rubbish about it being blessed by an elf maiden with purple hair. There's no way Patlon has ever seen an elf. Even if he had, who wants the blessings of an elf for their weapon? It would probably just make the axe giggle." He cast an annoyed look at Ayda. "Or refuse to cut down trees."

Alaric laughed. "Is Patlon a close cousin?" Dwarf families were vast and complex, with every relative outside immediate family, no matter how distant, called cousins.

"As close as they come. He's my uncle's son. We've been like brothers since birth." He paused. "Or we used to be."

Alaric let a moment pass. He considered using *augmenta* on the dwarf, but these people were growing on him. He'd rather have Douglon actually trust him. "Did your break with him happen to involve a treasure map?"

Douglon stiffened. "How'd you know?"

Alaric shrugged. "You have a treasure map, but no cousin-like-a-brother here searching with you."

Douglon studied Alaric for a long moment. "If you're going to tag along with us, I suppose you should hear the story. It has some interesting parts, anyway, you might want to include it in your notes.

"Patlon and I were digging in the Scale Mountains looking for a diamond deposit that he had heard of when we found a strange piece of wall. It didn't enclose anything, just leaned up against the base of a cliff."

Alaric looked at the dwarf in surprise. That sounded an awful lot like the Wall at the Stronghold. But Douglon was talking about a place in the Scale Mountains, two days' ride to the west.

"There had been a rockslide on the mountain behind the wall, and part of the slope had collapsed, exposing a tunnel. It wasn't dwarf-made. It was too straight and smooth." He shook his head in disapproval. "Didn't take into account the natural flow of the mountain. Looked like something a human would dig. Anyway, the tunnel started at the wall—even though the wall had no door in it—and continued straight under the mountain." Here Douglon paused to gauge Alaric's response to this fact.

Douglon was describing a wall and tunnel exactly like that of the Stronghold.

"This sounds like a story worth writing down," Alaric said. "Do you mind?" At Douglon's nod, Alaric pulled out his book and a coal pencil. He quickly took down what the dwarf had already said.

"The tunnel led straight ahead several hundred feet under the mountain," Douglon continued, warming up to his story and his audience, "until it came out into a valley we hadn't seen before. It was just an oversized crack in the mountains, really, left behind when the slopes beside it were thrust up. But it was inaccessible except from this tunnel.

"In the valley were the beginnings of a tower. A circle of iron-laced sandstone. It rose about twenty feet before it stopped, as though the builder had been interrupted. Only one room on the ground floor had been completed. A dusty bedroom." Douglon leaned closer. "It had belonged to a wizard."

Alaric's mind was racing. Douglon had found a Wall, a tunnel, and a valley complete with the beginnings of a new Stronghold? In the Scale Mountains? More questions than he could voice swirled in his head.

"A wizard?" he asked finally.

Douglon nodded. "It was full of wizardy things. There were shelves of scrolls and pouches and boxes. The scrolls were written in runes we couldn't read. But the pouches and boxes, every one held some marvel. The boxes held things like a spinning top that bounced off the sides, a pile of ancient gold coins, three dried mushrooms that hummed. One pouch held bright blue beetles that smelled of rosemary, all dead. Another was filled with pure silver sand."

Douglon's voice grew quieter. "All these things were fascinating, but we found the real treasure on a shelf near the bed. Next to a book, written in runes we couldn't read, lay this." Reaching into his cloak, Douglon pulled out a worn roll of leather.

Alaric unrolled it, reading a short, scrawled paragraph.

It feels wrong to bury something of such value. Perhaps I should give the stone to them, but I can't bear to look at it. The memories haunt me. I will bury it in a place of honor and leave it behind. I pray this map remains useless, and I am never in need of finding it again.

The handwriting was the same as the scroll at the Stronghold. The page had been written by Kordan.

Alaric read and reread the paragraph, his heart pounding. The map really was to Kordan's Wellstone. The new Stronghold the dwarves had found must have been built by the old Keeper as well. What had he done? Left the real Stronghold and tried to continue as a Keeper by himself?

Alaric flipped the leather over. Time had faded the ink, and there were blotches where the leather had been soiled, but most of the map was decipherable. Several sets of runes, meticulously drawn dotted the page.

Alaric let his eyes wander over the runes. There was no doubt that this was written by a Keeper. The precision and clarity of the writing made him surprisingly nostalgic. Whatever their other faults, the Keepers could write.

The map showed a valley at the base of the Wolfsbane Mountains containing some buildings. Two rock formations were labeled. In the center of the map was a tree with a gem drawn beneath it.

"And the town is Kordan's Blight?" asked Alaric.

"Judging from the rock formations, yes," answered the dwarf. "But whenever this map was drawn, the town was much smaller than it is today. And Kordan's Blight is full of trees. How on earth do we know which one the map refers to?"

"These are the runes that Gustav translated?"

"If you can call it translation. Either Gustav is an idiot, or whoever wrote this was a lunatic. Everything is gibberish."

Douglon's finger stabbed at a point on the map where a cluster of runes stood. "This says: *The falling stars cool the turtle's back.*" Douglon glared at the wizard walking ahead of them on the road. "I'm willing to believe he's an idiot."

Alaric took the moment to study the runes. He could see what Gustav had translated, but the writing was off slightly. An extra tail here, an odd dot there.

These weren't modern runes at all. They were ancient.

The Keepers had some books old enough to use them, and each Keeper was schooled in how to read them, but they were too nuanced and open to interpretation to be of use for most things today. The fascinating thing about the runes on the map was that even though they were ancient, each was similar to a modern rune with a different meaning. Sometimes radically different.

"Falling stars" was a decent modern translation, but in the ancient language, it read: damned soul. "Turtle's back" should roughly translate to: a place of sanctuary. The word "cool" was a complicated rune that indicated vengeance and justice. That rune also had the sense of turning the entire phrase into a question. The amount of nuance that was drawn into the runes was impressive. After piecing it together, Alaric decided that what the cluster really said was, *Shall the soul that has been damned seek vengeance or discover a place of sanctuary?*

Alaric tried hard to hide the smile that kept creeping onto his face. First of all, the writing wasn't part of the map. It was just Kordan's musings. Secondly, almost no one besides a Keeper would be able to read the ancient runes. Barely anyone in Queensland read even modern runes. Gustav must be well educated to be able to translate the modern runes he had, but he would have them chasing after nonsense. Alaric marveled at the complexity of the writing.

Douglon reached over for the map, and Alaric forced himself to hand it back. He'd been so focused on that one set of runes, he'd barely looked at the map itself.

"So you ended up with the map," Alaric said, watching Douglon roll it up and tuck it into his pocket. "Did you give Patlon the rest of the treasure?"

Douglon looked uncomfortable. "Patlon thought we should take all the wizardy things home before following the map. But since the stone sounded more valuable than everything else we'd found, I wanted to go get the treasure."

Douglon's voice trailed off. He shook his head and continued in an offhanded way. "In the end, we split up. He took all the stuff we had found, and I took the map."

Alaric looked at the dwarf in disbelief. "He agreed to that?"

Douglon shifted. "'Agreed' might be the wrong word for it."

"Smoke!" Gustav shouted from a turn in the road ahead.

A dark plume of smoke was visible over the hill to their left, roiling up into the blue sky.

Ayda and Douglon began to run. Ayda outpaced him quickly, racing down the road.

"Kordan's Blight?" asked Alaric. The look on Brandson's face as he urged the slow carthorse forward was his answer.

"Take Beast," Alaric said tossing Brandson the reins. The blacksmith leapt into the saddle and galloped toward the smoke. Alaric climbed onto the lumbering cart and followed.

Once the carthorse plodded around the turn, the entire town was visible. A crowd was gathered before the nearest building, milling around under the sign with an anvil standing untouched at the road. The acrid smell of smoke cut through the air, and as Alaric drew the carthorse closer, he could feel the lingering heat from the fire. Nothing was still burning. What had been the smithy was now a smoldering pile of charred wood.

Brandson sat on Beast, staring at what was left of his home. There was nothing to be done.

CHAPTER TEN

AYDA WALKED UP to Brandson and put her arm around his shoulder. Gustav ran through the crowd, grabbing leftover buckets and throwing water toward the already doused building.

"It's a little late for him to decide to do something useful," Douglon said to Ayda.

Gustav tossed a large bucket full of water that splashed into a puddle near the front of the structure, not remotely close to any of the parts that were still smoking.

"Well, not useful exactly," Douglon said.

Gustav glared at the two of them. Throwing the bucket down, he stalked away.

"I'm sorry, son," a man said to Brandson. "'Twas burning good by the time anyone saw it. 'Twas naught to do but keep th' other buildings safe."

Brandson slid down from Beast and stood staring at the husk of his home. The roof was gone, and the walls were sagging. Behind the smithy, the remains of Brandson's living quarters let out swirls of smoke. The smith began to walk toward them, his arm raised against the heat, but he couldn't even reach what was left of the walls. Even from back where Alaric stood, waves of heat rolled off the building.

Alaric doubted there was anything salvageable, but something white caught his eye. He stepped up next to Brandson and found a light-colored rock leaning against the base of a burned wall. Chiseled into the stone was a symbol, or two symbols, one over the other.

"What's that?" he asked Brandson.

The blacksmith looked at the rock blankly.

"That wasn't there when we left," Ayda said, squinting down at it. "The top symbol looks like an axe. I can't tell what the bottom part is."

Alaric crept toward the rock, the heat burning against the exposed skin of his face. He knelt and wiped wet ashes off of it, using the bunched corner of his robe. Then he stepped back quickly, and the three of them peered at the rock, trying to decipher the shape.

"What did you find?" Gustav demanded. "Move over. Let me see."

"It's a dwarf," Douglon said from behind them.

"It doesn't look like a dwarf," said Ayda. "It looks like a lizard."

"It is a dwarf, lying dead, smited by the axe," Douglon said dully.

"How do you know?" Alaric asked. Ayda's description was more accurate.

Douglon stepped up beside them, glowering at the white rock. "Because it's Patlon's symbol."

Brandson stared into the bottom of his empty ale tankard. He hadn't moved since collapsing into a chair in the tavern. His expression had gone from depressed to bleary. Alaric, returning from making sure that Beast and the carthorse were stabled behind the tavern, joined the rest of them at a table in the corner of the empty dining hall. The entire building was stuffy and smelled of onions.

"Are you sure that was Patlon's symbol?" Alaric asked Douglon.

The dwarf nodded. "We invented it as children. He claimed that he needed a warning to scare his enemies. I never thought that would mean me."

"It might not," Ayda said. "Patlon didn't hurt anything of yours. But he did destroy every single thing Brandson owned. Even though Brandson is guilty of nothing but generosity and goodness."

Douglon looked stricken. "I'll rebuild the entire smithy," he said to Brandson. "Twice as big. With diamonds for windows."

Brandson grunted and everyone fell into an uncomfortable silence.

"So..."Alaric said to Douglon, "Patlon just let you have the map?"

"I told him I was taking it, and he said nothing." The dwarf shifted in his chair. "Course he was passed out at the time."

Brandson dropped his tankard to the table with a thunk and turned to the dwarf. "You didn't think to tell us that you'd stolen the map and a fire-wielding dwarf was going to come burn down my home?"

"I didn't think he'd find me! It took me months to figure

out that the mountains and rock formations the map was talking about were here. I have no idea how he found me."

"He has a point," Ayda said, and Douglon looked at her gratefully. "Who would have expected a dwarf to be that clever?"

Douglon's smile turned to a glare.

She brightened. "I know! His purple elf helped him!"

Alaric let out a laugh at that, and even Brandson allowed a small smile before dropping his face into his hands. Ayda wrapped her arm around his shoulders.

"If Patlon found the smithy, why isn't he still here?" asked Alaric.

"I'm sure he is, somewhere," said Douglon. "He prides himself on his hunting ability. Claims he can wait for a week without food or water or sleep if he's tracking his prey."

"I doubt he can go that long," Alaric said, "but if that fire was just set this morning, I'm sure he saw us come into town."

Brandson groaned. "What are we going to do?"

"There are five of us and only one of him. He's not much of a threat if we stick together," Alaric answered. "We need to find a way to talk to him."

"Brandson might need to sleep off all the ale before we plan anything," Ayda said.

"Where are we going to sleep? If we stay here, he'll probably just burn the tavern down on us," Brandson said, raising his head enough to glare at Douglon with one eye.

The tavern door swung open letting in a swirl of fresh air. They all tensed. Douglon stood, his hand going to his axe. Gustav hunched over, glaring at the door and raising his hands as though he meant to shoot lightning at whoever entered. Alaric turned as well, but it was only a milkmaid carrying an enormous jug.

She stopped when she saw everyone looking at her.

Ayda gave her a friendly wave. Douglon nodded to her, dropping back into his chair.

The milkmaid gave a self-conscious smile and carried her jug into the kitchen. She returned a minute later. Catching sight of Brandson, she paused. Her gaze flicked uncertainly to Ayda's arm draped over the smith's shoulder, but she pushed one of her long, brown braids behind her shoulder, smoothed the front of her dress, and approached the table.

"Brandson, I'm so sorry," she said.

Brandson squinted at her. A foolish smile crept across his face. "Milly?" He tried to sit up a little straighter, but kept listing to the side. Douglon gave the smith a small shove to push him back up.

"I saw the smithy," Milly said. "That's terrible. Truly terrible." Her voice trailed off, and she stood uncomfortably next to their table.

Douglon pushed an empty chair out toward her, and she dropped into it. When Ayda introduced Alaric, Milly nodded politely.

"You can all come out to the farm," she said. "There's more than enough room. You can stay as long as you need to."

"We can pay you, Milly," Brandson said.

"Pay me? For taking in my homeless neighbor? You had better not say that again, blacksmith."

Brandson shrank back in his chair a bit.

Ayda clapped. "We'd love to! Can I milk another cow?"

"That's not a good idea," Gustav interrupted.

"Why not?" Milly asked.

"I did a good job last time," Ayda said.

Gustav ignored the elf and leaned toward Milly, his dramatic whisper barely lower than a shout. "The fire wasn't an accident."

Milly's eyes widened. "Someone tried to hurt Brandson?"

"Someone tried to hurt *someone*," Gustav said, looking at Douglon.

The dwarf shifted uncomfortably.

"Do they know you're here?" Milly asked.

"Probably," Ayda said. "It's the dwarf's cousin. He dragged his family feud all the way here, and now Brandson's life is ruined."

Douglon grimaced, and Brandson let out a groan and dropped his head back into his hands.

"Well if he knows you're here, you're stuck. There's no way out of the tavern without being seen."

"We'll wait until dark," Douglon said.

"Or you could come with me," Milly said. "My wagon is parked against the stable. You could hide in the back, and I can drive you out of town."

"We're not going to endanger you, Milly," Brandson said.

"Then you're stuck here until nightfall," she said. "And with the full moon tonight, good luck sneaking anywhere."

The table was quiet for a long moment. Douglon glanced at Brandson, but the smith's expression was vacant. The dwarf turned to Alaric with a questioning look.

Milly seemed like a competent sort of girl. She was right about being stuck here. There wasn't another easy way out of the tavern that he could see.

"I don't know," Alaric began.

"Oh, stop dallying and go," Milly said. "You can each

take turns guarding my house tonight if it makes you feel better. There's a window in the stable, and the wagon's just outside of it. There should be plenty of room."

Brandson looked worried, but Milly shooed him toward the back door.

"Thank you so much, Milly," Ayda said.

"Go on. I'll wait a couple of minutes before I come out."

The rest of the group went quickly into the kitchen. Alaric glanced after them for a moment. It wasn't really necessary for him to hide from Patlon, but he was unwilling to let Douglon and his map out of his sight. Alaric paid the tavern keeper for a loaf of bread and a generous cut of ham. Then he set an extra gold coin on the counter.

"If a dwarf comes in looking for us, it would be helpful if you couldn't remember where we've gone," he said.

The woman picked up the gold coin and tucked it into her apron. "Where who's gone?"

Alaric smiled at her and followed the others out the back door of the tavern. When he slipped into the back of Milly's wagon, it smelled reliable, like hay and hard work. Like the stables at the Stronghold.

He pulled his legs up close, trying not to bump into the others. This was hardly the most dignified way he'd ever traveled. But he'd cram into a wagon half this size if it meant he got to see Douglon's map.

"Which tree?" Douglon asked. "The boring one right there?"

CHAPTER ELEVEN

"We can't leave Kordan's Blight," roared Douglon. "Not without my treasure!"

"Your treasure?" Gustav demanded.

"We can't stay here waiting for your cousin to murder us," Brandson tossed over his shoulder from where he sat adjusting the door on Milly's wood stove.

They'd arrived at her farm a couple of hours earlier. Milly, who already knew about the group's treasure hunting, had demanded that they explain about the smithy. She had taken it all in with surprising level-headedness. Once everyone had eaten and Brandson's ale had worn off, the conversation deteriorated into an argument.

The kitchen was dotted with cups and pitchers of fresh wild flowers, making the room smell and feel like a serene mountain glen. Except for the smell of half-eaten ham. And all the yelling.

Alaric sat at one end of the table, letting the group holler at each other. Douglon's map was spread out on the other end, too far away to read.

"If only we could understand the runes," Brandson said, gesturing at the map. "Then we could find the treasure and be done with it."

"Maybe we need to find someone who can translate them," muttered Douglon.

"Translate them!" huffed Gustav in outrage. "I have translated them. It is not my fault that you're too stupid to understand them."

"You don't understand them, either," Ayda said. "Which might make people wonder if you're a fraud."

"I don't have to wonder," Douglon said.

"There'll be no talk like that around my table," Milly said. "Gustav is as much my guest as you two are, and I'm sure he's doing his best."

"Sorry," Douglon muttered, crossing his arms and settling back in his seat.

Gustav snorted and rose from the table, turning his back to them and staring into the fire.

"May I?" asked Alaric, pointing to the map. He tried to keep his voice level.

Gustav shot him a suspicious look.

"Sure," said Douglon, handing it to him. "Maybe you can see something we've missed."

"I doubt that," Alaric said, "but I've had a pretty thorough education."

"Of course," Brandson said, peering over the stove door. "I can't believe we haven't asked you yet."

"I'm sure I won't find anything the worthy wizard didn't." Alaric took the map and ran his fingers over the runes.

There wasn't much written on the map and none of it involved directions, but the structure was mesmerizing.

Each cluster of runes, its own sentence, ran into others complementing and subtly altering their meanings. There in the center of the map was the gem sitting beneath a tree.

"Do you see anything?" Brandson asked, his voice polite.

"There is something here," Alaric said pointing to large runes at the top of the map. "What do you make of this, Gustav?"

The wizard glanced where Alaric was pointing and snorted. "*The valley of Kordan*. That's one we understand."

"Yes," Alaric answered, "but this here, what you translated 'of' could have another meaning."

Everyone was looking at him.

"Literally it means: *which is the same as*," Alaric continued. "So instead of: *the valley of Kordan*, it would be: *that which is the same as the valley of Kordan*." He met five blank stares.

"Meaning," he said, "that there are two valleys. The valley of Kordan, which is what we're in, and the valley that is similar to it."

"We're looking in the wrong place?" asked Brandson, his face stunned.

"It's possible."

"Let me see that," snapped Gustav, snatching the map from Alaric's hands. He pored over the runes, holding the map inches from his nose. "I suppose that could be one interpretation," he said, "but it's hardly the most straightforward reading."

Douglon took the map back across the table and set it squarely in front of himself. "Another valley with these two rocks?" The dwarf pointed to two notations on the map. "There's the Rocks of the Bear at the top of the map, and Mother's Rock halfway down the left side."

"Mother's Rock?" asked Alaric.

Brandson nodded. "It's on the ridge west of town. It looks like a mother holding a child."

Gustav cleared his throat. "The legend says that a woman, Kessera, was so beautiful that an elf lord fell in love with her. They married, some say against her will, and a year later, she bore him a son. The elf was so jealous of Kessera's love for her child that he cursed them," he dropped his voice to a dramatic whisper, "and turned them to stone!"

"That's a charming story," Alaric said, glancing at Ayda. "What's the moral? Never marry an elf?"

"Never anger an elf," she corrected him.

"Probably good advice," Alaric said.

"Seems like an elf would turn someone into a tree rather than a stone," Douglon said.

"Elves turn themselves into trees," Ayda corrected him. "And it isn't a punishment. It's lovely."

"Anyway," Brandson said, coming up beside Alaric, "those two rocks put Kordan's Blight right in the middle of the map. The valley we are in is wider than the one on the map, but besides that—" Brandson cocked his head to the side, peering at the upside down map. "It's Bone Valley!"

Milly, standing next to Douglon, shook her head. "The rocks are in the wrong place."

"Not from where I'm standing," Brandson answered. He grabbed the map. "Bone Valley is over the ridge to the west of us—the ridge that has Mother's Rock. If we flip the map over, like this, so that Mother's Rock is on the east side of the map, instead of the west, then the map fits Bone Valley, complete with a set of ruins at its southern end named Bear Stronghold." Brandson grinned at everyone.

"You people need to stop naming things after bears around here," Douglon said, but he was grinning, too.

"Bear Stronghold wasn't named after the animal," Milly said. "It was a small fortress where the chieftain of a mountain clan defended his people from an attack. It is said he fought as fiercely as a bear."

Gustav grabbed the map. "Yes! That could be what it says. It is an old-fashioned word that today would translate to rock, but it has the idea of solidness and strength. I would say that 'stronghold' would be a fine translation."

Alaric had come to the same conclusion, but he was impressed Gustav had picked up on the nuance. Alaric felt his pulse quicken. Kordan's Wellstone was in the next valley. The antidote was almost within his reach. He rubbed the ruby at his neck through the pouch, picturing the darkness swirling around with the red light.

Douglon rubbed his hands together. "Well, at first light, we should stop wasting time and find our treasure. Brandson, please tell me there's just one lone tree in the center of the valley."

Brandson and Milly exchanged glances. "I'm not sure."

"It's right over the hill. Haven't you ever hunted there?"

"No one hunts in Bone Valley," Brandson said. "There aren't any animals. The lake there has no outlet, so the water's gone bitter. Besides…"

Everyone looked at him expectantly.

"It's supposed to be haunted," Milly finished.

"By what?" Douglon asked. "People who bury treasure?"

"By the ghosts of people who were killed by a dragon," Brandson said.

Gustav looked sharply at Brandson, his eyes eager. "A dragon?"

"A local legend about a dragon?" Alaric said, reaching for paper to write it down.

"It was a long time ago," Brandson said, "I don't know any more of the story than that a dragon came and ate people. But no one goes into Bone Valley today. I went over the top of the ridge on a dare when I was a kid, but I didn't go all the way down the other side. It was eerie. Part of the valley is forested, but it was unnaturally quiet."

"Well, ghosts don't scare me, and you'd know if there was still a dragon in that valley," Douglon said. "If no one goes there, then there's a good chance our treasure has been left alone. I say tomorrow morning, we go see what it's like over there."

"Yes," said Ayda. "Bone Valley sounds lovely."

CHAPTER TWELVE

THE SKY HAD BARELY BEGUN to lighten when they left the next morning. A mist skulked along the ground, and Alaric crept behind the others, beads of moisture clinging to him and dampening his clothes before they even reached the forest at the edge of Milly's farm.

Alaric's eyes were gritty from lack of sleep. After the others had finally gone to bed, he had lain awake, longing to steal Douglon's map and set out immediately, but it would be faster to stay with the others. Brandson could get them into Bone Valley more quickly than Alaric could wandering around in the dark. That fact didn't alleviate his anxiety to get moving. He had finally fallen asleep only to be woken up for his turn watching for Patlon.

The night had passed peacefully, though, and this morning, he carried one of the small packs Brandson had cobbled together for their trip. According to the smith, they'd reach the valley by dinnertime.

Douglon glared at Milly as she walked next to Brandson. "One more person wanting a share of the treasure."

"Maybe she'll turn out to be useful," Gustav whispered to the dwarf so loudly that everyone heard. "You never know who will. That's why I like to embrace the people around me."

Alaric tried to keep an incredulous look off his face, but Douglon didn't.

"You embrace me, and I'll break your scrawny neck," Douglon said.

"I don't want any of your treasure, master dwarf," Milly said over her shoulder. "I just don't want to be home alone when your cousin shows up."

"It's your fault that she's here," Ayda said, pointing to the dwarf. "Which means she should share your part of the treasure."

Douglon growled at her and trudged up the hill.

"How are you going to split up one gem?" Milly asked.

Alaric glanced around the group. Ayda didn't appear to be listening, but Douglon's face turned stony. They didn't really expect Douglon to share with them, did they?

"We're all friends," Brandson told her. "It will work out."

Gustav, on the other side of Alaric, gave a small snort, muttering to himself and shooting glances at Douglon.

As the ground rose, they entered a sparse forest smelling of pine and moss. Ayda picked small purple flowers, occasionally poking them into Douglon's beard. Holding a handful of flowers, she waited for Alaric to catch up to her.

"Are you going to put those on me?" he asked.

Ayda considered him for a moment, then she tossed the flowers aside and gestured to the flame that still hung around his neck. "You're better suited to fire than flowers."

Alaric had thought about removing the little flame, but it was so lifelike, he'd decided, cautiously, he liked it. "That's the second time you've said that. I don't feel well suited to fire."

"Of course you are. You have that tight burning core of anger. Or pain. Or guilt?" She waved the question away. "Whatever it is, it's deep, but it's bright."

That deep core was anger, and it flared at her attention. "Stay out of my mind."

Ayda laughed, "I'm not in your mind. I'm just looking at you. Can't you see someone's color?"

See someone's color? He didn't even know what that meant. "Let me guess, my color is red?"

"Fiery orange. But not all of you. Just that blazing center. Most of you is a tenacious green."

"Tenacious."

"Yes. Like a mossy stone under scuffling water. It's soothing, really. Except the fire part. You think the fire part is all there is, but that's not true. The anger is only there because of how much you love."

Right, that tenacious green love. "Does everyone have colors?"

Ayda nodded.

"What color is Milly?"

"A dauntless pitch purple. That first color the sky turns before the dawn."

"The color of the sunrise isn't usually called dauntless. Delicate or fresh, but not dauntless."

"Of course it is. The world is flooded with blackness every night before that purple glides over the horizon and presses it back to make room for the sun. No other color braves the darkness like that every morning, or holds it off as long every night."

Milly was walking next to Brandson, talking quietly with

him. She looked more like a farm girl than a dauntless sunrise.

"What color is Douglon?" Alaric asked.

"Molten coppery red. Like his beard. Molten enough to be dangerous, but still easily shaped."

Alaric laughed. "Easily shaped?"

"Yes. He's quite tender hearted."

"And Brandson?"

"Cozy brown."

"Gustav?"

"Oh, who cares about the wizard?" Ayda said, shrugging. "People are colors. If you can't see them, I'm not going to explain everyone to you." With that, she turned and headed up the hill toward Douglon.

Alaric shook his head at her. He was either getting used to the influence she exerted over him, or it was fading. The walk through the cool morning air left his mind feeling clearer than it had in days. He needed to consider what he would do once they found the Wellstone. He couldn't let Douglon, or Gustav, take it. Then Alaric would have to chase them, and he was tired of chasing things.

Alaric would explain who he was and what the Wellstone was. When Douglon heard how much Saren and the Keepers would pay him for it, he would sell it. And hopefully, Gustav wasn't a good enough wizard to even know how to use it.

They trudged up the steep ridge that separated Kordan's Blight from Bone Valley. It would have been impassible if Brandson had not known a game trail that wound up toward Mother's Rock. Even with the trail, Alaric was winded and hot before they were even halfway up.

Just before midday, they reached the highest trees, which

were stunted and twisted by the mountain winds. Alaric's back was sweaty underneath the pack Brandson had put together. The game trail turned back down the slope, leaving nothing above them but a steep slope of loose rock. Ayda had been lagging behind as they climbed, looking bored at the scrawny trees around them. At Brandson's suggestion, they all dropped their packs in the shade of the last trees, deciding to eat lunch before trying to scramble over the rocks. The sky, which had started out clear, was beginning to cloud over. With any luck, by the end of their meal, the ridge would be encased in cloud, hiding them from any watching eyes.

If nothing else, it would block the sun.

Milly and Brandson began to lay out some food.

Gustav stood at the edge of the trees, arms spread wide and eyes closed.

Alaric's skin tingled as though a warm wind had blown past him. He looked at the wizard in surprise. Gustav had just cast out, looking for the energy of living things around them.

"I sense no danger," Gustav proclaimed. "Neither ahead nor behind. I think our presence has gone undetected by the evil dwarf."

"He's not evil!" Douglon broke in, but at Brandson's annoyed look, he shut his mouth.

Alaric, who had been planning on doing what Gustav claimed to have done, considered the wizard. Casting out was different from manipulating energy. It was just a seeking, sending out a wave of awareness and feeling for the reflections sent back by living things. Alaric couldn't feel the reflections from someone else's wave with any accuracy, but he could feel impressions. Keeper Gerone had called it a sympathetic resonance. Alaric always thought it was more like eavesdropping on a whispered conversation. You couldn't hear the exact words, but you got a notion of how many people were talking.

Gustav had produced a wave, but it was clunky. Alaric doubted it had traveled past the first few trees.

So the wizard did have some familiarity with magic.

Alaric weighed his options for a moment. He did want to know whether Patlon was following them, but if he sent out his own wave and Gustav picked up on it, the wizard would know Alaric wasn't just a historian. Announcing that he was a Keeper right now, out of the blue, felt awkward. Unfortunately, the whole secret was beginning to feel awkward.

There was an art to casting out. Nuances of strength and speed and direction. Alaric kept his eye on Gustav and sent out the most subtle wave he could, sending it mostly downhill. Alaric felt the reflection of Gustav's energy, so some ripples had made it that way. But Gustav made no indication that he noticed Alaric's wave.

Alaric's wave made it a good way down the slope and all the way to the top. He came to the same conclusion Gustav had. There was nothing on the ridge larger than a squirrel.

The clouds had rolled down over the ridge by the time they finished eating.

After they had packed up, Ayda dusted her hands off on her dress and turned to the group. "Well, it's been lovely searching about with you people. You've all been entertaining, but I can't see any point in continuing this climb when I just have to climb back out tomorrow." She looked distastefully at the bare, rocky slope rising steeply above them. "I'm going to go find a nice forest with interesting trees."

Alaric turned to Ayda in surprise.

"You're leaving again?" Douglon asked, bored.

"You can't leave now!" Brandson said. "We're so close!"

"You know I don't care about your little stone," Ayda looked at the thin, wind-stunted pine trees around them. "These trees make me miss my home."

"You're not even slightly interested in whether we find the gem?" Douglon asked.

"Not really. I'm vaguely interested in seeing if the tree it was buried under is still alive, but not enough to keep climbing this endless slope."

It made sense, of course, Alaric thought. It was more surprising that Ayda was still with them than that she'd want to leave. Any normal elf would have run home months ago.

Alaric stood a bit back from the group and was the only one who saw Gustav, his brow drawn, step away from the others. The wizard focused his gaze on Ayda and his lips started to move. A moment later, his hand clenched in pain and his face reddened with effort.

Alaric looked back and forth between Ayda and Gustav. Was the wizard really trying to influence an elf? She would know it instantly.

But Ayda continued chatting with the others, unconcerned.

"But you're part of the treasure hunt," Milly said. "You can't leave the group."

Ayda gave her a skeptical look.

"She's right," Brandson said. "Right, Douglon?"

Douglon, whose scowl had deepened as the conversation continued, shrugged. "Doesn't matter to me. I'm here for a sparkling gemstone, not a sparkling elf."

Brandson shot Douglon a glare before turning back to

Ayda. "Please stay just a little longer. I wouldn't feel right if you weren't there."

Gustav stopped muttering and hid his shaking fist behind his back. He slumped, exhausted, against a tree.

Alaric could still see no sign that Ayda had noticed the wizard's attempts, nor was there any change in her attitude. Had the wizard even cast a spell?

"That makes no sense, blacksmith. You all will find your treasure, and I will find a forest with better trees than these. How could that feel wrong?"

Brandson looked around at the others for support, then turned back to Ayda and said, "We might need you. What if we need to talk to the trees? They might know where to look. They might remember a treasure… or someone digging… a really long time ago… or something," he finished lamely.

A small smile crept across Ayda's face. "I need to teach you a little bit about trees." But she nodded. "All right, I'll go over the hill with you."

She met Alaric's gaze and beamed. Alaric grinned back before he realized that the fog had returned. His grin turned to a scowl.

Maybe he should have encouraged her to leave.

They continued up, slipping on wet rocks in a dull grey mist. All around him, the endless grey was punctuated with thumps and curses and the skittering of rocks down behind them.

Reaching the top of the ridge in clouds so thick the group could barely see ahead of them, they hurried over, glad that no one in Kordan's Blight could have seen them leave and glad that the other side, although steep, was more grass and low brush than rocks. Brandson, after a short nervous glance toward the greyness filling Bone

Valley and an encouraging nod from Milly, led them down the slope.

Alaric brought up the rear of their group, focused on each step, concentrating on the slope before him.

With a shriek, Gustav tripped and tumbled down the hill, a blur of skinny limbs and a pointy hat. He fell a good way before his foot caught, yanking him to a stop with a yelp. He lay there stunned, his head lower on the hill than the white legs sticking out from beneath his robe. Gustav didn't move and Alaric peered down past the rest of them at the old man.

"Are you all right, Gustav?" Brandson asked.

"If he's dead, I get his share of the treasure," Douglon called out.

"Shut up," Gustav groaned, and Ayda let out a peal of laughter that echoed through the fog.

Gustav cursed and floundered, trying to right himself. As Alaric made his way down toward the old man, his own foot slipped, and he barely caught himself.

It was Milly who got to the wizard first, slipping and sliding down to reach him.

Gustav waved her away, scolding and complaining. Patiently, she ignored his protests and helped him untangle his foot, then retrieved his pointy, star-swirled hat, which had tumbled a bit farther down the hill.

He smoothed out his muddy robe.

"Thank you," he muttered to Milly as he crammed on his bent hat. "I'm fine," and he marched down the hill.

Milly waited while the others made their way down to her.

"You're too good, Milly," Ayda said. "Your kindness is wasted on that old man."

"Kindness can't be wasted," Milly replied. "If it needs gratitude, it isn't really kindness."

"It might not be wasted, but it's certainly unappreciated." Ayda glanced at Brandson who was watching Milly with bright eyes. "Or at least unappreciated by the wizard."

When the rain started, it came with huge drops that plopped onto Alaric's head and shoulders with irritating force. He pulled his cloak tight against his neck, but drop after drop found their way through, dribbling down his back. It took close to an hour before the ground leveled off and they reached the edge of a pine forest. Sunset was still hours away, but between the rain and the trees, they walked through a deep gloom.

With the pattering of rain sounding distant on the branches high above them, Alaric noticed the unnatural silence for the first time. There were no birds, no squirrels, not even many bugs. The forest smelled stale and forgotten.

Brandson caught his eye. "Creepy, isn't it?"

Alaric cast out a thin, subtle wave, unnoticed by Gustav, but found no animal larger than a bug. The trees held a deep, ponderous hum of energy, like a rumble of thunder.

Ayda walked by them, brushing her fingertips against their trunks and peering up into the canopy. "The trees are old. They've almost forgotten how to talk."

"How will we ever bear the loss?" Douglon muttered.

The rain fell on the canopy of the trees above them. The water cascaded down from above, here and there making the ground a patchwork of dry dirt and mud. They walked, their eyes mostly up, watching for the water and winding from dry patch to dry patch.

A dry crack from under Douglon's boot echoed through the forest. Everyone stopped.

The ground ahead of them was littered with pale sticks.

"These didn't come from the pines," Brandson said looking up at the dark trees around them. "They're not dark enough." He dropped down to one knee and picked up a stick. It crumbled in his hand. "Bones! They're all bones!"

A slight chill ran down Alaric's spine. As far as he could see, bones of different sizes poked up out of the ground like misshapen fingers trying to claw free of their graves.

The party stared in silence until Ayda spoke.

"What did you expect to find in Bone Valley?"

CHAPTER THIRTEEN

ALARIC KNELT DOWN. These weren't complete skeletons, just scattered bones. A lot of scattered bones.

Douglon crept backward, cringing at every crunch under his feet. "Where did they all come from?" he asked, an edge of panic in his voice.

"Quite a few of these came from chickens," answered Milly, moving some of the bones around with her feet.

"Chickens?" said Brandson.

"Some of them. But these over here are bigger. From a pig, maybe," she said, reaching down to pick up one of the bones.

"Don't touch it!" Douglon said.

Milly looked at him in surprise. "Why not? It's very old. Look how smooth the edges are."

Douglon didn't move any closer. Milly looked at him puzzled.

"They're just bones," she said.

"I know that," he said scowling, "but there are so many of them."

"This one's big. Horse, do you think?" Milly asked.

Alaric stepped in among the bones. Milly was right. They were all old. Broken edges were smoothed over from years of exposure to weather, and since little weather made it down beneath these trees, the bones must have been here a very long time.

A roundish lump lay half buried in the ground. "This one isn't a horse."

It was a human skull.

The sound of the rain above them lessened and the forest lightened. Alaric scanned the ground and saw a number of skulls.

"What happened here?" Milly asked.

Alaric caught sight of Gustav standing at the edge of the bones, squinting into the gloom. His befuddled expression slowly turned sly.

"There's only one thing that leaves carnage like this." Gustav's voice rang out so loudly that the others jumped. They all turned to look at him. All except Alaric. He knew what the wizard was going to say.

"A dragon!" the old man proclaimed, throwing his arms out and searching the treetops.

Milly took a step closer to Brandson, and everyone looked up toward the tops of the trees.

"A dragon big enough to eat a horse wouldn't fit in between these trees," Alaric pointed out. "And one shot of dragon fire would have burned up this entire forest. If these bones were left by a dragon, they were left here a long time ago, as Milly has already pointed out. Before this forest grew."

They considered his logic for a moment and nodded. All except Gustav, who glared at Alaric.

"It does look like the legend of Bone Valley's dragon has some truth behind it, though," Alaric said to Brandson.

"Can we please get out of here?" Douglon asked through clenched teeth.

Ahead of them, in the direction of all the bones, the forest lightened.

Brandson straightened. "I'm afraid there's no way out but through the bones." He stepped forward, cringing when his foot crunched down onto the eerie bed of bones.

Ayda and Milly picked their way through carefully, discussing the bones they came across. Brandson stepped through, gingerly testing each step before moving on. Douglon followed right behind Brandson, cringing and shuddering with each step.

"It was a dragon," Gustav said petulantly to Alaric.

"That's the most obvious answer," Alaric said. "And it fits with the legend of Bone Valley. But we certainly don't need to be frightened of a dragon from a hundred years ago."

Gustav scowled at him and continued ahead. Alaric shook his head. That old man certainly had a love for the dramatic.

The bones ended with the trees. The sun had broken through the clouds, and they stood at the edge of a meadow stretching across Bone Valley, dotted with stands of pine trees. Above them, the clouds were chasing each other on the wind. Snow-covered mountains soared above the western side of the valley.

"We'd better find a place to camp," Brandson said glancing at the sun, which sat low above the mountains. "Twilight is going to come earlier here."

"How about away from the bones?" said Douglon.

They struck out along the edge of the trees searching for some other shelter. The sun had dropped behind the mountains by the time they reached a little grove of pines set out in the middle of the meadow. After Douglon inspected the ground for any bones, they set up camp between the trunks.

Brandson carried an armful of wood for the fire. "I don't suppose you could do that thing again where you see if Patlon followed us?" he asked Gustav.

"Of course, my boy," the wizard answered. "I was just about to." Standing up tall and spreading his arms wide apart, the wizard closed his eyes and began to mutter, spinning in a circle.

Alaric watched him, keeping his face bland. He felt Gustav's wave limp past again.

"We are still alone," Gustav announced. "That monster did not follow us."

"He's not a—" Douglon started, but at Gustav's glare he stopped. "We'll set a watch tonight," he grumbled.

Alaric cast out his own wave without any movement or sound, but his findings agreed with the old man's.

Gustav ambled over to where Milly and Brandson were setting wood for a small fire. The wizard shooed them away. As he did, Alaric saw a glimmer of silver drop onto the wood. With a flourish, Gustav shouted, "*Incende*!" and stabbed his staff into the wood. There was a tiny spark and then an explosion as the wood burst into flames. Milly scrambled back and stifled a scream. Smiling in satisfaction, Gustav strode away from the flames, waving them back to the fire.

Alaric knelt to rummage in his pack, trying to hide his smile. Fire powder! The old man had used fire powder and passed it off as magic. Alaric thought for the hundredth time that he should give up everything else and bring fire powder to Queensland. It was prohibitively expensive, but the wealthy in countries far to the south sprinkled the silvery powder in ovens and over wood. A quick rap would ignite the powder and result in what had occurred in their own fire. How had Gustav managed to get ahold of some?

"Amazing, Gustav!" exclaimed Milly.

"Wondrous," Alaric agreed.

The evening stretched out, perfectly quiet, as the group settled down around the small fire. It was a little eerie that there were so few noises, and Alaric found himself constantly straining to hear something. Anything.

Brandson volunteered to take first watch and ambled to the edge of their small pine grove. Milly watched him for a moment. Seeing Ayda's encouraging nod, she prepared a plate of food and took it over to him.

"Thanks, Milly," Alaric could just hear Brandson say to her.

"She's a nice girl," Ayda said, following Alaric's gaze.

Alaric nodded.

"I think Brandson should marry her. I've been trying forever to get the two of them together."

"Marry her?"

"Yes. Brandson is lonely. He has been since his parents died," Ayda said, her face thoughtful. "I think he needs a more satisfying family than a bunch of misfits."

"Who are you calling a misfit?" Douglon asked.

"You," she laughed, stepping over to him and poking another flower into his beard.

Alaric glanced around at the ground but didn't see any flowers. Where did she find these things?

"Alaric is a handsome man with good prospects," Ayda

said, "and I'm— Well… me. So the misfits are you and the crazy wizard."

Gustav harrumphed and stood up from the fire, stalking away to sit on the opposite side of the camp from Brandson.

"I'm glad you're here, Milly." Brandson's voice drifted through the darkening trees.

"Me, too," she answered. "Those trees over there are lovely."

"The oaks?" Brandson said. "They are. Strange to see a stand of oaks when the rest of the valley is full of pines."

Alaric looked up and caught Gustav whipping his head around toward Milly.

Alaric waited for a grand announcement from Gustav claiming to have solved the riddle, but the wizard hunched back around and studied his fingernails.

So Gustav didn't plan on sharing his knowledge with the rest of the group. That was interesting. Alaric settled himself back against the tree. What was the old man's plan?

For a long time, Alaric rested against his tree, watching Gustav who was busy looking bored. The Wellstone was close. It was past time to let this group know that he knew what the 'oatry' clue meant. With that, there'd be nothing to stop them from finding the treasure. Tomorrow morning, Alaric decided, he would tell everyone he was a Keeper. It might not be precisely true, but it was as good of a title for him as anything else. The nagging guilt of lying to this group had become too strong to ignore. It would be a relief to tell them.

One by one, the others fell asleep. When Gustav hadn't stopped snoring for at least an hour, Alaric allowed himself to close his eyes as well.

It was still dark when Alaric awoke to a shriek. From across the campsite, Gustav ran screeching toward the fire. He reached the group and bunched up his robe, catapulting himself over the fire, white bony legs still pumping in mid-air.

"Dragon!" he yelled as he barely cleared the small fire and landed, legs still pumping as he raced through their grove of trees and toward the grass separating them from the main forest.

Alaric leapt up and searched the clear, moonlit sky with his eyes and mind. The night was quiet and empty.

Then an enormous power burst into the valley. A dragon shot through the night sky. Dark red flashes glittered off its scales in the moonlight. It flew in front of the moon, and for a moment, its thin wings glowed scarlet. It was massive, its wings blocking out ragged sections of the stars as it soared across the sky. It turned and dove, making straight for them.

Gustav, still shrieking, had reached the grassy meadow and ran toward the main woods.

Alaric's blood thrummed with the energy of the dragon. *A dragon!*

Milly screamed and cowered behind a tree. Brandson threw his arm around her.

"Gustav!" yelled Brandson, "Get back here!"

But the old man ran heedlessly on.

"Idiot!" Douglon swore.

Alaric snapped into motion, running to the edge of the grove, searching for a spell to protect Gustav.

But the dragon reached the wizard first. The dragon's roar shook the ground, and the blast of energy created as it produced its fire knocked Alaric off his feet.

Its massive body hurtled through the air, spraying out a jet of flame, which enveloped the old man. The huge jaw opened, and the teeth snapped shut around Gustav. The dragon spun around, shooting high into the air and leaving behind empty, charred grass.

CHAPTER FOURTEEN

A DRAGON—A real dragon! And Gustav…

But there hadn't been a dragon in Queensland for a hundred years.

Silence reigned in the valley. The clouds had cleared, and the wet grass glinted silver in the moonlight. Alaric stood with everyone else, frozen, staring at the scorched ground where Gustav had been.

High above them, the dragon roared. The sky lit up with red flames, startling them all into action.

Alaric scrambled to his feet and moved to the edge of the trees, searching the sky. He caught sight of the dark shape spiraling impossibly high before turning back toward them. What were they going to do against a dragon?

Alaric glanced around at the group. Brandson held his knife uncertainly. It was a knife for skinning animals, not fighting a dragon. Douglon hefted his axe, which was a *little* better. But the two looked small and insignificant. Milly ran to the fire and smothered it with dirt. Alaric gave her an approving nod. Looking around for a weapon, she grabbed a frying pan.

Alaric noticed in passing how clear his mind felt, and he glanced at Ayda. She was focused on the sky.

Don't fight a dragon, Keeper Gerone would say. *Leave that sort of business to warriors. Distract it and flee.*

Distract it with what? They were in an empty valley. But they certainly weren't equipped to fight it. Not this group. Douglon was the only one even close to a warrior. There was no archer. No one even had a sword. Alaric could protect them somewhat, but only from the fire. He had no defense against dragon teeth.

"Any ideas?" he asked Ayda.

"Befriend it?" she offered.

Useless elf.

"If he lands," Douglon said, "we might have a chance to injure it and drive it off." His voice didn't hold any real hope, though. "Stay in the trees until he does."

"What if he sets the forest on fire first?" Milly asked.

Alaric gathered some energy. He began to weave an invisible shield over the nearby trees, enclosing the group in it. It wouldn't stop the fire completely, dragon's breath was too hot, but it would protect the trees from enough heat that they shouldn't burst immediately into flames. And hopefully, it would stop the flames from reaching them down on the ground. His hands began to burn as he stretched the shield farther. He had guarded Douglon, Brandson, and Milly from the heat and was turning toward Ayda when she flashed him an irritated look.

"I don't need your help," she said. "Take care of the others."

"Sorry," he said, pulling the shield away from her and anchoring it above the rest of them.

"Here it comes!" Douglon warned.

A rushing sound began high above them, then plummeted down.

Douglon was right. Any chance they had of even injuring the creature depended on it being on the ground.

Maybe a strong wind could ground it. Alaric began to gather energy again, pulling it in as fast as he dared, feeling the pressure of it building inside of him. He wove a web across the space between their grove of trees and the main forest, containing a portion of air. When the web was complete, he drew energy out of the air above it, pulling out the heat, making it colder and colder. The cool air pressed down on his web, getting heavier the colder he made it. He drew out more and more heat until the air was frigid. An erratic wind began to move at the edges of his web, and the trees on either side where he had anchored it bent down toward the ground.

The dragon pelted toward them. An ear-splitting roar cracked the night.

Alaric's hands were in agony, and his arms burned as he forced more and more energy into the net. He stretched clawed hands forward one more time. The grass at his feet withered as he pulled energy from it to replenish his own. The leaves of the nearest tree shriveled. Alaric reached farther, searching for more strength to put toward his task.

The dragon sped down along the grass. With a surge, Alaric tore his net off the trees and let the cold air plummet down. The dragon, caught in the draft, crashed to the ground. But in a moment, it bunched its legs and launched itself back into the air.

He caught a glimpse of Brandson's knife as he threw it. It tinked harmlessly off the red scales of the dragon's belly and tumbled into the grass.

Alaric sank back on his heels, his stomach dropping. His arms were like rocks in his lap, and he had barely affected the dragon. The trees Alaric had protected were smoking, but one more pass would light them like torches.

The dragon roared high above them.

Ayda came over to Alaric. It took most of his strength to lift his head and look up at her.

"I thought you'd do better than that," she said, looking a little disappointed. "You didn't do much better than the wizard."

Alaric stared after her, unable to move as she stalked toward the grass where Gustav had disappeared.

"You stupid elf!" Douglon shouted, watching Ayda walk toward her destruction. "It's a *dragon!* Get back here!"

Ayda ignored him and kept walking. With one last look at the sky, the dwarf rushed after Ayda spewing curses.

Ayda shot him a furious glance and flicked her hand at him.

The dwarf jerked to a stop. Thin roots had snaked up out of the ground and wrapped around his feet, growing and hardening over his boots. He shouted at Ayda, waving his axe wildly and tugging with all his might at his stationary feet. He took his axe and chopped at the edges of the roots. For every root he cut through, another slithered out of the ground.

Ayda continued walking into the open grass. Brandson began to run after her, but at another dangerous look from the elf, he stopped and backed up next to Milly.

The dragon's roar came closer, and the sky lit again. On

Alaric's chest, a flash of light reflected off the flame that Ayda had frozen for him.

Maybe the elf standing in the center of the charred circle of grass wasn't so vulnerable.

But then the dragon appeared, impossibly huge and fast. The rush of wings grew louder, and the world glowed red. Milly screamed and hid her face in Brandson's shoulder as the dragon hurtled toward Ayda.

Alaric couldn't pull his gaze away. With the dragon bearing down on her, Ayda was nothing more than a golden wisp in the moonlight.

Ayda waited, looking up at the descending monster, watching until it was so close that the flames were inches from her face. With a wave of her hand, she cast the flames away, solidifying them and sending them splintering into countless pieces. They landed on the ground near Alaric's feet with the ringing of a thousand tiny bells. The grass was covered with glinting shards of deep red.

Enormous jaws crushed the end of the flame, which had solidified while still in the dragon's mouth, and the creature shot back into the sky.

Ayda looked pleased at the pile of hardened flames. "That was pretty." She crinkled her brow. "I think I'll make the next set blue. There's much too much red over there now, don't you think, Milly?"

Milly, staring with her mouth wide open, said nothing.

"Yes, blue." Ayda turned to see the dragon approaching again.

This time, the beast dove near to the ground farther up the valley and raced toward her. With its blood-red belly skimming the grass, it waited until it was right on her before spewing out flames. Another wave of her hand diverted the flame, this time, turning it a brilliant blue as it hardened.

Milly screamed as the dragon bore down on Ayda. But the elf, with an exasperated flip of her hand, sent the dragon tumbling over her as though it had caught a clawed toe on a rock. The dragon plunged to the ground behind her, crashing down on its back. The valley shook, and Alaric ducked, shielding his head from the branches and pinecones that rained down on him.

In a breath, the dragon twisted back to its feet. Crouched with its chin brushing the ground, the beast let out a low, vicious hiss.

Ayda cocked her head to one side.

"You're not going to try the fire again, are you?" she asked.

The dragon flared its nostrils but did nothing. It seemed to be contemplating the same question. Alaric slowly let out his breath, but drew it in again when Ayda walked toward the beast as though he were an angry house cat who needed soothing.

"Sir Dragon," she began, "if I may call you that since I don't know your proper name. I'm afraid that you have attacked a group that would have been better left alone."

The dragon stared at her with a mixture of hatred and confusion.

"We realize that you are a truly terrifying beast and that there are few who would dare to stand against a beast such as you, but we are among those few." She had reached the dragon now. Although the dragon's chin was on the ground, the top of its nose was shoulder height to the elf.

"It's not just me," she continued. "There's a fearsome dwarf warrior in those trees." The dragon flicked its eyes toward the trees. Douglon, who had been slouched in shock, his feet still frozen, straightened himself up and gripped his axe.

"There's a young blacksmith who is quite strong and equally determined." Brandson stood taller. "And there's a milkmaid with a frying pan. Between you and me, I don't think she was planning to cook over dragon fire." Milly hid the pan behind her back.

"And, if you had gotten by all of us, there is still a magic worker in those trees who I had *assumed* was fairly adept." She cast a critical look at Alaric.

Alaric felt Douglon, Brandson, and Milly look at him as well. The dragon turned intelligent eyes toward Alaric for a long moment.

Ayda stretched her hand out to touch the dragon's snout, but its eyes whipped back toward her and narrowed. A loud, threatening growl rumbled deep in its chest.

Ayda paused. Douglon made a strangled noise.

Alaric's heart was in his throat, waiting for the jaws to open and Ayda to disappear.

She dropped her hand back down, and the dragon's nose inched forward. Its head lashed forward, and it snapped its teeth. Ayda jerked back, crying out and grabbing her arm. Blood seeped through her fingers.

"A little help?" Ayda said, bracing herself as the dragon's snout drew closer again.

"What am I supposed to do?" Alaric hissed at her.

The dragon growled again, vibrating the ground. The breath from its nostrils swirled Ayda's hair. The dragon's eyes lit for a moment, watching the golden sparkles from her hair.

Distract it. Right. Dragons liked sparkly things.

Alaric pulled some energy in from the trees near him again and, ignoring the fact that his hands were still throbbing, began to pour energy into the air behind Ayda's feet. The air warmed and rose, lifting strands of her hair with it. More and more locks lifted and swirled around her head. In the middle of the moonlit grass, she looked like she was surrounded by sparks.

The dragon's eyes glazed slightly.

Alaric crept forward, feeding energy slowly into the air and gathering more at the same time until he thought he would burst with the pressure of it. When he was right next to the dragon's neck, he stopped feeding the air near Ayda and braced himself.

This was going to hurt.

The dragon blinked as Ayda's hair stilled. Alaric pushed both hands onto the dragon's scales at the base of its neck.

The dragon twisted and lashed out at Alaric, his claw tearing through Alaric's shoulder. Pain ripped across Alaric's arm. He dove to the side while Ayda yelled, drawing the dragon's attention back to her. Alaric scrambled back close to it and slammed his palms against the dragon's neck.

"*Paxa!*" Energy surged out through his palms, searing his skin as it poured into the dragon.

The dragon's entire body relaxed.

Alaric dropped to his knees and fell forward. Blisters formed on his palms, and his arms ached too much to move. Blood was running down his left arm from his shoulder. His head swam, and it took him a moment to realize he was leaning on the dragon's neck.

He used his elbows to push himself off the monster. Brandson, Milly, and Douglon were staring at him in amazement.

Ayda let out a whoosh of air. "That's better," she said, her voice quavering slightly. She reached out to touch the dragon's snout, but wrinkled her nose when she saw the blood on her hand. She wiped it off on her dress, leaving a dark stain, then set her hand on the dragon's nose.

Its eyes softened, and it made a sound less like a growl than a purr.

"Yes, I like you, too," she said kindly. "But it's time you were going. I'm afraid that we can't all share this valley and since we have some business here..."

Brandson cleared his throat.

"Oh, right," Ayda said. "We would appreciate it if you would leave the next valley alone also. It is our home, of sorts." With a final pat of the dragon's nose, she turned away.

The dragon blinked at her.

"By the way, what is your name?" she asked, turning back to it. She paused, her head cocked. "Anguine? Well it was lovely to meet you, Anguine. You are a very fierce dragon. I did think the old man you ate would have caused you a bit more trouble," she said with a crinkled brow. "I guess he wasn't too calm under pressure." The dragon shifted, and Ayda fixed it with a piercing gaze. "I see," she said. "Well, off with you."

Turning her back to the dragon, she walked back to the others. The dragon shook its head once. The clawed foot near Alaric flexed, and he scrambled back away from it. With one final confused look at the departing elf, it vaulted itself into the sky and disappeared northward toward the mountains.

CHAPTER FIFTEEN

ALARIC SANK BACK against the nearest tree trunk and watched the red glint of the dragon disappear over the mountains. At least it had flown west toward the Roven Sweep and not south into the heart of Queensland. Although the nomads on the Sweep were going to have a tough time dealing with it.

The gash in his shoulder burned, and his arms hung down on his lap, aching. He gingerly turned over his palms and saw a circle of blisters on each, shiny and taut in the moonlight. He rested his head back on the tree trunk and closed his eyes.

His mind churned up questions he was too exhausted to consider. A dragon? Here? Where had it come from? *Paxa* had worked on it—had anyone ever tried that before? Had a Keeper ever touched a dragon before? And survived? He'd have to send the Shield a letter. Alaric closed his fingers slightly, but the blisters shot searing pains across his palms. Writing a letter might have to wait.

"Ayda?" Milly's voice sounded far away and weak. "Is it gone?"

Alaric heard someone rekindle the fire and realized he was shivering. Part of the pain in his fingers, he realized, was because they were ice cold. The active part of his brain pointed out that was to be expected after pushing so much energy out of them. The exhausted part told it to shut up. He heaved himself forward and using his elbows, managed to get to his knees. The fire flickered through the trees, an impossible distance away.

Then Brandson was there, tugging Alaric to his feet and half leading, half dragging him to the fire. Alaric sank down close to it.

Milly stepped over to him and, with a wary look, handed him a piece of bread. He smiled gratefully at her. The smile she gave back was strained. He tore off a piece of bread that seemed to weigh as much as a boulder. One bite at a time, he ate, waiting for his strength to return.

Alaric could feel blood dripping down his arm. In his pack was tucked a salve that would help. It would help with the burns, too. He eyed his bag all the way across the campsite, another impossible distance.

Ayda would need some, too. He glanced at her, but her arm looked clean and whole. Her dress was spotless and white.

"That was amazing," Milly said in a hushed voice, glancing from Ayda to Alaric.

Ayda beamed at her. "Thank you. It's been some time since I've seen a dragon, but they are all the same. Always attacking with fire and teeth."

"They really should attack with something dangerous," Douglon said.

Ayda laughed a silvery laugh. "Exactly. And I am sorry about the whole tied to the ground thing," she said, motioning to the tree that Douglon had been stuck under. "But I'm afraid you would have been less handsome if that dragon had singed off your beard."

Douglon muttered something and stroked his beard, running his hand over the flowers Ayda had stuck in earlier. He brushed them out in disgust. "I guess we owe you our lives," he said grudgingly.

"You're welcome," she beamed at him.

Milly studied Ayda for a moment. "I've never heard of anyone who could do what you just did with the fire."

"Everybody has the same magic," Ayda said. She gestured at Alaric. "He could have done the same thing."

All eyes turned to Alaric, and a heavy silence filled the trees.

"So you're just a royal historian?" Douglon said.

Alaric started to shrug, but the shooting pain in his shoulder stopped him with a gasp. "That's part of my job."

Douglon scowled and the others waited.

Alaric sighed. "I'm a Keeper." The title didn't feel completely false.

Brandson and Milly gasped.

Douglon's scowl deepened. "Didn't it occur to you to mention that?"

"It's not something we announce," Alaric said.

"You're after the gem, aren't you?" demanded Douglon. "You were going to steal it."

"Douglon!" Brandson said. "Alaric's a Keeper! He wouldn't do such a thing!"

The title didn't feel completely true, either.

"Yes, he seems very noble," Douglon said.

Alaric sighed. Turned out having his secret revealed wasn't much of a relief after all.

"You, of all people, can't be upset at someone keeping his personal history to himself," Ayda said to the dwarf.

"It's all right," Alaric said. "He has a right to be angry. I should have told you sooner."

"Is Ayda telling the truth?" asked Milly. "Could you have done that with the dragon fire?"

Maybe. If he had a thousand years. And a thousand Keepers.

"I don't know," Alaric said after a short hesitation. "Certainly not with as much style."

"Why did you join up with us in the first place?" Douglon demanded.

"I was interested in your group because you lived in Kordan's Blight, and I was looking for information about Kordan. He was a Keeper."

"He was?" Milly asked. "The stories of him aren't very… Keeper-like."

"Maybe you people don't know what Keepers are like," Douglon pointed out.

"Neither Kordan nor I are model Keepers," Alaric admitted. "But Kordan started out as one. He did leave the Keepers after he lived here, though."

"How did you know we were looking for Kordan's gem?" Douglon asked.

"I didn't."

"You expect us to believe you just happened to come across a group looking for a treasure you're also looking for?"

Alaric shook his head. "I know. The chances of that are…

nonexistent. But I had no idea who any of you were or what you were looking for. I have no explanation."

Douglon gave him an incredulous look.

Alaric's hands were throbbing, but the bread was starting to help. "I will offer you what I promised for the gem."

"Why so generous?" asked Douglon.

Alaric hesitated, but there was nothing to be gained from secrecy. "Because the gem we are looking for is that valuable to me. To all the Keepers. I believe what we are going to find is called a Wellstone. To you, it is a treasure, and a treasure is worth money. To me, it is an artifact to be studied."

Douglon harrumphed and turned his scowl toward the elf. "What did you do to the dragon?"

"I befriended it," Ayda answered.

There was silence for a long moment.

Ayda shrugged and gave a small, self-conscious smile. "Everyone likes me, if they just get close enough."

Douglon snorted, but the words had the ring of truth in them. Everyone *did* like Ayda. Even Alaric liked Ayda, despite, well, despite everything.

"Do you think the dragon will return tonight?" Milly asked Ayda.

"Oh, no. He agreed to stay away as long as we are in the valley." The elf scrunched up her nose. "I suppose I didn't tell him to leave us alone after we left, but I don't think he'd try again."

Alaric reached for a skin of water, but the tear in his shoulder sent a lance of pain down his arm and he groaned.

"Alaric," Milly said, rushing over, "I forgot you were hurt."

She worked the ripped fabric away from his shoulder and cringed. The cut was deep and ragged.

Ayda stepped over and glanced at it. "That's not too bad."

"It feels bad," Alaric said.

Ayda reached past Milly and pushed her hand against the wound. Pain knifed through his shoulder and he gasped. But a warmth flowed out of Ayda's hand along with a tightening sensation, and the wound knit itself back together. In a moment, the pain was gone, and Ayda stepped back, smiling. There was nothing on his shoulder but a white scar and a lot of leftover blood.

Alaric rotated his arm gingerly. There was no pain at all. He looked up into Ayda's face, stunned. How had she done that? It took the body days, weeks to heal a wound like that. The amount of energy expended was enormous. Yet Ayda had done it effortlessly.

"We do not have the same magic," he said.

Her face darkened, and an odd look crept into her eyes.

"Yes, we do. Just in different amounts." She caught sight of Alaric's palms and frowned, "Those I can't do much with. A cut just needs to be cleaned out and pulled back together. But a burn is different. I could heal them, but it will leave terrible scars. Scars you might not want on your hands."

Alaric had met a man once with a burned hand. The scarred skin didn't stretch right, he couldn't grip anything well. Alaric thought of not being able to hold a pen. "I'll just wait for them to heal."

"I can do something about the pain, though," Ayda said. She set her hands on Alaric's palms. Her fingers felt cool against his flaming skin. A numbness spread across his hands, and the pain receded. He let out a sigh of relief.

Milly brought over some strips of fabric and began to

bandage Alaric's hand. At his questioning look, she gave an apologetic shrug. "One of Gustav's shirts."

"I can't believe he's gone," Brandson said, poking a stick into the coals.

It had all happened so quickly. So finally.

"If the dragon had to eat anyone," Ayda said, "I'm glad it was the wizard."

"Ayda!" Brandson said, aghast.

"It's true," she said. "I'll take the next watch in case that dwarf did follow us and decides to attack us tonight as well." She wandered over to the edge of the trees. "Although, after the dragon, a dwarf will be boring."

Brandson stared after her.

"You can't expect too much from her," Alaric told him. "Elves don't attach to anyone who's not an elf. It's astonishing that she stays with you at all, but she won't feel the same sort of bond to the group that you do. No matter how long she spends with you."

"I'm not sure that makes me feel any better," Brandson said, watching Ayda disappear between the trees.

Alaric managed to stand and get to his blanket. He sank down and rested his head on his pack.

Douglon crashed and clattered around on the other side of the fire, moving Gustav's belongings out of the way so he could move his own sleeping roll closer to the fire. He dropped Gustav's shovel on his foot and swore before throwing it into some nearby bushes. "I thought wizards were powerful, but Gustav obviously wasn't. That Mallon turned out to be a fraud, too. Wasn't he killed by a forest fire?"

"Mallon was *not* a fraud," Brandson snapped. "He controlled whole cities, killed thousands with his armies and sent diseases that—" Brandson's voice broke. He took a deep breath. "Diseases that murdered thousands more. Among them, my parents."

The clearing went quiet. Douglon cleared his throat. "Mallon never came near the dwarves. We knew he had an army and was attacking your cities, but I didn't know…"

"There are few families in Queensland who didn't lose someone," Milly said. "Mallon seemed unstoppable."

Alaric nodded. "There are some wizards with power, but not many."

"Aren't Keepers wizards?" asked Douglon.

"Not primarily. We know how to manipulate energy, but it's not our first priority. Actually, historian is closer to the mark. The official term used by the crown is 'Advisor and Protector of the Realm.' We see magic as a tool, one of many, that can be used to keep Queensland safe." Alaric was surprised that he had said 'we.' And that he had meant it. It had been a long time since he had thought of Keepers' ideals in a positive light.

"Most minor wizards, like Gustav, are independent. Some are Shade Seekers, a group who use what the Keepers, and probably most everyone else, would call darker magic. The magic is more important to them than anything, and they are not against killing for it. Mallon was a Shade Seeker, but no one had ever heard of one as powerful as he was. We had no defense. He controlled or destroyed at will." He looked into the woods after Ayda. "Ayda must know what happened, but I don't know what the elves did. We didn't know of anything that could stop him. I assure you whatever killed Mallon the Rivor, it wasn't a forest fire."

"Maybe Ayda killed him," Milly whispered.

Alaric felt a chill.

"Maybe Ayda ate him and stole his power," Douglon whispered.

Milly stifled a giggle.

"Why do you call him the Rivor?" Douglon asked.

"The first town that Mallon took over was along the edge of the Scale Mountains," Alaric said. "It was home to the gem cutters' guild. Mallon entered the town alone, found the town leaders and… turned them into his instruments.

"The people reported to the king, and the word they used for it was riving. It's the word for when a gem cutter cracks or damages a stone so deeply that it's worthless. It was an accurate description for what he was doing to people's minds. The name stuck."

Douglon looked troubled. "Seems the dwarves underestimated him."

Silence fell over the group. Alaric's eyes closed. He felt like he was falling, falling through the earth, falling into sweet, inescapable sleep.

But his mind still spun. Ayda, dragons, Gustav, Mallon. Thoughts chased themselves pell-mell around his mind.

His perfectly clear mind.

Alaric's eyes snapped open. He was tired, unbelievably tired, but his mind was alert. Not the least bit of fuzziness remained. He looked again in the direction Ayda had gone and took a deep breath, reveling in the new lightness. Was she done trying to influence him? He should have fought a dragon with her days ago.

His eyes sank closed.

Despite the events of the night before, Alaric stirred with the others at dawn.

"This is the day!" Douglon said. "We'll find the gem by lunch. Let's take another look at that map."

"After we bury Gustav," Milly said firmly.

Everyone paused.

"What would you have us bury?" asked Douglon, eyeing the charred bit of grass where the wizard had met his end.

"Well, fine, not bury then," said Milly, "but he deserves some sort of funeral."

"Yes, he does," Brandson agreed.

"Can't we pretend the dragon was a grand funeral pyre?" asked Douglon.

Milly gave him a withering look.

"Brandson," she said, "please go find something we could use as a tombstone. And go help him, Douglon. We're going to do something for the poor old man."

Brandson nodded and headed into the trees.

"We'll need something to write with," Milly said.

Ayda pulled a charred stick from the fire and offered it to Milly with an amused smile.

"What's she gonna write?" Douglon asked Brandson as they walked away. "'Here doesn't lie the body of a wizard who didn't beat a dragon'?"

Milly scowled after the dwarf. She turned to Alaric. "Can you think of anything else we should do?"

He was taken aback for a moment at being asked, but she looked so earnest that he shook his head. "I think the tombstone is perfect."

A few minutes later, the five of them gathered on the scorched grass and watched as Brandson shoved a large flat stone into place. Milly knelt before it and raised her stick to write.

She paused. "How do you spell Wizendorenfurderfur?"

Douglon shrugged. "Just put Gustav."

"Right," Milly agreed. "Gustav the Wondrous."

Ayda tried to hide her smile until Douglon whispered, "He wasn't a wondrous runner."

Milly ignored them both and finished. Standing back with the others, she cleared her throat.

"Gustav is gone and we'll miss him," she began. "We'll miss his... um, knowledge and... um... that way he could start fires. He was a noble wizard… At least, I think he was." She paused, looking at the others. At Douglon's grin, she flung the stick to the ground and glared at them all. "Oh, for pity's sake, I barely knew the man! You stone-hearted scoundrels say something!"

Ayda laughed and stepped forward. "Well, old man, none of us believed you were much of a wizard. I guess you proved us right."

"I, for one, will miss you," Brandson said. "My house was too quiet before you came. And you were an excellent cook."

Milly slipped her hand into Brandson's.

"Um," Douglon began, searching for something to say. "Even though it makes no sense, thanks for the tip about the 'oatry.'"

"What about an oak tree?" asked Milly. "Didn't we see oak trees last night?"

Brandson and Douglon stared at her.

"Oak tree!" they both yelled and rushed off toward the campsite.

Milly gave the tombstone one last apologetic look then

followed them, leaving Alaric and Ayda at the makeshift grave.

Ayda cocked her head and looked at Alaric. "Do you think the wizard knew the treasure was so close by?" She looked at Gustav's tombstone and gave a thoughtful, "Huh," before she turned and walked back toward the camp.

Alaric followed her and reached the campsite as the others were gathering shovels.

"Does anyone see Gustav's shovel?" Douglon asked, rummaging in the bushes where he'd thrown it.

"You don't need another shovel," Brandson said. "C'mon!"

The excitement was contagious and Alaric hurried after them. He set his bandaged palm against the pouch at his neck. Kordan's Wellstone was buried nearby. The antidote. Alaric's heartbeat raced ahead as well. He cast out, feeling the stand of trees ahead of him and one old, ponderous oak.

All thoughts of wizards and dragons and strange elves disappeared in a breath. Once he had the antidote and reached Kordan's Blight, it would take three days to reach Evangeline. Two if he pushed Beast hard. He could wake her. Heal her.

He rushed to catch up to the others.

Only Ayda trailed behind.

It was a large group of trees with one, near the center, reaching above the rest.

"It must be there!" Brandson said. "Under the oldest one."

Ahead of him, Douglon, Brandson, and Milly threaded their way through the oaks. The largest tree was massive, its trunk wider across than Alaric's reach, thick roots snaking across the ground. Branches spread out, sheltering an area as large as a house.

"Ayda is going to explode with excitement when she sees this tree," Alaric heard Brandson say as he walked around the trunk.

"Where should we dig?" asked Milly.

No one answered her for a moment.

From the other side of the tree, Douglon started swearing loudly.

Alaric finally caught up, stepping carefully over the jutting roots as he rounded the trunk, only to see Brandson and Douglon leaning on their clean shovels next to a freshly dug hole. Alaric joined them and peered in. His stomach dropped.

The hole was rough as though it had been dug in a hurry. It was about three feet deep and was completely empty. Even the small indentation at the bottom, which clearly used to hold a box.

It was gone. Kordan's Wellstone was gone.

Alaric felt fury rising inside of him, looking for a target. He raised his gaze and found one.

Leaning against the trunk above the hole was a pointy, star-covered hat and Gustav's shovel, now covered in dirt.

CHAPTER SIXTEEN

GUSTAV WASN'T DEAD.

He had survived the dragon.

He had dug up the Wellstone.

Alaric's mind crashed up against a single thought. The Wellstone was gone.

Ayda rounded the tree and took in scene before her… and the pointy hat. "Stupid wizard." She kicked the hat, sending it tumbling down into the hole.

"He's alive." Brandson's voice was a combination of shock and hope.

"I'm going to kill him." Douglon swung his axe, glaring through the trees.

"The wizard's long gone," Ayda said. "He has no more use for you or your map, dwarf."

Douglon growled and slammed his axe into a nearby tree. Ayda shot him a disapproving look. She flicked her hand, sending the axe spinning out of the tree. Douglon snatched it back up off the ground.

"He has no use for any of us now," Ayda said, giving

Brandson a small smile. "Our milkmaid's not the only one who wasted kindness on that old man."

Milly walked up to Brandson and slipped her arm into his.

"I can't decide if I'm glad or furious," Brandson said.

Douglon stomped past them. "...lying, cheating, back-stabbing, two-faced..."

Alaric stared into the empty hole. Gustav had duped him, had duped all of them.

"Gustav must be a powerful wizard if he escaped from the dragon," Milly said.

"He escaped," Brandson said, "and let us think he was dead." Anger began to simmer behind Brandson's eyes.

"He didn't escape the dragon," Ayda said. "He used it to fool us. I think it's his pet."

"Gustav has a pet dragon?" Brandson asked, the anger now moving beyond simmering.

Ayda shrugged. "What would you call it if you had a dragon that did what you wanted?"

"Dangerous," Alaric said.

"When I was talking to the dragon, I got the feeling that it knew the wizard."

Douglon fixed Ayda with a venomous glare. "You knew Gustav was alive?"

"No," Ayda said. "Just that the dragon knew him. I didn't ask if the wizard was still alive."

Douglon opened his mouth and sputtered. "You didn't *ask?*" His voice rose louder. "You didn't think to tell us? You didn't think—"

"Dragons eat people," Ayda interrupted, casting a bored look into the hole. "And I never cared for the old man." With that, she turned and walked back toward the campsite.

"I hate that elf," Douglon said, slamming his axe back into the tree. "I *hate* her."

Brandson was staring after Ayda, his mouth wide open in shock. He looked at Alaric. "Would she care that little about any of us dying?"

Alaric watched Ayda disappear through the stand of oaks. "Most likely. Elves don't usually care about anyone but other elves."

Brandson rubbed his hands on his face and growled in frustration. "Gustav betrays us. Ayda doesn't care about us. Why couldn't normal people have fallen into my life?"

"Look!" Milly slid down into the hole. "Something glinted down here."

"The gem?" Douglon asked, pushing past Brandson to get to the hole.

Brandson pulled Douglon back with a dangerous light in his eye. "If it's the gem and you decide to steal it because none of us matters to you either, I will track you down and chop off your beard."

Douglon looked at Brandson with raised eyebrows. He shook his head. "Anything we find, Brandson, we share." He held out his hand to the blacksmith.

Brandson let out a long breath. "Sorry." He shook the dwarf's hand.

"It's not the gem," Milly gave them an apologetic smile. "Just this."

She held up a small medallion of some sort. Brandson took it and helped Milly back out of the hole. It was bronze, hammered flat into an oval and inscribed with runes. Two off-centered lines, one vertical and one horizontal, split the oval into four sections.

Alaric leaned forward to study the piece. What appeared

to be incomprehensible runes grew sinister the longer he looked at them. A letter placed oddly, the way the shape of the runes seemed to suggest images. The symbols tugged at his mind, drawing him in.

He tore his eyes away from the mesmerizing symbols. The oval called to him. "That thing's dangerous."

The others looked up at him in surprise.

"It would be best if you threw it back into the hole and covered it up," Alaric said. "Or better yet dig a new hole for it then forget where you bury it."

"It was buried with the treasure. It could be valuable," said Douglon. "Gustav must not have noticed it in the dark."

"That was not buried with the Wellstone." Alaric's voice was harsher than he intended. He took a deep breath. He glanced again at it. It hummed with malevolence. "Those markings are corrupt. I don't know exactly what it says, but it is evil. Very evil."

"It still might have been buried with the gem," Douglon pointed out. "The stories of Kordan aren't pleasant. Maybe your Keeper went bad."

Alaric felt as though he had a rock in his gut. This medallion couldn't have been Kordan's. He had done some questionable things, but certainly nothing this evil. Alaric reached up to feel the pouch at his neck, feeling the echoes of Kordan's actions in his own life.

"Wherever it came from," he said, again pulling his eyes away from the medallion, "it is evil. You should get rid of it. Destroy it. If it will let you." He turned away from them and walked back to the camp.

At their campsite, Ayda was building up a cook fire. He stood aimlessly for a moment at the edge of the clearing. Gustav had the Wellstone. The knowledge felt like lead in his stomach. On the far side of the clearing, Gustav's pack leaned against a tree. Alaric knelt down by it and dumped out the contents. He wasn't sure what he was looking for, except answers.

There was nothing to find until a small, clay bottle rolled out of one of the many unmatched, poorly darned socks. Alaric worked the cork out, and a sharp metallic smell cut through the air.

Fire powder. It's a good thing Gustav hadn't had this with him during his dragon stunt. A bottle, even this small, ignited by dragon fire would have caused an explosion big enough to kill Gustav, the dragon, and the rest of them, too. Alaric put the bottle in his pocket and pushed the rest of Gustav's things back into his pack. Footsteps approached behind him.

"If you think this thing is dangerous," Milly said, "we would like you to destroy it. It does seem a little... dark." Douglon and Brandson nodded behind her.

Ayda glanced over at them. "What are you doing with the wizard's medallion?"

"This is Gustav's?" asked Brandson. "What is it?"

The medallion really wasn't Kordan's. A wave of relief washed over Alaric.

"I don't know, but he was very protective of it. I saw it one night when he was rummaging through his bag. I asked if I could see it and he hid it." Ayda hunched her shoulders and scrunched her face into an imitation of Gustav. "*No one can touch it! NO ONE! GET AWAY!*"

Douglon laughed, reached over and set one finger on the medallion. "I'm touching it."

Ayda let out a peal of laughter and took the oval from Milly.

"If Gustav cared about it so much," Milly said, "isn't it odd that he left it behind?"

Douglon shook his head. "He's an idiot. It's not surprising that he screws up anything. The only not-surprising thing is that he succeeded in stealing our treasure from us."

Ayda sat down, turning the medallion over in her hands. "I think these are part of the design," she said to Alaric, pointing to the thick lines cut across the oval.

Alaric reluctantly sat down next to her. Ayda held it out to him, but he shook his head. "I don't want to touch it."

"It keeps trying to pull me in, too." She held the medallion so Alaric could look at it. "See these small tails on the lines? They connect the different strings of runes to each other. Like the ugliest flower chain I've ever seen."

Alaric looked at the lines and felt himself pulled into the medallion. It was a gentle sinking, like falling asleep, but at its core, it felt malevolent. He braced his mind against the pull and studied the runes. Ayda was right. The entire design drew his eye in a serpentine path around the oval. There was no specific starting point, just a twisted loop.

The longer he looked at it, the stronger the pull.

Alaric blinked and looked away. "You're right. The lines are important. It's some sort of instructions. I can't read all of it, but it talks about sacrifice, death, and"—he cast a troubled look at the medallion—"bleeding the life out of someone."

Ayda crinkled her nose and tossed the oval to the ground near the fire. She wiped her hands off on her dress and stood.

Alaric's eyes were drawn back to it. It looked like bronze, but it was missing something. Warmth, maybe. It was too muted to be bronze, as though it sucked in the light that hit it instead of reflecting it. It sat there, a blemish in the dirt, too dark to fit into the sunny day.

"So Gustav really is… evil?" Brandson sank down beside him. He looked hard at the medallion. "When we found out he was alive, I hoped… I don't know what."

"I haven't seen anything this dark since Mallon was alive," Alaric said.

"Did you know Gustav was really a wizard?"

"Yes, but I thought his powers were minimal," Alaric said.

"I thought he was an idiot," Douglon said dropping to the ground beside them.

"Maybe he's a genius," Milly said. "If he played a role that well for so long."

"Impossible," the dwarf said. "He's too much of an idiot."

Alaric looked back down at the medallion. It sat dull and slightly too dark. The dirt around it looked wholesome by comparison. Disconnected thoughts swirled in Alaric's mind. This dark thing was Gustav's. He *hadn't* seen anything that dark since Mallon. The dragon couldn't have been Gustav's pet. Dragons weren't pets. Gustav must have been controlling it. Gustav was good enough at manipulating things to control a dragon.

Thoughts of the oval, the dragon, and Gustav flitted through Alaric's mind. His perfectly clear mind. His mind that had been fuzzy since the moment he had laid eyes on Ayda. Which was the exact moment he had laid eyes on Gustav. And his mind had been clear since Gustav had disappeared with the dragon.

The truth snapped into place.

How had he not seen it?

"Gustav is a Shade Seeker," he said.

Across the clearing, Ayda froze. Slowly, she turned toward him, her face dark and frightening. Something terrifying glinted in her eyes. "My, my. We did underestimate the old man, didn't we?"

CHAPTER SEVENTEEN

GUSTAV WAS A SHADE SEEKER. If there had been any doubt in Alaric's mind before about whether he was still a Keeper, the fact that he had traveled for four days with a Shade Seeker and never noticed settled it.

To have pulled that off, Gustav must be far more powerful than Alaric had thought. And the wizard had even fooled Ayda. She had figured out Alaric was a Keeper the first night he traveled with them, but she had lived at Brandson's with Gustav for a quarter of a year. The thoughts swirled, dragging him farther into doubt. How was he going to find the Wellstone?

Douglon had tried to destroy Gustav's medallion. He'd stomped on it, hit it with his axe, thrown it into the fire, but nothing had any effect on it. While the group numbly gathered their belongings, Alaric wrapped it in a cloth and buried it in the bottom of his pack. The oval didn't exert any pull on him unless he looked at it, but the knowledge that it was there weighed down his pack in an unsettling way.

"Patlon might find us if we go back to Kordan's Blight," Brandson pointed out.

"Doesn't matter anymore," Douglon said. "We don't have what he's looking for. Whenever he shows up, I'll talk to him. The sooner, the better, as far as I'm concerned."

The group trudged back toward the village. Brandson tossed out idea after idea as to Gustav's whereabouts, each as unlikely as the next. Douglon kept up a perpetual rumble under his breath, cursing the old wizard in every conceivable way and kicking rocks as he walked. Milly and Ayda, less gloomy than the others, pulled ahead a little and chatted.

"Not all trees are worth talking to," Ayda explained to Milly. The elf was like a glitter of sunlight passing among the trees. "Whisperwillows are silly, and oaks think too highly of themselves, but a lot of trees are interesting."

Douglon rolled his eyes and kicked the next rock at a tree.

"Can elves really change into trees?" Milly asked. "Does it feel… strange?"

"No, it's lovely. You can drink in the sunshine, and rain on your leaves is the most beautiful feeling in the world."

"I doubt it," Douglon muttered.

Brandson walked up next to Alaric. "Are you going to follow Gustav?"

Alaric nodded. "I need the Wellstone. It holds information that I desperately need."

"What kind of information can a stone hold?"

"An antidote."

Brandson glanced at him, but didn't press further. "How will you find him?"

"I don't know. Shade Seekers have a keep at Sidion. If I

can't find Gustav there, maybe I can find some information about him."

They had walked into a small clearing when Ayda spun toward the north and froze, her eyes boring through the trees. Alaric turned almost as fast, catching a snippet of a tune on the breeze. The others halted as well. The next gust of wind carried the sound of a whistled, jaunty tune.

"That's not Patlon," Douglon said. "Dwarves don't whistle stupid songs. Sounds more like an elf if you ask me."

Ayda ignored him, and Alaric motioned him to be quiet.

Another breeze brought the whistling back to their ears. This time, a throbbing hum could be heard as well. A low purr moving on the air like a warm blanket, wrapping around the things it passed.

"That's lovely," said Milly, pushing past Alaric and taking a step toward the trees.

Alaric grabbed her arm, making the blisters on his palm scream.

"Get her out of here!" Alaric commanded Brandson. "Caves! Are there caves nearby?"

Milly pulled her arm away from Alaric in irritation.

"Bear Stronghold's not far," Brandson said.

The humming and whistling grew closer. Milly smiled and took another step.

Alaric stepped in front of her and grabbed her by both arms, trying to hold on to her without hurting her, or his own hands, any more than he needed to. She shoved against him, glaring at Alaric, but he didn't let go. "Take her," he told Brandson.

"Knock it off!" Brandson said stepping between the Keeper and Milly.

"That is a borrey," Alaric said. "Milly's in grave danger."

"Just mischievous little sprites. No danger," scoffed Douglon.

"Borreys are all male," Alaric said. "That humming you hear is a mating call. It will draw Milly in, she won't be able to resist. They use women to reproduce." Milly was trying to get past Brandson, her eyes fixed on the woods. "The woman does not survive the process."

Milly attempted one more step toward the noise, but Brandson grabbed her.

"Get her to a protected place in the Stronghold," Alaric instructed. "She won't want to go. Get her there and keep her there however you can. And do it fast. Build a fire across the opening. A big one. Borreys hate fire."

Brandson nodded and began to pull Milly across the clearing.

"Help him," Alaric told Douglon. "You may need to carry her."

Douglon hesitated, glancing at Ayda.

"I'm in no danger," she said.

"Go," Alaric urged the dwarf. "Brandson will need your help. We'll come find you. Take this." Alaric pressed Gustav's small bottle into Douglon's hand. "It's Gustav's fire powder. Sprinkle a little on something then strike it with a stick or a stone. It will ignite."

Douglon took the bag and snorted. "This was how he started his 'magical' fires?"

"A little bit goes a long way," warned Alaric.

Douglon flashed a wicked smile. "Will it kill the borrey?"

"Probably not, they're hard to kill. But it should hold it at bay. We'll try to give you some time."

Douglon nodded and ran toward the edge of the clearing where Brandson stood tugging on Milly's arm and pleading with her to follow him. The dwarf ran up, tossed Milly up onto his shoulder and darted off through the trees while she shrieked and pounded on his back. Brandson stared after them in shock.

"Show me the way!" the dwarf bellowed as he ran. Brandson ran after them.

Alaric nodded in approval, then turned back to Ayda.

"And you are still here because…?"

She was watching the woods in the direction of the whistling. "I don't think I'm in any danger. I can help."

Alaric didn't know if borreys took elves for mates. He stood beside her, facing the coming creature. The humming grew louder, and Ayda's eyes glazed. She shifted toward the trees.

"Ayda!" Alaric's voice cracked like a whip. She blinked and looked at him. "You can't be here. Run!"

"Too late," Ayda said, seeing a flicker of movement deep in the trees. She stepped back, her eyes wide.

"I can't protect you," Alaric said, desperate. "If it takes control of you. You'll fight me, too."

"I know," she said, clenching her jaw against the hum. She turned and focused on Alaric. "I can change. Can you help me change back?"

"I can help," Alaric said. The whistling was getting louder. "But you don't have time."

"Of course I do. You've restored an elf before?"

When would he have had the chance to restore an elf from a tree back to their elfin form? "No. But I understand the process."

"Understand the process?"

"You'd be doing the hard part, right? I just have to anchor you with an image to help you snap back to…"—he waved his hand at her—"...this. But you're out of time. I saw Prince Elryn change into a tree, and it took almost five minutes. The elves thought that was fast. I can't hold the borrey off that long."

Ayda looked at Alaric sharply. "You were at the Tree of Hope when Elryn changed?" The humming grew still louder, and Ayda slapped her hands over her ears. Then she squeezed her eyes shut and hummed loudly, drowning out the sound of the borrey. She reached her arms up and took a deep breath in. Closing her eyes, she breathed out. Her feet and toes lengthened, followed by her arms and fingers. Her toes wriggled down into the earth, splitting into roots digging into the dirt. Her legs and torso thickened into a trunk. Her hair flowed along her branches and burst into bright green leaves. By the end of the breath, she had transformed into a slender, silvery tree. Only her face, an oddly tree-like face, remained. It had taken mere seconds. Alaric stared at her dumbfounded.

"An elf, Keeper," she said to him, her voice barely audible. "Help me change back to an elf."

He looked blankly at her for a heartbeat. "Can elves change into anything else?"

"No," she answered, and the tree mouth twitched into a small smile as her face hardened and faded into the trunk.

There was a rustling at the edge of the clearing, and a short young man with wide-set green eyes stepped out of the trees. The creature might have been mistaken for a human except that its sandy hair did not cover the top of its ears, each of which split into two sharp points. The throbbing hum was louder now, emanating from inside the creature. The thing stopped whistling and took a deep breath, smelling the air. A wide smile spread across its face, revealing pointed teeth. Its eyes lit on Alaric, then scanned the rest of the clearing.

"Good morning," the borrey greeted him.

"Good morning," Alaric responded, leaning against the Ayda tree. In his pocket, his fingers began tracing protective runes, concentrating on the magic and trying not to be distracted by the borrey.

"Beautiful day." The creature continued speaking pleasantly even as a small crease of annoyance appeared between its eyebrows. It began walking around the clearing peering into the surrounding trees. "I thought I heard you speaking with a woman as I approached. Have you no companion?"

Alaric looked around the empty clearing. "Just me and the trees."

The borrey turned toward Alaric, its face hungry. Its eyes fell on the Ayda tree. It looked at the silver trunk with its bright green leaves, and its brow furrowed. The creature walked closer. "Do you often talk to trees?"

"Well, not all trees. Whisperwillows are silly, and oaks think too highly of themselves, but some trees are interesting."

The borrey moved within inches of the Ayda tree. Alaric continued to lean against the tree, but his fingers quickened their tracing of protective runes. The energy burned his fingertips and flowed across his blisters like scalding water. The borrey breathed in, its nose brushing the bark of the tree. Then its eyes flashed open and it drew back. Alaric pushed away from the tree quickly as the borrey shot him a look of fury from eyes that were now seething red.

"I wonder what happens to the elf if you kill the tree?" The borrey flexed its hands, and sharp claws flashed out. With a snarl, it stabbed toward the base of the trunk.

Alaric made no move, but an inch from the trunk, the claws deflected as though they'd hit an invisible wall.

"I'm afraid I can't let you do that," Alaric said. "I'm fond of this tree."

The borrey stepped back, eyeing the Keeper. "Not bad," it said, moving forward again and breathing the scent of the tree. This time, the claws flicked out, not at Ayda but straight at Alaric's gut. When they reached his shirt, they twisted to the side again.

"You cannot stop me." The borrey fixed him with a chilling look. "You cannot hurt me. I will wear you down, destroy you, and then deal with the elf."

The creature closed its eyes and took a deep breath, drawing itself up. Alaric braced himself for an attack, but the creature's eyes snapped open.

"Ahhhh," the borrey sighed, relaxing. "You are protecting more than the elf." It lifted its head and smelled again. "A human woman... young.... close."

Alaric tensed, and the borrey's lips curled into a grin.

"How will you protect the human when you are here?" Light glinted off pointed teeth as the borrey flashed a smile. Then it turned, dropping to all fours, and raced off after Milly.

CHAPTER EIGHTEEN

ALARIC SPRINTED through the woods after the borrey already out of sight ahead of him. The ground kept rising and his lungs burned. He was never going to catch the creature.

Even if the others had managed to find a safe place to put Milly, what were they going to do against the borrey? Its skin looked human, but was tough as boiled leather. Douglon's axe *might* hurt it, if he could hit it. But the borrey's reflexes would outmatch the dwarf.

The other problem was that if they ran the borrey off from Milly, it could still return to Ayda. It didn't take much imagination to figure out that damaging the tree would damage Ayda.

No, the borrey would have to be chased off for good. When a borrey found itself in life-threatening danger, it transported itself back to the place of its birth, ice caves in the far north.

Unfortunately, there was a good chance that he, Brandson, and Douglon would not be able to produce that level of threat. By the time Alaric reached Bear Stronghold, he was going to be exhausted. Even if he could think of a spell to use, it was going to be hard to find the strength. He couldn't just trap the creature. They were too close to Kordan's Blight. The borrey would ultimately get free and just pick a new victim in the village. Somehow, he was going to have to generate a legitimate threat.

Early in Alaric's years at the Keepers' Stronghold, they had covered the topic of borreys. Alaric remembered how dissatisfied Keeper Gerone had been.

"Is the transport willful or instinctual?" he had asked. "We do not know. There is too much we do not know! We need to send someone to study them. But borreys never make it high enough on the list of dangers to warrant any attention.

"They are not dangerous to the public at large, but I'm afraid that for the unfortunate woman whom the borrey captures, it is always fatal.

"Borreys are rare and only mate every twelve years, but still… If you find yourself defending such a woman, my only advice for you is fire. Lots of fire."

First a dragon. Now a borrey. What was it about this group that drew exceptionally dangerous trouble?

If Douglon had managed to get a fire lit and Alaric was close enough, he could make it burn brighter. The flame Ayda had solidified into a necklace hung from his neck and glinted in the sun. This was a bad time for her to be unavailable.

Alaric swore for the hundredth time and pushed farther up the hill. He finally reached the edge of the trees. Above him, stretching out in both directions was a rocky cliff face. Sitting partway up the cliff was a stout wall enclosing two towers. There was a narrow arch cut into the wall, and the borrey crouched in front of it. Douglon stood before the doorway, swinging his axe with Brandson off to the side.

There was no fire anywhere. Alaric ran toward the path that wound up to the Stronghold. He rounded the first turn as an enormous explosion rocked the ground, shaking the Stronghold and knocking him to his knees. Alaric's palms slammed against the ground, and his blisters burst. He gasped in pain.

An inhuman shriek of rage echoed off the rocks, and Alaric saw the silhouette of the borrey cringing back from an enormous wall of flames. Behind Brandson, a section of the Stronghold wall cracked and crashed down in a cloud of dust and rock. Alaric shoved himself back up and ran closer. The borrey was on a small ledge in front of the entrance. On either side of the ledge, the ground dropped off steeply. Douglon and Brandson had chosen a good place. The borrey howled at the wall of flame in front of him.

"What troubles you?" bellowed Douglon over the fire. "Afraid you'll burn your pretty hair?"

The borrey snarled and dropped to all fours as it paced.

That fire wouldn't last long on the rocky ledge. Once the fire powder burned up, there would be no fuel to keep it going. Already, the flames were shrinking. If Alaric could get closer, he could add more energy to the fire, make it bigger.

"Come, pretty boy," Douglon called, "come meet my axe. Do you fear a little fire? Like a common dog?"

The borrey hissed, its long claws reflecting the firelight. The flames between Douglon and the creature sank lower.

The borrey crept closer.

From the edge of the wall of fire, Brandson started throwing stones. The borrey paused to glare at him, but every stone flew wide of the creature. Douglon shouted at it again, drawing its attention back to him. The flames were shrinking quickly. In a matter of moments, the borrey would leap across them.

Brandson was still throwing rocks. The blacksmith had never looked so incompetent. The stones would not have done the borrey any real harm, but Brandson had thrown a half dozen already, and each had sailed over the creature's head, landing an arm span behind him.

"Where's your aim, boy?" Douglon shouted, taking a step back toward the wall.

Brandson swore and scrambled about for another rock.

Alaric reached the ledge behind the borrey. He started to gather some energy to add to the fire. He could see nothing living around him, though, and he himself was exhausted. He was too far from the borrey to steal any of his. He began drawing from his own energy when Brandson threw a rock in a high arc toward the Keeper.

"Alaric! Get back! The powder!" Brandson pointed to Alaric's feet.

Alaric looked down an instant before the stone landed and saw the sparkle of fire powder. He dove behind the nearest boulder.

There was a deafening explosion when Brandson's stone hit the fire powder. Alaric lay there stunned, the world strangely muffled and a dizzying pressure in his ears. He shook his head to clear it and scrambled to his knees. Leaning around the boulder, he saw an arc of flames behind the borrey trapping it in a cage of fire. Alaric's hearing began to return, and he heard the borrey scream in rage as it spun around, finding itself encircled in flame. It stepped forward, hissing and spitting at Brandson.

Tucked in behind the boulder with Alaric was a stand of

brown scrub brush. It was alive, barely, but that was something. Alaric drew the *vitalle* from the scrub brush and pushed it toward the fire. His hands seared as though they were in the flames themselves, but Alaric forced himself to focus on the fire, pulling every last bit of energy from the scrub brush. The flames rose higher and brighter. Douglon and Brandson stepped back and shielded their faces.

The next moment, lines of fire powder leading in toward the borrey ignited and streams of flame shot toward it. Alaric poured all the energy he could find into the fire, his outstretched hands clenched as the pain seared through them.

The borrey turned, cringing away from the fire. It raised its head and let out a piercing shriek. One last pile of fire powder ignited right next to the borrey and it screamed again. Looking around frantically, it raised its hands to the sky and let out a howl. The flame flickered brightly for a second, then a thunderous clap reverberated through the air. Alaric felt the boom deep in his chest.

The borrey was gone.

Alaric cut off the flow of energy, and the ring of fire weakened. Through the flames, Brandson peered at him. Alaric lifted his hand slightly in a wave.

Brandson threw his arms into the air and let out a shout. Douglon bellowed something and pounded Brandson on the back.

When the flames died out, Brandson crossed over the blackened lines on the ground to clap Alaric on the shoulder.

"Don't know where the rotten beast went," Douglon said with a wicked grin, "but we sure pissed it off."

Brandson looked around. "Where did it go? Where's the rest of the powder?"

Alaric shook his head, "No need for that. You two have managed to pull off the only solution to a Borrey attack. You sent it scurrying back home, far, far away."

Brandson grinned.

"In that case, well done us." Douglon glanced at the black scorch marks then at Alaric. "Thanks for the help with the flames."

Alaric nodded. A line of pus and blood ran out from under one of his bandages. "It's a good thing the flames didn't need any more help."

Douglon looked down the slope, "Where's the elf?"

"She's… waiting down in the valley. Where's Milly?"

Brandson cleared his throat and his eyes flicked toward the tower. "Uh, she wouldn't stay inside, so…"

"We had to tie her to a post." Douglon shook his head. "For a little thing, she put up a good fight."

"She was pretty mad." Brandson pulled up his sleeve, showing long, red scratches running up to his elbow. "I guess we should go untie her," he said, not moving.

Douglon grunted and looked through the arch in the wall, not moving, either.

Alaric heaved himself up. "She'll be fine now that the borrey's gone."

Alaric followed the others into the Stronghold. The air inside the wall was thick with dust, and their feet crunched on loose rock spilled across the courtyard from the collapsed wall. A shriek and sounds of a scuffle came from inside the leftmost tower.

"Milly!" Brandson shouted as he rushed inside followed by Douglon.

Alaric dragged his feet forward after the others, trying to hurry.

A loud clang rang out. "Stay back, you... you... you..." Milly yelled.

Alaric made it to the doorway of the tower. The inside was dark and stale. Brandson and Douglon stepped inside and Alaric followed, slumping back against the wall next to the doorway. As his eyes adjusted to the gloom, he saw Milly brandishing a frying pan.

"Milly," Brandson pleaded, "we had no choice. It was for your own good."

"Tying me to a rock?" she shrieked. "In a room with a monster?"

"We saved your life," Douglon pointed out. "Where'd you find a pan?"

"The monster was outside the walls," Brandson said, his arms spread out in a placating sort of way as he inched closer to Milly. "Put down the pan. Please. It's okay. We fought it off." A little bit of pride crept into his voice.

"Outside?" she asked. Her voice rose an octave. "Outside?"

She took a long, shuddering breath, then, as though talking to children, she said, "While you two *heroes* left me tied up in here, this monster"—she waved the frying pan at a lump on the floor—"crept out of the dark and tried to kill me! If you hadn't tied such pathetic knots, I'd be dead!"

The form on the floor shifted and groaned. A hand rose and grabbed its head. Alaric could make out a beard and deep-set eyes.

There was a creak of leather as Douglon approached, holding his axe. "Get up slowly."

"Drop your axe, you meathead," the figure grumbled. "You're so slow with it, I could sit up, eat a meal, and saunter out of the tower before your blow ever fell."

Douglon's eyes narrowed. "On your feet! Now!"

The figure raised its head, wincing. It was a dwarf. With a moan, his head fell back to the floor.

"I'm afraid you'll have to kill me here, cousin. It seems I'm not quite ready to rise."

Alaric slid down the wall to sit on the floor. If he weren't so exhausted, he would laugh.

Douglon gestured to the dwarf on the floor. "Everyone, meet my cousin, Patlon."

CHAPTER NINETEEN

ALARIC SAT against the wall of the tower, exhausted. The split blisters on his palms throbbed. The more his eyes grew accustomed to the dim room, the more he could tell that Patlon must have been staying here. There was a large fireplace along the far wall with a scattering of cooking supplies near it. Milly stomped over to it and dropped the pan with a clatter, while Douglon hoisted Patlon up against one of the thick posts supporting the ceiling.

Milly took the rope out of Douglon's hands. "If you tie him up, he'll be out in no time. You can't just tangle ropes together and call it a knot."

Patlon let out a low chuckle as Milly tugged and tied the rope. "He's always been terrible at knots."

"You'd best shut your mouth, cousin," Douglon said. "You're not well thought of here."

Brandson rummaged through Patlon's cooking wares and brought a piece of thick-crusted bread to Alaric. "You look a bit worn out."

When Alaric lifted his hand to take it, Brandson's eyes

widened at the bloody bandage. "Here." He tore off a piece of the loaf.

Alaric took it gratefully and sank his teeth into the bread. It was dry and coarse and possibly the most delicious thing he had ever eaten.

Brandson and Milly unwrapped Alaric's hands one at a time before rewrapping them in clean bandages. Alaric ate the last bite of bread and flexed his hands. It was going to be days before his hands were useful.

Leaving Brandson, Milly, and Douglon to watch Patlon, Alaric began the long walk back to the clearing with the Ayda tree.

When Alaric reached the tree, one thin branch brushed across the top of his head.

"It's nice to see you, too," he answered. "I didn't realize you could control your branches. I suppose it makes sense, though. The branches are sort of your fingers, aren't they?" Where sunlight trickled through the pale green leaves, her bark was glimmering silver. "What kind of tree are you?"

The tree quivered a little.

"You invented it, didn't you?"

It quivered again.

"Well, don't drop any seeds. I don't think the world is ready for a forest of Ayda-trees.

"We scared off the borrey. But then we found Patlon hiding where they stashed Milly. I don't know if I can trust the dwarves not to kill each other, so let's change you back."

Alaric reached out his hand toward the trunk but paused at the thought of putting his blistered palm on her trunk. As far as he knew, he wasn't going to contribute any energy to this process, just provide Ayda with an image of herself, something she could focus on. Still, it took some effort of will to put his aching palm on the trunk.

"All right," he said, "I've got you fixed in my mind."

He stood still for several moments, eyes closed, mind focused on an image of Ayda. When nothing happened, he glanced up. She was still a tree. A tree reaching toward the sun and swaying in the breeze with more exuberance than the others.

"Ayda! Pay attention."

The tree settled down a bit. Alaric focused on Ayda as an elf again.

No energy flowed out of his hand, but where his skin touched the trunk, the warmth of his hand leeched out, leaving his fingers ice cold. He gasped and tried to pull his hand away, but it was fixed on the tree. His fingers grew white until they were as pale as the trunk.

The coldness moved up his arm, the warmth being leeched out from deep within muscle and bone. It crept higher, and Alaric tugged on his arm with his other hand.

A branch snapped down and swatted the Keeper across the cheek. Alaric looked up at the tree, realizing that he had lost his focus.

He froze. The tree was not turning back into Ayda. Instead of resolving down into her body, the branches were stretching out farther, solidifying into a disjointed tangle of limbs, eyes, and gaping mouths. Directly above his head, a tortured face emerged out of the wood, its mouth open in a silent scream. Branches stretched out into clawed hands and twisted legs. Eyes bulged out, wide and sightless.

Alaric stared in horror until another branch stung him across the arm. Squeezing his eyes shut, he dragged his focus back onto the idea of Ayda, desperately holding an image of her as an elf in his mind. The cold seeped into his chest. He clung to the image of Ayda as his knees buckled and he dropped to the ground.

The darkness stirred sluggishly and warm hands pulled at him. He dragged his eyes open to see Ayda, once again an elf, standing over him.

"Now I know why we use elves instead of humans as our anchors," she said, her voice far away. "I almost sucked the life right out of you." She knelt down next to him.

He couldn't breathe, his body was heavy and dull, and blackness flowed into the edges of his vision. Ayda took his numb, white hand and held it close to her mouth. She breathed across his fingertips. Warmth surged up his arm like a wave. It flowed into his chest, and Alaric's lungs drew in a rush of air.

Alaric sat up as though he'd just woken up from a long sleep. His vision was clear, and every trace of exhaustion was gone. Only the burns on his hands still hurt, and even that pain was deadened. He looked up at Ayda. She was fair and glittery and normal. Or as normal as Ayda could be. "What happened?"

"I drew too much out of you," Ayda said as she sat down beside him.

"I didn't know I was contributing to the process."

"You weren't supposed to," Ayda said. "I just needed an image to grab on to."

Alaric rubbed his fingers, which were now back to their proper color. "Well, the grabbing hurt more than I thought it would."

"It shouldn't have. Sorry. I wasn't paying quite as much attention as I should have been. You see, there was a lovely sunbeam that I had caught in my upper branch, and..." She paused and smiled at Alaric's glare. "I didn't notice how hard I grabbed."

"Do you know of any other time when a human was used for an anchor? What if I hadn't been able to bring you back?" Alaric asked. "Were you just willing to live out the rest of your centuries as a tree?"

"You aren't just a human, you're a Keeper. That makes you slightly more useful. And you make it sound like it would be bad not to change back. I like being a tree." She looked exactly as she always had, with no trace of disjointed limbs or eyes.

"You were terrifying," he told her. "I thought the anchor was just a focus because trees are distractible. What were all the arms and legs and faces? I didn't know you could change into anything other than...you."

"I suppose in a way that is me, too."

She was a monster with dozens of limbs and heads? Alaric opened his mouth to ask more, but at the dark expression on Ayda's face, he paused.

"Now," she said briskly, "it is easy to get distracted as a tree, but did you mention Patlon?"

Alaric groaned and stood. "Oh, I almost forgot. He was making camp inside the Stronghold. I'll be amazed if they haven't killed each other yet."

They started across the clearing.

"You seemed surprised that I was at Prince Elryn's changing," Alaric said. "It was during my years at court, so I attended with Queen Saren. I don't remember meeting you there, but there were a lot of elves."

Ayda continued walking for a moment before answering. "I wasn't there."

"Really? Were there many absent?"

She shook her head. "Only one."

"Where were you?"

She ignored the question. "You understand what the ceremony meant?"

"It named Elryn heir to the elven throne. Sometime you need to sit down with me and explain the elven royal family tree. The Keepers are always annoyed that we can't pin down exactly how you are all related, and no elves ever explain it. But Elryn is King Andolin's eldest son, right? Isn't it your custom for the eldest child to be the next ruler?"

Ayda laughed, "The custom is not mine, but it is what my people do. We aren't as bound by the idea of inheriting the throne as you humans are, but more often than not, the crown is accepted by the eldest child." She shrugged. "I had a role to play in the ceremony that I wasn't interested in. So I left and let someone else do it."

Alaric snorted. Elves didn't shirk responsibilities. Whether it was because of a sense of communal consciousness or just a cultural trait, they accepted their roles in elven society without complaint. True, there was little structure to the elven culture, but Alaric had never heard of one refusing to do what was asked of them.

"Ayda, sometimes when you talk, you sound more human than elf."

"That's what my father said. He blamed it on my mother."

Alaric looked at her in surprise. "Was she human?"

Ayda's peal of laughter rang through the trees. "Do I look like my mother was a human? You're a Keeper, so you must have heard of Ayala."

Alaric stopped. "Queen Ayala was your mother?"

Ayda nodded and stopped as well. She turned toward him and smiled a patient little smile.

"If she's your... then you..."

Ayda nodded encouragingly.

"Princess Aydalya?" he asked in amazement.

"At your service," she curtsied. "I am Aydalya, daughter of Queen Ayala. First born of King Andolin, elder half-sister to the crowned Prince Elryn."

"Elder!" He stared at her for a long moment. "You should have been named heir!"

"That was the role I didn't want."

CHAPTER TWENTY

PRINCESS AYDALYA? Not only had he found an elf, he'd found the only living elf princess. What was Princess Aydalya doing wandering around the northern edges of the kingdom with a bunch of treasure hunters?

"My brother was the better choice for heir," she continued. "His mind was built for ruling and planning and listening." Ayda reached up and touched a leaf. "Mine is... less steadfast."

"More human?"

Ayda laughed again, "That's what my father would say."

"So, your mother was captured by goblins and rescued by the human, Boman. She then lived with him for the rest of his life."

"For forty years, yes," Ayda said. "When she returned to the forest, she had developed some human-like tendencies. When she married my father, he said she proved that humanness was contagious. When I was born, he decided it was also hereditary." She looked ahead to where the forest still blocked their view of the caves. "May we continue now, Keeper?"

Alaric fell into step beside her again. She was Princess Aydalya. Even traveling with Queen Saren to the elves, he had barely received more than a nod from King Andolin. Elves just weren't interested in humans. A few elves had been assigned the job of making the human visitors comfortable, and they had been polite but distant. His mind swirled with questions for her.

"So was that when you left your people? The day of the ceremony?" It was hardly the most important question, but he needed somewhere to start.

"No. I went to the southern edge of the Greenwood for that day only. Once the ceremony was finished, I returned." She was silent a long moment. "I thought I had ended any plans my father had for me."

"He had another?"

Ayda's face shadowed again. "He didn't plan it, but he still forced me into a terrible fate."

"More terrible than becoming queen?" Alaric asked wryly.

Ayda took a deep breath, and the trees around them stilled. Alaric glanced around uneasily.

"More terrible than you can imagine," she answered.

The moment passed, and the forest breathed again.

They walked in silence for several minutes. Alaric kept a watch on her from the corner of his eye. It was unnerving that she walked so soberly beside him. His mind still shot out question after question. She was an elven princess who had first refused the throne, then left her people. Each of those facts alone demanded a long explanation, but she was walking so pensively, he couldn't bring himself to ask.

"The elves thought that Elryn had changed into a tree very quickly," he said, looking for a new subject, "but it took him several minutes."

A smile cracked her somberness.

When she didn't comment, he continued, "They said Elryn was faster than any elf they had ever seen."

"It drove him mad!" she said, bursting into laughter. "He had praise heaped upon him for how fast he could change, and the whole time, he knew what I could do. When we were children, we used to race. If you can call it a race."

"He never told anyone?"

She shook her head. "It wasn't his secret to tell. Until today, no one else has seen me change."

"How do you do it? Are you some sort of… elf prodigy?"

Ayda's laughter rang off the nearby trees. "Hardly. I've always been mediocre at everything. Except changing. And I don't know why I'm so fast at that. Elryn says he has to coax his body into changing shape. For me, it's like stretching. At any given moment, I think my body would rather be a tree."

"You're good at that freeze-the-fire trick," Alaric motioned to the flame that still hung around his neck.

Ayda's smile faded from her face. "That's a more recent skill."

"I've never seen anything like it."

She sighed. "Neither had I."

"What is it?" Alaric raised the flame toward her. "Is it flame or stone?

"It's a flame still. Well, it has the potential to be a flame still. Or maybe the longing to be a flame."

"Can you turn it back into a flame?"

Ayda's eyes widened. "Oh, you don't want that. The potential it has keeps building up in it. I changed one back, once. It had only been still for a few minutes, but when I changed it back, it quickly grew to several times bigger than it had been. The one you have has been still for so long, it would be huge if I changed it back."

Alaric held the flame as far away from him as the necklace would allow. "Is it going to happen on its own?"

Ayda laughed. "No, it takes some very specific manipulating to coax it back into a flame. It couldn't do it on its own."

She turned away from him and continued walking. Alaric cast out toward the flame to see if he could detect any energy, but it was completely dormant. He let the flame fall back down onto his chest, hoping he wasn't carrying around some sort of bomb.

"What do you want Kordan's treasure for?" Ayda motioned to the pouch hanging beneath Alaric's robe. "It has to do with Evangeline, doesn't it? Can it raise the dead?"

Alaric grabbed the pouch, protecting it against his chest. "Evangeline's not dead!"

Ayda raised an eyebrow. "She's not really alive, though, is she?"

Alaric pulled the pouch out of his shirt and loosened it. He dropped the warm, swirling ruby out into his hand. "Still alive," he answered, "but still sick."

Ayda's eyes widened. She leaned toward the Reservoir Stone but made no move to touch it. The light filled his palm, casting red light over his hand and Ayda's face. There was a pulse to the swirling, like a heartbeat. Alaric let his eyes follow the currents diving and dancing from one irregular surface to another for a moment. It was several breaths before the dark line surfaced. It stretched out longer than before. Alaric clenched the ruby in his hand before returning it to his pouch.

"Kordan's treasure is a Wellstone that holds the antidote I need to heal her."

"What will you do with the ruby?" Ayda asked.

"Wake her up." He shook his head.

"Do you know how?"

"I understand the process."

Ayda let out a short laugh. "That worked out well for you last time. Maybe I should be there in case you almost die again."

Alaric scowled and walked faster.

"The real question is," Ayda continued, "why did the wizard steal the Wellstone? I doubt he has a wife in a crystal box."

"Stay out of my head!" Alaric snapped.

She skipped a little to keep up. "You think about Evangeline constantly."

Alaric stopped.

Ayda stopped, too. "I don't try to listen, you know, but sometimes you shout your thoughts at me. And your thoughts of Evangeline are usually so sad. Although sometimes they're sweet. Like this." Ayda reached out and touched Alaric's arm.

Alaric stood in the Napon market. The southern sun poured down on the awnings slung between booths, lighting the stalls in hues of reds and yellows. It was still too deep in summer, too stiflingly hot, for there to be many shoppers. The few vendors that bothered to open booths today called out lazily in deep, southern accents.

Alaric set down another bottle of ink. Just a dark bluish black, like the others. The vendor called after him, dropping the price as he walked away, but Alaric gave him a smile and moved on. In the corner of the next booth sat a mismatched collection of little glass bottles filled with inks. Alaric held several up to the light to see their color. Behind him, he heard Evangeline ask a question.

"Six coppers," the vendor said. "Six coppers for the pretty flower bowl."

"Six?" Evangeline laughed. "Two coppers for the pretty flower bowl."

She was holding a small, clay bowl. The red clay formed an almost round bowl with a blue and yellow flower painted on the inside. It was a happy bowl, if not a high quality one. Two coppers was generous.

The vendor shook his head. "Six coppers. Flower bowls are six coppers."

Alaric turned back to the inks, hoping to find a red.

"Four coppers?" Evangeline's voice was less certain now.

"Six." The vendor's voice was firm.

The last bottle Alaric held up to the light was dark blue. Red ink was too rare to find in a naponese tourist market, but it never hurt to check.

He turned to find Evangeline behind him, smiling and holding the bowl. The pottery vendor flashed him a big smile, and Alaric put his arm around Evangeline's shoulder as they walked away. Her shoulders quivered with little laughs.

"You bought it?" The bowl was not even close to being round.

She looked up at him ruefully. "He wouldn't change his price."

Alaric laughed. "He didn't need to."

"I know," she laughed, "but shouldn't he have at least pretended to bargain with me?"

"He bargained very well." Alaric held his hand out for the bowl. "I think you're the one who didn't really bargain."

She laughed and gave it to him. "It didn't quite go as I had planned."

"Why didn't you walk away?"

"Because I like the bowl," she said, considering the colors painted on it. "The flower reminds me of the sky and sunshine."

Alaric held the bowl out in front of them and squinted at it. "Well, I do see blue and yellow. What exactly does the brownish red clay remind you of?"

"Someday," she said, taking it back and admiring it, "it will remind me of a naponese market I visited with you. It will remind me how great Keepers are always rummaging through the things around them, looking for what they need—whether it's knowledge or red ink. And it will remind me that maybe sometimes, it is better to stop rummaging and just ask someone." With a flourish, she produced a small glass bottle.

Alaric reached for it in astonishment. He held it up toward a ray of sunlight trickling through the fabric above them. The ink inside glowed like dark red wine. "This is perfect!"

"You can repay me at dinner tonight. When they request a story from you, tell Tomkin and the Dragon. I love that one."

"I will." Alaric kissed the top of her head. "I have the best wife."

"Yes, you do."

He glanced at her out of the corner of his eye. "Do I want to know how much you paid for this?"

She grinned. "No, you do not."

"I like that memory," Ayda said. "You two are so happy."

Alaric yanked his hand away from Ayda. "Stay out of my head!"

Ayda resumed walking. "Keep your thoughts to yourself."

Alaric followed her, off guard. It was his own memory she had shown him. He was partly furious that she knew it, partly heartbroken because he and Evangeline had been happy. He watched Ayda walk ahead of him, settling on an emotion somewhere near irritation. "Can you read everyone's mind as easily as you read mine?"

Ayda crinkled her brow. "No, yours is the clearest. Maybe because it's more… open? You could read my mind if you wanted, couldn't you?"

"I could try."

"Maybe that's why, then. You've trained your mind to reach outside of itself, so to me, it's open."

"Wasn't Gustav's mind open?"

Ayda cringed. "No." She paused. "Maybe that's why I never thought he was a wizard. Even Brandson and Douglon occasionally shout their thoughts when they're excited, but Gustav was always shut tight. I assumed he was just incredibly boring."

Alaric wished he knew how Gustav had done that. Add that to the list of questions he had for the wizard.

"Maybe he wants the Wellstone for a different reason than you do." Ayda said. "What else is in it?"

"Records of Kordan's work. He worked with seeds and…" Alaric reached for the ruby again, "he created a stone like this one. An emerald."

"Maybe the wizard is after that knowledge. Maybe he needs to bring someone back from the brink of death, like you do."

"Who would a Shade Seeker want to wake?"

Ayda stopped walking and spun toward Alaric.

Her eyes burned and her hair darkened until it was the

deep red of a glowing coal. Waves of heat radiated from her, pushing Alaric back a step.

Her hair lifted, blown by a wind Alaric couldn't feel, and sparks whipped out from the ends. She clenched her fists, and Alaric took another step back.

When she spoke, it was in a deadly whisper that shook the ground beneath his feet.

"He's going to wake Mallon."

Her hair lifted, blown by a wind Alaric couldn't feel and sparks whipped out from the ends. She clenched her fists and Alaric took another step back.

CHAPTER TWENTY-ONE

ALARIC STARED at Ayda and took yet another step back. She seethed with fury, her eyes glinting with cold light.

Wake Mallon?

Mallon was dead.

Ayda reached down, picked up a stick, and stared hard at it. She muttered angrily and began stalking up the hill.

Alaric followed behind her, a fear stealing over him that he hadn't felt in years. Was it possible that Mallon was still alive? He had disappeared and all signs of his power had ended. What could cause that aside from death?

He opened his mouth twice to ask her a question, any of the questions he had, but each time, she shot him such a glare that he shut his mouth again.

The stick in her hand shifted until it was a perfect likeness of Gustav's face and pointy hat, with a distinctly idiotic expression.

She hissed a vicious-sounding word and crushed the visage into her palm sending an explosion of splinters out from her tiny white hand.

Alaric hung back a moment, letting her move up the hill away from him. He stared at the settling shards of wood then watched the elf warily as she continued toward the Stronghold.

Ayda stopped and turned to wait for Alaric. He approached her with every sense alert, waiting for something terrifying to happen, but her hair was golden again and the fury had settled to the back of her eyes.

"I'm going to kill him."

"Oh." Gustav or Mallon?

Ayda looked straight into Alaric's eyes, and he braced himself for… something. But she just smiled a humorless smile.

"I like you, Alaric." She gave an elfish lilt to his name that caught his attention. It was the first time she had ever spoken his name. With that word, something changed. The glow that surrounded Ayda faded slightly, and she looked more concrete, more solid.

"I'm going to kill that idiot wizard before he can wake Mallon. You can come with me, if you'd like." Ayda turned and headed toward the Stronghold. "Bring whomever you'd like along," she tossed over her shoulder.

When they reached the others, the smell of roasting meat drifted out of the Stronghold along with echoes of laughter.

"So much for killing each other," Alaric said as they walked in.

"She dragged King Horgoth out," Patlon was saying, sitting next to the others by the fire, "by his beard!"

Douglon howled with laughter and pounded on the floor. Brandson was doubled over, and Milly wiped her eyes.

"Did he marry her?" Milly asked.

Patlon nodded. "That evening."

Alaric cleared his throat, and Douglon waved him over.

"Patlon, this is Keeper Alaric. He's been traveling with us."

Patlon nodded his head in greeting.

"And the elf is Ayda."

Patlon smiled at her. "My axe was blessed by an elf," Patlon said, lifting up his purple-shafted axe for Ayda to see. "Do you know any purple-haired elves?"

"Pella's hair was purple once," Ayda said, walking over to run her fingers along the purple wood. "It changed with the seasons."

"Her blessing did something to the wood, and it's near unbreakable. Do you—" Patlon paused. "Do you think she'd remember me? It was many years ago."

Ayda looked at the axe for a long moment. "She remembers you. Elves don't forget."

Patlon sat up straighter, throwing a smug look at Douglon.

Ayda turned back to Douglon. "Speaking of not forgetting, aren't we very angry with Patlon? I vividly remember a burned smithy."

"He's offered to rebuild it," Brandson said. "Twice as big and closer to the river." The blacksmith grinned. "And he's going to give me enough dwarfish rock steel to make five knives."

"One of which I get back," Patlon added. "I didn't mean to burn it down. I've been here for several weeks, hunting about near these rocks, but I just recently learned that Douglon was here. I went to confront him at the smithy, but I upended a bucket of ashes, and before I knew it, the whole place was ablaze."

"And so you stopped to carve a threatening symbol on a rock for us to find?" Alaric said.

"I had made it already," Patlon hedged, "and the damage was done. I figured I could at least make Douglon mad."

Douglon waved off the apologetic look from his cousin. "The rockslide has settled, cousin. No worries."

"You haven't told me if you've had any luck with the treasure, though," Patlon said.

Douglon leaned forward. "We found it."

Patlon looked eagerly at the others for confirmation.

"We almost found it," Brandson said. "But it was stolen by someone we were searching with."

"You found the treasure, then someone you trusted stole it?" Patlon asked Douglon, deadpan. "How dreadful for you."

Douglon glared at him. "It was stolen by a powerful wizard."

Alaric raised his eyebrow. That was more credit than Douglon had ever given Gustav.

"Then let's go find him!" Patlon rose and hefted his purple axe. "Where would he go to sell it around here?"

"We are not going to find him by wandering aimlessly," Alaric broke in. "He's a Shade Seeker."

Patlon looked around quickly. "You forgot to mention that."

"Well," Douglon said, "If you knew him, you'd forget, too. He's sort of bumbly."

"I think it's safe to say that the bumbling was an act," Alaric said.

"I don't know," Brandson said. "He lived with us for months. It was very convincing."

"The only non-bumbly thing he did was steal the gem out from under us." Douglon said.

"And sic his dragon on us," Ayda said.

"He has a dragon?" Patlon asked, dropping back down onto the floor.

"And he's not going to sell the gem," Alaric said. "He took it for a specific reason."

Everyone turned toward him except Ayda. She turned her back on them and looked out the door.

"Ayda thinks he took it to raise Mallon," Alaric said.

The room went perfectly still.

"Mallon?" said Milly faintly.

"He stole a gem to raise the Rivor from the dead?" Douglon looked at Alaric as though he was joking. "Is he going to buy him back from the underworld?"

Patlon chuckled. "I didn't realize the dead were for sale."

"He's not dead," Ayda said, still facing the door, her back stiff.

"Of course he's dead," scoffed Patlon. "Even the dwarves know the story of how he strode into the Greenwood to conquer you but your people destroyed him."

Ayda turned slowly from the wall and passed her gaze over each of them, ending with Patlon. Each one of them drew back at her expression. When she looked at Patlon, he wilted.

"I was there when he was bound," she continued, walking to Patlon and towering over him. Her face grew dark, and she seemed to stretch taller. "He is not dead," she ended with a whisper.

No one breathed for a moment.

"Bound?" Alaric asked, finally.

Ayda turned away from Patlon. "For lack of a better word. The Rivor can't be killed or trapped like a mortal. He's only connected loosely to his physical body. Not enough of him inhabits his body for hurting it to cause him any real harm."

The others exchanged puzzled looks.

"How did your people bind him?" Alaric asked.

"We made a net to catch him and drew it close around his body. Then we froze him there."

"In ice?" Patlon asked.

Ayda gave a short laugh. "No, it's not like he's stuck in a crystal box."

Alaric scowled at her.

"It's almost impossible to stop a will that strong, but we set his mind on a path that leads back to itself. He is fighting to get out, but the route he is taking is circular. The hope is that he cannot escape."

"So that is why all of his spells ended?" Alaric said. "Because his will is confined to himself now?"

Ayda nodded. "He could spread his will far from himself. He could attach it to a person and leave part of it there. It took my people a long time to figure out what he was doing. It was Prince Elryn who first detached one of Mallon's spells from someone.

"The spell needed somewhere to go, though, so it attached itself to Elryn. He was able to destroy it by transforming into a tree. This is where we got the idea of how to defeat him. We realized that if we could collect all of the spells and destroy them at once, there would be nothing left of Mallon outside of his own body. He would be mortal.

"That is when I began to travel," Ayda continued. "I visited every town I could find and marked any cursed people I found."

"Marked?" asked Douglon.

"In a way another elf could find, yes. I was returning from the far south, but not yet home when the elves began. It was earlier than planned, but there was no doubt. I could feel elves, hundreds of them, stretching out toward the marked ones." She looked far away and fell silent.

"Did it work?" Milly asked timidly.

Ayda blinked and looked around.

"Yes, but the Rivor arrived too soon, and the battle began before they had destroyed all the spells. Mallon was gravely wounded… but at a terrible price." Ayda turned back toward the wall. "All of my people were lost."

"No!" Milly said.

Alaric listened, stunned. All of the elves were dead?

The room was silent.

Ayda sighed. "I was too late. When I got to my people, they had taken Mallon's power onto themselves, but it was too much. My people were dead, and Mallon was senseless, but alive. I tried to kill him, but nothing I could do harmed his body. He was trapped, but not defeated."

She took a deep breath and looked around. "I carried his body to the Elder Grove, an ancient place. It is surrounded by the oldest trees in the forest, which will let none but elves enter. It took a bit of convincing for the trees to let me take him there." Ayda smiled sadly. "I left him there, secure in their deep magic, in the hopes of discovering a way to kill him."

Alaric realized he had been holding his breath and let it out. This was why no elves had been found in eight years. It wasn't that they were being secretive. Ayda was the only one left to be found.

CHAPTER TWENTY-TWO

A GREAT LOSS swept through Alaric. He knew there had never been many elves in the Greenwood, but he couldn't believe all but Ayda were gone.

Patlon frowned. "You know, I had discounted them as rumors, but we've heard news that nomadic tribes have been gathering in the Scales."

Alaric turned sharply. "Do nomads usually come into the Scale Mountains?"

"The last time was eight years ago when they joined with Mallon. I think those rumors need some investigating." Patlon slapped Douglon on the shoulder. "Cousin, you'll have to chase the single, solitary, old man by yourself. I need to go face hordes of vicious nomads."

Alaric nodded. "Tell King Horgoth to tell Queen Saren what the dwarves know."

Patlon raised an eyebrow. "I can't tell the High Dwarf what to do."

"Well, tell him I told you to," Douglon grumbled. "Tell

him to get off that ugly throne and start doing something useful."

Alaric raised an eyebrow at Douglon's brashness.

Patlon winced. "It won't be any better coming from you. In fact, it would be a lot worse. It's going to take me a little time to smooth things over between you and Horgoth."

"Smooth what over?"

"Your banishment," Patlon said apologetically.

"My *what*?"

"Well, I might have mentioned to Horgoth that you stole the map from me."

"How does that get me banished?"

"He thought that we had intended to bring him the treasure. He decided that you had stolen the map so you could keep the gem from him, and I couldn't correct him without saying that neither of us had ever considered giving it to him."

"Why would we?"

"Exactly! Since when do we drop all the treasure we find off with him? Did we give him the gold from that crown?"

"Or the barrels of whiskey from the monastery?" Douglon added.

"Don't worry, cousin," Patlon said. "I'll smooth things over with him. It will be taken care of long before you get back there."

"What will happen to you if it's not smoothed over?" Brandson asked Douglon.

"Jail," Douglon said.

"Well," Patlon tugged nervously at his beard. "Actually, he would be executed."

"You said banished," Douglon said in a low voice.

"Did I?"

"But execution isn't the penalty for breaking a banishment. It's the penalty for treason."

"I didn't mean for him to leap to treason," Patlon said, holding his hands out to keep Douglon back. "But somehow, Horgoth convinced himself that you were collecting wealth so that you could set yourself up as High Dwarf."

"What?" Douglon shouted. "You got me banished by convincing Horgoth that I wanted to be king? And he *believed* you?"

"I didn't do anything! You know how he is," Patlon said, inching backward. "He's always been a little insecure about your claim to the throne."

"Douglon has a claim to the throne?" Brandson asked.

"It's nothing," Douglon tossed the words at Brandson and turned back to Patlon.

"Sort of," Patlon said, leaning around his fuming cousin to look at Brandson. "Douglon's grandfather was the twin brother of King Horgoth's grandfather. There's this interesting story that draws into question which twin was actually born first. Douglon's grandfather had six toes on one foot, and one midwife claims—"

"Enough!" roared Douglon. "I do not want to be king. Neither did my grandfather. I hope Horgoth has a litter of sons so that their family line is indestructible. I would chop off my beard and live with an elf before I would submit to sitting day in and day out on that ugly throne. I cannot believe Horgoth believed you!" Douglon looked plaintively at his cousin. "He really charged me with treason?"

Patlon winced. "In front of a full court."

Douglon dropped his head into his hands. Then he looked back at his cousin. "And how exactly are you going to smooth this over?"

Patlon began tugging at his beard again. "I'm going to have to tell him it turns out you were just waylaid and you're on your way to bring it to him now."

"I'm not giving that treasure to my addle-headed cousin! Even if it were mine to give."

"If you can think of another idea," Patlon said, "let me know."

"King Horgoth dislikes wizards, doesn't he?" Alaric asked.

"Hates 'em," Patlon said.

"Tell him the treasure belonged to a wizard and Douglon was bewitched."

"Ooh! That's good! Then you're innocent, Douglon!"

"And Horgoth will never want the treasure," Douglon said, nodding at Alaric.

"Good, because he can't have it," Alaric said. "I need it."

"You?" Patlon asked.

"It's a Keeper's Wellstone, and I'm a Keeper." The claim rolled off his tongue almost easily.

"I keep forgetting that Kordan was a Keeper," Douglon said. "He seemed so evil."

"Did you hear that from anyone besides Gustav?" Alaric asked.

Douglon narrowed his eyes.

"No," Ayda answered for him.

"Kordan was a Keeper," Alaric said. "I have read the records of his work. He wasn't evil. There was an accident while Kordan was performing some magic, and a boy died, despite Kordan's efforts to save him."

Ayda leaned toward Douglon and whispered loudly, "Kordan sounds diabolical."

"Shut up," the dwarf said. He turned to Alaric. "What do you need the Wellstone for?"

Alaric almost gave a generic answer about Keepers loving knowledge. But as he reached for the pouch at his neck, he realized that he *wanted* to tell them about Evangeline.

As the silence dragged on, the faces of his companions grew concerned. Looking from face to face, something loosened inside of him and he began to talk. He told them of meeting Evangeline, marrying her, of the stupid accident when she had been poisoned, about how he had searched and searched for an antidote and finally had real hope that it was held in Kordan's Wellstone.

There was silence for a long moment.

"Oh, Alaric," Milly said quietly.

"I didn't realize Keepers married," Brandson said.

Milly smacked him in the arm. "What Brandson *means* is that is terrible and we will do everything we can to get the stone back."

"Not many Keepers marry," Alaric said. "Most spend too much time stuck in the Stronghold or libraries to meet anyone. But it happens occasionally."

"Do you think Gustav knew Kordan was a Keeper?" Brandson asked.

"I'm sure of it, if he knew about the Wellstone," Alaric said. "Although I don't know where he heard about it."

Patlon looked at them all curiously. "What story did Gustav tell you about Kordan to get you all to look for the treasure?"

"Douglon was the one looking for the gem," Brandson explained. "Gustav was already at my house when Douglon showed up."

Patlon tilted his head in confusion. "But Gustav's been looking for it since last summer." He stopped and snapped his mouth shut.

"You're getting old, cousin," Douglon said dangerously. "Brandson didn't meet Gustav until last winter. How do you know that Gustav was looking for the treasure before that?"

"You knew Gustav," Alaric said.

"'*Knew him'* is a little strong," Patlon began.

Douglon growled.

"I met Gustav last summer while I was hunting," Patlon said quickly. "He was sneaking along a game trail, and I almost shot him. We got to talking, and he told me he had found a cave the night before with veins of silver in the walls. He'd scraped some off for his potions but had no need of the rest of it. He gave me directions to it and said he was seeking a different sort of treasure. He had heard rumors of a valley with no beginning and no end. It was said to hold both treasure and magical objects."

"He told you about the valley where we found the map?" Douglon asked. "And you never told me?"

"I was going to, but when I followed the old man's directions to his cave with 'huge veins of silver', all I found was one streak so thin it was barely visible. I had spent my whole hunting day on a wild goose chase." Patlon's scowl turned a little sheepish as he looked at Douglon. "I didn't feel like telling you I'd been duped. Then when we really did find the valley, it seemed too late…"

"You never saw Gustav again?" Alaric broke in before Douglon could answer.

Patlon shook his head again, then paused. "Now that you ask… maybe." He tugged absently on his beard. "After you ran off with the map, Douglon, I stopped by the tavern at the river crossing and had a drink. Partway through the evening, an old man came in and sat near me. Hulgrat and Swenrich were there, and"—he glanced at Douglon—"I may have been telling them about what you did."

Douglon growled again.

"You stole from me!" Patlon exclaimed.

"The old man?" Alaric reminded him.

"Yes, well there was something familiar about him, but I couldn't seem to look at him clearly enough to figure out what. He just sat nearby, and I had the impression he was listening. Then at one point, I looked over and he was gone. I honestly haven't thought about him again until right now. But now that I think about it, he did remind me of Gustav."

"It was him," Alaric said. "Shade Seekers have a way of affecting what people focus on. They call it influence. Gustav could have manipulated you until you didn't care enough about him to pay attention."

"Then he knew I had the map," Douglon said, "months before I ever met him."

Alaric nodded absently, struck by an idea. Influence. Gustav used influence. The questions that had been fluttering through his mind since he met this group settled. Answer after answer burst into light.

"If Gustav is skilled at influence, that explains everything." Every single thing. "It's easy to make people not notice someone they weren't looking for in the first place, like an old man in a tavern, but I think Gustav's influence may range far past that.

"I think Gustav is the reason you are all together," Alaric said. "If he had tracked Douglon near Kordan's Blight, Gustav could have used influence to draw Douglon to him."

"No one drew me," Douglon objected.

"If Gustav was good at it, you would have thought it was your own choices that guided you," Alaric said. He gestured to Milly, "It's similar to the magic the borrey used."

"That doesn't explain why Ayda is here," Brandson pointed out.

"They both came to you at about the same time, right?" Alaric asked. "Then it makes sense. An influence spell to draw someone isn't one that Keepers use, but I understand the concept." He ignored Ayda's snort. "You can draw a specific person if you know a great deal about them. The better you know them, the more specific to an individual the spell will be, but it will work over a smaller distance.

"Gustav knew little about Douglon. Just that he was a dwarf, really, but since Douglon's probably the only dwarf within two days' walk, Gustav could afford to be vague. Since he didn't know how close Douglon was, he would have wanted to make the spell as general as possible. I'm guessing he drew any intelligent, non-human. That would bring Ayda as well."

"You might be right," Ayda said. "I hadn't planned on going to Kordan's Blight, but I never thought much about it. I have a hard time paying attention to things sometimes."

Douglon rolled his eyes. "Sometimes?"

"And it explains why I just couldn't focus on him. Ever," Ayda said. "I thought he was just boring, but I could barely look at him."

"I'm sure he knew you would notice too much about him if you did," Alaric said.

An irritated line creased her brow. "That's why I don't know what color he is, why I didn't ask how the dragon knew him, why I never wondered about the wizard at all."

"So Gustav kept drawing Ayda back whenever she left?" Brandson asked.

Alaric groaned. How had he not seen any of this? That's what Gustav had been doing in the woods when Ayda had wanted to leave. It wasn't Brandson that had convinced her to stay at all. Gustav had used his influence. "I thought elves were hard to influence," he said to Ayda.

She winced. "That's another thing my father said was human about me. I'm easy to fool."

Milly looked at Ayda, her brows drawn together. "Why would he keep drawing Ayda back? He needed Douglon's map, but what did he need Ayda for?"

Alaric looked at Ayda. Why did Gustav want her there?

Ayda shrugged. "Maybe he just liked me."

"That can't be it." Douglon shook his head. "He must have had some other crazy reason."

Ayda ignored him and looked to Alaric for an answer.

"I'm not sure," he said. "Maybe it was because you have such unusual powers." Alaric certainly felt better knowing where Ayda was. Maybe Gustav had noticed the same sort of thing; the idea that Ayda had the potential for something extraordinary. Or devastating.

"So if Gustav was just after the treasure," Brandson said, "why not just steal Douglon's map?"

"He couldn't read it," Alaric said. "The runes on that map are complicated. To anyone other than a Keeper, they would say the gibberish Gustav read. Shade Seekers study runes, but not to the extent Keepers do. I'm not sure anyone studies ancient runes the way Keepers do."

"Which means," Ayda said, "not only did Gustav draw the map to him, but he also drew one of the only people on earth who can read it." She smiled sweetly. "I think it's reasonable to think that Gustav drew you as well."

Alaric snorted. That old wizard hadn't drawn him. He had already been seeking information about Kordan. His own journey had brought him here.

Except here was finally an explanation for the ridiculous coincidence of finding this exact group. Gustav had drawn them together. And it explained the slight fuzziness Alaric had felt the whole time they were together. It was Gustav, subtly controlling everyone's decisions for his own gain. Alaric had never heard of anyone using influence so subtly.

"A troubling idea," he said. "Gustav seems to use influence as a kind of net, sending out ideas of what he wants and then drawing in whatever it catches. What's even more troubling is that it still might be working. Borreys are ridiculously rare. What are the chances that we would stumble across one right when we decide to follow Gustav?"

"Do you think Gustav's still around then?" Milly asked.

"I don't know why he would be," Alaric said, "but he could have set things in motion before he left. It's still a big coincidence, but every other coincidence so far has been Gustav's doing."

"Well," Brandson said, "there's one thing Gustav didn't plan. In attempting to collect a team to find his treasure, he's also brought together the perfect group to stop him—dwarves who know what the nomads are doing, a Keeper who knows about the Wellstone, and an elf who knows where Mallon's body is."

Alaric looked around the group as they all nodded.

"So where do we find Gustav?" Brandson asked.

Alaric felt the pressure as one gaze after another turned toward him. It would have been nice if he had an answer.

CHAPTER TWENTY-THREE

ALARIC LOOKED AROUND THE GROUP. "We're not on a treasure hunt in the safety of these hills any longer," he began.

"Yeah, nothing dangerous here…" Douglon muttered to Ayda.

Alaric ignored him. "Since Gustav is a Shade Seeker, he is most likely headed to Sidion."

At this, Milly paled and Brandson shifted.

"Do you know where it is?" Brandson asked.

Alaric nodded. "I haven't been to the Shade Seekers' Keep itself, but I've been close enough to know where it is. Douglon probably does too."

The dwarf nodded.

"It's not an easy place to get into." Alaric looked at Milly. "We need to go through Kordan's Blight and get horses. We'll drop you off at your home. Now that things are settled with Patlon, you'll be in no danger."

"Home?" Milly asked, one eyebrow rising. "You're not sending me home."

"I suppose I can't convince you to stay home, either, Brandson?" Alaric asked.

Brandson leveled a steely gaze at the Keeper. "Mallon killed my parents. I'm not going to just sit by and let Gustav bring him back."

"We may not be great wizards or powerful warriors," Milly said, "but we aren't just going to go sit at home while you all go off to stop Gustav. A lot of regular people like us are going to suffer if Mallon is raised. It's only fair that we should get to help stop him. You don't have to be some great hero to contribute something good, you know."

Brandson and Milly were sitting, chins raised, daring the others to disagree. Alaric nodded to them. "All right then. Does anyone have any ingenious ideas on how to stop him besides chasing him across the country? I think we have to assume he has the cooperation of his dragon, so he'll be moving a lot faster than we will on horses."

"Could you draw Gustav back here the way he drew everyone?" Milly asked.

Alaric shook his head. "An influence spell can prod someone in the direction that you want them to go, but once they realize it's happening, it's worthless. I don't think I could fool Gustav into thinking he wanted to come back and find us."

"Can you do something else magical?" Brandson asked. "Grab him and bring him here or make some sort of glowing trail to find him?"

"It doesn't work that way. Magic is pretty limited. Everything living has energy. Magic involves redirecting that energy. To do that, it has to travel through me. But it's like heat—a little is okay, too much burns." He held up his bandaged palms.

"But Keepers in the past have done amazing things," Milly said. "What about when Chesavia fought the water demon?"

"Chesavia was killed by the water demon," Brandson pointed out.

"Actually, she wasn't," Alaric said. "Keeper Chesavia died because she used too much magic. The demon was strong, too strong to be destroyed without Chesavia using more energy than she could manage. She knew it. She chose to continue past what her body could handle. She defeated the demon, but it cost her her life.

"Keepers aren't great wizards or powerful warriors, either. Chesavia was one of the few who single-handedly saved the day."

"Then what good are they?" Douglon asked.

"We work more with knowledge than magic. We spend a lot of time watching for trouble, searching out the truth if we find the rumor of any. Then we try to assemble the people that could do something about it and provide them with the knowledge they need."

"Well, that is perfect," Brandson said, rubbing his hands together. "We've definitely found trouble, and the group's assembled. Provide us with knowledge."

Alaric laughed and Douglon spread a map of Queensland out on the floor. At the top, in tiny detail, rose the Wolfsbane Mountains. The great river snaked south from them until it flowed off the southern end of the map. The Scale Mountains ran down the western edge, and the Marsham Cliffs lined the eastern side.

Patlon pointed out the location where the nomads were rumored to be gathering to Douglon.

"That's a huge valley," Douglon told Alaric. "It's well supplied with water. A large force could gather there."

"How many are there?" Alaric asked.

"No idea," Patlon said. "It's all just rumors."

"Isn't that near the entrance of Duncave? Haven't the dwarves bothered to see what's going on right above their heads?" Alaric asked.

Patlon shrugged. "Humans are always wandering around on the surface. It's hard to keep track of them."

"You need to convince King Horguth that he needs to," Alaric said. "Queen Saren needs to know if there's an army on her border. Douglon, where did you and Patlon find that valley with Kordan's tower and the treasure map?" He marked the area Douglon showed him on the map, west and a little south of Queenstown along the edge of the Scale Mountains. "I don't know why Gustav would go there, but he was looking for it when you met him, Patlon." Alaric turned to Ayda. "Gustav will need to get Mallon's body. Is it well hidden?"

"It's safe in the Elder Grove, but not hidden. I didn't know anyone would look for him. It might take the wizard some time, but he'll find it."

"I think we need to fix that," Alaric said. "I doubt we can hide him so well that Gustav will never find him, but we can buy some time. How long would it take us to reach the Grove?"

"Three or four days," Ayda answered. "But I don't know a way to hide him that a Shade Seeker won't figure out."

"I think I can come up with some tricks that should slow Gustav down." None of which would be pleasant. "I can at least guess how he'll go about looking. Can you show me where the Elder Grove is?" Alaric asked Ayda.

Ayda glanced at the map. "It wouldn't help you for me to mark it on the map. I'll need to take you there. It's near the northern end of the Greenwood."

Alaric looked over the map. "I think we should go there first. Gustav will have to spend time searching while we can go directly there. It might help us catch up."

"Then we'd better get moving," Douglon said.

"Is it safe to assume that Gustav has left Kordan's Blight?" Milly asked.

"He has no reason to stay," Alaric answered.

"Then, if we head out now, we can have one good night sleep in my house before setting out tomorrow."

The mood of the group was lighter as they headed to Milly's. Alaric could hear the dwarves' laughter ringing off the trees. Ayda walked along merrily near Milly, the two of them giggling and whispering to each other. In reality, they were in a far worse predicament than they had imagined when they trudged out of their camp that morning, but now they had a goal.

Brandson fell in beside Alaric. "Do you think we have a chance of stopping Gustav?"

If the wizard wasn't on a dragon, it would be a lot easier. "We have a chance."

Brandson was quiet for a moment.

"I was only twelve when the yellow plague broke out. My father got sick. My mother wouldn't leave him, but she sent me off to the hills with my uncle." He paused again. "No one who stayed in the village survived. My uncle went back with a group of men a couple of weeks later and burned it to the ground. Then he brought me to Kordan's Blight where the blacksmith took me in. My uncle left to join the King's army before the battle of Turning Creek."

Turning Creek. King Kendren's army had made their stand there against Mallon. The Rivor had brought legions of nomads and monsters no one could name. He had annihilated Kendren's army. The king himself had been wounded with a poisoned blade. Alaric had tried to save him, tried to find some way to stop the poison, to draw it out. The king had only lived for two days.

"I never saw my uncle again," Brandson said.

Alaric put his hand on the smith's shoulder. "We'll stop Gustav. And maybe in the process, find the way to kill Mallon."

Brandson nodded. "Good, because Mallon keeps taking people from me. My parents, my uncle, and now Gustav, too."

That night, the group sat around Milly's table. The room was warm and noisy, full of smells of roast chicken and hot cider. Douglon and Patlon spun tales of ancient treasures lost and found.

The fire in the hearth had burned low and the conversation lulled when Ayda turned to Alaric. "Tell us a story, Keeper."

There was enthusiastic agreement, and Alaric nodded. "Do you have one in mind?"

"Tomkin and the Dragon," Ayda said.

Evangeline's face, waiting expectantly the day he met her sprang up before his mind. Alaric looked sharply at the elf, but there was no mischief in her look.

"It's a night to remember better times," Ayda said.

Alaric looked into the fire for a long moment. He let his mind linger on the memory of Evangeline's face, the eagerness in her eyes. Outside, the night deepened, drawing the edges of the world down into the small, fire-lit room. Ayda was right. It was that sort of night.

He pulled his hood up over his head and looked down at the floor, remembering an inn and letting the room fall into silence before he began.

CHAPTER TWENTY-FOUR

PATLON PARTED from them early the next morning, choosing to head southwest, cross-country toward Duncave instead of following the King's Highway south.

Alaric retrieved Beast from the tavern's stables while Brandson borrowed several horses from his neighbors, leaving the slow carthorse behind. They headed south through a cool morning, following the road over sun-steeped hills and down into pockets of mist.

As they dropped into a long, low valley thick with mist, Alaric pulled out the ruby. In the dim morning, the core was the red of old embers, pulsing and breathing beneath the brighter streams of light. Droplets of mist clung to the surface, twinkling like blood-red stars. Alaric waited, watching the interplay of the currents of light through one of the faces of the rough gem. There was no break in the light and his hand tightened on the ruby. The energy spun beneath the surface in darker and lighter hues of red, but no black swirl appeared. His heart beat faster. The darkness had disappeared.

But then a wide band of light shifted. Deep in the core of the ruby, he glimpsed a knot of blackness before the light swirled back in front of it. Alaric felt his heart falter, and he clutched the ruby to his chest. The darkness was growing—slowly, but it was growing. And Gustav was so far ahead of them. How long did he have before the ruby went dark? How long could Evangeline wait for the antidote?

The road before them gamboled over hills and in and out of forests. At the top of each rise, Alaric scanned the sky as though he would find Gustav on his red dragon, just a short distance ahead of them.

They rose early and rode late each day trying to reach Queenstown by lunch the third day. Alaric had no doubt that Queen Saren would have her people keeping an eye out for him, but as long as Alaric didn't run into anyone he knew, they should be through in a couple of hours.

Alaric had a letter penned and ready to post to Saren in the city. She was going to be furious that he wasn't stopping. The fact that Mallon wasn't dead and might be a threat again soon wasn't really the sort of message to put in a letter, but he didn't want to take the time to go to the palace. Gustav was already too far ahead of them. The palace would mean councils and waiting and discussions and more waiting.

And explaining to Saren why her closest advisor had deserted her for two years without an explanation. He felt a pang of guilt at the idea of Saren, never quite sure of herself, carrying on for so long without a Keeper there for support. Probably, she had been fine, but the Court Keeper played a pivotal role in the politics of the palace. Without someone there who was obligated to work only for the good of the country, it was possible for things to become unbalanced quickly. Of course, he had thought that the Stronghold would send someone else to take his place when it became obvious he wasn't coming back. He'd always expected Keeper Will to be here.

The morning they approached the capital, a dark bank of clouds piled up against the western horizon. By the time they could see the city, sprawled out on both sides of the great river, the wind was sharp with the smell of the storm. They joined the slow plodding pace of wagons walking through clusters of houses and an increasing number of shops, toward the thick city walls.

When they rode through the city gates, the darkness of the approaching storm devoured the early afternoon sun, dropping the city into twilight. The winds rose, whipping dust and refuse down the streets in mad dashes. The flow of travelers continued doggedly into the city, funneling into busy avenues. All of the main thoroughfares in the city ran into the central market like spokes of a wheel. The quickest way through the city was straight through that market and out the avenue on the other side. There was no use fighting against the current of humanity moving in that direction.

It had been two years since Alaric was in the capital. The city hadn't changed. It had the same tumult of biting smells and jostling motion. Alaric had spent eight years at court, advising first King Kendren and then Queen Saren. Today, he felt like he was visiting a foreign city, wide-eyed and nervous. He searched the faces of the crowd, pulling back into his hood if he saw anyone who might be familiar.

When they turned into the open market square, the full force of the wind hit him, pelting his face with bits of rock and dust, and jostling Beast into the other horses.

The gale thrashed through a sea of booths and humanity. Vendors struggled to finish tying down their tents and their wares while thunder rolled over the rooftops. Alaric slid off Beast and pressed against him for protection. The others did the same, and he led them against the wind, pressing along the southern edge of the square until they huddled in the relative shelter of the buildings on the western side.

"We need to get moving," Alaric shouted above the wind. "Once we leave the city, we'll be back in the forest and the wind shouldn't be as bad."

The door of the smithy next to them crashed open, caught by the wind. A black-bearded dwarf exited, swinging an axe and watching it arc through the air with a pleased expression. Three palace guards fell into place behind him.

Alaric stepped back, letting Beast's head come between himself and the guards.

"Another dwarf!" Ayda said cheerfully.

Alaric could just see the dwarf glance at her, his brow knitting together in disgust when he saw the elf.

Next to Alaric, Douglon caught sight of the dwarf and let out a small growl. "Menwoth." His voice was steely.

Menwoth's mouth dropped open in surprise before fury filled his face. "Traitor!" he rushed at Douglon, axe raised. "Seize him! This dwarf is wanted by High King Horgoth!"

"Ambassador! Please restrain yourself, sir!" The lead guard's voice cut through the wind as he stepped forward, his own sword drawn.

Menwoth lowered his axe, but stood glowering at Douglon. "Arrest this dwarf." When the guards hesitated, he snapped at them, "I demand it. High King Horgoth has declared him a traitor. His execution awaits him in Duncave."

The guard, his uniform showing him to be a lieutenant, stepped up to Douglon. "You'll need to come with us."

Douglon's face darkened, and he reached for his axe.

Alaric set a hand on Douglon's shoulder and pushed back his hood. He stepped forward. "This man is not a traitor."

The guard looked at him dismissively. "If Ambassador Menwoth requests that we detain this dwarf, he will be brought to the palace."

Clearly, Alaric hadn't needed to worry about being recognized. "I don't know you, Lieutenant, but my name is Alaric. I'm the Keeper serving at Her Majesty's court." Well, serving might not be the exact word for it, but 'avoiding Her Majesty's court' didn't have as good a ring to it.

The guard looked at him sharply, taking in Alaric's not-quite-as-black-as-a-Keeper's robe. Alaric tried to look impressive, but judging from the guard's face, he wasn't succeeding.

"Keeper Alaric has not been at court for two years."

"Yes, well, I'm here now. And this dwarf is not a traitor. You can't arrest him."

The lieutenant's eyebrows rose and Menwoth sputtered, "That is for King Horgoth to decide, not some man claiming to be Queen Saren's historian."

"Keepers are well regarded here." There was mild disapproval in the lieutenant's voice. "Keeper Alaric is among the most respected men in our land."

"That means nothing to a dwarf," Menwoth said.

The guard narrowed his eyes at Alaric for a long moment. "I'm afraid, sir, that you'll need to bring your complaints about the detainment of this dwarf to Her Majesty herself."

Alaric clenched his jaw. Of course the guard shouldn't

just believe him. Alaric looked like a dirty traveler who happened to be wearing black. But still.

Douglon bristled. "I'm not a traitor, and you're not arresting me. If Horgoth wants me, he can get his fat head out of that throne room and come get me."

Alaric looked at the guards surrounding them. "Douglon, I'll talk to the queen. We'll sort this out."

Douglon growled.

Menwoth looked wildly at the guard. "You can't trust him! He wants Horgoth's throne! He's plotting to kill him!"

Douglon rolled his eyes. "The only dwarf here who wishes he had the throne is you."

Menwoth began to shake with fury. "I serve Horgoth faithfully. And I always have, which is why he trusted me with this position at Saren's court."

Douglon snorted. "He just wanted you far away from Duncave."

"Douglon," Alaric broke in, "just go with them so we can get this over with."

Douglon ground his teeth then nodded. At the lieutenant's pointed look, Douglon handed his axe to Brandson. The guards drew up around him and led the way through the wind-blown market toward the palace.

So much for getting through Queenstown quickly. Alaric took the reins of Douglon's horse and followed the others into the beginnings of the storm.

CHAPTER TWENTY-FIVE

THE AIR WAS heavy with the coming rain, and the wind smelled of the damp hills to the west. They were not quite halfway to the palace, leading their horses to keep pace with the guards, when the rain came. When it did, it was torrential. Alaric hunched down under his hood, pulling his cloak close. Within seconds, it was soaked through. Relentless fingers of wind wound around his neck, dribbling cold rain down his back, down his legs, and into his already sloshing boots. The crackle of lightning and constant rumble of thunder followed them as they hurried along the deserted streets.

They turned onto a wide avenue leading to the palace gates. Through the rain, the building was a grey, hulking shape behind grey, hulking walls. As they drew closer, the grey lightened into pale rock. They entered the palace grounds through an enormous portico and ducked into the nearest building, soaked to the bone.

Alaric stood impatiently, letting water drip off of him to puddle on the floor while the lieutenant ducked into a nearby room and returned with Captain Rold, captain of the queen's guard. Alaric felt an odd combination of relief at being recognized and guilt at being gone for so long that all this was necessary, when the captain snapped off a quick bow to him. "My apologies, Keeper Alaric. You understand that my lieutenant needed confirmation of who you were. Since Her Majesty will be most anxious to see you, if you could all hang your wet cloaks in here, I will take you to her immediately."

"This dwarf is a traitor," Menwoth said, pointing at Douglon. "I demand that he be thrown into the dungeon until he can be transferred to Duncave."

"Douglon is not a traitor," Alaric said. "It is just a misunderstanding."

"Yes, I understand there is some disagreement about a dwarf." Captain Rold turned to Douglon. "If you will come with me willingly to the queen right now, you will not be bound until Her Majesty has made a decision regarding you." He turned to Menwoth who was livid. "Your excellency, I will inform Her Majesty that you are anxious to discuss this situation."

With a curt nod at the other guards to fall in around them, Captain Rold started off through the palace. Alaric fell into step behind him, his boots squelching with each step. The others followed, leaving Menwoth dripping and swearing behind them in the hall.

Alaric followed the captain through the familiar halls of the palace, the sounds of the storm now muffled by the stone walls. When they reached a set of enormous doors, two guards snapped off salutes and heaved the doors open.

Entering the room was like walking into a map. Painted on the walls was a detailed map of Queensland. To the right of the door, the Wolfsbane Mountains dwindled into rolling hills at the northern end of the country. The great river wrapped around the room, meandering south until it passed into the southern kingdoms just to the left of the door. The large square table that filled the center of the room was inlaid with lighter wood showing streets and major buildings of Queenstown. This map, Alaric remembered rather than saw, since the clutter on the table obscured it.

"Your Majesty," the captain said, "Keeper Alaric."

A stout woman looked up from the sea of papers, which were drowning the city on the table. The queen glanced at Alaric for a moment before her eyes lit up and her mouth split into a broad smile. Alaric dropped into a low bow.

"Alaric!" She crossed the room to embrace him.

He had forgotten how short Saren was. Her head barely came up to his shoulders. She had aged more than two years since he had seen her. Her thick braid held much more grey than it had, and deep creases were carved between her brows. More than just a greeting, there was a deep relief in her words.

"It's been so long," she said.

Alaric opened his mouth, but couldn't settle on one answer to that.

Saren looked around at his companions, her eyes widening when she saw Ayda.

"Your Majesty," Alaric said, "may I present Aydalya, princess of the western elves."

Ayda curtsied gracefully, and Saren's eyes widened even further.

"My dear, you are most welcome! I was a child last time one of your people visited us. We are honored to have you as our guest."

Alaric introduced Douglon as well, and Queen Saren nodded her head at the dwarf. "We see far too few of your good people as well, master dwarf. Please consider yourself our honored guest." Saren looked at Milly and Brandson, who were hanging back behind the others. She gave them a warm, welcoming smile. "Are you going to tell me that these two young people are also royalty? A young king and his queen from the Winter Island, perhaps?"

Milly and Brandson both smiled stiffly.

"This is Brandson and Milly, blacksmith and milkmaid from the village of Kordan's Blight."

Queen Saren nodded to them. "Companions of Alaric are always welcome. My house is at your disposal."

At that moment, the door behind them flung open, and a tall, angular man strode into the room. The queen's eyes went flat, and the man, taking in the group before her, drew up short. A flicker of irritation crossed his face before he tossed off a bow so shallow it was barely a bob of his head.

Saren's smile grew icy.

"My apologies, Your Majesty," he said, striding forward to stand a step ahead of Alaric without glancing at him. "I didn't realize there would be guests at our discussion."

The man's fingers were weighted down with gold rings. A thick gold chain hung around his neck holding a ponderous disc printed with the seal of the Black Hills. He was a hand taller than Alaric, and he used his height to tower over the queen. He must be the son of the Black Hills duke who had governed when Alaric had been at court. Although no older than thirty, this man's face was already carved with arrogance.

The smile fell off her face completely as Saren lifted her chin to look the man in the eye.

"Duke Thornton," she began, "we've been honored this afternoon with important guests. We'll have to postpone our discussion until a later date."

Thornton kept his eyes on the queen, "Your Majesty, I'm afraid I have other obligations at a later date."

A surge of anger rolled through Alaric at the duke's arrogance. He stepped forward, positioning himself alongside Saren, facing the man.

The duke flicked an unconcerned glance at Alaric, then returned it to Saren.

"You're too new to court to recognize our guest, Thornton, so I'm sure he'll excuse your rudeness." Saren set her hand on Alaric's arm. "Allow me to introduce Keeper Alaric to you."

Alaric put on a courteous smile.

The duke stiffened and turned toward Alaric. He took in the Keeper's worn travel clothes with a slight raise of his brow. His expression remained haughty, and he gave the slightest nod in acknowledgment. "I didn't realize a Keeper was needed at court any longer."

Alaric didn't have to look down to know what he looked like. He wasn't even wearing his blackish robe any longer. His smile soured.

Saren's face took on a decidedly dangerous look. "There are many people at court who aren't needed, but a Keeper is not one of them. We'll find another time to have that discussion you were looking for. A time when Alaric is available as well." She turned away from Thornton and back toward the others.

The duke gave her a stony glare. He turned it on Alaric for a long moment before striding out of the room.

Saren watched the duke leave with a troubled expression

settling on her face. "Alaric, there are a few problems I could use your assistance with."

"Speaking of problems," Alaric said, glancing at Douglon, "we brought one with us."

The queen gave a tired sigh. "Of course you did."

CHAPTER TWENTY-SIX

"NOT JUST A PROBLEM, THEN." Saren frowned after Alaric explained the issue. "A problem with the dwarves, who are notoriously stubborn."

Douglon's brow creased.

"Don't scowl," Ayda whispered loudly to him. "It makes you look stubborn."

Saren gave Ayda a weak smile. "I'll talk to Menwoth."

"It might take more than that," Alaric said. "If Douglon isn't arrested, Menwoth has threatened to tell Horgoth that you shelter those bent on his overthrow."

"Menwoth did all this? He's usually so reserved."

"He has a special place in his heart for me, Your Highness," Douglon said. "I am closer to the throne than he is, and he feels that he deserves my place. In truth, he does. Menwoth has been working to make himself useful to the crown his entire life. I avoid the throne room like quicksand for fear it'll suck me in and force me to do something royal."

Saren narrowed her eyes. "Are you the dwarf who lined Horgoth's crown with lead before his coronation?"

Douglon laughed. "His head kept tipping to the side. He'd never worn the crown before, so he didn't know anything was wrong."

Saren allowed a small smile but shook her head. "This will definitely take more than a word from me to fix."

"Douglon is innocent, Your Majesty," Alaric said. "He can't be arrested."

Saren turned to the captain who still stood by the door. "Why *hasn't* he been arrested?"

"With Keeper Alaric and Ambassador Menwoth disagreeing, my lieutenant thought it best that you make the decision regarding his arrest."

The queen scowled at Douglon. "Menwoth will feel insulted. It might have made things easier if you'd just let him arrest you."

"I'm not keen on entering a dungeon, Your Majesty," Douglon said. "More people go into them than come out."

Saren shook her head. "The whole reason Menwoth is here is so we can reach some trade agreements with King Horgoth. It won't help anything if I harbor a dwarf they think is a traitor. Douglon is Horgoth's subject. I'm not willing to strain relations with Duncave over this. "

Douglon let out a low growl, and Alaric laid a hand on his shoulder.

Alaric said, "I assure you, Your Majesty, Douglon is not a traitor. A misunderstanding between him and his cousin Patlon was… misconstrued by King Horgoth. The matter is being cleared up as we speak."

"It will be your word against a royal decree from Horgoth. Your word won't be enough for Menwoth," Saren said. "The dwarves have no regard for Keepers. You are just another human to him. I would have to offer the ambassador something very valuable to get him to forget about this whole affair. Now that I realize who you are, Douglon, even that might not be enough. The hatred between you and Menwoth is almost legendary."

"I'm beginning to see that," Alaric said. "Douglon's problems often have a root in his personal relationships."

The dwarf had the decency to drop his eyes.

Saren rubbed the end of her braid while she contemplated Douglon. It was such a familiar motion that Alaric smiled. When she had first married Kendren, it had been her nervous habit, running her thumb down to the end of her braid while she tried to answer questions posed by the people who had intimidated her. But now, the motion was slow and calculating as she contemplated the problem before her.

Her eyes flicked to Alaric, and irritation flashed across her face. "What are you smiling about?"

Alaric smiled more broadly. "It's nice to see you again."

"It would be nicer if you hadn't brought problems with you." A small smile crept into her eyes, despite her sharp voice.

Alaric's smile faded. "This thing with Menwoth is nothing. We have a great deal to talk about. Urgently."

Saren's shoulders drooped, and she gave Alaric a tired look. "One problem at a time, please. Let's take care of this, and then I will clear my afternoon." She turned back to Douglon. "What if we took the question out of Menwoth's hands? Nurthrum arrives from Duncave sometime today for an annual discussion of our relationship with King Horgoth. He outranks Menwoth, doesn't he?"

Douglon considered for a moment. "Not officially, but

Nurthrum is older than the mountains. Menwoth would feel compelled to respect his decision."

"And would Nurthrum consider you a traitor?"

"He's got a clear head and can be reasoned with. I could convince him it's all a mistake."

Saren nodded. "Then until we can talk to him, you are officially my guest. I will hear grievances between you and Menwoth, and we'll make sure Nurthrum is present as well." She looked at the dwarf sternly. "Until then, do not leave the palace. Unless you want all of my resources, as well as Horgoth's, tracking you down."

Douglon grumbled something into his beard, but gave her a reluctant nod.

Saren let out a long breath. "Good. Alaric, there is a small council meeting tonight. Since you're finally back, I think I'll make it a full council. It will be a good way to get you up to speed."

"Your Majesty," Alaric said, "we're leaving at dawn."

Saren's eyebrows shot up. "Leaving? You just arrived."

"We were just passing through Queenstown. This thing with Douglon is the only reason we stopped."

Saren studied Alaric, her eyes hard. "Well, it's good to know that military force will bring you back."

"You will understand my need for haste once I explain to you what's going on."

"I expect an explanation of many things," she said curtly. "First, there are things that require my attention this afternoon. Let me take care of those, and I will send for you afterward."

She rang a bell on the table, and a smartly dressed steward entered the room.

"Send word to my full council that we meet tonight. And

see our guests to their rooms so they can change. Alaric, I'll send for you shortly."

The steward bowed and turned to lead them from the room.

Alaric bowed, frustration gnawing at him. Outside, he could still hear the thrumming of the rain. Even if he could get everyone out of the palace, this storm would make any progress slow. He resigned himself to an afternoon and evening of plodding through the cumbersome workings of palace life.

Alaric's feet could have found his room by themselves. At the end of a long hall of apartments and separated from them by a wide-open room with chairs and a large fireplace, a black door greeted him. This apartment had been his home for the eight years he had lived in Queenstown, advising first King Kendren, then his widowed queen.

Alaric stepped in to find it unchanged. Bookshelves dotted the room, shelves of scrolled maps filled one corner, and there were at least a half-dozen small tables and desks scattered around the large room. The doorway to the bedroom opened in the wall to his right.

He walked along in front of the bookshelf, running his hands over the spines of the books like greeting old friends. At the door to the balcony, he watched the rain pour down into the garden. Everything outside was too large, as altered as any garden would be after an absence of a couple of years. Alaric felt the time wash over him. The man who had lived here before had been so sure of everything, so confident in his place, his beliefs. Now, he felt more like one of the leaves careening by, tossed by the wind and battered down by the rain.

He washed and changed into clothes waiting in the room

for him before he returned to the window. Across the courtyard, a student of the apothecary hurried out of Ewan's quarters, ducking through the rain. Alaric's hand went absently to the pouch hanging at his chest. His fingers rubbed the stone through the worn leather bag.

He thought about going over there now, but knowing Saren would call him soon, he turned his back on the window and began to pace the room. A polite knock sounded, and he opened the door to the queen's grey-haired steward.

"Is the room acceptable, Keeper Alaric? If it doesn't suit you, we can find you another."

"No, Matthew," Alaric said, smiling at the man, "the room is perfect, just as it was when I left. If anything has changed, it has been myself."

"Her Majesty is pleased that you are back."

Alaric shook his head. "I'm not sure she's entirely pleased." Alaric looked around the room. It was *exactly* how he had left it. "I thought they would send another Keeper."

"As did Her Majesty."

Alaric sank down into the nearest chair. Of course the queen's last years had been hard. She had relied on Alaric heavily. And he had still left.

"Everyone has felt the absence of a Keeper. Having one here gives us all hope." Matthew bowed and left.

Alaric stared at the closed door for a long time.

CHAPTER TWENTY-SEVEN

AN HOUR LATER, Alaric followed a messenger all the way through the palace to the royal apartments where he found the queen reading at an immense wooden desk. The room smelled of blackberry tart and fresh bread.

"Alaric," she greeted him with an apologetic smile. She motioned him toward a table set with bread, fruit, and two enormous servings of tart. "Come eat, old friend. Let's start over, shall we?"

Alaric made her a bow, but she waved it away as she sat and began to serve herself. Alaric joined her, realizing how hungry he was.

"I see you have been well, Your Majesty."

The smile she gave had a hint of steel behind it. "I know you didn't plan it, but your return to the palace is timely. Some members of the council at tonight's meeting may find the presence of a Keeper at court to be detrimental to their plans."

So much for easing into the role of Keeper again. Alaric tore off a piece of bread. "I doubt my presence will make much difference. I am too out of touch with what is going on."

"Of course it will make a difference. By now, rumors of your presence have spread throughout the palace." Saren took a slow, savoring bite of tart. "The winds are changing already."

Her face was different than Alaric remembered. There was less youth and gentleness. Saren hadn't been ready for the throne when Kendren died. She had been raised the daughter of a noble family, one that spent little time at court. King Kendren had married her because she was kind and good and honest—too much of all these things to naturally take to the political games played around her.

"I'm sorry I left for so long," Alaric said.

Saren let his worlds hang in the air for a moment.

"Come now, Alaric," she said, an edge to her voice. "It's been two years. Where have you been?"

"When I left you to see if the nomads were allying themselves with the southern kingdoms, I had every intention of returning here when I was done. It took almost a year, but I found the rumors to be groundless.

"I didn't come back because on my way south, I met a woman."

The queen's eyebrow shot up. "A woman worth keeping you from returning to your queen?"

Alaric let the obvious answer speak for itself.

"Send for her."

Alaric flinched at the note of command. It was going to be hard to get used to being ordered about again. He took a deep breath to push down the irritation. "She's not here."

There was a long pause. Saren's eyes narrowed as she waited for him to continue.

"Her name is Evangeline. She was an innkeeper before she traveled with me." Alaric's throat tightened. "She's not here because she's dying. She was poisoned. She is… asleep while I search for the antidote."

Alaric looked at the bread in his hands. Across the table, Saren did not move.

"I have slowed the spread of the poison, but it is not stopped. It will take a long time, but it will kill her." Alaric met the queen's gaze, seeing the sympathy there. "That's where I've been. Searching through every corner of the world for an antidote, crawling through the darkest pits of humanity in search of anything that would help me."

The queen spun her wedding ring around her finger. "I often wondered, while Kendren was dying, if all the waiting and hoping and dreading was worse than the death would ever be." She didn't look at Alaric. "It turns out neither is better than the other. Mourning is just a continuation of the same dreadful waiting. Except now, I'm waiting for something that will never come."

Alaric looked at her, remembering when her hair was still brown, her eyes still young. "I think of your husband often. While searching for an antidote for Evangeline, I often found myself searching for an antidote that might have helped him, too, wondering if there was something else we could have done to save him."

She shook her head. "Such questions lead to madness. Kendren's wounds were not the kind that could be healed." She took a deep breath. "It is so good to see you, Alaric. The last time I saw a Keeper was when Will was here. That was not long after you left.

"His visit was over my birthday feast. Will treated us to stories three nights in a row." She shook her head and smiled. "I can still see the tales in my mind. Three old tales: Tomkin and the Dragon, The Fall of kin Elenned, and Mylen the Destroyer. That man can tell stories better than anyone I've ever heard."

Alaric smiled. "He could leave me breathless just telling me what was for dinner."

"He delayed his departure in the hope you would return."

Alaric felt a jab of guilt. Another person he'd let down. He picked up a small blueberry and rolled it between his fingers. "The last I knew, Will had gone to look for the elves. Evangeline and I were close to the Greenwood on the way back here when I decided to go look for him.

"We had been catching glimpses of the Lumen Greenwood whenever we crested a hill, and she had been giddy at the sight. We reached a village that had been plagued by a fire lizard." Alaric let the story spill out, telling her of the fire lizard and the arrow.

"I didn't know the villagers had poisoned their arrows." He raised his eyes to Saren. "They were all killed by the fire lizard. They hadn't told me."

Alaric looked at the table, the grain in the wood echoing the red lines that had wound their way up Evangeline's leg. "It took more than a day for any sign of the poison to appear. By that time…"

"I took her west, into the Scale Mountains to one of the deserted small keeps. I created a chamber around her, but even that does not stop the poison."

"I doubt there's anything in our own records that you don't already know about, but now that you're back, the entire library is at your disposal, of course. And anything else I can offer. Anything at all."

Alaric shook his head. "As I mentioned earlier, I'm not really back. I need to leave. The sooner the better."

Saren's brow contracted. "To go to Evangeline?"

"No, where I am going now affects the whole country." Alaric pushed his plate away. "Mallon was not killed by the elves."

Saren sat, pale-faced, while Alaric told her of Gustav and Mallon and the elves. When he told her of the gathering nomads, her eyes hardened and she rang a bell that sat on the table. The door opened and a guard appeared.

"Summon General Viso and the map keeper. Have the quartermaster begin preparations for a full army supply and deployment."

The guard bowed and left.

The queen smiled tightly at Alaric. "There's not much I can do against Mallon, but I will not be unprepared with a nomad army on my border."

The queen shoved papers off her table and began to unroll another large map.

"This news needs to be acted on. I'm moving the full council meeting to this afternoon. We'll convene in two hours." She glanced at him. "If—When you stop Gustav and heal Evangeline, you will come back to court."

He bit back irritation at the imperiousness of her demand. She waited for his agreement, but he couldn't bring himself to nod. He'd been too long on his own to have a knee-jerk agreement with the crown.

Saren turned her full gaze on him. "You were my closest advisor, Alaric. You were the one with the most influence over the nobles, the other council members, the people. And you left. The void you left in the court was swarmed by every power-hungry parasite that could reach it." The queen's voice shook slightly. "You have no idea the mess you left me in. There has always been a Keeper at court, Alaric. And with Will gone, there are no other Keepers the Shield can send to me."

Alaric shook his head. "You don't know the things I've done. I'm not sure I can be the court Keeper anymore."

"The world is falling apart, Alaric," Saren snapped. "We don't have the luxury of you falling apart as well. If you're not a Keeper anymore, you are the closest thing I have to one. And I need a Keeper. So whatever doubts you have, deal with them."

He opened his mouth, but she raised a hand to silence him.

Her eyes glittered with anger. "There is a full council meeting in two hours. I don't care if you feel like a Keeper, Alaric. Act like one."

CHAPTER TWENTY-EIGHT

ALARIC LEFT the queen's room and strode toward the apothecary.

There was a grim satisfaction in finding out that his return to court was as frustrating as he had expected. He'd spent too long making his own decisions and choosing his own path. He chafed against the commands of the queen.

Alaric took a calming breath. None of this mattered right now, anyway. He just needed to deal with Gustav. And he needed this blasted storm to end.

The rain had settled into a drenching downpour. Alaric pulled up his hood and dashed across the courtyard to reach the apothecary.

Ewan's door stood open, as always, and Alaric paused on the threshold, letting the water drip off of his cloak. The mossy smell of drying plants wafted out past him. Ewan, his white hair rumpled and his long beard braided to keep it out of his work, was hunched down on a spindly stool. Candlelight glinted off a honey-colored liquid as Ewan meticulously dripped it into a small clay bowl.

Alaric held himself still, not wanting to interrupt. He glanced around at the familiar chaos of the room. The table was littered with pages covered in tightly packed writing and peppered with diagrams. A fire burning in the large fireplace reflected off hundreds of glass vials and bottles.

Ewan set down his dropper and peered into the bowl. For a long moment, the only sound was the rain hammering on the roof, then a thin wisp of reddish smoke rose from the bowl. Ewan let out a whoop and grabbed for a nearby pile of papers.

Alaric laughed, and Ewan spun about to face the door.

"Alaric!" Ewan sprang to his feet and reached the Keeper in two long strides.

Alaric hugged his friend fiercely. The old apothecary's shoulders were nothing but bones.

"Everyone who's stepped through my door this afternoon has been giddy with the rumor of a Keeper in the palace."

"I didn't know it'd cause such a fuss."

"Yes, well, you always did underestimate yourself." Ewan motioned toward the corner of the room. "I hear you travel with an interesting group."

Alaric stepped around a silver apparatus and piles of papers on the floor to drop into the same smooth wooden chair that he always sat in. He leaned back in the chair and felt himself relax. How long had it been since he'd sat somewhere comfortable? Settling back, he told Ewan about his traveling companions.

Ewan's gaze searched Alaric's face. Whatever he saw there, the apothecary's face showed only warmth. "It is good to see you, Alaric."

"It's good to see you, too," Alaric answered. The apothecary had aged as Saren had. Not physically, it was something in his eyes. Something weary. "I know I've been gone too long."

Ewan's mouth twitched into a half smile, and he shook his head. "You were gone as long as you needed to be. There's no changing it now."

Alaric looked up at his friend, but he could find no reproach. Ewan wasn't the queen, wanting to bend him to her will. He saw only friendship. Something deep inside him loosened. A thread that had been twisted around his failures and doubts unwound, and the snarled mass relaxed the slightest bit.

"You don't look like a man who found what he was looking for," Ewan said. "What brought you back?"

"The most immediate reason I'm here is this blasted storm. But the reason I'm passing through Queenstown at all is rather troubling." Alaric told him of Gustav and Mallon and the elves. The apothecary's frown deepened as the story continued. "And so now I am here, trapped because of the storm and at the beck and call of the queen."

Ewan let the words hang in the air for a moment before he said, "Your absence has been hard on the queen. I'm afraid you'll have some more bitterness to wade through before she's done." There was no judgment in the words, just truth. "In the months after you left, a handful of nobles, led by Lord Leuthro, staged a coup."

"Leuthro? He's always supported the queen."

Ewan nodded. "That's one of the many things that made the situation even worse. Leuthro had positioned himself as Saren's closest advisor." Ewan shook his head. "When the truth came out about the planned coup, Saren had to charge him with treason."

Alaric sank back into the chair. "She had to execute him?"

Ewan nodded. "It changed something in her."

Alaric groaned. "And if I had been here, Leuthro wouldn't have been so bold. My entire absence has been a series of failures, each greater than the last."

Ewan shrugged. "I have no idea what your presence would have accomplished. But I know the queen felt very alone and very unsure of herself. It shook the foundation of her rule. Even today, there are pockets of trouble in the kingdom."

Alaric looked up at him sharply. "Who?"

"Currently, the most troublesome are a pack of southern dukes led by Duke Thornton of the Black Hills. No matter what Saren does, Thornton is in the middle of it, stirring up dissent and maneuvering to gain more power for the southern duchies."

"I met Thornton already." Alaric ran his hand through his hair. "He doesn't have the power to cause Saren much trouble."

"Maybe not on his own, but he's gained the loyalty of the southern duchies. He claims there are problems with bandits, but Saren suspects that he's just creating a stranglehold on the gold trade between Queensland and the south. He keeps demanding money for training more troops. Unless Saren complies, the trade routes stagnate. Gold prices are astronomically high and merchants and nobles are up in arms."

"Still, Thornton is in no position to make demands like that of the queen."

"Saren thinks he is. And he's blackmailed or bribed enough of the court to have gained himself an unreasonable amount of power."

Alaric shook his head and smiled. Here was something he could fix. "That's one problem I can easily solve for Saren. How long has this been going on with Thornton?"

"Since early last winter."

Alaric closed his eyes. "I should have come back sooner. There is so much Saren doesn't know. There's a treaty with the Black Hills duchy, but she probably doesn't know about it."

Anyone could have found the treaty with some research, if they had known to look for it. The problem was, no one but King Bowman and Gerone, who had been the court Keeper at the time, had witnessed the treaty. It would be stored in the royal library, but such an insignificant document would have been easily overlooked.

Ewan shook his head. "You have a ridiculous amount of knowledge stuffed into that head of yours. The Keepers were right to send you here to court."

"I wish I'd come back sooner…" Alaric looked at Ewan and felt desperation rise, "but I couldn't."

Ewan waited patiently. Alaric let the words spill out for the second time that day, telling of Evangeline and the poisoning.

Ewan listened as Alaric listed Evangeline's symptoms and the progression of the sickness. "There was no antidote." It was a statement, not a question.

"For each individual poison, yes there was. But not for the rock snake venom." Alaric pulled a small vial from inside his robe, a slip of paper that listed the poisons the villagers had used wrapped tightly around it. He handed both to his friend.

Ewan unrolled the paper and read the list. "May I use a bit of it?"

Alaric nodded.

Ewan held the small glass vial up before a candle and peered at it through bushy eyebrows. The liquid inside was a murky grey.

Perching on the stool by his workbench, he placed six separate drops on a large tray. Then with a clatter of glass and much muttering and clucking, he dripped, scooped, and mixed things into the poison. He soaked a small cloth with a white liquid then touched the corner to the poison. Black, rancid smoke rose from the point of contact.

"Remarkable," Ewan said, waving the smoke away. "These woodsmen created a masterpiece of a poison." He glanced at Alaric. "Her leg? The poisoned one?"

"Black and cold." Alaric squeezed his eyes shut against the image. "She has no feeling left in her foot. The blackness seeps up into her side."

"Lungs?"

"Full. It pains her to breathe."

"The blackroot would infect her spine."

Alaric nodded. "Her left side is weaker. Or it was back when she had the strength to move."

Ewan looked down at the tray before him. "The symptoms didn't appear until a day had passed because the blackroot weakened the rock snake venom. Neither would affect her until the looseweed had exhausted her body. She didn't seem poisoned at first because she wasn't. Just lethargic. But the looseweed would have weakened her body enough to let all the other poisons begin to work.

"The exhaustion could be treated with lionsroot, but once the symptoms of the other poisons appeared..." Ewan leaned back and peered at a dark, empty corner of the ceiling. He scratched absently at his beard. He shook his head and looked back at Alaric. "I can treat everything but the venom. For that I know of no cure."

"I'm on the trail of one," Alaric said, telling Ewan of Kordan.

When he finished, Ewan picked up the vial again. "Do the villagers make this often?"

Alaric shook his head. "They made it just for the fire lizard. They mixed every poison they could find. They had trouble even reproducing a list of the ingredients."

"Good. The thought of this poison being around is unsettling. Whenever you are done with it, it should be destroyed."

Alaric looked at the grey liquid. He was tired of carrying it. There was nothing left to learn from it. "I have no more need of it."

Ewan nodded briskly. He picked up a large glass vial full of a milky white fluid. Uncorking the poison again, he poured it in. The mixture fizzed, and Ewan held it at arms' length, turning his face away from the smoke. In a moment, the bubbles subsided, and he was left holding a vial of dark brown sludge.

Ewan walked to the fire, stoked it, then tossed the vial into the back of the fire place. The mixture spluttered and hissed before it caught fire. In moments, it was gone.

Silence filled the room like a heavy blanket.

Ewan sat back down across from Alaric. "With such a sickness, how is it that she still lives?" he asked quietly.

Alaric thought of the darkness that had spread up her leg, the way her skin had burned with fever.

He whispered, "She lives because I have done terrible things."

CHAPTER TWENTY-NINE

ALARIC STARED INTO THE FIREPLACE, watching the flames sweep across the surface of the wood, curling and burning the edges slowly and inexorably. He didn't want to remember it all, didn't want to voice the words, didn't want to taint this room. Those things were better locked deep inside.

Ewan sat silent and still.

Alaric let his gaze flick to the face of his old friend. There was still no judgment, just an invitation to unburden himself.

The words swelled, pushing their way up his throat, telling Ewan how he had traveled south looking for the antidote.

"I sent word to you here," he said to Ewan, "but heard you were in a small village at the southeast edge of the realm. After King Kendren's poisoning, I knew every book the library here had on the subject, so it wouldn't have been worthwhile to come back if you weren't here.

"I spent months traveling all over the south in increasingly desperate searches for anything that would help, but I found nothing. I was about to set out in search of you when I discovered that the mayor of Bortaine had an unusual interest in Shade Seekers. He had a small library of histories and writings of some of the lesser Shade Seekers. In several of the scrolls, there were mentions of revivals of those almost dead. I had exhausted every other place I could think of, so I went back to the Stronghold to see if they had any insight into the Shade Seekers' work. They were… unwilling to help with what I needed." Alaric paused. "So I left."

Ewan sank back in his seat, a slight nod the only sign that he understood the permanence of that sentence.

"I went to the library at Sidion."

Ewan's eyes widened. "The Shade Seekers let you in?"

Alaric shook his head. "There weren't any there. I don't know if there usually are, but I found it empty. Their library is in a tower at the southern end of a valley. They have a keep somewhere beyond it, but I didn't go that far."

It had taken all morning to direct a vine in between the library door and the wall, then swell it until the wood cracked. "I could only get into the ground floor. I didn't even see a way to go higher, although I'm sure there were more rooms above me.

"But the books I was looking for were all on the first floor. Their records of poisons were extensive and well organized, with antidotes listed and cross-referenced, but still I didn't find an antidote to the venom. But it didn't matter because what I was looking for didn't have anything to do with poison."

In that tower, he had pulled the dark blue book down from the shelf where it sat alone. The cover was lined with iron, and the volume felt heavier than it should have. The pages smelled of decay and unwholesome things. He had drawn back from the book for a moment. In the Stronghold, this would be locked behind the warning gate. Maybe locked up more than that. When he flipped open the book, he had found thick paper pages with ink that had sunk into the paper, as though it had corroded it.

Alaric glanced up at Ewan. "Keeper magic involves transferring energy between living things. Shade Seekers have no problem transferring energy across the boundary between living and inanimate things.

"But the balance between life and… not life always favors the dead. When the boundary is crossed, the living thing is always depleted, but the dead thing cannot be made alive. Keepers are leery of moving energy over that boundary because they value the living over the dead. Shade Seekers value power over both.

"I found a book explaining how Shade Seekers pull the energy out of a living thing. When they do, a stone is formed to hold the energy. Not quite a living thing, but not quite dead.

"They call it a Reservoir Stone and use it as storage for *vitalle.* They create these… monsters that guard their valley. The creatures are a crossbreed of human and animal. They store the *vitalle* of a human in one of these Reservoir Stones until they press it into a living animal." He grimaced at the memory of a bear he had seen from the library. It was lurching through the woods on misshapen legs, while it chewed on the hind leg of a small deer. The deer was still alive.

"Their use for it was repulsive, but the idea itself was fascinating. It was similar, in a way, to what Keepers do with runes. We infuse them with energy and store it there until the rune needs to work. Except instead of forcing the energy into something, the Shade Seekers allowed the energy to create a vessel for itself.

"I spent a week in Sidion and never saw another soul. When I returned to Evangeline, I found that, despite the trance I had put her in, the poison had progressed." Her face had been so pale he had thought her dead. The desperation of that day caught in his breath. There had been no hesitation, no debate as to the rightness of it.

Alaric pulled the ruby from the pouch at his neck. It filled his palm with a rich, red light. He fisted his hand and squeezed, letting its warmth seep into his fingers, then opened his hand and held it out toward his friend.

Ewan drew in a breath and leaned forward. He stared at the swirling light, his face a mix of horror and amazement. "Where is her body?" The apothecary's voice was barely above a whisper.

"The body lives when the *vitalle* is removed, but it lacks a will. It will neither eat nor sleep. And if I had left her body alone, the poison would have just continued to spread.

"The knowledge from the Shade Seekers opened up new ways of using *vitalle* that I had never considered. I created a crystal to encase her body, to merge with her, keeping her alive while it kept her from changing."

Ewan's eyes were wide and his face was very still. "You stopped her from… aging?"

"Not stopped, but slowed down. It will take years for her to age a month." Alaric dropped his eyes to the ruby. "But the poison needs much less than a month."

Ewan's eyes were locked on the ruby again. "How long ago…?"

"A little over a year."

His eyes lifted to Alaric's face. "You've carried that this whole time?"

Alaric nodded. "I needed to know how to stop the poison, so I traveled south. I tracked down the blood doctors in Napon, any that were competent."

Ewan's eyes went flat.

Alaric forced himself to meet his friend's gaze. "I studied with them for a time, learning about the poisons they used and the antidotes. Their methods are as brutal as we had heard. They perform all their experiments on prisoners, and if they run out of those, they round up the poor off the street.

"The elderly, women, children. There are death caves beneath the city where the fires that burn the bodies never go out. Even there, I found no antidote to the rock snake. So I left."

Ewan's face mirrored the repulsion Alaric felt. "I destroyed some things on my way out." He squeezed his eyes shut, banishing the memory of the cave, the stench of decay and blood, the constant background hum of moaning cut through with shrieks. "What I should have done was burn it down.

"After that, I went to Coastal Baylon and spent time at their library and at the university." The shelves of books there had been endless. "They have so much knowledge there. Books on every topic imaginable bursting off the shelves. And they research new things constantly. Building after building with labs and experiments and research. It's no wonder they have no regard for us. We're barbarians in comparison." He shook his head.

"The experiments they do with poisons, though, are gruesome." He pictured the long line of cells, the stench, the screams of the dying. "They use prisoners for study also."

Alaric shook off the memory. "They even have a small number of books on Keepers. In one, I found a reference to Kordan the Harvester. He was credited with having an antidote to the bite of a rock snake.

"So a few weeks ago, I came back to Queensland to see what the Keepers knew of Kordan. And you know the rest."

"Can you reverse this?" Ewan gestured to the gem that Alaric was still rubbing between his fingers.

"I think so." Alaric stared at the ruby. "I know how they take this energy and put it into another creature. I will put it back into Evangeline instead.

"None of it matters, though, unless Kordan really recorded an antidote and I can get to it. If I can't, my choice lies in leaving her asleep to die a lingering death, or wake her to a quick one. Painful, but quick. And I'm running out of time. The light in the ruby is beginning to fade."

Alaric tucked the ruby back into its pouch.

"I've been thinking of what Gustav wants the Wellstone for. Once he has learned the knowledge it holds, I think he will use it as a well of energy. If he fills it with *vitalle*, it will hold a great deal of power. Whatever his plan is to raise Mallon, it is going to take a lot of energy. And when Gustav fills the Wellstone with energy, if he really takes advantage of every bit of power it will hold, I am certain when he pours it out into Mallon, the memories in the Wellstone will be destroyed."

Alaric raised his gaze to his friend again, looking for hope that he knew he wouldn't find. "Gustav is so far ahead of us that I can't believe we are going to catch him. There is nothing to stop him from finding Mallon's body and waking him."

Alaric gripped the ruby through the pouch. He wasn't

going to get the Wellstone. After everything, the antidote was going to slip through his fingers. All the pain he had caused Evangeline, all the pain he had endured, all the people he had let down, it was for nothing.

Alaric dropped his head into his hands. "I should have let her die."

CHAPTER THIRTY

THE TRUTH FILLED THE ROOM.

It was useless to believe anything else. It was time to stop looking away from it. He faced it squarely.

"I should have let her die," he repeated. The words, even though just a whisper, opened something inside of him. Some dark corner that he had kept closed cracked open. He saw himself, withered and pale, coiled around the hope of an antidote. Wrapped so tightly that the beauty of that hope was gone. What should have been bright was crushed and deformed into something else, something unrecognizable.

"Maybe," Ewan said quietly, "but letting those we love die is no easy thing. Nor should it be."

Alaric did not move, but the coiled creature inside him unwound the slightest bit more at the apothecary's words. There was permission to stop. An invitation to stop turning away. To face what was done and release it. His actions could not be undone anymore than the poisoning. But he could let go of the mess he had made of it.

He met Ewan's sympathetic gaze. For the first time, the

words came out not as a desperate cry, but as a statement. "I should have let her die."

Ewan's eyes were wet, but he did not argue. "What will you do?"

Alaric took a deep breath and stared into the fire, watching the flame devouring the wood, leaving nothing but a small pile of ash.

"I will try to stop Gustav. But if I can't, then there is nothing left to be done," Alaric said, "beyond begging her forgiveness and letting her go."

Ewan motioned around the room. "Alaric, you know that everything I have is yours. If there is anything that I have that would help you in any way…"

Alaric gave a slight smile. "I've collected a fairly impressive store of medicinal plants for myself. You should come see it."

"Maybe you could bring it back here." At Alaric's silence, Ewan continued. "Whatever you decide to do, when it is done, please consider coming back and continuing in your role of Keeper."

"Continuing?" Alaric gave a bitter laugh. "I haven't played a Keeper role in… a lifetime."

"You're orchestrating a group of mismatched, powerful people to, what was it? Take care of some 'significant trouble brewing to the west?' That sounds very much like something a Keeper might do."

After a long moment, Alaric sighed. "It does, doesn't it?"

"You're rather good at it, you know."

Alaric stared into the fire. Yes, he was acting like a Keeper, but that is all it was. Just acting. What he wanted to do was go to Evangeline. "When I think of what will happen if we fail to stop Gustav, my first thought is that it won't be safe for Evangeline to be cured in such a world. Saving the world is lower on the list than saving her."

Ewan shrugged. "Heaped together, the world doesn't look like anything worth saving. It only looks valuable when we think of it in terms of those we love."

"Still. It's not a very Keeperish sentiment."

"It would be if more Keepers left their tower and loved someone in the world."

The apothecary rose and went to the fire. He puttered around for several minutes before producing two cups of tea.

Alaric sat with an empty mind. He let the familiar sounds and smells seep into him, filling an emptiness he hadn't realized was there.

"Reece died last year," Ewan said, still facing the fire.

Alaric's gaze snapped up to his friend.

"No! Ewan, I'm so sorry. I've been talking and talking, and I never even asked…"

"It was an infection in her lungs that wouldn't heal." Ewan looked out the window at the pouring rain. "I knew I couldn't fix it, but I still tried everything I could. I even tried things I knew wouldn't work. The darkest day was the one when I admitted there was nothing I could do."

Silence stretched out between them. Reece and Ewan had been married for years before Alaric had met them. Their marriage, with its easy camaraderie, was the first one Alaric had ever envied.

"She lived four more days. Four days." Ewan sighed deeply. "I wish I had some great wisdom for you."

Alaric could think of nothing to say. How had he not recognized the grief that rolled off his friend? Maybe because it was different from his own. There was no taint of hope in Ewan's. It was worn in, draping familiarly over him, bowing his shoulders. Is this what Alaric would look like in a year? Would this frantic, clawing grief that threatened him turn into something so quiet?

"May I pay my respects to her?" Alaric asked.

Ewan led Alaric outside and around the house, hugging the walls to stay out of the rain. Behind the apothecary, an enormous oak tree grew, dozens of huge branches twisting out in different directions. "I'm glad they buried her on the royal grounds," Alaric said.

Ewan nodded. "The queen herself ordered it and set the stone workers to make the headstone."

Alaric raised one eyebrow.

"Don't worry," Ewan said. "I talked her down from an eight-foot-tall angel to a stone marker."

Alaric laughed. "She's probably saving those angel plans for you."

Ewan winced. "I should design something for myself. Plans she'll feel obligated to follow after my death."

Beneath the oak, nestled between two enormous roots was a grey stone marker. It read, "Reece ~ Beloved wife and friend."

Sitting on top was a delicate, pale pink flower.

"Lambsbreath always was her favorite," Ewan said. "That's one of the last blooms of the season."

"When I first arrived at the palace," Alaric said, "it had been years since I had lived in a city. I told Reece I missed sprawling pine forests, that the city smelled stale. A week later, she appeared with a tray of dirt and moss formed into a little hill. She had planted a handful of pine tree shoots. She said it was my own forest, and anytime I needed to smell it, it would be on my desk. "

Ewan smiled. "She was proud of that little forest. You should have seen how excited she was when she thought of it."

"It worked. My desk smelled like pine trees every day."

Alaric leaned forward over the flower. He cast out to feel the *vitalle* from the grass around him, from the enormous oak and from the surrounding gardens. He laid his finger on the lambsbreath and found what was left of its own life. The edges of its petals were beginning to curl and wilt, the stem was dry. A trickle of energy swirled deep inside the flower, a combination of the white *vitalle* that made up its essence, giving it shape and scent, and the little veins of purple *vitalle* winding through it, letting the cut flower cling to life.

His finger began to tingle as he drew out the purple, separating strand after strand and gathering it just above the flower. A violet haze appeared and brightened.

The fog of purple flickered, and Alaric pulled small amounts of the *vitalle* from the grass beneath his knees, infusing the mist, giving it strength. The glow brightened again, tingeing the delicate pink petals with purple.

He set his other hand on the gravestone and felt the deep, slow essence of the stone. No energy swirled through it, no light, no color. But the stone was infused with its own dense sense of being.

It was this Alaric gathered, like collecting dewdrops. He felt down into the stone and stripped tiny beads of its essence out, pressing them into the glowing purple light above the flower.

His hand on the gravestone burned, but Alaric pressed it to the surface of the rock. He was almost done.

The bits of the stone he had added to the prick of purple light began to weigh it down. Alaric guided it back into the flower, spreading it along the surface of each petal and down the stem. The light diffused easily, flowing out into a lavender gauze covering the lambsbreath.

The flower pulled energy from him now, drawing what it needed. Alaric opened the channel wider from the grass through to his finger. He felt a blister begin to form on his fingertip where it touched the flower and moved more of his fingers to touch it, spreading out the pain.

The energy slowed, then stopped. He took his finger off the flower and pulled his other hand away from the gravestone. His palm where the skin was still new from the blisters in Bone Valley was a dark, angry red, and his finger had a long line of shiny new blisters stretching from the tip to the first knuckle.

Ewan was standing perfectly still next to him. Alaric gave him a small smile and nodded. Ewan hesitated, then reached out his hand to touch the lambsbreath which looked unchanged. When he turned back to Alaric, there were tears on his cheeks. "It's stone," he whispered.

"She deserves to have flowers year round." Alaric looked at the stone flower, its thin petals still a delicate pink against the tombstone. "Maybe not everything I learned from the Shade Seekers was useless, it's just a different way of thinking of the connection between things. Of course, there aren't many wholesome applications for turning living things to stone."

"You've found one."

The flower sat atop the grave, part of the stone. It would be there long past the time when he or Ewan would visit.

"Using the tools of a Shade Seeker doesn't make you one, Alaric. And the one choice of walking out of the Stronghold doesn't negate the thousands of times you chose to be a

Keeper. It is only one choice of many. We aren't defined only by our darkest choices. There is much more to us than those.

"Our pasts are complicated, what we've done, what has happened to us, but the beauty of life is that each day, we choose again which parts of that past we will allow to shape our actions. Most of the worst decisions in history have been motivated by love of some kind or another. The decisions you are haunted by certainly were. The path we take away from those choices is dependent on whether we let the choices compel us, or refocus on the love that motivated us in the first place.

"If you don't want to be a Keeper today, then don't be one. But if the only thing holding you back is choices you made in the past, well, those choices are done. Let the past inform your choices today, but don't let it rule them."

CHAPTER THIRTY-ONE

ALARIC STOOD before the mirror in a formal Keeper's robe. He had found the robe hanging in the closet of his room. It was just a black robe, hooded and reaching down to the floor. Even formal robes had no decorations, only a slightly thicker material.

Still, the robe gave Alaric pause.

The Keeper's robe he had worn when he left the palace had fallen apart almost a year ago. He had replaced it with the first black robe he could find, but it was the black of a storm cloud or a shadow. This robe was the warm black of the night, weighted with the night's stillness.

And there were pockets. Eight pockets just on one side. Eight pockets and nothing to put in them.

His mind slid back over the past year: the library at Sidion, the caves of the southern blood doctors, the dark searches for dark things, Evangeline's withered face always driving him on, a relentless, hollow fire.

The map hanging on the wall above the mantle was

shaded in grey over the areas Mallon had controlled eight years ago. It was a looming cloud seeping in from the edges of the country toward Queenstown. If Mallon were raised, that would all begin again, the death, the fear. Something deep inside Alaric rebelled against that cloud. There could be no more ruined villages, no more plagues, no more riving of the people. It didn't matter how far Gustav was ahead of them. Alaric would reach him and stop him.

Alaric turned back to the mirror. A Keeper blazed back at him, cloaked in black, eyes burning. He stepped back in surprise, and the fire died. A knock at his door pulled his attention away.

"The scrolls you requested from the archives, sir," a servant at the door said, bowing.

Alaric took the two small scrolls and glanced at them. At least there was something good he could do. It was satisfying to tuck them into one of his pockets. Over the servant's shoulder, he saw Ayda and Milly seated in some chairs outside his room.

"Did you ever meet Will?" Alaric asked, walking over to Ayda. "Saren said he had visited the elves last time she saw him."

Ayda cocked her head to the side. "Another Keeper?" She nodded. "Two springs ago."

"And in all of the vast Greenwood, he managed to find the one remaining elf?"

"I found him."

"Why?"

"Because he asked the trees to find me. He was very polite to the trees." She smiled. "He stayed with me for several weeks. The first night, he told me a tale of one of your ancient heroes. I'd never heard a human tell a story so well. We traded stories each night, besting each other. He said that the bards should sing songs of our battle."

"Did he tell you where he was going when he left?"

"To the queen, then the Keepers."

Why hadn't Will gone back to the Keepers after coming to the palace? And why hadn't he sent them a message explaining where he had gone?

Douglon and Brandson appeared, complaining about the rain. Alaric led them all through the palace to the council chamber. A long rectangular table filled the center of the room with enough chairs to accommodate a dozen people, but the chamber was empty.

At the head of the table stood Saren's throne-like chair. To the left of it, in the position reserved for the court Keeper, sat a chair shorter than Saren's but decidedly larger than the rest. Alaric raised an eyebrow. He'd never had a special chair before. This wasn't set up just for a council. Saren didn't want anyone to miss the fact that there was a Keeper back at court.

A door at the far end of the room was open, and raised voices came through it. He led the group through the door and into a smaller chamber reserved for the queen and her small council. Saren sat in a large chair, her husband's old chair. It was too big for her, but Alaric had never been able to convince her to get a different one. It made her look like a child pretending to rule. She hadn't taken it well when he'd told her that, though. Now Queen Saren was sitting in her too-large chair and looking troubled as Menwoth stomped back and forth in front of her, shouting.

"He's been charged with treason against King Horgoth!

He stole from the crown and is storing up wealth for the purpose of stealing the throne!"

Saren gave a little sigh of relief when Alaric and the others walked into the room.

Menwoth whirled around. "Why is that dwarf not bound?"

Douglon rolled his eyes. "Stuff it Menwoth," he muttered.

Saren held up her hand for silence. "I'm not sure how King Horgoth runs his court, but in mine, things are run in an orderly fashion."

Menwoth glared at Douglon but shut his mouth.

Another dwarf entered the room. His beard was streaked with grey, but his eyes were bright and he carried himself with the ease of a young man. Alaric had met few dwarves with grey beards. Nurthrum must be quite old, a fact that didn't seem to be slowing him down.

"Nurthrum," Saren greeted him. "Thank you for coming."

Douglon nodded respectfully to Nurthrum.

Menwoth looked sharply at the older dwarf and shot Douglon a smug smile. "I didn't know you had arrived, Master Nurthrum. I am so glad you are here. "

Nurthrum bowed to Saren. "Just this hour. I received a message from Her Majesty that there was an issue between some dwarves and she would appreciate as many opinions in the matter as possible."

"We have much to do this afternoon, gentlemen," Saren said, motioning for everyone to sit. "If someone could close the door, we can get this sorted out. Menwoth, if you could, in a clear and calm manner, explain your grievance against Douglon?"

Menwoth, with a quick glance at Nurthrum, stated his accusations again, this time, in a more subdued tone. Saren listened patiently, and Douglon, with a few snorts and shakes of his head, listened as well.

"Do you have anything to say, Douglon?" Saren asked when Menwoth had finished.

With surprising restraint, Douglon stated his own case.

"Nurthrum," Saren said, "do you have an opinion on this matter?"

The older dwarf bowed. "Your Majesty, I have known both of these fine dwarves since they were knee high. I do not doubt either of their stories. Anyone who knows Douglon knows that he has no interest in the crown at all. It has been a trial to King Horgoth on many occasions that Douglon is unwilling to do anything related to the throne."

Douglon straightened up proudly at this dubious support.

"I know that Menwoth also speaks the truth, that King Horgoth has indeed accused Douglon of treason before a full court."

"Then what are we to do?" Saren asked.

Nurthrum turned to Douglon. "I have your word that the accusations are false?"

"Good Grayven's Beard! Of course they're false!"

Nurthrum nodded and turned back to Saren. "I will inform King Horgoth that the charges are disputed. If Douglon will agree to come to Duncave as soon as he can to present his case to Horgoth, I will vouch for him until then."

Saren blinked in surprise at the easy solution. "Menwoth, are you willing to stand by Nurthrum's decision?"

Menwoth glowered at Douglon, his mouth clamped shut. He gave a quick nod.

"Excellent," Saren said with a relieved air. "Then we have a great many other things to discuss with the council. Thank you each for coming—"

"Excuse me, Your Majesty," Nurthrum said, "We may have a slight problem convincing King Horgoth that this is the right decision."

Saren leveled a gaze at the dwarf.

"Perhaps a gesture of good will to go along with the news?"

"What do you want, Nurthrum," Saren asked tiredly.

"Kollman Pass."

Menwoth looked quickly at Nurthrum, then a little too eagerly back at Saren.

The queen's eyebrows rose. "Kollman Pass? You want the only western pass out of my lands? In response to this situation? The High Dwarf has been trying to get Kollman Pass since before my husband died. I'm not about to hand it over to keep one dwarf out of trouble."

Nurthrum glanced around the room and his gaze stopped on Alaric.

"Rumors are flying about the palace, Your Majesty. They say a Keeper has returned and that he travels with elves and dwarves and that his presence here means there is great trouble on the horizon."

Alaric watched the dwarf closely. Whatever game Nurthrum was playing, it was working. Saren's eyes shifted apprehensively between the Nurthrum and Alaric.

"I was under the impression that it was important to you, Your Majesty, that Douglon retain his freedom in order to help the Keeper with whatever it is that is so urgent." Nurthrum shrugged. "If it is not, then let us drop this discussion all together and arrest Douglon. King Horgoth can have the headache of sorting all this out, and we can continue about our day."

Saren's eyes narrowed as she considered the dwarf for a long moment. A sense of foreboding began to gnaw at Alaric. Saren hadn't gotten any better at negotiating in the past two years. Nurthrum had cornered her. Saren couldn't give the Pass to the dwarves. It was the only pass through the Scale Mountains. No one in Queensland ever used it, but the army had an outpost there. It was the easiest way for nomads to enter Queensland. The dwarves wouldn't protect the pass. An army of nomads could be at Saren's doorstep before she had any clue.

And the small castle Alaric shared with Evangeline was on Kollman Pass.

Saren gripped her hands together in her lap. "Perhaps it is time for an era of cooperation between our people to begin. There are two watchtowers along Kollman Pass. I want one company of my soldiers for each tower and guaranteed safe passage to and from them. They will be limited in their activities to the immediate area of the towers."

Menwoth's eyebrows rose and Nurthrum smiled widely.

Alaric opened his mouth to object. That was a terrible idea. In practical terms, if the dwarves owned the pass, there were limitless ways they could trouble and harry the soldiers. This would end with Saren losing the Pass completely. She had backed herself into a corner.

Before Alaric could speak, Saren turned to him. "There is one more condition. When you are finished with your current work, Alaric, you will return to court and remain here until I dismiss you."

Alaric stared at her for a moment, then closed his mouth.

Nurthrum glanced at him in surprise, realizing at the same moment as Alaric that the negotiation had never been between the dwarves and Saren.

CHAPTER THIRTY-TWO

IT HAD NEVER BEEN Saren who was cornered.

Alaric couldn't let Douglon be arrested for treason just because Alaric was reluctant to come back to court. He clenched his jaw and gave Saren a short nod. "When I am done with what I need to do."

Saren let out a breath. "Nurthrum, draft up a treaty for the Pass. We will sign it, and you can take it to Horgoth with the news that Douglon will present himself and his case in Duncave as soon as he is finished helping Alaric."

Alaric watched Saren closely, realizing that the lines on her face looked less like exhaustion and more like experience.

"Now," Saren said, rising and heading toward the formal council chamber, "we have a council meeting to attend."

The dwarves filed out of the room, and Alaric set his hand on Saren's arm to stop her as she walked past. "You gave up Kollman Pass? Just to have me back here?"

Saren's brow snapped together. "Kollman Pass is just one of the pieces in a complicated agreement I am working on with the dwarves. I've been planning to trade the Pass to them for a very long time. Frankly, I never thought I would get the promise of something so valuable in return." She stepped past Alaric, the corner of her mouth curling up in a triumphant smile. "Once you're finally back, I'll take the time to explain it all."

Alaric stared after her for a long moment, holding down the irritation forming in his chest. She had trapped him. She had played into what everyone thought of her and she had trapped him. Worse, she had played into what Alaric thought of her, complete with sitting in the too-big chair. His irritation broke apart and came out as a huff that was very close to a laugh. His mouth twisted into a rueful smile. Reluctantly, he admitted she had won.

The council table was now full of soldiers in military uniforms, a small man rummaging through a pile of maps, and several others from the nobility. A woman with a large book opened on the table before her was glancing around the room and making notes. Brandson and Milly took seats at the foot of the table near the door. Douglon leaned against the back wall behind them. Ayda looked curiously at the people at the table and sat cross-legged on top of a huge chest that sat near a column close to the queen. Saren gave her a courteous smile as she took her seat, and Ayda beamed back at her.

Alaric walked over to his seat at the table and stood behind it. His black robe felt more conspicuous than before. General Marton, the stalwart leader of Saren's forces, gave him a friendly nod. It was nice to see a familiar face. There were empty seats at the end of the table next to Milly. The woman with the book opened, who must be the current court scribe, looked at Saren questioningly.

"Duke Thornton and the southern dukes were invited to the council," Saren said. She pursed her lips and tapped her fingers on the table. Then she glanced at Alaric. "Let's begin, anyway."

The woman with the book raised her eyebrow almost imperceptibly before raising her pen.

Saren cleared her throat and the room quieted. "Today, we welcome Keeper Alaric back to court after far too long without him."

Alaric nodded to the queen.

"We also welcome his companions Brandson, Milly, Douglon, and Princess Aydalya of the Greenwood. Ayda brings us the news we have long feared. She is all that remains of the elven kingdom. The rest of her people were destroyed by Mallon."

There was a collective gasp as the room looked quickly at Ayda and murmured to each other.

"Alaric brings us some more dire news," Saren continued, bringing the room to order. She turned toward him.

Alaric decided to begin with the most straightforward. "The nomads are gathering to the west."

The mapmaker started rummaging through scrolls, and the scribe began scribbling fiercely. "Where?"

Douglon walked up to the table. "They are rumored to be gathering in the valley below Mt. Dorten." He pulled a map closer to himself. "This map is terrible. The valley is here. You don't have it marked." He pointed at a blank space on the map. "It's large and flat with good supply of water and plenty of game. There are several ravines that lead to it from the Roven Sweep. A large force could gather there and be supported by the valley for the entire summer."

The mapmaker began to sketch the valley onto the map.

"Rumored?" General Marton asked.

Douglon nodded. "The dwarves have been finding evidence of them since early spring."

"And they have sent no one to check it out?" Saren asked.

"No, Your Majesty," Douglon answered, looking apologetic. "The dwarves don't think that the actions of humans are particularly important. I've sent my cousin to convince the king to look into it."

Saren considered the map for a moment, then looked at the court scribe. "Didn't Lord Horwen arrive at court yesterday?" At the woman's nod, Saren turned to the guard standing near the door.

"Go find Lord Horwen," Saren told him. She turned back to the room. "Horwen is Lord of Penchen. His lands lie here along the feet of the Scale Mountains. If anyone would have knowledge of that part of the mountains it would be he."

General Marton leaned over the map, asking Douglon questions while the mapmaker scribbled notes furiously. The general called for and then sent a half-dozen messengers out of the room on assorted errands.

A few minutes later, the door opened and the guard escorted an elderly nobleman into the room, his cane tapping on the floor as he tottered off a bow toward Queen Saren. His doublet was black velvet, emblazoned with a white hawk. She motioned him to the empty chair next to Milly. He tussled with his cane for a moment, thumping it against the chair and table, before sitting. Queen Saren introduced the lord to Alaric.

Horwen blinked. "A Keeper! How wonderful!"

Alaric bowed his head slightly toward the man.

Queen Saren addressed Horwen. "These good dwarves

bring news of nomads gathering here in the Scale Mountains."

"Nomads? Impossible," Horwen declared. "I've heard no such thing."

"How many scouts do you have in the mountains?" Saren asked.

"None. Nothing ever happens there."

Saren's lips tightened. "If you don't patrol, how do you know there are no nomads there?"

"My people tell me everything," Horwen said expansively. "And I've heard no news of any nomads."

Queen Saren's lips grew even thinner.

"Nevertheless, Your Majesty," Alaric said, "the dwarves are certain there are some nomads there." Alaric glanced around the room again. He took a deep breath and continued, "The reason the nomads are especially troubling is that we believe a Shade Seeker is attempting to raise the Rivor."

There was shocked silence for a moment in the room, then a rumble of conversation.

"What did he say about the Rivor?" Horwen demanded. "Speak up, young man! The Rivor died years ago."

"Maybe not," Saren said.

"Oh," Lord Horwen said. "Oh dear."

As briefly as he could, Alaric told the council about the sacrifice of the elves. Ayda sat close-lipped on the chest.

"How do you know this about the Shade Seeker?" General Marton asked.

"The Shade Seeker's name is Gustav, and he traveled with us for a while."

The general raised his eyebrow.

"No," Alaric answered the obvious question, "we didn't know he was a Shade Seeker."

"We thought he was an idiot," Ayda said.

"How did you figure it out?" Marton asked.

Alaric opened his mouth, but Ayda beat him to it.

"We had been looking for a treasure," Ayda began.

"Ooh!" Horwen said. "A treasure hunt!"

"We figured out that he really was a wizard when he stole it right out from under us," Ayda continued. "Alaric hadn't told us it was a magical treasure created by a Keeper long ago. It turns out the Shade Seeker had been controlling each of us, including Alaric, in order to find it." She shrugged. "Then the Shade Seeker flew off on his dragon."

The queen turned back to Alaric. "That's a lot of things that didn't go well, Alaric. Do you know where Gustav is now?"

Alaric paused. "Ahead of us."

"Do you know where he is going?"

Another pause. "I have some theories."

Queen Saren sighed and sank back in her chair.

"I thought that man was a Keeper," Horwen said loudly to Milly.

Alaric scowled.

"As did I," said the queen tiredly.

CHAPTER THIRTY-THREE

ALARIC REFUSED to drop his gaze from the queen's.

"I didn't begin this"—he waved his hand at the group—" treasure hunt as a Keeper. I fell in with a group searching for something I was interested in." He paused. "And I had nowhere else to go."

"Not even back to court where you belong?" she asked.

Alaric clenched his jaw, fighting to keep his voice calm. "I'm not done with what I need to do."

"There's more going on in the world than your problems," she snapped.

Alaric closed his mouth, fuming. The rest of the room was perfectly still. The court scribe's pen, scratching down the words, was the only sound.

"Stop being mean to Alaric," Ayda said peevishly.

The queen's eyes blazed as she turned to the impertinent elf.

"Yes, he did all those things," Ayda said. "He even helped the Shade Seeker translate some troublesome runes on the map so he could find the treasure."

Alaric glared at her, and she shot him a cheerful smile back.

"And, no, Alaric doesn't really want to be a Keeper. Well, most days he doesn't. At this point, he wishes he could pass this off to someone else or at least get some useful advice instead of having to explain himself to people who didn't even know there was a threat, much less know how to neutralize it."

The queen stood to face Ayda, and Alaric rose, too. Douglon pushed himself away from the wall where he had been leaning.

Ayda slid off the chest and stepped forward into the light of a large torch. The room flashed with coppery reflections from her hair. "But there are no other Keepers to rescue you," Ayda said in a quiet voice that filled the room. "And there are no other elves to sacrifice themselves to save your miserable race that did nothing but fall under Mallon's power."

Alaric glanced around the room. Every single face was staring at the elf. The scribe's pen hovered frozen over the paper. Even Lord Horwen's eyes were alert.

"So I'd suggest you stop posturing and ask Alaric what it is that he needs you to do in order to save your weak little kingdom from a threat that has destroyed far more powerful races than your own." Ayda held the queen's eyes a moment longer. Then giving the queen a cold smile, the elf sat back down on the chest.

Alaric let out a breath.

"Uppity little thing," Horwen whispered loudly to Milly.

The look Ayda shot Alaric was fierce and, dare he say, loyal? He bowed his head to her and she grinned.

Alaric looked back at Saren, making his voice as calm as

possible. "The nomads are gathering no matter what Lord Horwen's people tell him." Alaric nodded toward Horwen who was sitting back in his chair, looking confused. "And if Gustav succeeds in raising Mallon, you should be ready for an invasion."

The council door swung open, and Duke Thornton strode in, followed by two other smug young noblemen. Thornton tossed off the slightest nod to Queen Saren before dropping into one of the chairs. He looked around the table, his eyes falling on the scribe's book. Noticing that she had already begun taking notes, he scowled at the queen.

Alaric could almost feel the pressure of her fury pull away from him and refocus on the duke. Saren, her hands gripped tightly in her lap below the table, pierced Thornton with her gaze. "How nice of you to join us."

Thornton's eyes flicked to Alaric then back to the queen. He opened his mouth to speak, but the queen continued. "These dwarves bring news that nomads are gathering in the Scale Mountains because a Shade Seeker is attempting to raise Mallon."

Duke Thornton snorted. "The dwarves wouldn't know an army was gathering above them if the troops were stomping and shouting down every muddy hole they could find. And you expect us to believe that Mallon's been what? Sleeping for eight years?"

The two dukes next to him smirked.

"Duke Thornton," Alaric said, keeping his voice level as he targeted the duke with all of his own frustrations. He stood, reaching into his pocket for the scrolls he had requested from the library. "I knew your father."

Thornton gave him a bored look.

"I met your grandfather, Morlan, once as well," Alaric

said. "I hear that, unlike your father and grandfather, you're having a hard time keeping the southern passes safe."

Thornton raised an eyebrow. "The passes are crawling with brigands who worm their way up from the south to harass the gold merchants. My soldiers keep the passes open."

"Well, that is your job," Alaric said.

The table had gone quiet. The mapmaker was looking between Alaric and Thornton. The scribe was scribbling away madly, recording each word.

"Yes it is," Thornton answered. "And what exactly is your job, Keeper? Did you notice that while you've been away, the court has continued running just the same? Makes many of us wonder what it is you did when you were here. And it makes us wonder why you came back? Out of a deep loyalty to the queen, was it?"

The anger that had been growing since the meeting with Menwoth surged to the surface. Alaric forced his jaw to relax. Out of the corner of his eye, he could see Saren sitting perfectly still in her chair, her back stiff.

Alaric let his gaze travel around the room. The rest of the council sat waiting, barely breathing. It was impressive how much weight the young duke carried. Not a single person spoke up against him.

"As far as I've heard," Thornton continued, "wherever you've been and whatever you've been doing, Her Majesty was displeased with it. So if you haven't been serving the queen, what have you been doing?"

Alaric let out his breath in a laugh. Whatever this duke deserved, it wasn't an explanation of Alaric's actions. He opened his mouth to answer, but Saren spoke first.

"What Keeper Alaric has been doing is not the concern of a lesser southern duke."

The scribe smirked and wrote the queen's words with obvious pleasure. Thornton turned furious eyes on the queen.

"My apologies, Your Majesty," he said in a scathing voice. "This man is the first Keeper I've ever met, and I find him less impressive than I had expected."

"I, on the other hand," Alaric said, "am impressed by the power you've amassed in such a short time at court. The Black Hills are such an insignificant duchy that the nobles from there are rarely even noticed at court."

Duke Thornton's eyes went flat, but Alaric ignored him, unrolling one of his scrolls and spreading it out on the table. "But it doesn't seem to me that court is running quite as well as it did before I left and before you showed up. It seems to me that there is a bit of dishonesty and exploitation going on." He set his finger on a passage of the scroll and looked back at Thornton. "One of my jobs here is to make sure the truth of things doesn't get lost."

Thornton's eyes narrowed.

"For instance, I have a bit of truth here that deserves to be found." Alaric cleared his throat and read. *"I, Morlan, Duke of the Black Hills, do hereby bind myself as protector of the southern passes. My family is responsible, financially and militarily, for the safety of the three passes leading south from the Black Hills. All financial and military needs will be seen to by myself and my posterity, up to the exhaustion of our resources, before requesting assistance from the crown. In return, King Bowman graciously pardons my treason."*

Alaric raised his eyes to meet Thornton's stare.

"Do you know what this treason is he's speaking of?"

Alaric asked conversationally. Alaric spread out the other scroll and scanned down it. "King Bowman kept the matter fairly quiet. Here it is. *During the twelfth year of King Bowman's reign, Duke Morlan of the Black Hills was caught pilfering gold from the merchants along the southern trade routes. His men, disguised as highwaymen, robbed and murdered southern merchants, keeping the gold for the Black Hills family and using it to bribe members of the king's court. When caught, King Bowman generously forgave Morlan the charge of treason in exchange for repayment of the gold stolen, with interest, and Morlan's agreement to protect the southern trade routes with his own resources. From Midsummer's Day, year twelve of King Bowman's reign, the Black Hills duchy is responsible exclusively for the safety of merchants traveling the southern passes. Any losses experienced by the merchants will be repaid by the Black Hills treasury. This treaty is binding to Duke Morlan and his posterity for the duration of the duchy."*

Alaric glanced at Thornton. The duke's face was white with fury.

"That is an interesting bit of truth," Queen Saren said.

Thornton opened his mouth to speak, then shut it.

"If you had knowledge of this," Alaric said, walking around the table toward the duke. "Your recent actions would be treason."

Thornton's hands were at his side, clenched into fists.

"These copies are for you," Alaric said dropping them on the table before the duke. "If I were you, I'd work on how to convince the queen that you didn't know any of this, that somehow, your father neglected to teach you your family's duty. I'm sure Her Majesty will be requiring an explanation. Soon. The royal treasury is calculating how much money you have mistakenly accepted from Her Majesty to protect the passes you are responsible for. I suggest you contact your own treasury to begin collecting the funds."

Thornton shoved his chair back and stood up, glaring at Alaric. His two friends rose, too, backing up toward the door.

"And I also suggest you get that brigand problem under control quickly. Her Majesty will be checking with the gold merchants who enter Queenstown to make sure they've received safe passage."

Thornton turned blazing eyes to the queen.

She looked back at him calmly. "I'll send for you when I have time. Do not leave the palace."

Duke Thornton grabbed the scrolls, spun on his heels, and stormed from the room, followed quickly by the other two.

Saren sank back in her chair, a genuine smile spreading across her face.

Alaric bowed to her. It didn't make up for everything, but it was a start.

CHAPTER THIRTY-FOUR

WITH THE EXIT of Duke Thornton, the tension in the room dissolved. Alaric walked back to his seat amidst a sea of murmuring.

Saren cocked her head to the side. "Alaric, how did you find out about Gustav and what he was doing?"

"I was searching for some information from an old Keeper named Kordan when I met this group. Douglon had discovered the remains of Kordan's home in a valley in the Scales."

"The Keeper didn't live at the Stronghold?" Saren asked.

"Not at the end of his life. He left the Keepers and built his own home, west of here at the edge of the Scales. Douglon had found a map there to where Kordan had buried a Wellstone."

The queen and Lord Horwen looked impressed by this. Most of the other faces in the room were blank.

"What's a Wellstone?" asked General Marton.

"A gem that holds memories or energy. They are extremely rare, and it is what I had been searching for.

Unfortunately, it's what Gustav was looking for as well. To raise Mallon, Gustav is going to have to find a lot of energy and store it somewhere. The Wellstone would be the perfect tool for that."

"What are you planning next, Alaric?" Saren asked.

"We're going to the Greenwood to move the Rivor's body to a more protected place. It won't stop Gustav forever, but it will slow him down and give us more time to find him."

General Marton cleared his throat. "This Shade Seeker is in Queensland preparing to raise Mallon. So who is organizing the nomads?"

Alaric shrugged. "I have no idea. But I can't believe the two things are unrelated."

"It was Gustav!" Milly said suddenly. The entire room turned toward her and she shrank back into her chair. "I mean, it could have been."

Alaric shook his head. "He's been in Kordan's Blight for months."

"I know," Milly said. "But he told me once that before he came to Kordan's Blight, he traveled the Roven Sweep among the nomads. He said they loved him."

Lord Horwen was looking in amazement at Milly, "This is the queen's council, young woman! Not a tavern where peasants shout out rumors. Hold your tongue!"

"Lord Horwen," the queen said sharply, "she is welcome to speak. If I didn't allow rumors in my council meetings, we would have very little to discuss. Milly, do you think Gustav was telling the truth?"

She paused. "Well, I didn't. He also told me once that he could move the moon." She looked at Alaric. "That's impossible, right?"

Alaric nodded at her. "Definitely."

"So I thought he was just making more things up," she continued. "He doesn't seem like a man anyone would follow, but..."

"But what?" the queen said impatiently.

Milly looked at Alaric again. "He always gets what he wants. None of you really liked him, but you all did exactly what he wanted."

"He managed to influence us," Douglon said. "But he could hardly do that to an entire army."

"He wouldn't have to control the entire army," General Marton said, "just the leaders."

Alaric shook his head again. Gustav couldn't have done that, too. Could he? The idea had the unsettling feeling of being... probable. And if the dwarves were right, the nomads had been slowly gathering for months. Theoretically, Gustav could have set things in motion before going to Kordan's Blight.

"This wizard fellow doesn't sound as foolish as you all made him sound," Horwen said with a chuckle. "Sounds like an evil mastermind!"

General Marton nodded.

Saren nodded as well. "Whether Gustav is the mastermind behind this or not, it is clear that we face a threat. One we didn't even dream possible." She looked at the maps and then turned toward Alaric. "What do you need us to do?"

"Ready the army and send some scouts to figure out what the nomads are doing. If we can stop Gustav, I think the nomads will disperse. But if he is successful..." Alaric looked around the room, knowing he didn't need to finish. "We might as well put up a fight."

The queen nodded. "There are things to plan," she said to

the council. "You all know your jobs." The council members rose, talking among themselves and moving out of the room.

"You live in the Scale Mountains," Horwen was saying loudly to Menwoth. "You should come to the library with me. I've been studying maps of the mountains near my lands, but they are woefully incomplete. Your expertise would help."

Menwoth nodded. "I have spent a great deal of time with High Dwarf Horgoth's maps, sir. It is possible that I could fill in some gaps."

"He's never actually spent any time in the mountains, though," Douglon muttered to Brandson. Menwoth shot him a glare.

"Excellent!" the old man boomed, his cane tapping quickly on the floor as he walked toward the door with Menwoth. "It's nice to talk to someone of sense. I'm stuck with commoners so often. My steward sent me a message today claiming they've seen a red dragon over the Greenwood." He waved his arms around. *"Help, Lord Horwen! A blood-red dragon rides the sky at night!"* He shook his head. "Peasants! There hasn't been a dragon in Queensland since before I was born."

Menwoth snorted and the two disappeared out the door, his voice fading away.

Alaric's stomach dropped. Gustav was already west of here, searching for Mallon's body. Through the council chamber ceiling, the rain drummed loudly. Alaric growled in frustration. It was going to take them the better part of a day to reach the Greenwood, and Gustav was already there.

It was people like Lord Horwen and his nervous peasants who would suffer if Mallon was raised. People who didn't completely understand what was going on and who didn't have the power to do anything about it. The same people who Alaric had once spent a great deal of energy to protect. How had they fallen so far out of his view? Alaric looked in annoyance at the table spread with maps and papers. He needed to leave, to chase down that stupid wizard and stop him before he managed to pull off another thing he shouldn't be able to.

General Marton looked after the departing lord with a troubled face. "That's strange," he said. "We received a report of a red dragon seen in the area yesterday."

Alaric looked sharply at the general. "What area?"

"This area. Near the city. The report came this morning from a farmer whose land lies a half day's journey north of here." Marton looked thoughtful. "I sent a soldier back with him to check it out, but I admit I didn't believe him. If there's a dragon in the area, it's not acting very dragon-like."

"Gustav flies on a red dragon," Alaric told the general. "I'm sure Horwen's people are telling the truth. I expect him to be over the Greenwood looking for Mallon. But I can't imagine that he would come back east to Queenstown. There's nothing here for him. If your soldier finds anything, let me know."

CHAPTER THIRTY-FIVE

HOURS LATER, Alaric closed the door of his room behind him. He had offered Saren the help he could. The army would be assembled and some general plans were underway.

As the day had gone on, Alaric had felt more and more overwhelmed. Something about the seemingly unattainable expectations everyone had of him, and the constant reminders that if he hadn't been gone for so long, a good many problems could have been avoided. It all combined to leave him feeling like he was fighting against a cloud of guilt and judgment. Saren had ordered food brought to the council chamber, and they had feasted and talked and planned, but Alaric had spent much of the time wishing he could just return to his room for peace and quiet.

Night had fallen, and his room was filled with the comforting red light of a fire someone had lit in the hearth. On the desk, a single candle was lit for him, and Alaric didn't bother to light any more of them. When he dropped into the chair in front of the fireplace, he saw that his bag and cloak had been tidied up over in the corner. He let out a groan that he knew expressed more frustration than some cleaning deserved, but couldn't even the cleaning staff leave him alone for a single day? He had forgotten how diligent the servants were in the palace. After one incident, years ago, of a servant sweeping up and burning the tatters of an ancient scroll he had been trying to reconstruct, he had greatly curtailed their duties. It was going to be hard to come back here.

Having someone prepare a warm fire was nice, though.

A book on the mantle caught his eye, and he leaned forward to get a better view of it. It was one of several decorating the shelf along with candles and a vase of flowers. The rest of the books he was familiar with, but not that one. The title read, *True Light.* He heaved himself out of the chair, grabbed the book, and sank back down. He flipped open the book. The pages were blank.

He turned back to the cover. *True Light.*

Alaric picked up the unlit candle that was sitting on the side table. Touching the wick gently, he said, "*Verus lumen.*" A rush of energy barreled through his finger, and a tiny dot of bluish-white light appeared. Alaric forced his finger to stay steady while the energy burned through it, far more energy than a normal flame required. The light grew brighter, casting a stark white light. Alaric pulled away, clenching his finger for a few breaths until the pain faded.

He set the candle next to him on the table and opened the book to the first page. Silver words leapt into existence.

Brother,

I have a troubling matter and no one to turn to.

If it is you, speak your name.

Alaric stared at the words for a moment. "Alaric."

The writing shimmered slightly, but remained unchanged. Who had left this? No Keeper had stayed here since he left.

No, Will had been here. If this was from Will, what did he want Alaric to say?

Of course. "Alaric the Feckless."

The words shimmered, faded, and reappeared.

Speak your full name.

Alaric grinned. "Alaric the Feckless, Keeper of Trivia, Pawn of Queens."

The words shimmered brightly and then faded. In a breath, the entire page sparkled with silver writing.

Yes you are.

Brother,

I leave this message because I do not trust it to a raven. I have no time to return to the Stronghold myself. I have lingered as long as I dare. I hope you return soon.

I have been to the elves and met an elf named Ayda. She appears to be the last living elf. She said the elven people fought the Rivor and imprisoned him.

I have seen Mallon's body. He is not dead. In fact, he is still strong. The elves have his mind trapped, however, and he is not conscious of anything around him. I could find no way to wound the body.

Something must be done. Although Ayda was complacent, I believe the Rivor will find a way to escape. Without the elves to help, I fear his return would be unstoppable. Tell the Shield. We need to destroy Mallon now while he is weakened. Although how we are to do that, I have no idea.

The other thing that troubles me concerns the elf, Ayda. I spent three weeks in the Greenwood as her guest. I probably shouldn't have stayed so long, but you know how I love the elves. She didn't act as I expected—polite, but really just waiting for me to leave. Instead, she seemed genuinely pleased to have me around.

We spent the time in a contest of storytelling. The first time I realized she was unusual was when I was taking my time getting to the end of Isond and Gondrey's tragic tale. Ayda had been leaning forward, eager as a child, listening when suddenly she stepped… no, crashed into my mind.

I was powerless. She entered my mind as if it were her personal library, picked up the end of the story and stepped back out. It wasn't that she had done anything harmful to me, but the ease with which she'd done it and my utter lack of power to stop her were terrifying.

Several other times, always in a similarly negligent way, she displayed extraordinary power. But mostly she was pleasant. Pleasant and lovely. I know I found her lovelier than I should have, and I often wondered if she had a hand in that.

It was the day before I left when I saw what was truly troubling.

She had found a stone along the river and tossed it to me. The sunlight had caught in the stone, and when I held it in my palm, it started to collect my memories. Milky scenes chased each other through it. My hand on my old knife, writing that report about elves in the library of the Stronghold, throwing stones into a creek during my childhood. Each scene, although mundane, seemed to speak a sort of truth to me. Or perhaps a truth about me. As though the stone were sifting through my memories to find out who I was.

It was a Wellstone. I tried to direct it, but could get nothing coherent out of it. It was too wild. I realized that by studying it, we could gain insight into how our Wellstone thought—or whatever thinking is called when it's done by a rock. Perhaps that knowledge could help us decipher the visions from our own cut stone. Or teach us to ask better questions.

Thrilled with the possibilities, I lifted it up to Ayda, intending to ask if I could keep it. But as I lifted it toward her, I was practically blinded by the light that shone through it.

Through the Wellstone, I caught a glimpse of her standing alone in the center of a glen, power radiating out from her until the very trees bent away.

Then the real Ayda, who had been watching me curiously, shifted slightly. In that moment, the light in her was swallowed up by a darkness so deep and so complete that I was terrified. The stone pulled me into blackness—a very old, very angry blackness.

I knew that all was lost.

Then the Wellstone was knocked from my hand, and Ayda stood before me as lovely and real as ever.

"Those stones don't like me," she said, kicking it into the river. Then she looked at me, a look of piercing loneliness and sadness. "They expect the worst from me. As though one small thing that I carry could destroy everything else."

Please travel to the Stronghold and tell the Shield that the Rivor is not dead, but he may be weaker than he has ever been. Now is the time to act.

And tell him that Ayda—she should be watched. You may not understand this until you meet her, but there is something about her. When I am with her, I am incredibly fond of her. Still, I am afraid. Afraid of the darkness she carries. And not only her darkness, I am afraid even of her light.

I do not trust her. Find her, if you can, but do not trust her.

I will try to return to the Stronghold by year's end.

I wish you were here. I am out of my depth and crave your insight.

Your brother,

Will

Alaric sat back, his nerves thrumming with apprehension. He lifted the flame Ayda had frozen that still hung around his neck, watching it glint in the light.

Did he trust her? If he was honest, he had started to. And if he was honest, he had no reason to. She was hiding something about when the elves fought Mallon. She wouldn't explain to him why her magic was so powerful. Until the meeting with Saren earlier today, she had never even shown any loyalty to him.

Will feared that Ayda was manipulating him, and it was easy to see that she did manipulate almost everyone she met. But it had always felt relatively harmless, a childish desire to be liked. Was it more than that? Brandson and Milly obviously cared about her. Douglon, a dwarf, had overcome his dislike of elves to such an extent that Alaric wondered if there was anything the dwarf wouldn't do for Ayda. Even Gustav had seemed to like her.

The logical conclusion was that Alaric trusted her because she wanted him to.

And the darkness Will saw, what was that? Will was fun to the point of being reckless—at least the Keepers' idea of reckless. Yet there had been real gravity in his warning. The fact that Will had gone to such lengths to keep the message secret was astonishing.

Alaric was a little surprised he hadn't found a crumpled,

stained letter stuck to his door with tree sap labeled, "Secret information for Keeper Alaric."

Alaric sat back and rubbed his eyes. He shouldn't be mocking Will's Keeper skills. At least Will had noticed something off about Ayda. Alaric had been completely taken in by her. If this little side trip to the palace had done nothing else, at least it had shown Alaric all of the ways that he had missed things a Keeper should have seen.

A bell somewhere in the city tolled midnight. The rain had lightened to a pattering outside his window.

He looked again at the frozen flame necklace he had. Who was Ayda? He started to pull it over his head, but paused. There was something about the necklace that felt like it should be kept close. Maybe he shouldn't be trusting his own judgment any longer, but he let it drop back down next to the ruby.

This collecting of troubling stone necklaces was getting to be a habit.

CHAPTER THIRTY-SIX

ALARIC TURNED BACK to the book. Will's warning had filled the page, and Alaric, flipping idly to the next, was surprised to see a postscript spring into view, filling the page completely.

One more thing.

I go west directly. Beyond the Scale Mountains are rumors of a gathering war. A holy man walks among the nomadic tribes recalling them to the Rivor's banner.

A village that I visited near the Greenwood told me tales of a Shade Seeker who had served Mallon. An elderly man who still comes through their village, demanding food and money. Mallon had left him in their village the day he had gone into the Greenwood. They said the Shade Seeker had never harmed any of them and that he wasn't even particularly threatening, but they were still afraid. The fear Mallon spread still lingers, even after all this time. When the Shade Seeker left, some young men from the village followed him on a dare. He went to the Roven Sweep. I think this Shade Seeker is the one gathering the Nomads. Could he know the Rivor is not dead?

Was Will talking about Gustav? If Milly was right and Gustav had spent time among the nomads, then it could be. There were not many Shade Seekers, and it was highly unlikely there would be two of them interacting with the nomads.

But that would mean the wizard had been close to Mallon, trusted by him. Which meant Gustav wasn't an idiot at all. If Mallon found him useful, Gustav must be powerful.

The Rivor cared for nothing but power.

A cold knot sat in Alaric's stomach. He had underestimated Gustav to a dangerous extent.

Duke Thornton's estimation of Alaric's worth as a Keeper was feeling more and more accurate.

Alaric turned back to the book and flipped the page one more time, just to be sure he was at the end. He found one last line of writing.

Last I heard, the Shade Seeker was masquerading as some elderly western lord.

Lord Horwen.

The exhausted fog in his mind stirred. Lord Horwen was Gustav. The truth of it blew through his mind like a breeze, clearing away the cloud that had hung over him all afternoon.

Alaric dropped the book and swore. The wizard had done it again. He wasn't exhausted. He was being manipulated by Gustav's influence. Again.

Alaric dropped the book and raced into the hall, calling out for the nearest guard to take him to Lord Horwen's rooms. The guard ran ahead of Alaric leading him to Lord Horwen's apartment in a different part of the palace.

Alaric turned the doorknob, expecting it to be locked, but the door swung open. He ran into the lavish quarters. They were empty.

A servant girl stood inside, looking wide-eyed at the guard and Alaric.

"Where is he?" Alaric demanded.

"Lord Horwen left hours ago," she answered, shrinking away from his scowl.

The room was messy, trunks rummaged through, and drawers left open, as though it had been hastily vacated. Gustav was gone.

"Close the gates," Alaric commanded the guard. "Inform Queen Saren that Lord Horwen is an imposter. Search the premises for him." At the man's hesitation, Alaric snapped, "Now!"

If Gustav had left hours ago, it wouldn't matter, but Alaric had to do something. The guard raced off, and Alaric stepped into the room, letting his eyes roam across the mess. The room smelled earthy, like mud. Alaric looked around for the source and saw a grungy canvas bag tossed on a table by the window.

He walked over to it and saw smudges of dirt all over the table and chairs. He picked up the bag and under it found a wide-open box holding a grimy red handkerchief. Alaric stared at the box, his stomach sinking. He reached forward slowly and flipped the box lid closed, revealing the cover, carved with a sprawling oak tree.

He had seen this box before in the memories of the Keepers' Wellstone. It was the box Kordan had used to store the emerald he had created when he had tried to save that young boy's life. The emerald he had wrapped in a red handkerchief.

Alaric sank into a chair. This box, covered in dirt, was what Gustav had dug up in Bone Valley. A box containing an emerald. Not a Wellstone.

Kordan hadn't even buried the Wellstone in Bone Valley.

The book Alaric had found in the Stronghold had read: *I will store all of my memories in the Wellstone, and bury my treasure here beneath a young oak.* Alaric had assumed the treasure was the Wellstone, never thinking that Kordan would have valued the emerald after the boy had died.

Alaric's head thumped down on the table. It made perfect sense. Kordan had buried the emerald under the oak tree for the exact same reason Ewan had buried his wife under one, to give the boy a burial place of honor.

Alaric had been chasing the wrong treasure this entire time.

Alaric fell into bed in his own room. His body felt like it was made of stone, like it would be a simple thing to just lie on this bed forever.

The guards weren't going to find Gustav. He had left the palace hours ago. He was probably back with his dragon, a half day's journey north of here. But why had Gustav come to the palace? What did he want?

Alaric groaned and threw his arm over his face.

And where was Kordan's Wellstone? Alaric had thought back over everything, but he could think of nothing that had specifically said that the treasure buried in Bone Valley was the Wellstone. Alaric had supplied that idea all on his own. Of course Kordan would have buried the emerald. It had gone dark after the boy had died. Why would Kordan have kept a Reservoir Stone that didn't hold any energy?

Which meant that Kordan's Wellstone was probably in the place where he went after he left Kordan's Blight, after he left the Keepers. Kordan's Wellstone was sitting in the very tower where Douglon had found the map.

There was a polite knock at the door, and Alaric heaved himself into a sitting position before calling for them to enter. Matthew, the queen's steward opened the door.

"I'm sorry, sir. No trace has been found of Lord Horwen."

Alaric nodded.

"Her Majesty also wants you to know that your horses will be saddled and ready for you at first light."

"Thank you."

"If you need anything before then, anything cleaned or brought to you, please let us know."

"I think I will be fine, Matthew," Alaric said. "Besides, your conscientious cleaning crew already came by this afternoon."

Matthew's eyes narrowed as he looked around the room. Following his gaze, Alaric saw muddy stains on the tile by the door from when he had first arrived, drapes still pushed back unevenly from when he had first looked out the window, and a candle knocked over on his desk lying in a hardened puddle of wax.

"I sent no one to clean your room today," Matthew said. "And if any of my people had done this shoddy a job, they would be unemployed by now."

Alaric's heart stuttered. It was only his pack and his cloak that had been tidied.

He pushed himself off the bed and sank down next to his pack, dumping it upside down on the floor. He searched through the contents before swearing. It wasn't here.

Gustav had taken back his ominous medallion.

CHAPTER THIRTY-SEVEN

BY THE TIME the sky began to lighten the next morning, Alaric wasn't sure he had slept at all. His mind churned with the same thoughts that had plagued him all night. Ayda, Gustav, the Wellstone. The theme of Alaric's failure to see the truth of things wound through his thoughts. It was like a snake, hissing accusations and constricting tighter and tighter.

After taking leave of the queen who was already awake and in her study, Alaric went to the stables. In the east, the sun rose behind the remnants of the storm clouds, turning them a molten orange-red. The vibrancy of the morning felt like a personal affront to the despondency settled deep in Alaric's bones.

Their horses had been readied, and the others were preparing to leave when Alaric joined them. Alaric studied Ayda for a moment. She was chatting easily with Milly, her hair glittering with flashes of copper. Alaric readied Beast mechanically, realizing he had absolutely no idea what to do about Ayda.

He gathered the others together and told them about Gustav.

"I hate that wizard," Ayda said. "It's even harder to pay attention to him than it is to the rest of you. I couldn't even work up the interest to look at that lord."

Alaric had spent a good portion of the restless night wondering how he had missed noticing Gustav again. Alaric couldn't even reconstruct a good picture of Horwen's face. He mostly remembered his doublet with the white hawk. That and the fact that he was old and slightly daft. Horwen had seemed unimportant, a nuisance to be suffered. And the day had been full of so many distractions. Ewan, Saren, Duke Thornton. Gustav had taken advantage of all those things to distract him.

The nuance of the wizard's influence spell was staggering. A normal influence spell would distract someone by suggesting something particular to them. This is how you could recognize an influence spell. If someone suddenly had an overwhelming interest in mushrooms, or staring at a blank wall, it was a sign. But Gustav's was different. Somehow, he managed to cause each person to be distracted by the things they would most naturally be distracted by.

"I have never heard of anyone using influence in such a far-reaching, subtle way as Gustav does," Alaric said. "I'm not even positive he knows what his spells will draw. I don't think he expected to see us at the palace. I think he just casts out nets for things he needs and sees what is drawn in. Maybe a web is a better analogy. And he's the spider waiting to see what is caught. It's entirely possible that the fact we ran into Menwoth was Gustav's doing."

"Why was Gustav even at the palace?" Brandson asked.

"His official reason was studying maps in the library,"

Alaric said. "I'm guessing he was looking for some clue as to where Mallon might be in the Greenwood. The Keepers are on good terms with the elves, and we know barely anything about their woods. I can't imagine the Shade Seekers know anything at all."

They saddled up, all subdued, and headed out of the palace in silence.

"This isn't all bad," Milly said as they passed out of the western city gates. She ignored all the eyebrows that statement raised. "We missed our chance to stop Gustav at the palace, but we now know that he's not as far ahead of us as we thought."

"True," Alaric said. "And I think he may not be heading straight to the Greenwood. The stone Gustav dug up in Bone Valley was Kordan's emerald, not his Wellstone. The emerald was probably what Gustav was after all along, but after yesterday's council meeting, he knows that Kordan also had a Wellstone.

"I believe the Wellstone is at Kordan's tower where you found the map, Douglon. Gustav would have come to the same conclusion. A Wellstone would help Gustav hold all the energy he's going to need when he tries to wake Mallon. Since the valley with Kordan's tower is between here and the Greenwood, I think he'll go look for that first."

"That's the Wellstone you need, isn't it?" Brandson asked. "The one with the antidote for Evangeline?"

Alaric nodded. The thought of Gustav having the Wellstone rankled deep inside of him.

"It won't take long to stop there," Douglon said. "To get to the northern edge of the Greenwood, we'll pass right by the valley. It'll just take a couple hours to get to it and back."

As the day went on, Alaric kept Beast near Ayda. She

was riding quietly, not bothering Douglon or paying attention to the trees. Something was different about her this morning. Ever since she had defended Alaric in the council meeting, she was more open and honest. More present than she normally was. This morning, it felt less like he was keeping tabs on an unpredictable elf and more like he was riding alongside a friend.

Alaric tried to come up with ways of broaching the subject of the darkness Will had seen in her. But there really wasn't a good way to ask someone to share their deepest, darkest secret while you rode with them on a sunny morning. Not a way that seemed likely to work, anyway. It was Ayda who finally spoke first.

"Will you return to the palace when this is over?"

That agreement hung over him like a cloud. "I told Saren I would. After we stop Gustav and after I..."

"Let Evangeline go to sleep?" Ayda asked, not unkindly.

Alaric felt a knife blade of anguish in his gut. To 'go to sleep' was the elven term for death. "No, if we find the Wellstone, I'll wake her and stop the poison."

Ayda looked at him steadily, but said nothing.

Alaric refused to answer the unspoken doubt in her eyes. Unless the Wellstone was absolutely destroyed, he would not give up this hope. "Where will you go after this is over?"

Ayda's eyes swept southwest as though she could see the Greenwood past the miles of hills between them. "Perhaps it will be time to sleep," she answered, a dreamy, hopeful expression on her face.

Alaric turned sharply toward her. "Your kind of sleep? Or mine?"

"Your kind of sleep," she answered with a wistful smile, "will not cure the sort of weariness I have."

Alaric stared at her in amazement. "But you are the last of your people," he said. "If you die, everything of your people dies with you. Think of how much the world could learn, could benefit, from your knowledge!"

"That is my only regret," she said softly, "that the lore of my people will end. But not for the world's sake, for the fact that there will never be another elf who will learn it. We have never felt compelled to share our knowledge with the world. Why should I begin now?"

"But there can't be no more elves. The world needs elves."

Ayda snorted. "There haven't been any elves for eight years, and the world has barely noticed."

Alaric looked ahead without answering, and the two rode together in silence for several minutes.

"I can't continue like this." Her voice was full of exhaustion.

He glanced at her and saw her face drawn with pain. "Because all your people are dead?" He cringed as soon as the words were out at how insensitive they were. But she'd never expressed anything about this before.

She shook her head. "Because my people are not dead."

Not dead? He turned to face her completely, and she looked back at him. The rage was back, deep in her eyes. A small crease appeared between her eyebrows while she studied him.

Alaric braced himself. For what, he didn't know.

But she only gave a slow nod. "You are a Keeper, and my people's story should be kept." Her brow smoothed, and her face opened up somehow. The guarded look in her eyes dropped away. What he had taken to be rage was something worse. She was brimming with a deep, shattering pain. "Will you take the story of the elves?"

Alaric drew back from her, from her eyes. The depth of the pain and hopelessness there threatened to swallow him. She sat patiently, waiting, knowing the weight of what she asked.

He wanted the story, wanted it very much. But the suffering in her eyes was so cavernous, he was afraid to go near it. "I'm not a very good Keeper," he whispered.

"Then do it because you are my friend, Alaric," she said.

Ayda held out her hand to him.

Alaric's was shaking slightly as he reached out and took it.

CHAPTER THIRTY-EIGHT

HE RACED THROUGH THE TREES, their branches reaching for him, their murmurs of fear and confusion clinging to him. The ground below him was covered with life, tendrils of energy reached down into the dirt, the fragrance of moss and grass filled the air.

He looked down to see Ayda's feet leap over the slow, pulsing energy of a gnarled tree root.

He was in her mind, in her memory.

Ayda raced toward the last bend in the path before the clearing, the fear from the trees urging her on. When she turned, instead of being greeted with warm sunlight, she stumbled to a halt at the edge of a snarled forest.

Directly in front of her was an elf partially transformed into a tall birch. His torso melted into the trunk of the tree, his arms, past the elbow, were covered in bark. His eyes stared unblinking past her as he bent his will toward his goal.

She stepped back a moment, frightened.

"Just a changing," she said quietly to herself. A changing

was smooth and graceful. Like stretching. There was nothing frightening about it.

And yet she drew away.

A groan farther ahead drew her attention.

Another elf, partway through changing stared out of an aspen, his face stretched in pain. Why pain? Changing wasn't painful.

There was something terribly wrong. She stood before the tree, trying to understand. The deep pulse of energy that should have flowed through his roots was sluggish. She reached forward and touched the side of the tree, looking into the elf's tortured face. The life energy didn't flow; it swirled and dribbled and pressed in all the wrong places. And there was a darkness, a growing mass of blackness sending tendrils out, wrapping around what was left of the elf and smothering it.

She yanked her hand off the tree and looked around her. Every tree was the same. She could see it now, the blackness sitting inside each one of them.

She walked past one after another, each a tangle of elf and tree segments spliced together. There were so many.

Her gaze scanned the glen as she took faltering steps forward. Her eyes finally fell on the basin sitting at the foot of the steps to her father's house. The surface still bubbled slightly with the power of the links to the cursed ones, links to the people controlled by fragments of Mallon's will.

Ayda looked around at all of the half-changed elves. They should have used those links to pull Mallon's curses off the people he controlled and onto themselves. Once they finished changing into trees, the curses would be released, the dark energy returning to Mallon. Then, with all his power back inside of his own body, he would be mortal. Then, they had a chance to destroy him.

They just needed to finish changing.

Ayda ran toward the basin, ready to take one of the curses upon herself.

"Ayda, stop!" Prince Elryn called from the steps. He rushed to embrace her.

She clung to him, burying her face in her brother's chest, feeling his energy flow smoothly through his body. She hid against him for a moment, blocking out the other elves.

"I can help," she said finally, pulling away toward the basin.

He held her firmly. His face was pale, his eyes tense. Cornered. "I didn't think you'd make it."

"What's happening?"

Elryn shook his head and turned away, leading her up the stairs winding around the trunk of the greenwood tree to her father's house. As they climbed, Ayda could see that the glen was full of elves in different stages of changing. She paused in her climb. The elves stood or kneeled on the ground, looking ill or exhausted. Some looked dead.

"Elryn, what's happening?"

He stepped down toward her, gently took her hand, and began leading her up the stairs again.

"We don't know, exactly," he began. "We've collected the curses, but somehow, they are keeping our people from changing." He looked down toward the glen, dismayed. "There may be too much of the Rivor in one place."

Ayda stopped again, staring at Elryn. "They can't change as fast as you, so the spells have time to stop them."

Elryn looked stricken. "I didn't know it would make a difference."

Ayda began to run up the stairs, now pulling her brother after her. They ran to the top and into her father's house. Rushing through rooms created out of the tree itself, she ran into King Andolin's council chamber where she slid to a halt.

The king stood with his head bowed before a large window. Off to the east, smoke rose lazily above the trees.

"He has crossed the eastern border of the Greenwood," the king said. "He spreads fire and darkness. We have very little time."

Ayda looked at her father. His shoulders were bowed and his skin was white as moonlight.

"Who?" Ayda demanded. "Mallon? Is he coming here?"

Her father did not move. Elryn closed his eyes.

Ayda stared at the two of them just standing there. Mallon was coming to the glen. A seething rage grew deep within her. The darkness in the elves was his doing. He would not bring more of that darkness here.

"We have to fight him!"

"There will be no fight," the king said quietly. "There will only be death."

Ayda looked angrily at her brother and father. "Of course we will fight," she said. "Every elf alive is here. Why would we not fight?"

"Every elf alive is trapped," Elryn said. "Trapped in themselves having willingly taken on the power of the Rivor."

She stared at him, then looked out the window at the elves below. Those changing were still caught, others sat senseless on the ground or stumbled about as though in darkness.

"How many are free?"

Elryn looked at her. "Three."

King Andolin dropped his head into his hands.

"Father," Elryn said matter-of-factly, "it is time."

The king sighed deeply then straightened his shoulders and looked at Ayda. His eyes drew her in and surrounded her.

"I have always loved you, my daughter," he said, pulling her into an embrace. Then he stepped back and held her firmly by the shoulders. "Will you help me?" His voice was pleading. His eyes burned with the question.

"Of course," she answered. "Anything you need."

He opened his mouth for a moment, then closed it again. Turning abruptly away, he strode from the room followed by Elryn.

Ayda looked again at the eastern sky. The smoke spread across the blue sky like a stain.

She ran after them back down to the glen.

Elryn was standing at the eastern entrance of the clearing. He faced down the avenue that wound away under the tree, holding a longbow in his hand.

"What are you doing?" she asked, running up to him. She looked down at the handful of arrows stuck into the ground by his feet, waiting to be shot. "What are we going to do against him with a few arrows?" Still, she turned and stood next to him, facing down the quiet forest path.

"Not we," he said. "Me. Our father has need of you."

"I'm not leaving you," Ayda said. "You can't defeat him alone."

"Our father has need of you," he repeated. Then he pulled his eyes from the path and looked at her, smiling reassuringly. "I can if everything goes right. Now, go."

She hesitated a moment. Elryn's face was filled with…

something. Fury? Determination? Agony? He leaned forward and kissed Ayda on the forehead. "I love you."

His kiss burned slightly, as though she had been touched with a coal. Or maybe some ice. "And I love you." Her brother nodded and turned to face the avenue again.

Ayda ran to the king who was shepherding the elves into one large group. She began helping, guiding the ones that could walk to sit among the half-transformed trees. The ones that couldn't walk, they carried. Some rocked, curled on the ground like infants, some shrieked, some were bent and deformed, some had boils and sores.

As gently as she could, with tears spilling down her cheeks, Ayda herded them together.

"Someday," her father had told her the day she had refused to be named his heir. "Someday, you will realize how much you love your people."

And here, with the fire and darkness approaching from the east, she knew. She worked tirelessly, her heart breaking over and over.

When they were as collected as was possible with only a few of the half-formed trees sitting outside of a tight circle, Ayda sank down onto her knees.

Her father was pale.

"How do we protect them?" she asked.

He looked at her with desperate eyes. "I wanted you to be queen because there is a strength in you that is different," he said, coming to her and grasping her hands. Then he closed his eyes. "May that strength sustain you."

"Father?" she said uncertainly.

He dropped her hands and turned back to the circle of elves. Without looking, he waved in her direction. Ayda felt the air stir around her. She looked down and saw that her clothes had changed into a white robe covered in clear crystals.

The queen's gown.

"Father," she said with more steel in her voice. "This belongs to the queen."

King Andolin looked sadly at the closest tree. There, her face frozen in pain and confusion, stood Queen Alaine, not fully a tree but far from an elf.

"She's not dead!" Ayda cried. "And even if she were, you are still here and so is Elryn." She gestured across the clearing to where the crown prince still stood firmly before the eastern entrance. The smoke and darkness were almost upon him.

Suddenly, flames blazed out from between the trees, and a thin, black figure strode into the clearing. The air around him rippled slightly, and even from across the glen, Ayda could feel that the trees near him were filled with loathing.

"This will be your end, Rivor," Elryn said calmly.

Mallon laughed and looked across the clearing. "You don't have many to fight with you."

"We have what matters."

"Yes, I see you've collected my curses. You do realize that just means that now I control all of you as I once controlled others. I could take all your brethren and use them as my own personal army, if I needed an army. Or just set them to killing each other." Mallon smiled. "Or I could just leave them here to rot, haunted by my spirit for the rest of their long lives."

"That's what we were counting on," Elryn said with a smile.

Before Ayda could understand what he was doing, Elryn nocked an arrow and sent it deep into the Rivor's heart.

Mallon stumbled back a step, then stood straight and looked quizzically at Elryn. "Do you think you can kill me with an arrow?"

"Not yet," Elryn answered.

Ayda was distracted by the movement of her father as he reached his arms out over the elves. He closed his eyes, and Ayda felt the spirits of the elves fight to give him their attention. Each elf pushed aside the power of their curse for just a moment to answer the call of their king. She felt their agreement, but her attention was too divided between them and Elryn for her to understand what was happening.

"Aydalya," the king said gently.

She turned back to him just as he opened his eyes.

"It was our only choice."

She wasn't sure if it was an explanation or an apology.

At that moment, each elf gave a long sigh and toppled lifelessly to the ground. Thin wisps of light rose from their bodies, slowly curling toward the sky.

Ayda's breath caught in her throat in horror. "No!"

Her mind spun as a darkness tore out of each figure and rushed across the clearing toward the Rivor.

This was how they would defeat him. As each elf died, each curse was set loose and flew back to its master. Almost all of his power would be held again in his body, and that body would be mortal.

Mallon cried out and grabbed at his chest where the arrow sat.

Elryn smoothly drew another and sent it sinking in next to the first. The Rivor hissed and threw a burst of flame at Elryn. He screamed as flames engulfed him. Ayda took a step toward her brother.

Her father stepped between her and Elryn, stopping her.

The flames grew and a growing darkness spread out behind him.

A terrible blackness, solid and living, shot out of Mallon toward the prince. The Rivor dropped to his knees as Elryn raised one hand and the darkness shattered. Pieces shot off him and flew throughout the glen. Elryn faltered then collapsed. Ayda screamed his name. A sliver of darkness shot toward her father's back. She shoved him out of the way.

The shard spun deep into her chest. It stabbed into her, shooting out tendrils, wrapping and crushing her.

"Ayda" her father's voice was strangled as he reached for her.

Inside of her, the darkness spread, consuming her. She dropped to her knees, gasping for breath while everything inside her burned with darkness.

The king reached his arm out toward the wisps of light floating up from the elves. He breathed out a command, and the tendrils streamed over to Ayda, as though carried by a wind.

A flood rushed into her. Voices clamored and wept and commanded. An enormous weight settled on her and she fell to her knees. She clamped her hands over her ears to block out the roar, but it was within her, stretching her, deafening her.

There was a roar of fury, and the elves inside of her tore into the darkness, ripping the fingers of darkness out of her and shoving them into a small ball. Then they wrapped themselves around it, smothering it inside of her. With the darkness contained, the voices stilled and drew back to the edges of her mind, but they did not leave.

Fire spread across the glen. The trees burned, their cries of anger filling Ayda's mind.

Her father moved in front of her again, sheltering her from the backdrop of flames and darkness. Tears streamed down his cheeks.

"I will stay to finish this. You must leave, Ayda. You are all that is left."

She pushed at him, trying to get to Elryn. Past the king's shoulder burned a wall of fire. Mallon stumbled out of the flames, but the prince was gone.

"Ayda," her father's voice snapped her attention back to him. "Run!"

CHAPTER THIRTY-NINE

ALARIC BLINKED. He was staring at Ayda, their horses walking calmly along the road still damp from last night's deluge. Ayda dropped his hand. She looked down, letting her hair fall forward in front of her face.

"My people are not dead," she said softly. "But they are not alive, either."

Alaric couldn't find any words. The elves, all of the elves who had sacrificed themselves were inside of her. No wonder energy flowed out of her. She was like a dam holding back a flood.

"My people are bound to me. They exist in a half-life, a shadow world contained inside of me. They give me their power, but it bleeds them dry of their own... essence... their own souls. Yet they cannot die. They cannot change or heal or free themselves. They just continue, tattered remnants of a once formidable people.

"They crowd my mind. They fill everything. They infest..." Her voice trailed off. She picked a twig from her horse's mane.

Alaric's attention was caught by a movement of the stick in her hand. What had been nothing more than a sliver of wood swelled to the size of a nut. Ayda's hands still rolled it unconsciously between her fingers as it lengthened into a thin stick. The stick sprouted branches with tiny green buds.

"They saved me from being consumed by Mallon's darkness. I should be grateful." Ayda's features hardened. She squeezed the small tree, now clearly a maple, in her fist. "But they left me alone, and yet I'm never actually alone. I carry the weight of them always, every day, no matter where I am." Her voice rose. "I can't speak to them, but I also can't get away from their presence."

The little maple tree burst into flames.

She looked back at Alaric. Her eyes were dark with anguish. "So yes, when this is done, I will sleep. What was my life ended eight years ago."

Alaric pulled Beast away a step, looking at her warily. Catching sight of the burning tree, Ayda snorted in irritation and tossed it aside. As it fell, the flames solidified, just like the flame on Alaric's necklace, and a perfect model of a burning tree fell to the ground. She didn't even look back as the spot of orange disappeared behind them on the road.

"There is too much power…" she said. "Too much for one body. It flows out too quickly. It trickles out when I don't know it. This… person, this… thing that I have become is not a good thing. No one should be able to flatten hills or level a city on a whim."

"Like Mallon?" Alaric asked.

Ayda nodded. "And so I am still with you, and not sleeping yet." Her face grew pensive again. "I wasn't there when they began to fight him."

Alaric nodded, remembering her racing to the glen. "Would you have made a difference?"

"No. I was no stronger than the others. Weaker than many. I would have died like the rest. But my people sacrificed our whole race to try to destroy his power. I cannot stop before I have tried to do the same."

Ayda fell back into silence. Everything about her made sense now. The effortless way she performed magic, the tortured limbs and faces when she was changing back from a tree. And the fact that she was now part of this group, truly part of it, because she wanted to defeat Mallon. At least that was a goal that Alaric could trust. As long as he was trying to destroy Mallon, Ayda would be with him.

They rode on next to each other in silence. Alaric mulled over her memory for a long time. Will was right. Ayda did have darkness within her. Whatever blackness Mallon had attacked the glen with, a piece of it was inside her. If it weren't for the power of the elves, she surely would have been destroyed.

The only question now was what that darkness had been doing for the last eight years.

The Scale Mountains drew closer as the day went on, their barren slopes rising like jagged teeth. The lower foothills were carpeted with dark green pines, but the taller slopes were bare rock.

The western road ran up against the foothills of the Scales before intersecting a narrow dirt track that ran north and south along the edge of the range. They turned south and Douglon took the lead, walking off the road along the base of the slope, looking closely at every nick in the mountains. He stopped them several times while he explored small paths they came across, but came back each time shaking his head.

"Faster, dwarf," Ayda chided him. "I thought you'd been here before."

"I came from the mountains north of here last time, not from the east like this," Douglon said, glowering at her. "I only passed this way on the way out, and it was quite dark. But these hills are wrong. These were carved by a glacier. Kordan's valley was behind a mountain that jutted up from the west."

Alaric looked down the range of foothills that ran along the road. They looked like mountains, not carved mountains or jutted mountains, just mountains. But it wasn't much later when the dwarf gave a satisfied grunt and pulled over next to a barely visible path that ran through the trees toward the roots of the mountains.

Brandson gave a hoot and clapped Douglon on the shoulder as he rode into it.

The ground from the lowlands next to them ran smoothly up the front of the next hill. Down the ravine Douglon pointed at, Alaric could see the rocky backside did look like it had been thrust up out of the ground. Jutted fit after all.

Brandson called out that the trail had disappeared.

"How sure are you?" Alaric asked.

"As sure as I am that I'm a better woodsman than the blacksmith," Douglon said, grinning.

The trees grew close together, and the path wound into a narrow gap between two hills. The floor of the valley was dotted with large rocks and the thin path wandered slowly through them.

A small knot of anxiety formed in Alaric's chest as they drew closer to Kordan's valley. Kordan had walked down paths similar to Alaric's and had left the Keepers to begin a life here. What sorts of things had he created? Had Kordan built something better than the Stronghold?

A shout rang out from beside the path, and a man lunged at Brandson. Milly screamed as the smith was knocked off his horse, with his attacker landing on top of him.

Two more men attacked Douglon, one leaping off a large boulder to knock him from his horse.

Douglon shoved him off, then slid to the ground, loosing his axe. The men before him crouched down, spreading out and leveling swords at the dwarf. Their clothes were worn, and they had the wild look of brigands. Douglon swung his axe smoothly before him, keeping the men at bay.

Alaric reached toward the man who was straddling Brandson, choking the smith.

"Dormio," Alaric directed the burst of energy toward him. The man fell limp and collapsed on Brandson.

Swearing, the blacksmith shoved the body off him. He stood up, pointing his knife at the man.

"He's asleep," Alaric called out, sliding down off of Beast.

Brandson ran back toward Douglon. The dwarf had knocked the sword out of one man's hand and was facing the other. The weaponless man grabbed at Douglon from behind until Brandson ran up and pulled him off. The smith pinned the man's arms behind him, easily overpowering the thin brigand. Brandson pulled out his knife and thumped the man on the head, knocking him out.

Ayda had stopped up ahead on the path, watching a campsite. More men were tumbling out of the camp and rushing toward them. Alaric ran up next to her, lifting his hand to help. Ayda ignored him, smiling slightly and flicking her fingers at the bandits.

One man yanked to a stop when tiny roots shot out of the ground and wrapped around his feet. Another stumbled to his knees, blinked foolishly at them, then stood and wandered off into the trees. A third stopped, spun around, and started to grab at his companions, calling for them to stop fighting.

Ayda giggled, and Alaric let his arms fall as he watched her take care of them, one after another.

There was a howl and a thud, and they turned to find that Douglon had knocked out the last man who had attacked him and was turning, axe raised, to survey the area. The area had quieted, the bandits escaping off into the forest. Brandson went to help Milly dismount from her horse. Douglon glanced around, then walked back toward Alaric and Ayda, surveying the trees.

Brandson joined them, looking into the clearing and giving them all a grin. "Here's a group of bandits who won't be bothering anyone for a wh—"

Douglon shouted and lunged forward, shoving Alaric out of the way and back against a boulder. The dwarf dove in front of Ayda.

Brandson pointed up a tree, shouted a warning, and threw his knife up into the branches.

There was a soft umphing noise, and Douglon staggered. He spun slowly around, and Alaric felt his stomach drop as he saw the fletching of an arrow sticking through the dwarf's beard.

There was a series of crashes, and a body dropped lifelessly out of a nearby tree, Brandson's knife in his chest. The bandit's bow fell after him.

Ayda stood and stared at Douglon. The dwarf stumbled a step toward her then sank to his knees.

"Douglon!" Brandson yelled, rushing to grab the dwarf's shoulders and lay him gingerly on the ground.

Alaric knelt closer to look. The arrow was sitting in the center of the dwarf's chest. It quivered with each beat of the dwarf's heart.

Milly squeezed her lips together and held Douglon's hand. Brandson knelt next to her, alternately reaching a hand forward, then pulling it back.

Alaric's mind raced. He had to stop the bleeding, had to do something. He reached out, gathering energy from the forest around him. He felt it build in him, pressing against him like a flood.

Douglon's breath came in gasps, his skin was frighteningly white. With every breath, the arrow shuddered. Milly began to cry.

There was so much blood. Too much blood. Douglon was losing more life than Alaric could replace. If he tried, if he began, the dwarf would pull too much energy through him. More than Alaric could handle. And once the magic burned Alaric out, once the energy drained all the life out of himself and into the dwarf, Douglon would probably still die.

Alaric's mind spun helplessly. There was nothing to be done.

Douglon looked down at the arrow and let out a ragged breath. It ended in a gurgle.

CHAPTER FORTY

ALARIC SANK BACK on his heels.

Douglon looked at him, and his head jerked forward in a quick nod. The dwarf knew it was pointless. Milly held Douglon's hand with tears streaming down her face.

Ayda shoved Alaric out of the way. "Why did you do that?" she demanded of Douglon.

"Ayda!" Milly said aghast.

Douglon tried to scowl, but coughed, and his face crumpled in pain.

Ayda glared at him. "I didn't ask you to do that."

The pool of dark blood seeped into the ground beneath Douglon. The arrow moved less with each breath.

"Ayda, there isn't much time," Milly whispered.

Ayda waved away Milly's words impatiently. "Why?" she demanded again.

"Why?" Douglon's voice came out in a gasp. "Because you weren't paying attention." A spasm of coughing wracked his body. "You are never paying attention," he whispered.

Ayda stared at him uncomprehendingly. "But why did you do it?"

Douglon groaned. "Any of us would have."

She glared at the rest of them. "That's not true."

"Of course we would, Ayda," Brandson said.

"I would want to," Milly said. "I'm not sure I would be brave enough."

Ayda spun to look at Alaric.

"But *you* wouldn't," she said to Alaric. "You have… a lot of things to do."

Ayda was genuinely confused. The anger was back in her eyes, and she was leaning toward Alaric with the look that said if he didn't answer her soon, she was going to step into his mind and rip out the answer.

"I think any of us would try to save each other, Ayda," Alaric said, stepping back.

"Ayda," Milly said, watching Douglon's face grow pale, "I think the time is almost up."

Ayda dropped to her knees and leaned close to Douglon. She was so slight next to him. A sliver of bright copper next to the stocky dwarf. She reached out and turned his face toward her, her hand small and pale against his red beard. "But why?"

Douglon looked at her directly. "I would die for you a hundred times without regret."

She drew back slightly and her eyes widened. Milly and Brandson froze. Alaric felt suddenly intrusive, but he couldn't bear to move back, couldn't look away. Douglon lifted a hand toward her, but it fell back to the earth.

"But I didn't ask you to," she said helplessly.

Douglon rolled his eyes. "Never mind, I regret even doing it once."

"It might be time to thank him," Milly said softly as Douglon's eyes began to close.

Ayda shot Milly an annoyed look. "Stop it, Milly," she snapped. "He's not going to die." With that she reached forward and yanked the arrow from Douglon's chest.

Douglon's body lurched up off the ground, and a cry ripped out of him.

Alaric's whole body clenched. Brandson cried out and Milly fell back. Ayda ignored them all and pushed her hand against the dwarf's chest. She looked off into the distance for a moment, then lifted her hand. Looking distastefully at the blood on her palm, she wiped it on Douglon's shirt, then stood and stalked away.

From the ground, Alaric heard a cough. Milly scrambled back to Douglon's side.

Douglon coughed again, then struggled to sit up. He pushed his beard over and pulled apart the hole in his shirt from the arrow. The shirt was soaked with blood, but the skin beneath it was whole. A jagged scar sat in the center of his chest.

"What is *wrong* with that elf?" Douglon demanded.

"Douglon?" Milly asked, reaching timidly for his shoulder. "Are you… okay?"

Douglon took a deep breath. It sounded clear. The color had returned to his face. "I'm fine," he said, staring after Ayda.

Alaric shook his head. The ground where Douglon had lain was saturated with blood. There was no way the dwarf should be alive. What had Ayda done?

Douglon was glaring after the elf. He began to swear colorfully, then added in a few dwarfish terms, some of which Alaric didn't understand.

Milly still had her hand on Douglon's shoulder. "She saved your life," she pointed out.

"She let me lie on the ground bleeding and then tore an arrow out of my chest!" Douglon shuddered. "Do you have any idea what that *felt* like?"

"Well, n-no," Milly said. "But she did save your life."

Douglon let out a growl and continued to glare after Ayda.

The bandit Alaric had put to sleep began to stir.

Douglon turned his scowl toward the bandits' camp. "Why are there bandits this low in the mountains? They never come this low."

Alaric knelt down next to the bandit "What's your name. What are you doing here?"

The man blinked up at Alaric and grabbed for his sword lying nearby. Brandson kicked it away and stood beside Alaric, glaring down at the man.

"Name's Elrich, sir," the bandit said, shrinking away from them. "And we're here because we ain't got no other choice. We had a village of sorts farther up th' hills. But the nomads have been creepin' closer and closer. Simmon went scoutin', and he says there was thousands of them. They were filling all the valleys below the Pass, with more arriving every day. 'Twasn't a safe place for us to stay, you understand."

"And you're very concerned with safety," Douglon growled.

"Oh yes. We always tries to eat healthy and keep a double watch on the camp at night," he said earnestly to Douglon. "You never know what dangers are out there." Elrich's gaze flicked to the sky.

Douglon just stared at the man.

Alaric glanced up to the sky, too. "Elrich, are there dangers in the sky?"

Elrich chewed on his lip, then said quietly. "We saw a dragon."

"When?"

Elrich looked surprised at being believed. "Couple hours ago. Well, I see'd it, but no one else did, and they din't believe me."

"What time?"

"A bit after lunch. I was tendin' to the horses and glad I din't have the job of hunting because the forest had grown quiet—unnat'rally quiet. The horses was all spooky-like, too. While I was brushing down my own dear brown mare, she got so skittish she almost kicked me! Been together three years, and almost kicked me while gettin' her brushin'!

"That's when I sawed a flash of somethin' in the sky." He leaned forward conspiratorially. "Somethin' red."

Alaric nodded. "A dragon."

"'Twas, indeed, sir. I ain't never seen a dragon before, but that's what this was. Sure as my mama loves me, 'twas a dragon."

"Did you see it again?"

"No, sir, just for that moment, flying deeper into the mountains. But I reckon that's why the woods was so quiet. Ain't no creature done want to be near a dragon."

Alaric nodded. "Thank you, Elrich. You can sleep again," and he raised his hand toward the man.

"And Elrich," Brandson said, looking down at the man. "When you wake up, it's time to stop being a bandit. The next group you try to rob might not just put you to sleep."

Elrich shifted uncomfortably. "Go do something useful with your life."

Milly had walked up next to Brandson.

"Like what?" Elrich asked. "I dunno anything but stealing."

Milly gave the man a disapproving look. "Then it's long past time you learned something else."

Douglon heaved himself to his feet and rolled his shoulders, stretching out his chest. He stepped over to the top of Elrich's head and scowled down at him. "Did you know dwarves patrol these hills? I'm going to let them know that you attacked me. Your group here is going to wake up one night just in time to see the axes fall."

Elrich paled and shrank away from the dwarf.

"I think that's enough," Alaric said. He set his hand on Elrich's forehead. "*Dormio*."

The bandit sank back asleep.

"Let's keep moving," Alaric said. He looked at Douglon. "Are you okay to ride?"

Douglon nodded, stretching again. "I feel fine. Better than fine, really. Whatever Ayda did, it worked," he said, rubbing his chest.

"Does anyone know where she is?" Milly asked.

Alaric looked around but saw no sign of her.

"She's over there." Douglon retrieved his axe from the ground and motioned to the trees. "She's up in that big, strong oak."

Alaric's eyebrow rose. "The big, strong one?"

"I don't see her," Milly said.

"Well, she's there," Douglon said. "The oak is all excited about it."

Milly and Brandson turned to Douglon, too.

"It is?" Brandson asked.

Douglon turned slowly to look at them, the color draining from his face. "Good Grayven's Beard! What did that elf do to me?" He looked around at the forest, his eyes growing wilder. "I can feel them!" he whispered. "I can feel the trees!"

CHAPTER FORTY-ONE

"Of course you can," Ayda's voice rang out. "I couldn't put as much of myself into you as was required to save your bearded neck without giving you some perks."

"You put yourself…" Douglon looked at her, growing paler still.

"You were almost dead. There wasn't enough blood in you to animate a rabbit. And you're large. Well, you're dwarf-sized. But you had managed to dump most of your own life out onto the ground. I had to replace it with something."

Douglon was holding his chest protectively, cowering slightly as his eyes flitted around the trees.

"You're fine now, Douglon," Ayda said.

Douglon jumped slightly at his name, which she spoke with that strange elfish lilt she used with Alaric's. Had she ever said Douglon's name before?

Douglon looked at her sharply. "What?"

"You're fine now, Douglon." She was watching him impatiently. "So let's go."

When she said his name again, he relaxed a little but stood very still, watching her.

She let out a sigh. "You're the one who knows where we are going. We're waiting to follow you."

Douglon rubbed his chest and, giving the trees one last suspicious look, went to his horse.

He led them up the path, hunkered down slightly in his saddle. Any time a tree was right next to the path, he skirted along the other side, but it wasn't long before the trees dropped away and what had been the trace of a trail became nothing more than a narrow dry stream bed in a barren valley. As the trees disappeared, Douglon sat straighter in his saddle.

"We're almost there." He pointed to the layer of red-stained rocks that ran through the valley walls a little more than halfway up. "The iron layer is almost thick enough." He doggedly led them on while the way twisted left and wandered through another stone-dotted ravine. The layer of rust-colored rock grew a bit thicker just before the streambed turned right around an enormous boulder.

"Here we are," Douglon said.

Alaric turned the corner and stopped short. Ahead of him, set directly against the base of a steep slope, was a stone wall. It was not large, maybe a bit taller than he was, running thirty steps in either direction.

Unlike the grey Wall of the real Stronghold, this wall was made up of the dusty sandstone from the ravine. The stones were small and pieced together well, but not perfectly, leaving the top of the wall tilted and rippled.

Douglon turned left and headed along the wall to a twisted tree trunk growing against it. The dwarf approached the tree cautiously as though it were a wild animal. Gingerly, he reached out and set his hand on the trunk. His eyes widened, and he snatched his hand back. He shot Ayda a murderous look. She smiled proudly at him. He quickly tethered his horse to a low branch, avoiding actually touching it. Then taking a deep breath, he grabbed the lowest branch and clambered up, heaving himself over the top of the wall and away from the tree.

Alaric dismounted and brushed his hand along the wall. Though more crudely made, there was no mistaking the way the stones fit together, as though they had cooperated with each other. He ran his finger along the tiny space between two stones that held no mortar. This wall was made by a Keeper.

The others followed Douglon's lead, climbing the tree and jumping over the top of the wall. When the last of them was gone, Alaric stepped back from the wall.

"*Aperi.*" The familiar burst of pain in his hand was slightly stronger than the Stronghold Wall needed, taking more energy, lacking a little of its sophistication.

Off to his right, the stones shifted and the opening to a tunnel appeared. Not too far in it was choked with stone.

So much effort. So much energy had gone into making this. It wasn't a perfect replica of the Wall, but it would have been exhausting to make. Alaric glanced around at the barren slopes around him. There was nothing to pull energy from, either. Kordan would have had to find it all inside himself. It must have taken him ages.

The small voice in him that still spoke like a Keeper gave a disapproving grunt at all this energy spent and yet the job not done completely right. The other part marveled that it had been done at all.

The voices of the others floated over the wall, and Alaric stepped away from the tunnel.

"Cluda." He said, clenching his hand and watching the stone shift back to a solid wall.

Alaric scrambled up the tree and stood on the top of the wall. The slope behind it met the wall just a couple of feet from the top. A thin game trail meandered away from it around the base of the mountain. He hurried to catch up with Douglon who was leading the others down a wash in the slope. They crunched through the loose rock that filled the wash until they reached the gash of a rockslide in the mountain. At the base of the slide was a heap of stones and a dark hole where the ground had caved in.

Alaric joined the group peering down into the hole. Though stones littered the floor, Alaric realized it was the tunnel that had begun at the door in the wall and continued under the mountain.

Exactly like the one at the real Stronghold, the tunnel they climbed down into ran straight and dry underneath the mountain, ending at the edge of a valley. The tunnel wasn't as large as the real Stronghold's, but again, Kordan must have put an incredible amount of work into creating it.

Alaric followed the others slowly, running his hand along the rippled wall of the tunnel.

Something about this bothered him, but it took several minutes to figure out what. He had started to feel a sense of kindred with Kordan. A sense of someone else understanding his need to leave the Keepers. Someone else who knew he'd be cast out for the decisions he had made. Someone else who had left.

But Alaric wouldn't have done this. He wouldn't have

tried to be a Keeper, anyway. He didn't want to recreate a shadow of that life. He just wanted to live on his own.

He didn't want to be sent on missions and do research. He had loved those things before Evangeline. After her, it had all felt so pointless. How could he care about the intricacies of politics in southern countries when he needed to think about her? Countries were going to war with each other. It had always been so and would always be. The futility of trying to help a world bent on destroying itself had been too much.

By the time Alaric reached the end of the tunnel, he knew Kordan hadn't felt the same way. The beginnings of a pale tower rose a couple of stories into the air and stopped, as though it had been chopped off. Again, the main difference from the real Stronghold was the scale and the quality of the work.

But none of that mattered, because the Wellstone was here. He would have the antidote in his hands. His heart was racing and his palms began to sweat at the thought of it. He tried to hold the hope at bay, but it surged forward like a wave.

The group stopped at the mouth of the tunnel and everyone stood quietly, peering out into Kordan's valley.

"Gustav's dragon's not here, is it?" Milly asked.

Alaric stepped to the very edge of the tunnel and cast out for any *vitalle*. "There's no one here," he said.

"Do you think Gustav has been here yet?" Milly asked.

"I don't know," Alaric answered, walking out.

Like the Stronghold, this valley was enclosed by mountains, so none of the afternoon sunlight reached the floor of the valley. Unlike the real Stronghold, Kordan's unfinished tower did not rise high enough to reflect light into the rest of the valley, leaving it in a dim twilight.

Douglon started toward the tower, and Alaric followed right behind him. The others lingered near the tunnel. Even though the valley was empty, everyone spoke in hushed tones and kept looking toward the sky. Alaric glanced up at the clear afternoon sky, too.

Alaric followed Douglon to the empty arch at the front entrance of the tower. It was a poor reproduction of the Keepers' Stronghold. The very air was wrong. There was no sense of solidity to the place, no sense of peace, no sense of permanence. It was a child's attempt at a man's creation.

Something crashed against the wall inside the tower ahead of him. Douglon started swearing.

Alaric followed the short hallway to the center of the tower which was open to the sky. The beginnings of a ramp wound up against the wall starting on his left and ending at nothing. Douglon was staring at the back of the tower.

"Yes," the dwarf said. "Gustav has been here already."

Ahead of them, the entire back of the tower was destroyed, stones torn down and shoved away. Deep dragon-sized claw marks stretched like scars across the floor, through the rubble, and into the grass outside.

"That was the room we found everything in," Douglon said.

Alaric stared at the destruction, defeat flowing over him. He climbed over the fallen stones to stand in the center of the room. Following one claw mark, his gaze fell on a small trunk open in the middle of the floor, a long scuff mark in the dirt showing that it had been pulled from the rubble into the middle of the floor. Alaric stepped around it to see if any of the shelves on the far wall were intact. Behind him, Douglon grunted as he walked right into the trunk. Alaric turned to consider it. The brown trunk was unremarkable in every way.

With a little effort, Alaric forced himself to walk back to the squat, rustic trunk. He nudged the lid with his foot, flipping it shut, displaying a set of runes carved into the top. Influence runes.

"Have you ever seen this trunk before?" Alaric asked Douglon.

The dwarf squinted at the trunk. "It seems vaguely familiar."

Alaric pointed at the runes. "These were placed here to make the trunk seem unremarkable. I bet it was right here in the room when you and Patlon were exploring."

Douglon flipped the trunk back open, and Alaric knelt down next to it. Shoved into the back corner was a three-pronged silver stand, darkened with age.

Alaric sank down, his stomach dropping through the clawed floor. It was the stand he had seen in the Keepers' Wellstone. The stand that had held Kordan's own Wellstone. This trunk was where it had been stored. And now Gustav had it.

CHAPTER FORTY-TWO

A KNOT of desperation formed in his chest. Alaric looked around the room wildly, looking for the flash of the Wellstone. He stood up and scrambled over loose rock to reach the shelves that lined the wall.

The shelves were damaged, some hanging precariously, some lying on the floor. Scrolls and books had slid off onto the floor, but Alaric shoved them aside, searching for the glitter of the Wellstone.

It wasn't here. He sank down onto Kordan's bed, crunching the pebbles scattered across it. His eyes kept roaming the room, but it was hopeless.

Next to the head of Kordan's bed, a shelf was affixed to the wall. It held a small book covered with thick dust, but Alaric could see by the edges that it had been well used. He reached out and picked it up. After wiping it with the edge of Kordan's blanket he gently opened the cover.

A small cloud of dust puffed out. The smell of it stretched gentle fingers into his mind, drawing out memories of the Stronghold. The first books he had ever cracked open as a

Keeper had the same scent. Knowledge and magic and power. And hope.

The queen's library wasn't the same, somehow. Her books smelled like dust and paper. It was a nice smell, but not like this. This book, he knew, had more than just words poured into it. Before he read a word, he knew he had found Kordan's journal.

He flipped toward the back of the book and caught a fragment of another smell. One that gave him pause. Sharper fingers scraped across his mind.

It smelled like the books of the Shade Seekers. Those had more power, more whispering secrets, more lurking shadows.

When he had first read books in Sidion, the difference had struck him, and although a part of him had been wary, the larger part reached for it. He had been tired of the dryness of the Keepers' books, had needed the power and life he could feel in the Shade Seekers' writing.

Life. Alaric shook his head. No, it hadn't been life that he had found there.

Alaric turned back to the first page. Kordan's handwriting covered the page.

> *This valley is perfect. It is not as large as the Stronghold's, but it will hold what I need. I didn't stay to ask the Shield what he thought. I knew what they would think once they read the work. I have no place among them. But I will do what I can to redeem myself. Here, in this valley, I will create a new Stronghold. A place of learning and peace and—*

Alaric closed the book and dropped it into his pocket. He looked around the rest of the room, feeling the echoes of

Kordan's attempted new life. Now that he was here, now that he could see the tower and stand inside it, the place was a disappointment. Just a poorly made building dressed in the trappings of a Keeper.

And the Wellstone wasn't here. With a final look at all of Kordan's scrolls, Alaric climbed back over the broken wall and out of the room. He joined the others, who were waiting for him by the tunnel. Not waiting for them and not returning any of their sympathetic glances, he walked out of the valley.

Alaric climbed back over the wall and set out back down the ravine on Beast, urging the horse on as quickly as he could. He was pushed forward by the image of Gustav emptying the Wellstone of Kordan's memories. The others followed him quickly until they reached the road and turned south toward the Greenwood.

Alaric didn't feel hopeful that they'd reach Mallon's body before Gustav. The wizard was ahead of them at every turn. But maybe the Elder Grove would keep him out somehow. Maybe it wouldn't let Gustav take the body away.

It grew dark quickly. After Alaric had cast out to make sure there was no one in the area, the group made camp off the side of the road.

The campsite was subdued. Ayda was unusually quiet, while Douglon kept catching himself talking about the trees around them, then clamping his mouth shut and glaring at Ayda. Sitting near the fire, Alaric pulled out Kordan's journal and flipped through the first few entries.

Kordan had begun to build his tower, but had soon been distracted by other things. He had become increasingly obsessed with the idea of stopping death. He found wounded animals in the forest and brought them back to his valley to try to save them.

The more Alaric read, the more of Sidion he could smell in the words. Kordan had healed the foot of a small mouse, but the effort had almost exhausted him. He had poured out some of his own blood to do it and leached the power from that. The mouse had run off, but Kordan had been in bed for days.

Alaric's heart quickened. Was this the answer to Evangeline? Could Alaric sacrifice some of his own life for hers?

Alaric read of Kordan's elation after this success. He had stumbled onto the knowledge that, besides the spark of life that his magic could give, to really heal something, it required pulling that life from something else. He began with plants and tried to draw life from them to reanimate small bugs, but the plants provided barely any power. Alaric could believe that. The energy from the largest tree didn't compare to that of even a small animal.

Then one day, Kordan had found two wounded beetles. He sacrificed the one to save the other. It almost worked. Almost, but not quite. The bug was partially healed, but it died the next morning.

He found another beetle and caught a large, healthy spider. The beetle wasn't injured, so Kordan, unhappily, injured it, then killed the spider to save it.

Alaric reread the paragraph. Kordan's reluctance to hurt the beetle was plain, but he showed no qualms at all about killing the spider.

It succeeded and the subsequent experiments grew. Soon, Kordan was healing larger animals.

The lamb has walked away! It seems fine, and yesterday, when I found it, it was almost dead. A leg had been broken and there was a terrible wound in its neck.

As I watched it prance away this morning, I felt so much joy. That tiny creature, which would have died if left alone, will now grow and live.

But then I returned to the room and saw the body of the pig.

It was old, so I don't know why it gave me pause, but it did. When I entered the room, its vacant eyes were facing me, and for a moment, they looked reproachful.

I think I must need company if I'm feeling judgment from a dead pig. A dead pig that I would have barely thought about if I were killing it to fill my table.

I have thought about using its meat. Since I drained the blood for the magic, there's really no reason not to, but I find that I can't. He wasn't sacrificed for that.

I know that doesn't make sense. I even went to get the cleaver, but when I got back, there were the eyes again. I swear they were blaming me. Blaming me for counting the lamb's life as more important than his.

But that is what we do all the time, right? We kill animals to feed ourselves. We judge which animals are worth money and which are pests. We rank the value of lives all the time.

I'm just doing the same.

Alaric flipped ahead in the book until an underlined phrase stopped him.

The magic bleeds away some of the life.

During the spell, the magic itself bleeds away some of the power from the life that is being sacrificed. I can feel it. It's as though there is another force in the room. A force directing it all and taking its share of the power.

I have tried everything I can think of to stop the bleed. I have created runes to hold the power before using it. I have put the most protective spells I know around the two creatures to keep the energy between only them. But nothing works. No matter what I do, some of the power is lost.

And the greater the sacrifice, the greater the loss.

For the lamb, a larger animal worked. But for the horse last week, the large cow was not enough. He lived, but in great pain. In the end, it took an entire second cow.

I find that the Shade Seekers know this. I have visited with them and seen the creatures they have made. To make their monsters, they take a man, almost kill him, then revive him through the death of some creature. Every time they try to impart life, the source they use is… diluted before it creates the new thing. If you take a person and save him with a bear, you don't get a full human. You get a half-breed that is not as strong as a bear but still bear-like, with some remnant of human intelligence. But it is not the sum of the two. It is much less. This, of course, makes them easier to control.

This concept is essential to their work: The sacrifice exceeds the reward.

Kordan had studied with the Shade Seekers? Alaric felt his discomfort growing. Kordan was more like him than he had thought. The matter-of-fact way he had spoken of the Shade Seekers mirrored Alaric's own thoughts when he had first encountered their writings. Mirrored some of his thoughts still today. Yet reading Kordan's words made him shudder. Why exactly was that? Why was it harder to justify for Kordan than for himself?

Which makes me wonder, what would it take to heal a human? If a human body were close to death, what would need to be sacrificed to save it?

Alaric's breath caught.

What is greater than a person? It's not so much size as...vitality. Some undefined quantity of life. A large animal wouldn't work. I don't even have to try it. The vitality of the animal just isn't enough. But what would be?

I've thought long about this, and I think there are only two answers. The first is some sort of powerful, magical beast. Somehow, I think it would need to be intelligent also.

If one could catch a dragon, well, there's a chance that would work.

Alaric looked up from his book.

Gustav had a dragon. Gustav could raise Mallon by sacrificing the dragon.

The other answer is more difficult to accept. I believe the sacrifice of more than one person would do it. For instance, the death of two adults, I believe, could save a child from the brink of death.

Alaric drew back as he continued to read Kordan's detached calculations on exactly how many humans would need to be killed to save another.

A Keeper, however, being more than human and having magical qualities, would certainly be worth more than a normal human. Perhaps even enough to save one. But I don't think killing off Keepers in order to save common folk is the answer.

The sacrifice exceeds the reward. But by how much? Perhaps the Shade Seekers know.

Alaric closed the book and let it fall to the ground. Kordan didn't hold answers to his problem with Evangeline. Kordan played with death and life like a child, with no care for the value of either.

Alaric closed his eyes and remembered Kordan's tower. He thought of the smaller stones, the unfinished walls, the attempt to imitate the Stronghold, and the lack of goodness that had been there. When he walked into the valley of the real Stronghold, there was goodness and hope and a desire to battle the darkness, even though it would never stop coming.

But here, in Kordan's work, he found a man who was fiddling with the edges of that darkness. Trying to pull tendrils out into the light and failing to notice how much darkness came with it.

CHAPTER FORTY-THREE

"Could Gustav really use the dragon to wake Mallon?" Brandson asked Alaric the next morning. "I mean, having a dragon obey you is one thing. Maybe you can get the dragon to like you or something. But how do you get a dragon to sacrifice itself for you? Or stay still long enough to sacrifice it yourself?"

"I don't know," Alaric agreed. "The instances I've read of in which someone was paired with a dragon, it was more of an agreement between the two, not the person controlling the dragon. And those situations rarely end well for the person."

"I keep hoping that Gustav will annoy the dragon as much as he annoys everyone else, and that Anguine will take care of our problem for us," Douglon said.

"But it's possible to control it," Milly pointed out. When everyone looked at her she went on. "Ayda did it. Ayda got it to do exactly what she wanted."

Ayda shook her head. "When I touched its nose, I encouraged it to like me. We became friends. I asked it not to hurt us and to leave the valley, it agreed. But not hurting each other is the sort of thing friends do. I didn't ask it to kill itself."

"Would it have?" Milly asked.

Ayda looked off into the sky for a long moment. "I don't know. I can't imagine asking it to."

"Do you think Gustav could?"

Ayda looked at Alaric.

Alaric shrugged. "I'd say Gustav's using a form of influence on the dragon to get it to follow him. But I can't imagine the extent of influence you would need to use to have a creature like a dragon submit to being killed."

"Maybe he'll poison it or something," Milly offered.

"Dragons eat rocks and dead things," Brandson pointed out. "It's got to be hard to find something that's bad for their health."

"And he'd need the dragon healthy before sacrificing it," Alaric said. "The whole point would be to sacrifice a strong, powerful life to provide power for the Rivor."

Milly sighed. "Doesn't it seem like Gustav should be easier to figure out than all this?"

Everyone nodded.

"He probably doesn't know himself how he's going to kill that dragon." Douglon smiled wickedly. "I hope he's terrified about it."

Ayda grinned. "And he and the dragon will be communicating by thought, which means that if the wizard tries to think about the problem, Anguine will know it."

"Still," Alaric pointed out, "Gustav has everything he needs but the body, and he's moving much faster than we are." He glanced at Ayda. "Do you think it will take him long to find the Elder Grove on Anguine?"

Ayda's smile disappeared and her eyes turned instantly to steel. "I can get us to the Elder Grove by this evening."

She climbed on her horse and, neglecting the path, headed straight into the woods.

They followed Ayda through the trees at a brisk rate. Even though there was never a proper trail, the forest itself seemed to be obliging her as she drove a straight line toward the Elder Grove. There were never obstacles, there were convenient streams whenever they needed water, and the trees themselves seemed to lean a bit to clear a path through the woods.

Around lunchtime, Milly came down the line handing out pieces of bread and cheese.

"I didn't ask her if she wanted to stop for lunch," Milly said apologetically to Alaric.

The Keeper shook his head. "Don't blame you."

Ayda had sat straight in her saddle all morning. It was probably good that he couldn't see the expression on her face.

They reached a wide, slow-moving river by mid-afternoon. Alaric realized it must be the Sang River, the northern boundary of the Greenwood. They had come farther than he had thought.

Ayda didn't slow, just walked her horse directly into the river. The water never even rose to her horse's stomach, so the others followed her in.

When Alaric reached the other side, Ayda was frozen in her saddle, her head cocked slightly. The others huddled silently a short distance away from her. Ayda's hair blew slightly in a breeze that Alaric couldn't feel. She reached out slowly, hesitantly, and touched the nearest tree.

She began to breathe heavily. Then, terrifyingly, she darkened. Her hair, her skin against the tree trunk, the very air around her darkened. Beast and the other horses shied nervously. Alaric leaned forward to catch a glimpse of her face. It was drawn in fury. She closed her eyes for a moment, then her eyes flashed open. They burned a fiery red.

A cry ripped from the elf, and she spurred her horse forward, tearing into the woods.

Alaric tried to chase her, but drew up, having no idea where she had gone. The others piled up around him and looked around the woods.

"Where did she—" Milly began before she was cut off by a scream of rage.

The trees around them shuddered. The horses and riders all froze and looked in the direction of the sound. Alaric swallowed hard and pointed Beast toward it. He had to prod the animal twice before he would move.

Before long, he came to the edge of a clearing. Ayda was standing in a circle of destruction, her hands at her side and her head hanging forward. Her hair fell down around her face, covering it.

The ground was scarred with deep gashes of dragon claws between tufts of grass. A few flowers bravely stood amidst the destruction. Around Ayda, a ring of seven colossal trees lay torn down and flung outward. Their roots twisted up into the air like gnarled fingers grabbing at the sky.

The Elder Grove had been destroyed.

And there was no Mallon. Gustav had taken him already and was probably on his way back to Sidion by now.

Beast had taken a step into the clearing before drawing back under the trees. Alaric pulled him back a step farther.

He dismounted, but kept a firm rein on Beast, who was nickering nervously.

"Oh no," Milly breathed.

Ayda looked up at them, her eyes burning red. They all drew back an extra step.

Ayda walked slowly to each huge trunk and put her hand on it for a long moment.

"The dragon destroyed them," Douglon said quietly, his eyes wide. "It ripped them up by the roots." He looked warily at the trees around him. "They're so angry." He closed his eyes as though concentrating. "It was beautiful here." He opened his eyes again and they glinted with wrath. "Gustav made the dragon rip them up by the roots."

Ayda walked by each tree again, splintering off a piece of each. Stalking in a wide circle, she stabbed them into the ground, like an upright circle of miniature spears.

Stepping into the middle, she held her arms out and closed her eyes again. The ground began to rumble and the sticks swelled. Before Alaric understood that they were growing, the sticks were up to Ayda's knees. Then her shoulders, then she was hidden from view by the hedge of trees that surrounded her.

But these trees weren't like the fallen ones. The trees that lay on the ground were green and gentle. The new trees, which were now nearing the height of the rest of the forest, had a vicious look to them. Their leaves, a malevolent dark green, had serrated edges and between them shot out thick crimson thorns.

The trees expanded, digging up the earth with roots stretching out toward the edges of the grove. The horses tucked themselves farther back into the forest. When the trees reached a height well over that of the rest of the forest, they stopped.

"I've never been afraid of trees before," Douglon said quietly.

Alaric craned to see between the trunks, hoping Ayda would come out. He certainly didn't want to go in after her.

A moment later, the thorns nearest them parted and Ayda strode out. She walked toward Alaric, and he fought to keep Beast from bolting.

Everything about her was dark. Too dark for an elf.

Her eyes still burned red and her face was terrifying. Alaric stood his ground, but everything in him wanted to run. She walked right up to him until her face was inches from his chest. It was like looking down at a fire demon.

"Yes, it is too dark for an elf," she said. "But I think it's time you stopped expecting me to be an elf."

She reached up and lifted the pouch at his neck gently with her fingers. Alaric's gut clenched as she tapped it, causing the ruby to bounce against her fingers.

"After all, I've stopped expecting you to be a Keeper." She let the pouch drop, and looked into his face again. "Take me to the wizard," she hissed.

CHAPTER FORTY-FOUR

DOUGLON LED the way through the forests heading north. No one spoke much and Alaric found his mind wandering.

Gustav had a dragon. He would reach the Shade Seekers' valley in a matter of hours. Crossing the hills and valleys like they would have to do was going to take more than a day. By the time they reached him, it would be too late. And even with Ayda, Alaric didn't think they stood much of a chance against Mallon once he was raised.

All of them were drooping in their saddles when Alaric finally called a halt. Ayda looked at him stonily and dismounted.

As the camp lay quiet, Alaric stared at the sky. The stars above him twinkled peacefully. The stars always seemed more unattainable when he was unsettled. He took a deep breath trying to draw in their serenity. He waited for the soothing sense he got from the night sky to settle in, but it refused.

There was no way they were going to reach Sidion before Gustav revived Mallon. No way. He was probably preparing right now. Tonight might be the last night of peace that Queensland would know.

He let his gaze wander through the sky. If only he could look at the stars long enough, his mind would calm. Their light was so constant, so emotionless. No, not emotionless, serene. They burned with a serene hope because they burned so purely. And if there could be that much purity in the universe, maybe it outweighed all the mess down here.

Alaric's eyes scanned west and his chest tightened. The starred sky outlined a deep V in the mountains to their west. Kollman Pass.

Through that pass, a half-day's journey would take him to her. She was lying there, only hours away from him.

He wanted to go, to gather his things and slip off to the west. To stop this futile hunt for a wizard who kept beating him.

His eyes lingered on Kollman Pass.

He could go to her. He could see her again. If he followed Gustav, if he found the Rivor awake, there was no way they would survive it. Not even with Ayda.

Not even if Ayda would go back to being Ayda and stop growing darker and darker. He didn't need the Wellstone to see the darkness in her, and the thought of bringing her closer to Mallon was terrifying.

They were on a hopeless journey. Five eclectic travelers stood no chance against Mallon. This journey would be their death.

But he could be with Evangeline by dawn. He could hold her again.

The familiar ache flared up inside of him. That could not last, either. She had been in so much pain, how could he wake her again without the antidote? Could he sit with her and let her die?

Not that it mattered any longer. Even if he could cure her, he would bring her back to a world enslaved to Mallon.

Alaric sighed and closed his eyes against the Pass. No, he would see this to its inevitable finish. Perhaps between himself and Ayda, they could… wound Mallon. Slow him down. Give the world time for…

What?

Still he would go. He would try.

A humorless smile twisted his face. How Keeperish of him. Perhaps there was more Keeper left in him than he thought. Reading Kordan's journal had reminded Alaric of what true Keepers valued. Their ideas had regained that ring of truth.

Alaric rolled onto his side, turning his back on Kollman Pass. He was going to need some sleep. This journey to his death was bound to be exhausting.

Before dawn, Ayda was up again, commanding the others into their saddles.

Alaric called for everyone's attention. "This evening, we'll be nearing Sidion, and we're going to meet some trouble." They were all looking at him: Brandson and Milly attentively, Douglon nodding, and Ayda looking scornful. "The Shade Seekers have a particular way of dealing with their enemies. They capture them, almost kill them, then revive them by putting them into an animal. It creates something new. Something monstrous."

Milly's eyes were wide.

"I've encountered some of them," Alaric said, "and they are dangerous. Some of them look human, some of them look like animals, but most are some sort of combination. The Shade Seekers use them to protect their valley. I'm not positive that there will be any other Shade Seekers there, but Gustav will be, and I think it's safe to say that whatever creatures are there will be doing what he wants. We may encounter them as early as this afternoon, so we should be cautious."

"We're not going to catch up with Gustav, are we?" Brandson asked.

Alaric shook his head. "I don't think so. It wouldn't take very long to get to Sidion on a dragon."

"Then we'll be too late?" Milly asked.

"Possibly."

She looked uncertainly around the group. "But… if we're too late, won't he have raised the Rivor by the time we get there?"

Douglon looked grim. Ayda glared toward the north.

"That's possible, too." Alaric looked around the group. "We're not far from the road back to the capital. Anyone who's not interested in going to what's most likely a death trap is free to leave." He looked at Milly closely. "In fact, we should let the queen know what's going on. You and Brandson could get there by tomorrow morning and—"

"Are you ever going to stop trying to send me home?" Milly demanded.

"I've only tried it once before. And it's an even better idea now than it was then."

"Don't make her get a frying pan," Douglon said with a grin. Then he prodded his horse forward, and the others followed.

Alaric held Beast back. His eyes found Kollman Pass again. It stood clear against the pale morning sky. In the dawn light, it looked close enough to touch.

He cast out, trying to feel her life. But it was too far. He felt vibrant sparks of birds and creatures, but even if he could reach all the way to her, he wouldn't find that. He would find only the dimmest flicker, barely surviving.

"I'm sorry," he whispered.

For what? For not being able to save her? For putting her near the poison in the first place? For the fact that he was about to follow the others into the trees instead of going back to her?

He closed his eyes and sighed and released Beast to follow the group, bringing them back into view.

It was only hours after lunch when the first creature attacked. Douglon, who had been riding in the lead, was bowled off his horse by a shaggy creature approximately the size of a wolf. Brandson was there in a moment, his knife out and through the creature almost before they were on the ground.

Brandson heaved it off the dwarf revealing a vaguely wolf-like face over a misshapen body. Ayda came up and knelt down beside the creature. She set her hand on its head and closed her eyes for a moment.

"This was a man once. Long ago. So long ago, the memory of it has almost left him."

She looked at the rest of them. "We can't kill any more of these."

"Can't kill them?" Douglon said. "Wait until one jumps on you."

"No," she said firmly. "These aren't evil. We can't kill any more unless they are too far gone to save."

"If we can't kill them, what exactly would you like us to do?" Douglon demanded.

"I'll take care of them," Ayda said. "You just make sure you don't kill them. But keep Milly and the others safe."

"Sure," Douglon grunted. "We'll just play with them 'til you take care of it."

She ignored him and remounted her horse.

It was several hours before they encountered the next monster. They turned a corner, and there in the path was a lion. A lion with wickedly intelligent eyes. It hunched before them, growling slightly. The group froze, the horses shifting in fear. Ayda walked forward. As she got close, the lion crouched lower.

"It's going to attack," Douglon warned, his voice low. He slid to the ground and pulled out his axe as he moved over as far to the side as the trail would allow.

"It's fine," Ayda said.

She took one more step, and the lion lunged toward her. She flicked her hand, and a shimmery blue net appeared in front of the lion. It roared once and the net flickered out. Then the lion hit Ayda and drove her to the ground. Douglon cried out and rushed forward.

Milly screamed from the back of the group. Alaric whipped around to see a huge ape hanging down out of the tree, pulling Milly up out of her saddle. Brandson was racing toward her, his knife out.

Alaric dropped to the ground and grabbed a moss-covered rock. He thrust some energy into it, igniting the moss, and threw it at the ape. The rock hit the creature in the shoulder, and it dropped Milly back into her saddle. She spurred her horse away as the ape dropped to the ground to face Brandson. Alaric gathered energy, looking from

Brandson to Ayda, who was pinned beneath the lion, holding it back with one hand.

"Don't kill it!" Ayda yelled at Brandson.

Douglon rushed forward, but a swipe of the lion's paw threw him against a tree.

"Sleep," Ayda commanded, setting her hand on the lion's forehead. The beast stumbled slightly then toppled to the side.

Ayda shoved its legs off of her and raced back to Brandson.

Alaric lit another rock and hurled it at the ape.

The ape bellowed at Brandson and swung an arm out at him. Brandson fell back, letting out a cry as the ape's nails dragged across his calf.

Ayda rushed past him to stand in front of the beast. It bellowed at her as she reached out and placed her hand between its eyes.

"Sleep," she commanded quietly.

The ape leaned closer, his mouth open, breathing fury into her face. She stood calmly before him for a moment before he blinked then sank to the ground.

Brandson was leaning heavily against a tree with blood dripping down his leg.

Ayda walked up to him and touched his leg gently. Then she stood and walked over to where Douglon still lay stunned.

Brandson's eyes widened, and he stood, gingerly putting weight on his leg. Then he pulled his tattered pants to the side and looked at his leg, which held only a dark red scar.

"A scar?" he said dumbly.

"I can heal it," Ayda answered tartly. "I can't make it so that it never happened."

"No, I didn't mean—" Brandson protested. "It's wonderful!"

Ayda smiled slightly.

Douglon stood slowly, shaking his head to clear it. "How long are these things going to sleep?"

Ayda looked at them sadly. "The rest of the day. They're terribly sad, aren't they?"

Milly looked at her as though she were crazy. "That thing was going to carry me off into the trees!"

"That ape used to be a farmer. I could see it in his mind. He refused to give a Shade Seeker his only pig. They took him and did this." She paused. "He had a wife and a tiny baby."

Milly's brow crinkled. "Can you… put him back to normal?"

"No," Ayda answered. "There's not enough of him left in there."

Milly looked at the ape sadly, then tentatively reached out her hand to stroke his head.

"Is there nothing you can do?" she asked, looking at Ayda, then Alaric.

Alaric looked at the two creatures and shook his head. What was there to be done? They couldn't be restored to what they once were. They were too changed.

Ayda cocked her head to the side and crouched down before the ape. Placing both hands on the sides of his head, she closed her eyes for a long moment. Finally, she opened them and shook her head.

"I thought that maybe I could cut the Shade Seeker's hold on him. But he's too much monster now for it to make a difference. He can do nothing but hunt and kill. What was a man has been long forgotten."

"Of course it has," Milly said softly. She reached out to take the ape's enormous hand in her own, avoiding its long, red nails. "How could it not be? We become what we act like, don't we. And after so much time, what would be the point of remembering?"

There was a pulse to the swirling, like a heartbeat. Alaric let his eyes follow the currents diving and dancing for a moment. It was several breaths before the dark line surfaced.

CHAPTER FORTY-FIVE

ALARIC WATCHED MILLY, her words echoing through his mind. *We become what we act like.*

Kordan shouldn't have made his own Stronghold. He should have come here, to the Shade Seekers. It was a Shade Seeker Kordan had ended up acting like, not a Keeper.

Alaric reached up and rubbed the ruby at his neck. And where, he thought, should he go himself?

Light from the setting sun stretched out across the path.

"We need to keep moving," he said.

Quietly, the group remounted and, skirting the sleeping lion, continued into the valley of the monsters.

The sun sank lower as they went. Ayda rode in the center of the group with Milly so the elf could get to the front or back of the line easily. Alaric and Brandson led, and Douglon took the rear. Every few minutes, Alaric cast out, looking for monsters, but found the forest near them empty. But far off in the woods, he caught glimpses of large creatures.

"We might want to find a place to camp before it gets

dark," Brandson said, looking warily around him. "Somewhere that might be defensible."

A few minutes later, the trail went by a cluster of large boulders with a small clearing inside of it. There was only one way into the rocks making it the most protected place they'd seen all day. The group set up camp in the fading light.

"How much farther?" Ayda demanded.

"Only an hour or two," Alaric said. "But we can't do it at night with all the creatures here. We need to stay someplace we can defend. Tomorrow, at first light, we'll go to the keep."

Ayda glared at him. "We're wasting time," she hissed as she walked away.

They set a fire at the entrance to the clearing to light their camp as well as hold off any but the bravest beasts.

"I'm sure the animals know we're here already," Alaric told them. "But we can try to dissuade them from bothering us."

They took shifts on watch, two at a time, while the others attempted to sleep. Milly and Brandson took first watch, and Alaric lay wide-awake. He was exhausted, but he couldn't sleep. Every few minutes, he could hear rustling outside the ring of boulders. There were creatures out there. Whether the fire would hold them off or not, he didn't know. There were enough people here and the fire, so they might be held at bay, but Gustav certainly wouldn't want to be disturbed, and since things seemed to work out the way Gustav wanted…

Alaric must have dozed off eventually, because he woke to a scream by Milly. He sat up and saw her pointing into the darkness, but he could see nothing. Then the shadow on the top of the largest boulder slithered, and a head lifted off the rock. Its eyes glinted back firelight, but its body was all shadows.

Brandson stepped in front of Milly and drew his knife. Douglon leapt up and held his axe, but backed slowly away from the boulder. Alaric stood, too, and stepped back as a black lizard slithered down the rock to the ground. Ayda stepped forward. The beast snapped its head toward her and dropped low. It hissed deep in its throat, causing lines of molten red to glow beneath the dark scales of its neck.

A fire lizard. Alaric's breath caught and his palms began to sweat. This one was larger than the one he'd fought when Evangeline was poisoned. That one had been sleek and fast. This one was thick with strength. Its head, slithering smoothly on a thick neck, was almost as high as Alaric's waist. Alaric began to gather energy from the trees and grass around him.

Ayda stepped forward purposefully and held out her hand toward the beast.

The lizard crouched down, ready to spring.

"Ayda," Alaric whispered, "please be careful. That's a fire lizard."

"You're not a lizard," she said softly. "Do you remember who you are?"

The beast paused and cocked its head. Then it crept closer. The lizard's snout was inches from Ayda's hand. Ayda knelt down and leaned forward, reaching out her hand slowly. Its eyes slimmed to slits and it drew in a breath.

"Ayda—" Alaric whispered in warning.

But the elf pushed her hand forward and closed her eyes. She set her hand on its snout.

The lizard's eyes snapped open wide and a deep growl began in its chest.

"Can you remember?" Her voice melted through the air.

The growl stopped. The creature blinked. It sniffed Ayda's hand several times, then sank back onto its haunches.

I remember, elf, a voice rang out in Alaric's mind.

Milly, Brandson, and Douglon started and looked at the lizard in amazement. He must be speaking into all of their minds.

Ayda smiled warmly. "I'm Ayda. May I?" she asked, reaching for its head.

The lizard, which had drawn back, gave a stuttered nod and closed its eyes.

Ayda place her hands on either side of its enormous head. She closed her eyes as well, and the two stayed like that for several breaths. When the creature finally opened its eyes, they were clearer.

Ayda stepped back and gestured around the circle. "This is Keeper Alaric, Douglon, Brandson, and Milly."

No one relaxed, but Milly peeked around Brandson. "What is your name?" she asked, her voice a little higher than normal.

The lizard shook its head.

"It has been too long," Ayda said quietly. "He has been changed for so long that he can't remember who he was before." She looked at the others. "It's been a very long time. Maybe a hundred years."

The creature's eyes were wary. A hundred years. A hundred years trapped in the body of an animal. Most of the Shade Seekers' monsters were crossbreeds of humans and common animals. They had normal sorts of lifespans. But to cross someone with a fire lizard? Fire lizards were a relative of dragons. They lived for centuries.

The creature lifted its head and looked directly at Alaric.

A Keeper, his voice rang out slowly in Alaric's mind again. *It has been a long time since I saw a Keeper.*

Alaric stepped forward. He could find nothing to say.

Do you know my name?

Ayda and the others were watching expectantly. The creature looked at him desperately.

"Ayda would know more than I would," Alaric answered. "She can enter your mind easily. I don't know if I can."

You're a Keeper.

Alaric opened his mouth to object, but Ayda cut in. "Don't tell me, Keeper, that you don't understand the concept of how to do this."

Alaric shot her a glare. "I've done it before," he snapped. "Just not the way you do. My way involves permission. And I can only see what he wants me to."

"Well, this man wants you to see his name. There was too much in there for me to look through. But maybe your way will work."

Taking a deep breath, Alaric stepped forward and reached out toward the lizard's head. The creature reached forward as well. Alaric's hand touched the small, black scales on the side of his face. The lizard flinched away, then moved his head back against Alaric's hand. The scales were smooth and warm, like river stone lying in the sun.

Alaric took another deep breath. Closing his eyes, he reached out tentatively toward the man's mind.

What he found was the mind of an animal. There was hunger and watchfulness and the feel of the earth beneath his feet, the rock beneath his tail, the smell of the people in front of him. He was a beast, but he was intelligent. His mind held caution and planning, and through it all wove bright strands of anger.

Alaric moved carefully, following the anger deeper into the creature's mind until he found a place that was full of fury. There were snippets of memories there. Memories of mountains and trees, of people.

But that was all he could find. Impressions of life and sadness. Regret. The rest of the mind was closed firmly.

Alaric pulled himself out and let his hand fall off the scales. "I'm sorry."

The lizard shook his head slightly. *It was long ago.*

Milly, who had been peering intently at the lizard walked closer to him. "I think you are quite lovely."

The creature snorted softly but bowed to her.

"If you don't remember your old name, do you have a new one? Is there something we can call you?"

The lizard considered her for a long moment. *You may pick one for me.*

Milly gave him an uncertain smile. "You're so very black, like the color of night. Alaric, is there a word that mean darkness, but in a good way?"

"Nox?" he offered.

"Yes," Milly said. "Nox. Will that do?"

That will do very well. Nox sounded pleased.

"How did you end up like this?" Ayda asked.

This fire lizard. The Shade Seekers were going to hurt it. I tried to stop them. They weren't pleased.

"Were you a Shade Seeker?" Alaric asked.

I don't think so. Nox paused, then shook his head. *I don't know. The Shade Seekers talk to me. Many of the other beasts have forgotten how to speak. They use me to control the others. We stay in the valley and attack anyone who comes here without the Shade Seekers' permission.*

"Then why aren't you attacking us?" Milly asked.

"I could tell the Shade Seekers' control over him had weakened," Ayda answered. "It wasn't hard to break."

The lizard bowed his head to her. *I owe you a great debt.*

"Why has their control weakened?" Alaric said.

Maybe because they are all gone from here. Except the one who is here now. He has appeared once before, but did not stay long.

"The Shade Seeker who is here now," Ayda said. "Where is he?"

At the keep, Nox answered. *He passed through the woods late this afternoon.*

"He came through the woods?" Alaric asked in surprise. "Not on his dragon?"

Dragon? There has been no dragon near here.

"Are you sure?"

He looked levelly at Alaric. *I am sure.*

"Of course you are. Sorry." Alaric exchanged glances with Ayda. "We thought he was on a dragon."

"Then he's not far ahead of us!" Milly said. "We're not too late."

Too late for what?

"The wizard is trying to revive the Rivor," Ayda said, her eyes glinting.

Nox growled again, deep in his chest, and his eyes went flat. *That should not happen. The Rivor lived in this valley for years. During that time, the other Shade Seekers disappeared one by one, and the Rivor's power grew. He killed many creatures, too.*

"Mallon killed the other Shade Seekers?" Alaric asked.

Nox nodded. *Many of them.*

"Can you take us to the keep?" Ayda asked.

Nox nodded. *The Shade Seeker will do nothing until morning, though. Raising a creature is a long process, usually requiring hours of preparation and more than one Shade Seeker. Alone, this wizard could not do all of the preparations he needs in the dark.*

Alaric agreed. "The runes he needs to write are extensive. But there's another reason. If his dragon isn't here, then Gustav has nothing to sacrifice."

He had only a donkey and a wagon. In the wagon was a large object wrapped in cloth.

"Mallon's body," Milly said. "What will Gustav sacrifice that is powerful enough?"

He has summoned all the creatures in the valley to meet at the keep tomorrow at midday.

"All of them?" Milly gasped. "He's going to sacrifice all of you?"

Nox's eyes glared into the darkness. *He could not do that. A single Shade Seeker would not be strong enough to control all of us at once.*

"We keep assuming he can't do things," Brandson said.

The Shade Seekers all together could command us to kill ourselves, perhaps. But not one alone. And not one like this.

"Gustav is particularly good at influence," Alaric said. "Maybe he plans to have you kill each other."

"Take us to him tonight," Ayda demanded.

Alaric shook his head. "The other creatures will be out in the dark."

This valley is dangerous at night. Even were I to be with you, we might encounter more monsters than I could fight.

"I'm not afraid of monsters," Ayda said quietly.

"There's very little chance that we are going to make it safely through the valley tomorrow during daylight," Alaric said. "We can't risk it at night. Especially knowing that Gustav isn't going to do anything immediately. He won't start until close to midday tomorrow when the creatures come. He needs something to sacrifice."

Ayda glared at him, her eyes burning into him. Alaric swallowed hard and braced himself for… something.

She finally let out a long breath. "Fine," she hissed. "I'll take watch." And she stalked off past the fire and into the darkness.

The rest of the group looked at one another uneasily.

"She's a little angry at Gustav," Milly said to Nox, smiling apologetically.

Indeed. The elf is powerful and lonely. And angry. Do you think you can stop the Shade Seeker?

"We're not here to stop him," Ayda called back over her shoulder. "We're here to kill him."

CHAPTER FORTY-SIX

"NO WE'RE NOT!" Brandson protested. "We're not here to kill him." He looked around the group. "Are we?"

"No," Milly said. "We aren't. We're here to stop him from raising Mallon."

Douglon let out a short laugh. "We're here to kill him."

"Alaric," Milly appealed to him.

Alaric took a deep breath. "I would rather not kill the old man."

"You won't need to," Ayda said.

"It should be easy enough to stop him," Alaric said, ignoring her.

Ayda snorted again. "Because it's been so easy to stop him all the other times?"

"This is different," Alaric said. "We know where he is, and we know what he is planning. Even if he gets everything set up before we get there, he will be relying heavily on the runes he draws before he begins. He won't be able to begin until the monsters arrive for him to sacrifice. That should give us plenty of time. And we will stop him this time."

"Oh," Ayda said, her eyebrow arched, "so we finally have a Keeper in charge. It's nice that you've decided to break away from wallowing in your past long enough to commit to something. Tell me, Keeper, how do you plan on stopping him from doing this exact same thing again sometime when we aren't following him?"

"We're going to take the Rivor's body and destroy it."

"Don't you think I've tried? What do you think I've been doing since my people fought him? I don't know if he can be destroyed."

Alaric nodded slowly. "Maybe not. But we can try again. Together."

"It is the Shade Seeker who wants to raise him," Ayda pointed out. "There's a simple answer to how to keep him from trying again. He wants the power that the Rivor can bring to him. He is not nice, nor does he care for any of us. He used us, manipulated us, destroyed my home." Ayda's eyes glowed with fury. "And he will pay for it."

"We'll stop him, Ayda," Alaric said.

"Stopping him isn't enough."

Alaric turned to Nox. "Is there a way for us to enter the keep unnoticed?"

There's an entrance in the back. It will not take long to reach it tomorrow morning. The Shade Seeker shouldn't be able to see us approach.

"Then we should get some sleep," Alaric says.

Ayda glared at Alaric, then turned and stalked over to the fire.

One more day and this would be done.

Morning couldn't come soon enough.

Unfortunately, dawn's early light came a little too late.

The sky had turned a dauntless pitch purple when Douglon shook Alaric awake.

"She's gone," Douglon hissed.

Alaric sat up and tried to focus on the dwarf. "Who's gone?"

"The stupid elf. She's gone. She left sometime during the night. She never woke anyone for the next watch." Douglon scowled into the forest.

Alaric looked around. Ayda was nowhere to be seen. Alaric swore, jumping to his feet. "He's still doing it," he said, slamming his pack together.

The others stared at him blankly.

"Gustav doesn't have his dragon," Alaric said, "so he drew something more powerful to himself. He drew Ayda."

Everyone had slept soundly, even Nox, who had curled up in front of one of the gaps in the boulders. That must have been Ayda's doing as well. Alaric felt like he hadn't slept that deeply in years.

"How long ago do you think she left?" Milly asked.

"As soon as we fell asleep… Or more accurately, as soon as she put us to sleep," Alaric answered.

Brandson tried to stand, but cried out and fell against the boulder next to him. Milly ran over to him as he slid back down to the ground. She pulled up the leg of his pants and drew in a quick breath. The skin around the scar where the ape had gashed him had turned dark red.

Alaric went over to look at Brandson's leg and swore again. Not just an infection. The ape's nails must have been poisonous. He hadn't thought of looking at it last night. He couldn't leave Brandson like this.

"We need to drain this. It should be quick."

Alaric sent Douglon off in search of a couple of plants while Milly began boiling water.

I can follow the elf's trail, Nox offered.

Alaric nodded.

With a rustle, Nox slithered over the nearest boulder and into the forest.

Alaric took his knife and held it in the fire. He turned to Brandson. "I'm sorry. This is going to hurt."

He washed Brandson's leg thoroughly, then took his knife and slid it carefully through the center of the scar. Greenish pus seeped out while Brandson bit back cries of pain. Douglon returned, and he and Milly began making a paste while Alaric directed them. Once Alaric had drained out as much pus as he could, he rinsed the wound with water and pressed the paste onto it. Then he ripped up a shirt for some bandages and wrapped the leg.

It felt like ages before Brandson was ready to be helped to his feet. Milly slipped under his arm to stabilize him.

Nox wasn't back yet, but they hurried, packing up their things as quickly as they could. Ayda must have reached the keep hours ago. Alaric slammed his things together. Ayda *should* be more than a match for Gustav, but she had been so angry. Dread anchored deep into Alaric's gut.

Milly let out a loud gasp. Alaric looked at her in alarm, wondering what had happened. She was staring wide-eyed at something behind him.

"Good morning," a nasal voice said from outside the rocks.

Alaric spun around.

Gustav was standing just beyond the coals from last night's fire. He still wore his blue robe with the swirling stars, but it was rumpled and dirty.

Douglon growled and pulled out his axe.

"You came back?" Brandson said.

"That was unwise," Douglon said, stepping toward the old man.

"*Alligo*!" Gustav shouted, waving his arms dramatically toward them.

Alaric started to laugh at the ridiculous motion until he felt his legs freeze to the ground. The paralysis moved quickly up his torso. He grabbed for the pouch at his neck just as his arms went rigid. Only his head was free to move.

Behind him, he heard Douglon grunting against the spell as well.

Alaric felt the humming of the magic focused on the ground around his feet. He began to gather energy to attack Gustav.

"*Liquo*!" Gustav shrieked, this time waving his hand frantically at Alaric.

Alaric felt the energy drain from him, sinking down into the ground. As fast as he could gather it, it ran out of him.

Gustav shook his hands out and looked at Alaric warily for a moment. Then he grinned.

"Don't try to fight me," Gustav said, motioning to the top of the boulders surrounding them.

There was a slither and a scraping of claws as monstrous creatures crawled up onto the tops of the rocks. On the boulder closest to Alaric, an enormous badger appeared. It scraped long, black claws against the rock as it leaned toward them. Instead of the black eyes of a badger, it had human eyes, light brown and shrewd. On other boulders sat a long, mottled snake, a small bear, and a golden-haired lion, all looking at them with unnerving intelligence.

"Gustav?" Brandson asked. "What are you doing?"

Gustav didn't look at Brandson.

Alaric strained against the magic holding him in place. He pulled in energy again and again, only to have it drain out just as quickly into the ground beneath his feet.

"What do you want?" Alaric demanded through a clenched jaw.

"I want peace and quiet to finish my work. And you weren't going to give me that. So I'm afraid you'll need to stay here. I'm leaving my creatures here to keep you under control."

"You mean to kill us," Douglon growled.

"Not yet. I'm not sure you all won't still be useful to me for something. So for now, I've commanded them to leave you alone as long as you remain inside the boulders. If you try to leave, I'm afraid they will kill you." Gustav studied them all. "And after everything, I find that I'm a little fond of all of you."

"Well, we hate you," Douglon said. "Where's Ayda?"

Gustav smiled. "Ayda has agreed to help me in my work."

"She wouldn't," Milly said.

Gustav flashed her an irritated look. "Ayda is helping me. And with her energy, there is nothing to stop me."

"She's not working with you," Alaric said. "Even your influence couldn't convince her to help you. You're using her."

Gustav smirked.

"I'd be careful," Alaric warned. "Ayda isn't someone to trifle with."

"Ayda will be no trouble," Gustav said, waving off Alaric's words. "And neither will you. Now if you'll excuse me, I need to take your weapons."

Gustav walked slowly up to Douglon, reaching tentatively toward his axe. When Douglon didn't do anything more than snarl at him, Gustav took the axe from his hand.

Brandson stared at the wizard, a mixture of anger and hurt in his eyes. Gustav walked past him quickly, not meeting his eye and took Brandson's knife from his saddle and two more knives out of Douglon's. The wizard held them pell-mell across his chest and walked out of the ring of boulders.

"I'm afraid it's time for me to go," Gustav said, hoisting the weapons up higher in his arms with a clatter. He looked at each of them for a long moment. "Um, goodbye."

As Gustav stepped out of the ring of boulders, Alaric threw his entire will against the spell holding him still. His hand holding the pouch jerked forward, breaking the cord that it hung from and leaving the pouch hanging from his clenched hand. Nothing else moved. He was filled with fury.

"Let me see the Wellstone." Alaric's voice broke with desperation. "Before you do it. Please let me see the Wellstone."

Gustav paused and turned back. "What do you need the Wellstone for?" He tilted his head as he looked at Alaric's hand. "What do you keep in that pouch?" Dropping the weapons to the ground, Gustav walked back between the boulders and stepped up to Alaric.

Alaric reached for energy, but again, felt it drain away.

He strained against the immobilizing spell, but could do nothing beyond grind his teeth furiously at the old wizard.

Gustav ignored him and pulled the pouch out from Alaric's stiff fingers. He pulled open the strings and dropped the rough ruby into his hand.

CHAPTER FORTY-SEVEN

GUSTAV'S MOUTH FELL OPEN. He slowly raised his eyes to Alaric in disbelief. "A Reservoir Stone? I thought you had been drawn to me because I needed you to read the map. But you were drawn to me because I needed a Reservoir Stone."

Gustav looked at the ruby in wonder.

"Now, I don't need Kordan's emerald. I'm not particularly good at creating Reservoir Stones, you understand. And since I haven't been able to find any other Shade Seekers since I came back from the Roven Sweep a year ago, I started looking for Reservoirs that already existed. When I heard that Keeper Kordan had buried an empty one, I knew I could use it. Just fill it with someone else's energy.

"But this Reservoir Stone still swirls with the flame of a sacrifice. It will be so much easier to add energy to this one than to Kordan's dead emerald." Gustav flashed a wickedly gleeful smile toward Alaric.

"It will be messy and leaky, but enough energy should

get to Lord Mallon to wake him up. When he's awake, he can find other sacrifices himself."

"Hm," Douglon grunted, "I wonder where he'll find one of those."

Gustav's brow creased. "He won't sacrifice me. I'm the only servant loyal enough to help him return."

"I'm sure he'll be very grateful," Alaric said, glaring at Gustav with more fury than he had ever felt.

"Oh, you've made it so easy! It's already holding a sacrifice!"

"It's not a sacrifice!"

Gustav looked at the Keeper in surprise. "You don't even know what you have, do you? You don't know the power this holds."

The old man's fingers were wrapped around the ruby like a parasite.

Gustav's smile spread. "A Reservoir Stone is a vessel, a vessel to hold the power of a life which has been sacrificed until it is poured into someone else. They are Mallon's specialty. He has used dozens of them. Absorbing the power of other strong men, including any Shade Seekers who weren't useful to him, made him almost invincible. He strengthened himself by the sacrifice of others."

Alaric's stomach clenched. "She is not a sacrifice."

Gustav's eyes widened, then he burst out laughing. "You sacrificed someone you know? You proved in Queenstown that you weren't much of a Keeper, but that is even darker than I expected. Thank you, by the way, for bringing my medallion to Queenstown. I had thought it lost. My task is much easier with those instructions."

Alaric strained against the magic, his breath coming in gasps.

"Why did you do it?" Gustav asked curiously, looking at the ruby.

The words rose unbidden. "I had no choice. I needed time. I needed time to save her."

"Save her?" Gustav's brow creased. "You didn't save her. You sacrificed her. Shade Seekers don't pull the life out of someone to save them. They pull it out to sacrifice them. Then they use the energy for themselves." Gustav raised his gaze back up to Alaric's face. Sudden understanding filled his face, turning to a look that almost held compassion. "You didn't mean to sacrifice her, did you?"

"She will not be a sacrifice!"

Gustav looked at Alaric hesitantly, then he began to speak almost kindly. "She already is. Whatever she was before this—whoever she was—she isn't here any longer. At least not all of her."

Alaric stopped struggling. He looked from Gustav to the ruby. The old man couldn't know that. He didn't know what he was talking about.

"Too much of her has been lost," Gustav explained. "Too much energy is lost when the vessel is created. The Reservoir holds the life energy of a person, but not enough of it to make a whole person again. *The sacrifice exceeds the reward.* I thought even the Keepers knew that much."

Gustav looked at the Reservoir Stone closely, then closed his eyes. Alaric felt him cast out toward the energy in the ruby. A wave of fury rose at the thought of Gustav's mind brushing against her.

Gustav looked up at Alaric puzzled. "There's not much life here at all. Whatever you planned on doing, this does not hold enough life to do it."

Alaric glared at the old man's wrinkled hand grasping the red stone.

"It's certainly not enough for what I need." Gustav shrugged. "But I can add more. Every little bit helps, I suppose." He tossed Alaric's leather pouch on the ground and dropped the ruby into his pocket. With one final look at each of them, Gustav stepped out of the circle of rocks and disappeared.

The ruby. Gustav had his ruby. He had Evangeline.

Alaric's gut felt like ice.

His wife was going to be sacrificed to Mallon.

Fury built up in him. He strained against the spell holding him in place. It was as though he had been turned to stone.

Douglon was swearing and grunting behind him.

Gustav was getting farther away and Alaric couldn't move.

His rage boiled over into a roar as he reached out gathering energy as quickly as he could, only to have it drained out into the ground once again. Alaric ground his teeth and gathered more, faster. He drew from the ground, from the trees, from the embers of last night's fire. He reached into the boulders and pulled the slow, dark solid *vitalle* of the rock itself.

The energy from the boulders held. Before it could drain out, Alaric focused his energy on the ground around him.

"Lacero!"

The energy stabbed down into the ground, slicing Gustav's spell, tearing out of Alaric's palm like a knife. He fell to his knees.

Gustav's spell to drain his energy must have been focused at his feet, because Alaric felt a rush of *vitalle* flow into him. He turned to the others. Quickly, not noticing the pain, he cut through the spells, setting the others free.

Douglon ran through the opening where Gustav had stood, lunging for their weapons. A shriek rang out above them, and an enormous vulture swooped down out of the treetops in front of them, diving for Douglon. The dwarf raised his arm to defend against the attack. Talons ripped across it.

From the woods behind the boulders, Nox lunged for the vulture, his jaw closing on one of the bird's legs. The vulture gave a scream, but Nox yanked the bird out of the air and the two tumbled into the trees. The forest beyond the rocks swayed with the crashes of their fight.

Douglon scrambled back into the circle of boulders, holding his arm to his chest. He swore loudly, glaring at the beasts poised at the tops of the boulders.

The group backed up to the center of the clearing, standing with their backs together. Alaric glanced around the clearing. Their weapons were still outside the ring of boulders. The only weapons within reach were long, thick sticks by their feet. Those wouldn't hurt anything.

Atop the boulders, four monsters shifted, watching them with glittering eyes, content to stay there for now. There had to be a way to get them to leave, to break Gustav's control over them. He reached down slowly, picking up the four closest sticks.

"Those aren't very good weapons, Keeper," Douglon growled.

Alaric held them together and reached up to touch their ends.

"Incende."

The sticks burst into flame. He handed them out to the

others before shaking out his hand. Then Alaric cast out his mind toward the badger, its mind full of stealth and power. It knew the people below it were of little consequence.

Alaric felt the tether on its mind, the thin leash of control of what was left of the Shade Seeker's control. With a quick burst of energy, Alaric snapped the tether.

The badger twitched, then lifted its head and sniffed the air. Alaric took a step toward it, raising the fire closer. The badger shied back, then dropped off the back of the boulder.

The other animals crept forward. The snake slithered toward them and dropped to the ground, coiling itself into a loose pile. Milly held her torch out toward it, pushing it back against the rock as it hissed.

"Keep the bear back," Alaric called to Douglon and Brandson.

The two of them stepped toward the boulder with the bear, holding their torches out ahead of them. The bear swung its head back and forth, watching them but shying back from the fire. Alaric held his own torch up toward the lynx. Before the cat could spring, Alaric broke the Shade Seeker's hold on its mind. He shoved the torch toward it until the cat turned and jumped down the other side of the boulder.

He turned to the other two creatures, doing the same thing until they disappeared into the woods as well.

Alaric's hands were burning. He picked up the leather pouch Gustav had dropped and followed Douglon to the gap between the rocks where Gustav had left. Warily, Douglon stepped out. Nothing moved in the woods. The others followed him out, gathering their horses and weapons.

There was a loud rustling in the trees, and Alaric spun

toward the sound. Nox's head pushed out from the undergrowth. He shook his head, shaking a vulture feather off onto the ground. *I followed the elf's scent to the keep. She is there.*

"Let's go," Douglon said.

Nox led the way up the valley through the forest. Alaric moved up next to Douglon to check his arm. The cuts were deep and the dwarf grimaced in pain.

"Where's the stupid elf when you need her to heal something?" Douglon asked.

CHAPTER FORTY-EIGHT

ALARIC PULLED out some of the cloth strips he had leftover from when he'd bandaged Brandson. He looked ahead, searching for any sign of the keep. The way things were going, no one in the group was going to make it there unharmed.

Several times, Alaric caught the sound of creatures skirting the forest near them, but it seemed that Nox's presence deterred them. Whether they were intimidated by the fire lizard or whether they thought Nox was escorting them to the keep, he didn't know.

The keep is just ahead of us.

Almost immediately, the path turned sharply and they found themselves at a large tower at the corner of the keep, crumbled off above the first floor. Nox stood quietly by the door while Alaric opened it.

Good luck, Keeper, Nox said, hanging back.

"Will you come with us?" Alaric asked.

The lizard shook his head. *I don't think I can help beyond this. I want to leave the valley before he calls us all to the sacrifice. I have spent too many years being the Shade Seekers' slave.*

"You weren't their slave this morning," Alaric said.

For that, I thank you all. I am free, but I have forgotten who I am, and I'm not sure I want to remember. I do not think I was good even before the Shade Seekers enslaved me. And by now, I have done too many dark things for them to forget. I just want to leave before the Shade Seeker has the chance to enslave me again.

Alaric nodded. "Thank you for your help."

"Yes," Douglon said, motioning to his arm. "Thank you."

"A friend of mine told me that we're not defined by the darkest parts of our past," Alaric said, remembering Ewan's words. "We can leave them behind as easily as we leave our best moments. We're not confined to be what we have been."

Some things are too much to come back from, he answered. *That's a very pretty idea. I'm not sure it works that way, but it's a pretty idea. Good luck to you all. And Keeper, I'm glad you are here. Your presence here brings hope.*

"Don't get too excited," Alaric said. "I'm a terrible Keeper."

Well, we're not confined to being what we have been, you know. The lizard's laughter echoed in Alaric's mind. *Good luck to you.*

Nox turned and disappeared into the trees, and Alaric entered the tower. It consisted of a large circular room with several old chairs. Stairs reached up toward the broken roof. Across the tower, another door opened into the keep. The tower was so large that they brought the horses in and closed the door behind them.

Brandson sagged down against a wall and slid slowly to the floor. Milly rushed over to him and lifted his pants again. Dark streaks of red radiated up his leg.

Douglon fell heavily into a chair of his own, his arm held protectively to his chest.

Alaric looked at the two of them. "You can stay here with the animals," he began.

"Shut up." Douglon shoved himself back up and walked over to Brandson, offering his good arm. Brandson took it and tried to stand.

Alaric sighed at their stubbornness.

"We're not staying behind," Brandson said.

Alaric nodded. "Then let's go find Gustav. And Ayda."

With no way of knowing where they were headed, Alaric randomly picked the corridor to their left. The walls around them were crumbling, and water ran in little rivulets along the floor of the damp hall. They crept stealthily down hall after hall, but the keep remained silent.

After several more turns, a large archway appeared ahead of them. Alaric paused a little back from it and cast out into the large room beyond it. The room was empty. They walked into the silent room and looked around. It was a great hall. It was deserted and, like the rest of the keep, in the process of crumbling to dust.

Alaric looked around, comparing it to the Stronghold, which would probably last for centuries. He couldn't imagine this keep lasting more than a few rainy seasons.

Sunlight fell on the floor from open doors at the end of the hall.

As they approached, they could see a large courtyard.

Outside, someone was grunting and swearing.

They crept forward until they reached the door. Alaric peered out.

The center of the enormous courtyard had been hastily cleared of leaves and twigs so that the area around a white altar was clear. At this distance, the sides of the altar looked lumpy, but Alaric couldn't quite make out why. There was a circle of runes on the ground, drawn in black winding around the altar. The noises were coming from the other side of it. Gustav had to be over there, although Alaric couldn't see him.

On top of the altar, set far to one corner, were Gustav's medallion and the Wellstone, which was glowing and humming gently. Sparks sputtered between the two. Alaric studied the Wellstone. It didn't seem bright enough yet for Gustav to have filled it. The flashes of light were normal. Gustav must be planning to fill it once the spell was begun. Alaric blew out a quick breath in relief. The cure was still there.

A loud grunt came from the other side of the altar. Gustav's head came over the top as he strained to lift something. The top of another head came briefly into view before Gustav swore and the head fell out of view with a thunk.

Gustav stood, breathing heavily, and gave the body a kick. A foot flipped into sight around the end of the altar. Gustav stomped off past the altar, leaving the body where it had fallen against the altar.

"Is that...*Mallon*?" Brandson asked quietly.

Alaric bit his lip to keep from laughing.

"He is a little bit of an idiot," Douglon whispered.

"Those markings on the ground are runes," Alaric told them. "They form a circle around him. Gustav will use them to store the energy of the spell while he creates it. He'll be relying heavily on them. If we erase a couple, he might not be able to complete the spell."

The others nodded.

"Once he begins the spell, the circle of runes will glow

blue. From that point on, they'll have a life of their own. We won't be able to damage them any longer, nor will we be able to take away any of the things he's using. It will all be tied together. So we need to stop him before he begins." Alaric peered as far around the door as he could without stepping out. "Anyone see Ayda?"

Douglon's brow contracted. "I think she's past the altar."

"How do you know that?"

Douglon cringed. "What did she do to me? I can *feel* her." He shook his head. "Sort of."

"I haven't heard any noise from her," Milly said.

"Wouldn't blame him if he gagged her," Douglon said.

"There's no way Gustav got a gag on Ayda," Brandson whispered.

Gustav returned to Mallon's body. He unrolled a bundle of fabric spilling out a flash of green and something bright red. Kordan's emerald and Alaric's ruby.

The fury Alaric had been feeling since Gustav took the ruby rose again.

Gustav bent down, out of sight behind the altar. When he stood back up, the stones were gone.

Alaric imagined the ruby sitting on Mallon's chest, swirling slowly. He took a deep breath, forcing the emotions back and watching Gustav closely.

"Let's go," Alaric said.

Gustav dusted off his robes and looked around critically at his runes. He stepped over Mallon to look closely at the medallion on the altar. Gustav took a deep breath, shook out his arms dramatically, raised his voice, and began to chant.

Alaric stepped out into the courtyard.

In that moment, he saw two things.

The first, with the circle of runes stretched out awkwardly to include her, was Ayda.

Sort of.

Anchored firmly in the rocky ground of the courtyard stood a tree with pale green leaves and glimmering silver bark.

The second was the dull bluish glow of the runes as Gustav began the spell.

CHAPTER FORTY-NINE

ALARIC'S STOMACH dropped as the circle of runes glowed blue.

The runes stretched around the Ayda-tree, standing still and bright in the courtyard. How had Gustav managed to get her to change?

Alaric strode out toward the wizard.

Gustav's head snapped up. His mouth froze open in the middle of a word. Shutting his mouth and swallowing hard, he looked down, finished saying the word, then carefully set his foot next to one of the runes on the ground to mark his place. Finally, he looked back up at Alaric, glaring.

"Good morning," Alaric said. He walked along the circle of runes, studying them. They were redundant to the point of being ridiculous. "I see you've decided to be overly cautious. Most of these runes are unnecessary, but"—the smile he flashed at Gustav felt vicious—"every little bit helps, I always say."

Douglon stomped out into the courtyard, his face set like stone, and Gustav's gaze flicked to the dwarf. Douglon looked at Ayda. "Stupid elf. No wonder I can feel her." Douglon cocked his head to the side. "She is *really* angry."

Gustav darted a nervous glance at Ayda.

Douglon made a little strangled noise, and Alaric looked at him quickly. The dwarf's face was twisted in revulsion, and he was looking at the altar. Alaric followed his gaze, realizing that the sides of the altar looked lumpy because they were composed entirely of bones. Skulls of different shapes and sizes leered out in all directions across the courtyard.

"That is unnecessarily creepy," the dwarf muttered.

Milly came up beside him, letting Brandson lean on her shoulder. Brandson stared hard at the wizard. Gustav met his gaze for only a moment before dropping his eyes back down to the string of runes.

"Nice to have the group back together." Douglon pulled his axe out.

"How exactly did you get Ayda to change into a tree?" Alaric asked conversationally, knowing Gustav couldn't stop the spell to tell him. Alaric kept walking slowly around the circle of runes, deciphering each one.

Saying that Gustav had been overly cautious was an understatement. Any other time, it would have been funny. Runes were double and triple written to make sure there could be absolutely no doubt as to their meaning, yet each individual mark was sloppy.

"You really aren't very good at runes, are you?" Alaric asked. "You weren't pretending with Douglon's map. These are awful."

Gustav glared harder, then turned and looked intently at the runes directly before him and began to mutter again.

"Afraid to talk to us, Shade Seeker?" Douglon asked.

"He can't," Alaric said, smiling. "He's begun the spell. If he does anything besides read these excellent runes he's worked so very hard on, the spell will unravel. Or worse, mutate."

Douglon sniggered. "Maybe I should throw my axe at him. Think he can read and dodge at the same time?"

Gustav's head whipped up again, and he pointed frantically to some runes set off from the others.

"Ahh," Alaric said, glancing toward the runes. "He has put some protection in place. You probably can't actually touch him. Even with your axe. Were you nervous someone would disapprove of what you're doing here, old man?"

"Gustav, what are you doing?" Brandson asked quietly. "Mallon killed my parents."

Gustav looked up at the smith and a flicker of doubt crossed his face. But he brushed the doubt away with a scowl and turned back to reciting his spell.

Douglon growled and threw his axe straight at Gustav. The blade hit an invisible wall and rang out, bouncing away from the wizard and landing near Douglon's feet.

Gustav jumped back, glaring at Douglon.

"Yup," Douglon said, picking up his axe. "He's protected."

"Why *are* you doing this?" Alaric asked Gustav. "Everyone was perfectly happy thinking Mallon was dead and gone. What possible reason would you have for raising him?"

Gustav narrowed his eyes, then went back to work.

"I'm actually interested," Alaric said. "Power? Prestige? Did Mallon promise you a dukedom?"

"You had better things than that when you had these

people's friendship," Milly said. "Somehow, I doubt you'll get that from Mallon. You picked the wrong side."

"Mallon just needs a puppet," Douglon scoffed. "Most people would have been smart enough to cut the strings when Mallon disappeared."

Gustav's face was red. He clamped his mouth shut and shook his head vehemently.

"Do you hate the entire world so much you just want to see it die?" Brandson asked. "Even those who thought of you as a friend?"

Gustav opened his mouth to Brandson, then snapped it shut in frustration. He turned toward Alaric and stared at him intently. He pointed to his own head, then to Alaric's. The old man was pointing and staring so frantically that Alaric almost laughed.

"You want me to read your mind?"

Gustav nodded vehemently.

"Okay," Alaric said, "I can't say I don't have a morbid interest in what I'll find."

He closed his eyes and reached his mind out toward Gustav. The wizard stood perfectly still, his mind still focused primarily on the rune at his feet, but there was one image sitting prominently in Gustav's mind. A tall, angular man stood on a hill, the Greenwood spread out before him. It was Mallon, his glittering black eyes looking impressed and pleased. The Rivor's face showing clearly that he saw Gustav as useful—valuable even.

Alaric pulled back out of Gustav's mind and opened his eyes. The wizard stood before him, chin raised, eyes blazing defiantly. He looked old, and Alaric was struck by the great loneliness that Gustav carried within himself.

"There are better things to crave than being useful to a man who sees everyone as a tool," Alaric said.

Gustav looked at him for a long moment, his face indecipherable. Taking a deep breath, he continued to read the runes.

"I need some time to read all these runes," Alaric told the others. "Distract him. Do anything you can think of that will slow him down. But don't get too close. I don't know what other sorts of protection he's set up."

Douglon grunted and moved directly across the runes from Gustav, training his gaze at the wizard and pacing him step for step. Gustav attempted a sneer, but it looked rather sickly.

Milly and Brandson whispered together for a minute before Brandson sat down with a groan and Milly ran toward Douglon and Gustav, tossing something shimmery on the ground near the runes before grabbing Douglon's arm and scooting them both back. Brandson tossed a small rock to the same place. Flames burst from the ground, shooting higher than Gustav's head. The wizard jumped back.

"This fire powder is great," Douglon said. "You could have saved Brandson a lot of work, though, by lighting his forge with it every morning."

"What's the word he used when he pretended it was magic?" Milly asked.

"*Incende!*" Brandson shouted as he tossed another stone into some powder.

Gustav leaned forward, trying to concentrate on the runes amidst their distractions.

"Can you read through fire?" Milly said. She walked close to the next rune past Gustav and threw some fire powder directly on in. Brandson grinned and threw a rock, sparking a flame that obscured the rune for several seconds before beginning to die down. Gustav snarled at Milly and had to wait until the flames were low enough for him to stomp out so he could see the rune again. Meanwhile, Milly moved to the next rune and sprinkled on some powder.

Alaric continued to decipher runes until he reached those that stretched out around the Ayda-tree. The more runes he read, the more his sympathy for the wizard disappeared. "So this is how you chose to name Ayda?" he asked, joining the efforts to distract Gustav. "*'The enclosed creature'*? That's vague. Really, all you needed to do was assign an energy rune to Ayda near the beginning, then refer to it here. You should rely more on your mental focus and less on descriptive runes. Let's erase these and start over. We could probably use a third of the runes you've scribbled here.

"And watch this one. It looks a bit like 'pig' instead of 'blood.' That could make things interesting."

Gustav slapped his hands over his ears as he leaned down closer to the runes and kept muttering.

"Will it work?" Milly asked from across the circle.

Alaric sighed. "Surprisingly, it will." He pointed to the rune about Ayda. "He must have originally meant the dragon when he wrote 'creature.'" Alaric turned to Gustav. "Where is your dragon, by the way?"

Gustav kept his eyes on the ground, muttering quickly as he crept around the circle.

"Did he find out what you intended to do with him?"

Gustav ignored him. Douglon had taken to pacing near Gustav, growling. Gustav was trying his best to look only at the runes, but with each growl, he flinched.

Alaric had reached the rune that would draw energy from Ayda to reanimate Mallon. He was close to the Rivor's crumpled body. Mallon's long legs were akimbo and his gaunt cheek was shoved against the altar so that a skull leered out over his black hair. Sitting on his chest was Kordan's dark emerald. And next to it, its red currents swirling unperturbed, sat Evangeline's ruby.

Alaric stepped closer to read a particularly messy rune, the rune he had been looking for. There it was, drawn out on the ground, a rune set to draw the latent energy out of Evangeline's Reservoir Stone. The energy that swirled in the ruby, the little life Evangeline had left, was now bound to Mallon. Alaric stepped forward again to pick up the ruby, but paused. Even if he removed it from the circle, the rune was linked to the ruby. It would still claim the energy. In a matter of minutes, the Reservoir Stone was going to darken, the red light seeping out of the ruby and into the still body below it.

Alaric glared at the rune as though he could burn it off with sheer force of will.

The spell was going to work.

He was too late.

The rune circle was complete. It was ridiculously overcomplicated and messy, and not even remotely close to being a circle, but it was going to work.

The Wellstone sat on the altar just waiting for Gustav to call it out and fill it.

The Ayda-tree was firmly rooted in the flagstones of the courtyard. She was unmovable. And as long as she stood inside the rune circle, it would be her life's energy that Gustav would sacrifice to wake Mallon.

The runes called out Mallon's name, so removing his body from the circle would do no good.

Gustav had protected himself from weapons and interference.

Alaric was going to have to sit here and watch that wizard do exactly what he wanted to do, destroying what was left of Evangeline in the process.

And once the Rivor was raised? There was no way Alaric was going to be able to fight him alone.

Alaric sank down to his knees.

After all this, he was going to fail.

A rustling behind him caused him to turn. Nox had slithered up behind him, looking grave. Gustav's eyes lit up for a moment seeing the lizard approach, but when Nox settled down next to Alaric, Gustav scowled again and went back to his runes.

Alaric almost asked what had brought Nox back, but he realized that, in the end, it didn't matter. "You should leave. There's nothing we can do to stop him."

I heard what you said, and I have an idea.

Alaric looked at him, the vaguest stirrings of curiosity rising in his heart.

The rune that speaks of Ayda, Nox began, scooting up alongside Alaric. The lizard's voice was quiet in Alaric's mind. *We could…*

Nox paused thoughtfully, then let his head sink down to the ground. *Never mind, it won't work. You would think that after all these years, I would stop trying to fight the Shade Seekers.*

Alaric looked at the enormous lizard head settled next to him and thought about the long years that Nox had been enslaved here. Years with no hope. And just when Alaric had offered him some, it was pulled away.

Alaric glanced up at Gustav to check his progress, knowing the wizard was moving inexorably closer to finishing the spell.

Inside the circle of runes, the wizard let slip a sly smile.

CHAPTER FIFTY

ALARIC GLARED at Gustav who went back to muttering and moving with terrific slowness around the circle.

The ruby still swirled on Mallon's chest. Alaric's hands itched to go pick it up. But it wouldn't matter. The Reservoir Stone was called out by the runes. If he picked it up and ran as fast as he could, maybe he could get it far enough away that the spell wouldn't drain it. But what would be the point of that? With Mallon raised, everyone would die sooner or later.

It made no difference. He might as well let her go this way.

His mind recoiled from the idea. Let her be absorbed into the power of a man who murdered and destroyed? There was a big difference between living in a dangerous world and being devoured by evil.

Alaric looked back at Nox, something tugging at his mind. The lizard was so despondent. Not that Alaric could blame him. Still…

Nox was just lying there. He had decided to come back to

help, but now, he was just lying there. And Alaric was considering letting Gustav use Evangeline to raise Mallon.

Gustav was going to get exactly what he wanted. Again.

Alaric's head snapped up.

They were doing exactly what the wizard wanted them to do. Again.

Some of the haze in his mind stirred sluggishly.

Alaric looked at the ground behind where he knelt. Not that he was going to find anything. There was no point.

"No," he said out loud and shook his head to clear it. He focused again on the ground.

There behind him was a thin line scraped carefully through the dirt. It crossed right behind Alaric, went under Nox's neck, and wiggled off around the circle.

Taking a deep breath, Alaric tensed all his muscles and lunged backward. It felt like he was pushing through mud or quicksand. With a final heave, he toppled past the line.

Fresh air hit his face and he took a deep breath. The haze in his mind scattered.

An influence ring. That stupid wizard had tricked him again. Alaric grabbed at Nox's neck and yanked at him. The lizard glared toward him and left his head still, lying on the ground inside the ring.

Alaric tugged again but there was no way he was going to move the creature.

"Nox," he urged, but the lizard turned away.

Alaric stepped back. "Sorry about this." He swung his foot as hard as he could, kicking the lizard in the most vulnerable place he could find, the area covered in smaller, thinner scales right behind his front leg.

The fire lizard let out a roar and whipped around faster than Alaric had thought possible.

The Keeper threw himself backward and scrambled away from the enormous head lunging toward him. He heard Milly scream.

The jaws, wide open, froze inches from Alaric's face.

"Nox?" Alaric asked nervously.

The lizard closed his mouth slowly and pulled back, blinking.

"There's an influence ring there," he pointed at the thin line drawn on the ground running around the outside of the rune circle, trying to explain. "Gustav was using it to make us feel hopeless. We needed to get out of it."

Nox turned to look at the wizard and growled. Gustav was staring at them, the color draining from his face.

"At least now I know how he planned to keep his dragon still while he sacrificed it," Alaric said.

The rune that is applied to Ayda just calls out a creature, so if we could get her out, we could replace her with a different creature, right? Nox asked. *Can you get Ayda out of the rune circle?*

Alaric looked at Ayda. One of Ayda's branches hung a few inches outside of Gustav's influence ring. He couldn't move her as a tree, but he could certainly help her change back to an elf. How had he not thought of this sooner? Alaric shot a venomous look at Gustav. It was impossible to think clearly around that stupid wizard. The wizard opened his mouth to shout at him, but then snapped it shut again.

Alaric stretched out a hand to touch the Ayda-tree, but froze, remembering the last time he had helped her change. He reached out with his mind to find other sources of energy. He reached for the dense forest just outside the walls of the keep. He took a moment and felt all the life and energy sitting in those trees. Past Gustav's protective wall, he caught a glimpse of the energy that was the wizard.

Alaric grabbed onto that as well. Keeping ahold of that energy, he fixed a firm image of Ayda in his mind then touched a leaf on the nearest branch.

His hand clenched the leaf as a rush of power surged through his body so fast that his knees buckled. The trees along the wall of the keep withered, and Gustav fell to his knees with a yell. In a rush of fury, the tree transformed almost instantly into Ayda. Alaric fell to the ground.

He could feel fury rolling off Ayda in waves as he tried to catch his breath. She caught sight of Gustav and began to stalk toward him.

Gustav had frozen kneeling next to the altar and was looking at Ayda open-mouthed, white as the bones next to him.

"Ayda!" Alaric called. "Get out of the rune circle! He's going to sacrifice you!"

Ayda's step faltered. She dropped her eyes to the runes and to Mallon's body propped awkwardly against the altar. Gustav turned away from her and stared desperately at the runes, chanting again.

Ayda stopped and stood still. Then her shoulders sank in despair as all of the fury drained out of her.

"Ayda!" Alaric yelled. "Gustav is doing this to you! There's an influence ring making you feel like that! Come out!"

But Ayda didn't move. She stood motionless.

Gustav cast one final glance at her then bent over and began muttering faster. He was approaching the runes that had surrounded the Ayda-tree and still enclosed the elf. Once the wizard read them, it would be too late to get her out.

There was one answer.

Alaric looked once more at the ruby swirling on Mallon's chest. He knew, deep inside of him, that Gustav was right. There was not enough life in the Reservoir Stone to bring back Evangeline. He wanted to grab the ruby and run. Run all the way back to Evangeline and save her, fix everything, undo all the pain and suffering and death. But the reality of it all sat heavy on his chest, crushing him with the weight of all the dark things he had done—all in vain. There was no way to save her. There never had been.

Alaric gave the ruby one last, long look before turning away. He had spent a year trying to save her, not caring if the rest of the world burned. And all this time, there wasn't enough of her left to bring back.

He couldn't save the ruby, but maybe he could keep the world from burning. If Ayda were sacrificed, Mallon would gain all the power of the elves. The solution here, the only solution, was to give Mallon a weaker sacrifice. A sacrifice that Ayda could easily best.

Milly and Brandson were still busy trying to slow Gustav using the fire powder, so Alaric called Douglon over to where he stood. "Stand near the edge, but don't cross the influence ring. I'm going to shove Ayda out. You may need to grab her and pull." The dwarf nodded and positioned himself as close to her as he could. Alaric walked back around next to Nox.

And how will you get out, Keeper?

Alaric gave Nox a tight smile. "Ayda's sacrifice would be so big that Gustav would be able to raise Mallon easily. My sacrifice will be much smaller. The sacrifice exceeds the reward."

Nox's eyes flashed. The lizard twisted his head to look at Mallon. A low growl started deep in the lizard's chest.

Gustav continued reading.

There was no time left. Alaric cast a lingering look at the ruby swirling on Mallon's chest. Then he took a deep breath and filled his mind with the desire to get Ayda out of the rune circle no matter what. He focused on that idea until there was nothing else in his mind. With a shout, he threw himself across the influence ring.

Alaric's legs slowed, as though he were running though water, but his momentum crashed him into Ayda. The two of them faltered, but she didn't fall.

Alaric felt his heart slow. The futility of his actions crashed in against him, and no matter how much he clung to the idea of getting out of the circle, the edge was too far away. He would never make it.

He stood there next to Ayda, both of them encircled by the runes. Douglon, Brandson, and Milly were shouting and waving, but Alaric could barely hear them. It didn't matter. It would all be over soon.

Gustav bent over and began reading faster.

Alaric fixed his gaze on the swirling ruby. He had never imagined that he and Evangeline would both die at the same time.

A roar shattered the haze, and a huge force slammed into Alaric's side, shoving him sideways into Ayda. The two of them tumbled away, to the other side of the circle.

Douglon grabbed for them, pulling them clear.

Nox sat inside the circle. He looked pleased, but as Alaric watched, the lizard's eyes faded and his head drooped down to the ground.

Ayda sat up and started back toward the creature, but Alaric grabbed her arm.

"We'll never get him out. If we cross the influence ring,

Gustav will control us again and all three of us will be trapped."

"But... Nox..." Ayda said, looking at the runes around him.

You were right, Alaric. This is the answer, Nox said, his thoughts coming sluggishly to them. *The wizard has his creature, a much weaker being than either of you.*

Alaric shook his head. "Nox, focus on us. Come out."

Nox looked at Alaric through his dark, reptilian eyes. *I remember.* His thoughts staggered out to Alaric, desperate and reaching. *The sacrifice exceeds the reward. I remember that emerald. I remember my name. I remember why I chose to forget it.*

Nox opened his mind and Alaric saw a boy, writhing in pain. A man held a snake and the boy's mother wept. He dropped down next to the boy and cradled his head, pouring energy into him. A green light pulled out of the boy's body, the child screamed. Then the light condensed into an emerald that dropped heavily onto the boy's chest.

Alaric pulled his mind away. "Kordan?"

CHAPTER FIFTY-ONE

"KORDAN," Alaric repeated, his mind spinning.

You were right, Kordan said, *I have made many choices I regret, but those choices do not control today. Today, I choose to be a Keeper again. I choose to stand up against something evil instead of toying with the edges of it.*

Alaric shook his head again. "This isn't the answer. The spell will kill you."

It is the only answer. The spell will claim a creature, but he needs a creature at least as great as a human to revive Mallon. I am the only one here who is not. Even if I have enough energy to revive him, the Rivor will not rise powerful. He will be a shadow of himself.

"It will kill you," Alaric said again weakly.

Kordan nodded. *I thought I had died a useless death many years ago. If my death will stop this, it will be more than I ever imagined.* He looked at Alaric intensely. *Give me this chance.*

Alaric looked at the lizard again, then nodded. "I've been searching for your Wellstone, searching for anything I could find of yours. My wife…" His voice dropped to a whisper. "You have the antidote for rock snake venom."

Kordan fixed Alaric with a long stare. *Acadanthus leaves,* the words slipped weakly into Alaric's mind. *Acadanthus leaves boiled to a strong tea.*

Alaric stared at the lizard. "Does it work?" he whispered.

Kordan nodded. He bowed his head briefly to his newfound companions before turning his head and glaring at Gustav. Gustav was looking at Kordan frantically. Every time Kordan's eyes began to sink closed, he would shake his head vigorously and growl, re-fixing his glare on the wizard.

"This still hasn't stopped him," Douglon pointed out.

"No, but Kordan is right. If Gustav can raise Mallon with just the energy that Kordan has, Mallon will be terribly weak." He glanced at Ayda.

Ayda was looking at Kordan with tears in her eyes. She looked up at Alaric, fury building again.

Alaric nodded. "Yes, get angry."

Ayda stalked around the influence ring until she stood as close as she dared to Gustav. She glared at him, her fingers flexing. The courtyard darkened and a breeze swirled through it.

The wind didn't ruffle Gustav at all.

"Your spells protect you for now, wizard," Ayda said. "But when you are done, you will no longer be safe."

Milly helped Brandson over to where Douglon stood.

"Be ready," Alaric said. "When Mallon wakes up, we need to attack. I have no idea what he'll be capable of. Gustav should be exhausted. I doubt he'll be able to do much. But focus on Mallon. There will be time to deal with Gustav afterward."

They moved closer to the edge of the influence ring, closer to Mallon's body.

"Your ruby," Milly said, looking toward where it rested on Mallon's chest.

Alaric's heart clenched. "Even if I pull it out of the spell, it won't matter. This rune links the spell to 'the stone with latent energy,' meaning the Reservoir Stone."

"Can you replace it with something else?" Milly asked.

"Yes," Alaric said with a short laugh. "If you have another stone with latent energy."

Milly's shoulders slumped. "You can't just leave it there."

Alaric looked at the swirling red light. A matching flash of red reflected off his chest. He looked down at the flame Ayda had frozen. The stone with the potential to be a flame. Alaric grabbed the necklace and yanked it off his neck. "I'd say the potential to explode into flame qualifies as latent energy."

He just needed to overcome the influence ring and reach Mallon's body. He began to fill his mind with Evangeline, with how desperately he wanted to see her again. Bracing himself, he stepped over the line and strode toward Mallon's body.

The ruby swirled weakly. Too weakly to do anything. Would he ever see her again? Despair crashed over Alaric. He couldn't bring himself to pick it up.

A flash of fiery red from Ayda's flame dangling in his hand caught his eye.

You are better suited to fire than flowers, Ayda had said. *You have that tight burning core of anger, or pain. Or guilt. It's deep, but it's bright.*

He reached inside himself, looking for the anger. He found it, a burning core of fury. Clinging to it, he tried to shake the haze of Gustav's influence, but the anger just kept leading him to despair.

He had to let go of the anger. What else had Ayda said? That the anger wasn't all of him. That the anger was only there because of the love he had. Ewan had said the same.

They were right. He was angry because Evangeline was dying. And he *loved* her. He was angry because the role of Keeper didn't feel right, but that role sat inside the deep well of knowledge that he *loved*.

There was more there than the anger. There was more there than the decision to save Evangeline, to create a ruby, and to turn his back on the Keepers.

No one is defined by a single choice, the Shield had said. *With each day, we decided anew who we are, what we will grow toward. Alaric has chosen to be a Keeper a thousand times in a thousand ways.*

A thousand times in a thousand ways. Alaric pushed away the despair. It was time to choose to be a Keeper one more time. Right now.

This time, when Alaric looked for strength to fight the influence ring, he didn't reach for his anger. He reached for the things he loved. The things that made him who he was: Evangeline, his life as a Keeper, the queen, Ewan, Ayda, Douglon, Brandson, and Milly. He found them, a solid, indestructible foundation beneath the rushing despair of Gustav's influence ring and beneath the fire of his own anger.

He anchored himself to that foundation. This moment was his to choose, and he would choose to follow his own mind, not Gustav's.

The despair receded.

Alaric reached down and picked up the ruby. He almost

dropped the flame in its place, but paused. He didn't want the flame touching Mallon, either. Instead, he set it on the altar. Then, clinging to the truth that this moment was for him to choose, he stepped back out of the influence ring.

Alaric clenched the ruby to his chest until the rough edges dug into his hand. He could still feel its warmth. Her warmth. But it was so faint compared to what it had been.

Gustav was sweating and panting. He stared at the ruby in Alaric's hand.

"Gustav," Brandson pleaded. "Don't do this."

The wizard shuddered.

Alaric walked along the outer edge of the influence ring until he stood next to Ayda, close to the wizard. "Not going how you had planned? Well, you can't stop now."

With a shaking voice, Gustav picked up reading where he had stopped and walked the last short distance until he had gone all the way around the circle of runes.

The runes suddenly glowed a vivid blue. The Wellstone burst into light and sent a rush of scalding white energy at Mallon's body. The flame from Alaric's necklace remained unchanged. There was no life inside it for the spell to take. The runes on the ground grew brighter and brighter until both Ayda and Alaric stepped farther away. Gustav sank to the ground, exhausted.

"No," Brandson said, a broken whisper.

With a sigh, Kordan's head settled to the ground. His eyes stared lifelessly across the courtyard. Alaric felt a pang of regret, and Ayda let out a small groan.

A moment later, there was a rustle from the side of the altar, and Mallon's legs stirred.

Ayda began to breathe furiously, and Alaric, after a glance at Gustav, who was lying senselessly on the ground, reached forward and rubbed his foot across the influence ring. The line rubbed off and the influence ring was broken.

"He's too exhausted to keep it up," Alaric said. Grinning, he strode across it with Ayda on his heels.

Their motion roused Gustav who cast a frightened glance at them then rushed to Mallon. The wizard shook him and started yelling for the Rivor to awaken.

With a groan, Mallon opened his black eyes and slowly turned his gaze on each of them in turn.

Douglon let out a war cry and rushed toward the Rivor, his axe raised. Mallon's eyes narrowed, and he hissed at the dwarf. Douglon went flying backward, crashing into a heap against the keep wall.

Brandson hobbled forward a step and threw his knife at Mallon. The Rivor swatted it away and with a look, knocked Brandson flat on his back.

Ayda and Alaric paused.

Mallon focused his eyes on Gustav, then flexed his hands. A smile spread across his face. He pulled himself up, leaning on the side of the bone altar.

"Well done, servant," he said, his voice cutting through the courtyard.

Gustav dropped into a fawning bow.

Ayda, who had begun to shake with fury, stepped forward. The Rivor's eyes fell on her. He studied her for a moment before his grin widened even farther.

"Very well done," Mallon murmured. "You have even brought one who holds some of my soul."

Gustav looked in surprise at Ayda. "She what? I didn't… um… I thought…"

"Shut up, wizard," Ayda said, never taking her eyes off Mallon.

"Come to me, my child," Mallon commanded. His body still leaned heavily on the altar, but his voice burned with power.

Ayda lurched forward as though on a chain. Her hands clenched into fists at her sides, but her body was dragged slowly forward.

The Rivor looked at her hungrily. "Come closer. I am still weak, but the darkness you hold will change that. The darkness you have kept for me all of these years."

Alaric looked at Ayda in fear. This was the darkness Will had warned him of. The darkness he could almost see sometimes.

"Come to me," Mallon called to her. "I will give you power even an elf cannot imagine."

Ayda cast a frightened look at Alaric. Her feet stepped forward again.

In desperation, Alaric held her eyes and opened his mind up to hers. He felt her presence in his mind as her gaze clung desperately to him. He saw her, standing in the Greenwood while the elves died around her. She was tiny and dim and alone.

Her eyes glazed over.

Alaric threw images at her. The image of her standing in Queen Saren's council, defending Alaric. The moment when Douglon had told her he would die for her, lying on the ground with an arrow in his chest. The time she had held out her hand to Alaric, willing to share the story of how her people died. Ayda chatting with Milly as they walked along a road. Any image he could think of to show her she was not alone.

Ayda's eyes refocused on Alaric, and he could see her thoughts clear. She smiled, then turned back to Mallon.

"Come!" he commanded, his voice growing harsher.

"You want your darkness back?" she asked him sweetly. "It would be my pleasure. I am *tired* of carrying it."

A flicker of uncertainty crossed the Rivor's face.

Ayda held out her hand and took a deep breath. Breathing slowly out, she formed her hand into a claw. Inside the claw, a swirl of darkness appeared surrounded by wisps of light. Tendrils of black kept slipping out, reaching between her fingers, but then the light pulled them back in. The light slowly tightened, spinning the dark into a ball of utter blackness.

Alaric could feel it pulling at him. He leaned back, pulling away from the void she was holding. A single tendril of black snaked out toward him, but just as fast, a finger of light snatched it back and trapped it in the ball.

The lights were the elves—what was left of the elves that had been trapped in Ayda.

Mallon shifted backward, his eyes widening.

Finally, Ayda looked up and smiled. "A gift from my people."

With that, she gave the ball, engulfed by light, a nonchalant toss.

It tumbled through the air and landed next to Mallon on the altar. The Rivor drew back. He reached out to touch it, but a spark from the light whipped out at his hand, and he drew it back sharply.

"Keep him near it," Ayda whispered.

Alaric gathered as much energy as he could in the space of a breath. Before Mallon could step back, Alaric reached his hand toward the Rivor. "*Alligo!*" He hissed the same spell Gustav had used to keep them rooted to the ground this morning.

Mallon froze, everything below his head locked into place. Gustav, at the very edge of the spell's range, bent over and tugged on his feet, struggling to move them. Both of them cursed and struggled against the spell.

"That won't last long," Alaric said. He could already feel fractures in the spell holding Gustav's feet.

Ayda was staring at the white lights wrapping the ball of darkness. "They need more power, more energy."

Alaric looked desperately around for something, anything. There was nothing to draw from. The courtyard was stone. There wasn't even a fire to pull energy out of. His eyes fell on the frozen flame sitting on the altar.

"Would the potential for a big fire help?" he asked, nodding toward the frozen flame sitting on the altar.

Her eyes widened and a wild grin spread across her face. She took the flame and turned back to Mallon. He was still looking uncertainly at the dark ball spinning on the altar completely enclosed in a web of light.

Ayda walked up to him and looked him squarely in the eye. She pointed to the bundle of light encasing the dark ball. "You did not destroy my people. I just want to make sure you understand that it was the elves that defeated you." She glanced over her shoulder toward Alaric and the others. "With a little help."

Then Ayda held the tiny crystal flame in her palm. She blew on it, setting it to quivering. It burst into a living flame.

Mallon's eyes widened and she smiled at him.

"Everyone knows that darkness is only dark until you throw in a little light," she said and tossed the flame at the altar. It landed on the little ball of darkness and light, spreading out and dancing over the surface.

Ayda turned and walked over to Kordan's still body. She kissed his scaled head gently then turned toward Alaric.

Alaric stared at her for a moment. Her face was bright and easy. Nothing about her sparkled or flashed, yet she looked more alive and real than he had ever seen her.

"We should go," she said, glancing at the flame that was spreading across the ball of darkness. "Quickly."

CHAPTER FIFTY-TWO

ALARIC CALLED TO DOUGLON, who was stirring against the wall. The dwarf staggered over and helped Alaric drag Brandson to his feet. The three of them stumbled back toward the keep, following Ayda and Milly.

At the door of the keep, Alaric paused and looked back. The others crowded behind him, watching breathlessly.

The blackness was spreading, now covered in orange flame. The white lights that had held it in a ball were stretching out, reaching for each other and creating a web that stretched over the darkness. Mallon strained back against Alaric's spell. He shot spell after spell at the ball, trying to destroy it, but each one was merely absorbed, swelling the size of the darkness trapped there. Gustav snapped his feet free and raced to Mallon, clutching at his arms and tugging at him, but the Rivor didn't move.

"Gustav!" Brandson yelled, "Get away from there!"

Gustav looked toward Brandson for a moment, then went back to pulling on the Rivor.

With a rush of noise like a great wind, or a blazing fire, the ball shot out into an enormous size, enveloping Mallon, Gustav, the altar, and half of the courtyard.

The orange flame, which had been stretched almost to invisibility, flared up. The web of white lights joined with it, creating a shell of brilliant white fire. Alaric shielded his eyes from the searing brightness as a wave of heat rolled over him.

There was a low trembling in the ground. The circle of darkness and flame collapsed down with a concussion like thunder. The ground shook and debris shot out from it, pelting Alaric with pebbles and spreading a thick cloud of dust.

The earth shuddered, and the nearest wall of the courtyard trembled and collapsed. Alaric and the others lurched away from the keep, shielding their heads from the stone and rubble raining down.

The ground rumbled for several more seconds, stones continuing to fall from the keep, then slowly, everything fell silent.

No one moved for a long moment, then Alaric stepped quietly through the haze toward the place where Mallon had been. A breeze stirred the cloud of dust and revealed a gaping hole in the ground where the altar had stood. It spread halfway across the courtyard and was deeper than Alaric was tall.

There was nothing inside it but rubble. No altar, no Gustav, no Kordan, no Mallon.

Ayda stepped up next to him and beamed. She drew a deep breath and flung her arms out. "It's gone!" she sang.

"What was that dark thing?" Milly asked.

"A piece of Mallon," Ayda said, "He infested me with it the day my people sacrificed themselves." She smiled impishly. "I just gave it back to him."

"Gave it back?" Douglon asked.

Ayda smirked. "Well, I gave it back surrounded by a web of my people."

"Your people?" Milly asked faintly.

"What was left of them," Ayda answered. "They were very angry. And then we added some fire." Her smile widened to a grin. "Turns out that's a destructive combination."

"Turns out?" Alaric asked. "You didn't know?"

"I didn't know for sure, but I had a suspicion. You could say that I understood the concept of what would happen."

"However you did it, it was well done." Douglon motioned to the crater. Then he grimaced and pulled his arm back protectively to his chest.

Ayda looked at him in exasperation. "I only left you alone for one night." She walked up to the dwarf and grabbed his arm.

Douglon grunted but didn't pull his arm away. "I don't need you to fix it," he grumbled. "It'll be fine."

Ayda touched the wound gently. Douglon let out a sigh of relief and Ayda patted his cheek sweetly. "Now stop getting hurt."

"The lights around the darkness," Milly said, still looking puzzled at the great hole in the ground, "were they...?"

Ayda sobered. "The elves have held the darkness in check for eight years. They continued to hold it until the flames destroyed the darkness."

"And destroyed them?" Alaric asked.

"And them."

Alaric looked at the pit, a surge of loss rolling through him. So many elves destroyed. Not that they had exactly been alive before, but the price of killing Mallon had been a heavy one. Next to him, he caught sight of Ayda's face, blazing with pride.

"It's all they wanted," she said. "To destroy him. They've waited for too long."

She breathed deeply again and laughed. Seeing Alaric's sober face, she leaned over and kissed him on the cheek. "Don't be so serious, Alaric. This is a good day. The best day in a very long time. We've won. And the only losses on our side today were those who went willingly."

Alaric looked cautiously at Ayda. "So are all the elves… gone?"

Ayda wrinkled her nose. "No, not all of them. Just some." Then she cocked her head slightly. "The ones that are left do seem a little more withdrawn than usual, though."

"Perhaps they can be, now that they don't have to hold the darkness back."

Ayda nodded. "Perhaps. They are small and tired now." She sighed. "And I suppose they will be bored for the rest of my life."

Alaric smiled. "Maybe we can find some other great force of evil to fight."

Brandson groaned quietly, and Ayda looked at him, noticing for the first time that he was slumped against the wall.

She walked quickly to Brandson and knelt down next to him.

"Can you fix it?" Milly asked, her voice breaking a little.

Ayda sat back on her heels and looked helplessly at Milly. "I'm sorry. It's animal poison. I can heal wounds. That's just putting things back together. But poison—poison spreads and… and things aren't broken, they're changed. I don't know how to change them back."

Brandson groaned.

Alaric walked up to Brandson and knelt across from Ayda. He gently lifted the pants Milly had cut open out of the way so that he could see the wound more clearly. There were streaks of dark red climbing up his leg and the flesh was hot.

"We need to get him some medicine," Alaric said. "Let's get him to his horse."

"What are we going to do?" Douglon demanded. "Find some sort of poison doctor out here in the middle of nowhere?"

Alaric grimaced. "You already have."

They all looked at him blankly.

"Evangeline was poisoned. What do you think I've been studying this whole time?"

"And you have antidotes stashed nearby?" Douglon asked.

Alaric sighed. "Let's get Brandson to his horse. It should take less than a day to get to my castle."

"You have a castle?" Milly asked.

Alaric smiled weakly. "Well, no one else has claimed it for over a hundred years, so yes. I have a castle."

They just kept looking at him.

"And Evangeline is there. And all of my research on poisons."

Then Brandson moaned and the group jumped into

action. Alaric and Milly each ducked under one of Brandson's arms, helping him walk. Douglon led the way back through the keep, shoving any large debris out of their way. They reached the room with the horses and Brandson sank into a chair.

Alaric led Beast to the doorway and cast out to see if any monsters were nearby. The explosion must have scared them off, because there were no large life forms down in the valley. Everything he felt was far off on the hills.

"The valley is relatively safe, for now. We should hurry."

Alaric and Douglon helped Brandson claw his way up onto his horse. Douglon mounted his horse next to him and tugged and pushed the smith into a better position on his saddle.

"Sorry," Douglon muttered gruffly, his eyes showing far more concern than his voice.

"Here," Alaric said, moving next to Brandson. "Someone will need to ride next to him to make sure he doesn't fall, but I think I can help him a little."

Closing his eyes, Alaric took a deep breath and recalled spells he hadn't tried in a year.

He found the one that he'd first tried on Evangeline. The one meant to slow the spread of the poison. It sat in his mind discarded where he had thrown it when he was furious that it couldn't work well enough.

Taking a deep breath, he set his hand on Brandson's leg and whispered the words he couldn't quite bring himself to say out loud.

When he opened his eyes, everyone was looking expectantly at him. Brandson moaned again.

"I don't think it worked," Douglon said.

Alaric ignored him and closed his eyes again. It had

worked. He could feel it. He could feel the energy stopping the spread of the poison, blocking it at the edges. He felt the smallest bit of poison slip through his net and knew that Brandson's time was still limited. But now, he might have the time he needed.

Then Alaric reached up and held his hand toward Brandson's face. "*Dormio,*" he told the blacksmith, and Brandson's head slowly slumped down on his chest, his brow relaxing and his breath calming.

Milly, eyes wide in alarm, rushed up to him.

"He's fine," Alaric assured her.

"He's not fine," Ayda pointed out.

Alaric glared at her again. "He can't feel the poison. And I slowed the spread of it, too. We should have several days before..."

Milly nodded tersely.

"Then what are we waiting for?" Douglon demanded.

The group headed out of the valley with Milly riding behind Brandson, helping to keep him seated. Douglon rode alongside, ready to help if needed.

Alaric led them south, back out of the valley and along the same trail they had taken to get there. That night, when they set up camp, the exhaustion of the last few days settled heavily on him. He could sense Kollman Pass getting closer. For Brandson's sake, he wanted to rush, but his own desire to get back there was steeped in reluctance.

The ruby hung around his neck again, its weight familiar but no longer comforting against his chest. He now had the antidote for the rock snake venom, but it didn't matter. If the energy in her ruby wasn't enough to bring her back, what good was an antidote? The swirls of red light felt fragile and delicate.

He was never going to be with her. This would be the end. He would heal Brandson and send them all on their way. And then? Then the only question was whether he would wake her to say goodbye or just let her slip painlessly away.

CHAPTER FIFTY-THREE

THEY ROSE EARLY the next morning, trying to reach the castle by evening. As they saddled the horses, Alaric looked at Ayda. "You never told us how Gustav managed to trap you as a tree."

"I was stupid," she answered. She glanced at Douglon with a rueful smile. "I wasn't paying attention."

"That's surprising," the dwarf answered.

"I had reached the courtyard and could see that the wizard was planning something, because there were some runes scratched into the ground, but I couldn't see him anywhere. It was still dark and as I wondered what to do, four creatures came slinking toward me from all directions."

"And let me guess," Douglon said, "you didn't want to kill them, so you turned yourself into a tree."

Ayda looked guiltily at him for a moment, then giggled. "That's exactly what happened." Her face sobered. "They were so sad. They were so lonely and twisted, and they were only attacking because they were commanded to. I didn't know where the wizard was, but they hated him. They hated the keep, and they hated themselves. The only thing they didn't hate was me." She paused. "But they couldn't stop."

She took a deep breath. "So I couldn't kill them. And I couldn't free them fast enough. I would have needed to touch each one, and I didn't have that much time. But they all were supposed to attack an elf. So I figured that if I were a tree, maybe they would be able to give up. And they did." She shrugged. "It seemed like a good idea until the wizard stepped out of the shadows."

"She just loses the big picture," Douglon explained to the rest of them. "It's not that she makes bad decisions, she's just never paying attention to the big picture."

"And how were you expecting to get back to your own shape?" Alaric asked her.

"I didn't see another choice," she answered. "But I did know you all were close by. You wouldn't have left me as a tree, Alaric."

They pressed on, hoping to reach Kollman Pass in the early afternoon. Alaric spent the day focused on Brandson, contemplating which herbs he would use to fight the poison. He concentrated on the fact that he would need to notify the queen of what had happened. And that he'd need to send Douglon to the dwarves as soon as he would consent to leave, which wouldn't happen until Brandson was healed. Which led him back to his consideration of the antidotes.

What his mind refused to land on was her. The image of Evangeline lying in the crystal filled his mind, but he refused to look at it. Every other time he had envisioned her, he had been driven by hope, driven by ideas of how to heal her. But now…

The sun was lowering toward the horizon when they

finally reached the road that led to his castle. They turned a corner in the broken old path and there it sat.

It was small and grey. It had three turrets that rose to different heights and was surrounded by a storybook wall. There was even a drawbridge and a moat. Milly gasped and Ayda clapped in delight at the old castle glowing in the afternoon light.

When they entered, Alaric led them to the tower that held the bedrooms. He told them to choose whichever they liked. They lay Brandson on a luxurious bed in one of the higher rooms.

Alaric saw Brandson safely to the bed and renewed his spell to help him sleep. Then he asked Milly to get some water from the kitchen and headed toward his workroom.

He walked up the stairs, his steps getting heavier as he approached the carved door on his left. He paused beside it for a moment, raising his hand to touch it. But instead, he let his hand drop and continued up the stairs at a brisker pace.

He pushed open the next door on the right and entered his workroom. When the smell hit him, he took a deep breath. It smelled like herbs and dust and medicine. And even though everything in there was meant to stop poison, to restore life, he couldn't hold back the thought that the room smelled like death.

It was lined with tables and bookshelves. He lit a lantern that hung from the center of the ceiling and banished the dark thoughts from his mind. Moving from shelf to table to shelf, he collected things quickly, setting them onto a small tray. When he slipped one round nut into his pocket to keep it from rolling around the tray, it dropped to the floor. Alaric looked down at his robe. It was torn and filthy, the pocket ripped straight across the bottom. He shrugged out of it and tossed it into a corner. The cold of the castle stones seeped into him.

Next to the door hung a black Keeper's robe. It was clean and it was warm. Alaric reached out tentatively and lifted it off the hook. He slid his arms in, and the robe draped over his shoulders like a blanket, wrapping around him and welcoming him home.

He picked up the nut, put it in one of the many pockets of this robe and headed back to Brandson's room, closing the door of the workroom firmly behind him. He passed the carved door again without pausing.

In Brandson's room, Alaric sat quietly at a table, measuring and mixing while the others stood awkwardly around Brandson's bed, sometimes looking at their sick friend, sometimes letting their eyes roam around the room.

There wasn't much in it, but the furniture that was there was carved of rich wood. The bed was covered in thick blankets and fluffy pillows. There were dark red drapes that hung at the balcony. Someone had started a fire in the fireplace and set a kettle above it.

Ayda walked over to the balcony and looked out.

"This place is beautiful," she said.

Alaric grunted, measuring out exactly fourteen simbo seeds.

She opened her mouth as though to say something else, but after glancing at Alaric, fell silent.

When he was finished mixing, Alaric used Milly's water to make a thick paste, then brought it over to Brandson. Gently, he cleaned the wound out again. He smoothed the paste over the wound and bound it with a fresh bandage. Then he gave Milly some leaves and asked her to brew Brandson some strong tea from them.

With all those tasks done, Alaric sank back onto the chair at the table and watched Milly coax the tea down Brandson's throat.

"That's all I can do," he said quietly. "I think the antidote will help, but we won't know until at least tomorrow morning. Every four hours, he should drink another cup of tea.

"How do you know what antidote to use?" Milly asked from her seat next to Brandson, holding his hand again. "Don't you need to know what he was poisoned with?"

"Sometimes, that matters," Alaric said, "but there are combinations of herbs that are good at fighting a broad range of poisons. I gave him the strongest blend I know of for animal poison." Alaric sighed and looked down at his hands as he cleaned the paste off of them. "I spent many months researching antidotes for animal poisons, specifically against the rock snake. So I am now quite familiar with the antidotes to most of them. There are very few that don't have a known antidote, and most of those are reptiles."

Ayda turned and looked directly at Alaric.

"May I see her?" she asked.

Alaric's heart clenched. When he didn't answer, Ayda took a step toward him, her eyes kind.

"She is your wife, Alaric. May we meet her?"

At the word wife, Alaric flinched. He looked around the room at the others. They stood looking hopeful and uncomfortable. Their faces were so familiar that suddenly, he wanted them to meet her.

He stood slowly and walked out into the hallway, turning up the stairs. He heard the others following after him. This time, when he reached the carved door he raised his hand and pushed.

A wave of fresh air hit him. The doors to the balcony

were open and the room was flooded with evening light. There were pots of flowers in the corner with blooms growing cheerfully, Alaric's painstakingly created spells keeping them in a state of perpetual summer. Two small trees grew in blue pots on the balcony, just outside the doors. The drapes on the balcony rustled free of dust. The floor was smooth, clean stone.

And in the middle of the room, up on an intricately carved table, lay Evangeline, encased in a thin layer of crystal. Alaric walked up to her, his gaze still heavily on the floor. He walked up to her side, only able to focus on her hand.

It looked smooth and soft as it lay perfectly still. He set his hand against the crystal and his heart almost stopped.

By contrast to his own, her fingertips, halfway up each finger, were blue.

The group behind him filed in. Douglon held back by the wall while Ayda and Milly approached the crystal.

"She's beautiful," Milly said.

Alaric stared at her fingertips.

Ayda set a hand on the top of the crystal, above Evangeline's face. She closed her eyes and stood perfectly still.

"Nice to meet you, Evangeline," she said softly.

Alaric lifted his eyes to Evangeline's face, serene, free of worry.

"Is the crystal what's keeping her alive?" Milly asked quietly.

Alaric nodded. "Partially. The crystal is keeping her body from aging, or at least making it age very slowly." His gaze dropped to thin, small runes that were marked with ink on her neck. "And there are spells that are protecting her body, giving it strength."

The room fell silent. Alaric sank into a chair next to Evangeline and dropped his head into his hands. With quiet rustling, he heard the others leave.

The room was silent for a long time. There was a noise by the door, and Alaric looked up to see Douglon still standing in the back of the room. He had lowered his axe to the ground before him and bowed his head in the dwarfs' posture of mourning.

At Alaric's movement, Douglon looked up. Then he nodded to Alaric, picked up his axe, and left the Keeper in peace.

Alaric was a little surprised to realize that he was glad they were all here. They brought a warmth and life to the castle that had been missing for too long. Alaric sighed and leaned his forehead on the crystal.

His eyes caught on her blue fingers again and his heart lurched. He pulled a small pouch out of one of his pockets. Acadanthus leaves. He'd had them in his workroom all along. Acadanthus vines grew on holly trees, wound so tightly into the tree that it was all but impossible to pick holly leaves or berries without also getting acadanthus leaves. So he had sorted them into their own bag and tossed them on a shelf. He'd never heard of them having any sort of medicinal use. He took out some leaves and dropped them into a kettle hung over the fire.

It doesn't matter, his brain told him. *Providing the antidote to the poison does nothing but heal this husk of a body. You still won't be able to get her back.*

He pulled the boiling kettle off the fire to let the leaves sit until he could smell the acadanthus tea. He stood before his wife, running his hand over the thin layer of clear crystal that encased her.

It won't work, his mind whispered. But he had to know. Somehow, he had to know if it could have worked. All of the other poisons were taken care of. It was just the venom left.

Was it wrong to keep trying things when nothing would truly heal her?

The smell of the acadanthus leaves filled the room.

He had to know.

Alaric took a deep, shuddering breath. He closed his eyes and laid his hands on the crystal right above her heart. He reached out to feel the energy there, the ponderous essence of the crystal that he had placed around her, through her.

Alaric focused on the structure of the crystal where it touched her body. "*Amoveo.*"

The crystal vanished.

CHAPTER FIFTY-FOUR

Evangeline lay still, but her chest began to rise with shallow breaths and a weak, slow pulse was visible in her neck.

Alaric poured the acadanthus tea into a cup. Using a small medicine dropper, he dripped the tea into her mouth, watching her neck for signs that she was swallowing. After he'd fed her half the cup, he dredged the leaves from the kettle and mashed them into a paste. He lifted her dress up to just above her knee where the swollen, black wound gaped. Purplish red streaks wound up her leg. He began to gently clean and drain the wound, focusing his mind completely on the task, working at it until it was as clean as he could get it. He packed the wound with the paste of acadanthus leaves and wrapped her leg with clean bandages. Then he resumed his seat next to her and filled the dropper again with tea.

The next morning, Alaric awoke stiff. He had fallen asleep in a cot near Evangeline. It was his bed whenever he was at the castle. The morning sunlight was behind the mountains, and Evangeline's room was still dim. He lit a candle and brought it close to her.

She still slept. He set his hand on her forehead and drew in a sharp breath. It was cooler. Not completely back to normal, but her fever was definitely lower. He set the candle down and unwrapped her leg. Underneath, the lines reaching up her leg had faded to a dull red and the swelling was almost gone.

It was working.

He put some more acadanthus leaves in the kettle, his stomach in knots. It was working.

He pulled the ruby out of the pouch at his neck and laid it on the pillow near her head. The Reservoir Stone did not hold enough life to wake her up. Seeing her here, seeing how little of her was left, he knew Gustav had been right.

He dropped his forehead down on the edge of Evangeline's pillow. Healing her would take the sacrifice of something healthy, something strong. But maybe that price could be paid, somehow. Maybe…

He lay there for hours until Milly came to let him know there was lunch in Brandson's room. He stood and stretched, dragging his mind back to the present.

Alaric was pleased to see the smith sitting up and talking with the others. His leg looked better and his fever was gone. Brandson smiled gratefully at Alaric and thanked him. The group chatted with each other while they ate the cold sausage from last night's dinner. Alaric found himself staring out the window.

Finally, he excused himself and went back to Evangeline's room.

He pulled his chair close to the table and sank into it, taking her hand.

It was time. With the crystal gone, he imagined that the blue had moved infinitesimally farther up her fingers. He cast out to feel the *vitalle* in her body. It was so weak and thin that he could barely sense it. Next to her head, the *vitalle* in the ruby was similarly thin. There was no way that energy would be enough to fill her whole body.

There was no point to this waiting, this lingering. There were only two choices. One was to let her die, the other to sacrifice someone else to save her…

She'd hate him for it, but it might give her a chance.

"Forget what you are planning, Keeper," Ayda said softly.

Alaric whipped his head toward her. She stood just inside the door, watching him with large, troubled eyes.

Alaric looked at the elf with narrow eyes. "I told you to stay out of my head," he said flatly.

Ayda gave a short laugh. "I don't need to read your mind to know what you are thinking." Then she walked over to the other side of Evangeline. "Your sacrifice would be more than useless. It would be cruel."

Alaric glared at Ayda, saying nothing.

Ayda held his gaze. "There is too much death in her, Alaric," she said gently. "All of the life inside of you will not wipe it out. Your death would bring her back barely, but only to be trapped in a broken body. She would revive to find herself in pain and you dead beside her. Then she would still die herself."

Alaric dropped his head into his hands, his fingers digging into his skull.

"There are worse things than death," Ayda whispered.

Alaric looked up at her. Ayda's face was strangely taut. She looked at him sadly.

"Alaric, there is only one thing left for you to do."

"I can't even say goodbye." His voice sounded like someone else's, as though the words tore themselves out of him. "If I wake her, she'll be in so much pain."

The room was silent for a long time.

Ayda moved first. She went to one of the pots of flowers and snapped off a few blossoms, then she stepped out onto the balcony, walked to the potted trees and set the flowers near the base of each trunk. With a whisper, the blooms began sending out tendrils, winding their way up the trunks with thin green vines, sprouting out tiny buds every few inches until the trees looked like they were about to burst into bloom.

She touched a few buds on each tree, and the breeze brought in a soft smell of spring. Ayda stood looking out, with her back to the room. Finally, she nodded and turned to Alaric.

"I can help," Ayda said. "We can help," she gestured to herself. "I can make it so she doesn't feel much pain." Then she looked at him intently, clarifying. "I can't take all the pain away, but whatever she feels should be mild, compared to…"

Alaric looked at her, a faint flicker of hope igniting.

"You could remove the healing spells and wake her," Ayda continued. "All these spells have served their purpose. They gave you the time you needed to look for the antidote. But they serve no purpose now."

No purpose. The words rang dully in Alaric's head. But there was a way. Gustav had done it, Kordan had. The flicker of hope turned to fury. Why did he not have enough life? Where could he find more?

You cannot find more. What would you do? Sacrifice us all? Ayda asked, her voice speaking quietly in his mind.

Alaric's head whipped up and he glared at her. He shoved at her presence in his mind, pushing her away, but she stood firm. Standing just on the edge of his mind. Not invading him, but not leaving, either.

This is not what you want.

The words rang in his mind, echoing the Shield's words. *This is not what you want.*

But he did. He wanted it more than anything.

"No," Ayda spoke firmly out loud. "You do not.... and neither does she."

Alaric's eyes tightened. "How would you know what she wants?" he growled.

Ayda looked down at Evangeline, warring emotions crossing her face. Then she looked back up at Alaric her expression wretched. Reluctantly, she spoke.

"Because she's not really asleep."

CHAPTER FIFTY-FIVE

ALARIC'S BLOOD FROZE. Evangeline wasn't asleep?

Ayda continued softly. "I can feel her mind. She's not really awake, and she can't move, but she's not sleeping, either. She knows she's been alone and she knows that now you are back."

Alaric shrank back in his chair. He looked at Evangeline's face, smooth and peaceful. She knew she'd been alone? His hands began to shake. He had left her alone for so very, very long. "Is she in pain?" he whispered.

Ayda was silent for a long moment. "Not in terrible pain."

The breath rushed out of Alaric as guilt clenched inside of him. He had left her here alone and in pain.

"She's happy you are here and she wants to see you," Ayda said. "And then she wants to rest."

Alaric slipped forward out of the chair and reached for her with trembling hands. "I'm so sorry." He leaned his head against her forehead and felt the decision click into place. He couldn't sacrifice himself for her. She would still die. He couldn't sacrifice others for her. No matter what Kordan or Gustav thought, that wasn't something you could calculate, the worth of one person versus another.

The Keepers had been right. This power to pull the life out of someone was not used for a reason. Not because of some antiquated rule, just because the shifting about of people's lives couldn't be done with a clear conscience. It couldn't be done well.

Alaric was tired of not doing things well.

He was tired of feeling angry toward the world, toward the Keepers. Tired of distancing himself from a way of life that he had loved and respected. Tired of living in a desperate world of questionable actions. Tired of fighting against the truth that there were some sicknesses that couldn't be healed.

He wanted the truth back.

And the truth was she was awake and she was dying.

This had gone on far too long.

He nodded at Ayda. "How long can you keep her from feeling the pain?"

Ayda looked at him for a long moment. "For as long as she needs it."

Alaric felt tears start to fill his eyes and he nodded. "Thank you." His gaze dropped back down to Evangeline's fingertips. "It won't be long."

Ayda nodded and picked up Evangeline's hand.

Alaric looked at the ruby. The red light swirled slowly through the stone and it pulsed, slightly warm in his hand. Every breath or two, a swirl of darkness touched one of the irregular surfaces.

He leaned and focused on the thin lines that he could just

see on her neck. He began to read them quietly. The runes at her neck glowed a dim blue.

The first words were rough, but as he continued, focusing all of his attention on the thin runes, his voice strengthened and the glow on the tiny lines began to fade.

He narrowed his focus, just concentrating on each line in her skin. He spoke until it faded, releasing the power held there, then he moved on to the next. One by one, moving slowly along the faint path, releasing branches that snaked off, releasing the ones that protected her heart, releasing the ones protecting her mind, releasing the lines that protected her life.

Energy trickled out of his hand, so little needed to end what had cost him so much energy to build.

When the last line faded, he stopped. Nothing had changed. The ruby still swirled slowly. Evangeline lay still, but now he could feel her body living.

Alaric set the ruby on her stomach. Reaching toward the ruby, feeling the energy that spun through it, he began the process of pulling it out and letting it fall back into Evangeline's body.

It happened more quickly than he expected, the amount of *vitalle* in the ruby was so much less than it had originally been. In the span of a few breaths, the ruby sat dark and cold. He moved it off to the side, then set his hand on Evangeline's forehead.

"Excita," he said gently, feeling the rush of energy flow out of his palm.

Evangeline gasped a weak, shallow breath. Her body twitched and her brow drew down in pain.

Alaric heard a strangled noise and realized it was his own breath. He grabbed for her hand and leaned over her.

Her fingers were ice cold. Evangeline's body began to thrash, her head tossing from side to side, her back arching.

Alaric remembered. He remembered the pain she had endured. He remembered how inadequate his skills had been to give her comfort. He remembered knowing she was going to die. And he remembered the terror of that idea.

Then Evangeline's body relaxed. She breathed heavily, for a few breaths, but even that began to calm. Alaric looked at Ayda. She was using both hands to hold onto Evangeline's. The elf's eyes were shut, her brow drawn slightly.

A small sigh escaped Evangeline's mouth, and Alaric whipped his attention back to her.

Her eyes were open and looking at him.

He felt his breath catch in his throat and he leaned close to her.

"I've missed you," she whispered.

Alaric reached out and brushed her hair back from her face, bringing his forehead down on hers. She closed her eyes and smiled.

Alaric pulled back, unable to take his eyes off her, but unable to speak. He wanted to apologize, to tell her how much he loved her, but he could barely breathe. He just gripped her hand and stared at her face. She looked so peaceful, so normal. Her cheeks had regained some color and her eyes were bright.

Evangeline looked at Ayda, and Alaric opened his mouth, but no words came out.

Ayda, whose face was pale and drawn, gave a little snort. "I'm Ayda," she said. "I've been traveling with your husband for a bit. Fighting dragons, saving the world, things like that."

Evangeline gave a weak smile. "That's the sort of thing

he does." She looked down at her hand encased in the elf's small hands. "You're pulling the pain back, aren't you?"

Ayda gave her a tight, tired smile.

"Thank you," Evangeline whispered.

Alaric stared at her for a moment. She looked so healthy. He hadn't seen her look so healthy in… so very long. He barely remembered that her skin was always a little golden. It had been pale and waxy for so long.

"Evangeline," Alaric said, his voice barely audible, "we don't have much time." His hands gripped her so hard that he had begun to drive away some of the coldness. "I'm so very, very sorry. I couldn't…" He found himself floundering. "I found the antidote. But it's not enough. I'm so sorry." He reached for her face. "I've missed you every second."

"And I you," she said, her voice growing a little stronger. She looked at him with those clear eyes and smiled. "It wasn't your job to stop death, Alaric. Even great Keepers can't do that."

"They should be able to," he whispered.

"I'm glad I met you, Alaric," she said softly. "And I'm glad you will soon be free of"—she looked down at herself—"of this burden. You should have more of a life than this."

"He saved the world just yesterday," Ayda said. "Fought a great wizard and defeated Mallon."

Evangeline raised one eyebrow. "Not to take away from your victory, but wasn't Mallon already dead?"

"Mostly," Alaric said, smiling slightly.

"Well," Evangeline said, "it's been a long time since you've done Keeper things. You should ease back into it. Maybe you can work your way up to fighting someone who is fully alive."

Evangeline's eyebrows drew down suddenly, and she looked over at the hand Ayda was holding.

"Whatever you're doing," she said to the elf, "it's working. I feel... wonderful."

Ayda smiled again, but her face was pale.

A noise near the door caught Alaric's attention. Brandson and Douglon were standing against the wall, looking as though they would like to sink into it. Milly had tears in her eyes.

Evangeline glanced at Alaric. "I think I could sit up."

Alaric looked at her in surprise and noticed a strong pulse in her neck. He pulled up her hand and saw fingertips pink and healthy. Evangeline lifted her head, and Alaric quickly reached an arm behind her to help her sit.

Suddenly, there was a strangled yell and Douglon threw himself across the room.

The dwarf reached Ayda just as she toppled to the floor.

CHAPTER FIFTY-SIX

EVANGELINE TOOK a deep breath and stretched her hands. They looked healthy and strong. Alaric reached down quickly to see where the arrow had pierced her. Instead of the scabbed, swollen, black thigh he had seen for the past year, he saw smooth, clean skin with a small scar sitting right above the knee.

"Ayda!" he breathed, turning toward the elf. "How?"

Ayda lay in Douglon's arms, her face white, barely breathing.

"What have you done?" Alaric demanded.

Ayda smiled weakly.

Douglon's arms gripped her tighter. "You stupid elf," he whispered. "You stupid, stupid, stupid elf."

Evangeline was sitting steadily so Alaric pulled his arm away from her and knelt next to Ayda.

"It turns out," Ayda said, "that there is someone who had enough life in her to heal your wife."

He reached out and took Ayda's hand, which was ice cold. Her fingers were snowy white.

"Oh, Ayda," he says quietly, "you didn't."

She smiled weakly at him. "You were willing to sacrifice yourself. Is it so strange that I should do the same? You know, sometimes people break away from wallowing in their pasts long enough to commit to something."

"But… you're the last elf."

"What better reason is there?"

"You sacrificed all your people, too?"

"My people agreed to die eight years ago. Their lives have not been their own since. I have needed them for many things. I needed them to hold back the darkness. I needed them to take that darkness and destroy Mallon. And now I needed them to heal Evangeline."

"But…"

"I told you I wanted to sleep," she said quietly.

A sob tore out of Douglon, and Ayda looked up at him. She reached up and lifted his chin a bit so that she could see his face. There were tears streaming down his cheeks. His eyes bored into the elf, and now it was Alaric who felt suddenly intrusive. But he didn't want to move and break the moment.

"You stupid elf," Douglon said.

"You can stop looking at me like that, Douglon. It's just a charm," Ayda said. "Just a charm to burn off some of this power."

She looked around the room again, her brow puckered slightly with guilt. "I had too much power. It kept leaking out." A short giggle escaped her, sounding bitter. "I kept dropping little flames without knowing it. I was afraid I was going to burn down the world."

She looked back at Douglon and continued, an edge of self-loathing in her voice, "So I created a charm that worked constantly. A small, steady stream of power that would trickle out in the hopes that the destructive things would stop. Now animals like me, trees talk to me constantly, and even dwarves can set aside their disgust for us a bit.

"So you can stop looking like that Douglon. What you're feeling is just the charm. When I'm gone, the feelings will be, too."

Douglon had looked at her steadily the whole time she had been speaking, not moving. Alaric searched his face for some sign of his thoughts, but the dwarf just stared at Ayda with that burning intensity that made Alaric feel intrusive again.

"It's not a charm," Douglon said finally. His words were so quiet that Alaric found himself leaning forward. "I know about the charm. Everyone knows about the charm."

Ayda turned her head quickly around the room. Brandson nodded slightly. Milly shrugged and looked apologetic. When Ayda turned toward Alaric, he smiled slightly.

"Well," she said petulantly, "just knowing about it doesn't keep it from working."

"It's not working now." Douglon had not looked away from her face.

Ayda's eyes snapped back to him.

"It hasn't worked since you destroyed Mallon."

Alaric shifted slightly. That could be true. Ayda had been much less sparkly since then.

"The charm wanted me to think your eyes were darker and your hair glittered more than it does." He ran one dark hand across the golden curl that spilled over her shoulder. "And that you were taller than you really are."

She let out a small laugh. "I'm short, you know. For an elf."

Douglon let a small smile curl up the corner of his mouth. "Dwarves aren't particularly attracted to height," he pointed out. "It only works when you are around. I never think of you as tall when you are too far away."

"See?" she said, reaching her hand up tentatively to touch his beard.

Douglon stared at her a long moment. "The charm would make me want you to stay because I would think the room a gloomier place once you leave. But what do you think it is that makes me know now that the room really will be gloomy with you gone?"

Douglon reached up and pressed her hand against his cheek. Ayda's eyes widened slightly.

"What do you think it is that helps me to know that I love the real color of your hair, not that awful glittery nonsense you try to make me *think* you have?"

Alaric barely dared to breath for fear of interrupting. Out of the corner of his eye, he saw Milly reach over and hold Brandson's hand.

"What makes me wonder whether I'll ever return home again? Whether it wouldn't be better just to travel with you?"

Ayda was looking up at him, her eyes wide, her hand still pressed against his cheek. Alaric could almost see her slip into Douglon's mind. The dwarf sat perfectly still.

After a long moment, Ayda drew in a long breath. "I'm sorry," she whispered. "I didn't know."

Douglon shrugged, but his eyes burned into her. "That's because you are never paying attention."

Ayda reached up behind him, reaching for his axe blade. "It was selfish of Patlon's elf to choose purple. She thought only of herself. You, Douglon, should have red," she said to him, reaching her hand out to touch the handle of his axe. From the tip of her finger, tendrils of red fire spread along the axe handle, freezing to look like real flames.

"There you are," she said sweetly, sinking a little lower against him. "Now it's an unbreakable axe."

Douglon looked back at his axe handle, then cupped Ayda's face gently in his hand. She met his gaze and something passed between them.

She looked around the room, finding Brandson, Milly, and even Evangeline's eyes.

Finally, Ayda turned to Alaric and he felt her mind. He drew back slightly when he felt how weak it was. It was just an elven mind, a plain, weakened, elven mind.

Alaric sat very still, his mind probing hers slightly. Her mind was so very small, its power almost depleted. He found himself casting around for something to do, some way to give her more power, some strength.

Stop it, her voice snapped through his mind. *I have made my choice. My people are finally gone. It took them all, in the end, to replace all of the death that was in Evangeline. They were so much weaker than they had once been. Stop feeling sorry for them. There was never going to be a different ending.*

Alaric shook his head, but she continued.

Thank you. All I wanted, all we wanted, was to destroy Mallon. And I would have failed without you. Healing Evangeline is my thank you.

Alaric felt her mind waver, then it slipped back out of his mind, leaving him feeling empty.

Ayda smiled weakly at him, then sank back into Douglon's arms. Her head drooped forward, and a curtain of golden hair fell across it.

Douglon let out a shuddering sob and pulled her close, but she did not move again.

CHAPTER FIFTY-SEVEN

THE SUN SAT low over the mountains, the sky stretched out overhead in a clear blue that felt serene, but empty. Alaric stood with his arm around Evangeline on the balcony of the room he had always intended to share with her, near the top of the tower. He listened to her speak, but her words were interrupted by the thrumming of her heart and the sound of her breathing. He cast out wave after wave just to sense the blazing core of energy inside of her. Beneath his arm, she leaned against him, warm and secure, not quite strong enough to stand on her own. But she was alive. Her face was bright and animated and so very alive.

"You're doing it again," she said, her smile teasing.

Alaric blinked and laughed. "Sorry. I have no idea what you just said." He pulled her around and kissed her. She wrapped her arms around his neck, kissing him back. "It's just that your alive-ness is so distracting."

"Alive-ness? Is that a technical Keeper term?"

"Yes. Don't be intimidated by my sophistication."

She looked at him curiously. "Are you still a Keeper?"

Alaric dropped his forehead down to hers. It had taken some getting used to, learning that she hadn't really been asleep all that time. He had been terrified that she'd be angry, but when they'd had their first moments alone, she had just stretched her hands out, flexing her fingers and then touching his face. "I'm too happy to be mad," she'd said. "I know what you did and why. Besides, it wouldn't be entirely fair if I'd just gotten to sleep while you were spending all that time tortured." But she had smiled when she said it, and just like that, the issue was dismissed, dropped back into the realm of things in the past that are over now.

She knew all the things he had spoken to her during her long sickness. All the confessions of failure, all the fury at the Keepers for not helping him, all the anger, all the desperation. All the times he had sworn he was done being a Keeper.

"I'm not sure I'm the same Keeper I used to be, but… yes, I still am one. I have some ideas about how things need to change at the Stronghold, but I think there's a chance it can all work out reasonably well. How do you feel about spending some time at court?"

Her eyebrows rose. "Well, I'm fancy enough for it." She gave a little curtsey in her old traveling dress and bare feet, holding onto his arm to steady herself.

He smiled. "It's busy there and there are some horrific people, but I think you'll like Saren. And Ewan is there.

"At some point, I need to go see if I can figure out what happened to Will. When he left the palace, he was headed to the Roven Sweep to look into something with the nomads. But he should have been back a long time ago."

"As long as we don't volunteer for any fire lizard hunts on the way," she said, "I'm willing."

Alaric rested his chin on her head. There were too many emotions swirling inside him to pick just one. Evangeline was right here, standing, talking, breathing. But in a room below them, Ayda lay still and cold.

He let his mind stop spinning. He breathed in the scent of Evangeline's skin. He felt the cool breeze and the cooler stones of the balcony. He listened to the quiet rustling of the world.

In the midst of all the emotions, he felt a small green shoot of peace begin to grow. It was a peace tinged with sorrow and loss, but it was rooted in a profound rightness.

Ayda was laid out peacefully on Evangeline's table.

Alaric and Douglon had moved it to the balcony, and placed one tree on each side of her, their blooms just waiting to burst open.

Douglon stood stationed at her feet.

Alaric stepped up to Ayda's side, his arm still around Evangeline.

Milly straightened Ayda's dress and touched the ring of purple flowers that encircled her waist.

"These flowers are still alive!" she said, looking closely at one tiny daisy-like bloom. "How long has she worn this?"

Brandson stepped forward, his eyes red. His brow drew a bit and he said, "I think always."

"She was wearing it the day we met her," Douglon said.

"They're beginning to fade a bit at the edges," Milly said.

The very edge of each petal was curling. Alaric looked at Douglon, and the dwarf nodded.

Alaric traced some runes in the air above Ayda's body, letting the slow energy pour out of his hands. A shimmer appeared. It stretched until it encompassed all of her, then hardened, perfectly clear.

Alaric set his hand lightly on the crystal. Beneath it, Ayda's body lay perfectly still.

"Will it keep her like this forever?" Milly asked quietly

"Not forever," Alaric said. "But for a long time. It should take years for even the flowers to wilt." He studied the flowers for a moment. "I don't even know what sort of flowers those are. I wonder if they have any healing properties?" The question came out more out of habit than curiosity.

Evangeline peered down at the little purple flowers. "Those are Lumen Daisies. They grow everywhere in the Greenwood."

Alaric raised his eyebrow. "You've never been in the Greenwood."

Evangeline's brow creased and she looked up at Alaric. "I know. But I also know that these flowers have no medicinal value and are a favorite gift among the elves. They symbolize... home."

Alaric stared at her, an idea taking hold of him. "Why was the Elder Grove so powerful?" He tried to keep his eagerness under control.

"Because it was the burial ground for the first elven king and queen. They sacrificed themselves to the woods to create a place of power."

Alaric took both of her hands. "How much do you know? How much did Ayda tell you?"

Evangeline shook her head. “I don't know. I didn't know I knew any of that until you asked.”

Alaric grinned at her. “That's okay. I have a lot of questions.”

THE END

THE STORY CONTINUES...

The Keeper Chronicles continue in Book 2: **Pursuit of Shadows**, which tells the trouble Keeper Will has been having while Alaric's been searching for the Wellstone.

The prologue of **Pursuit of Shadows** is included at the end of this book.

FROM THE AUTHOR

Hello! Thanks for reading ***A Threat of Shadows.***

Alaric's story was my debut novel, and even several books later, I'm still terribly fond of these characters.

Being my debut, though, I made some mistakes.

The largest of which is that I wrapped up Alaric's story too well, tying up loose ends and giving him a—if not perfectly happy ending, one that hopefully satisfies.

But in wrapping it up, I left nothing to draw you on to book two, **Pursuit of Shadows**.

In my defense, I never really expected anyone to read ***Threat***, so why would I waste energy convincing a non-existing audience to continue on?

And yet here you are, one of the wonderfully kind people who gave an unknown author a chance, and enjoyed her debut enough to at least read the entire thing.

And I find myself in the unlucky predicament of having offered you nothing to convince you to pick up Book 2.

Except this:

Nearly everyone brave enough to grab book 2 loves it more than book 1.

We do leave Alaric and company (for a while at least) and join Will, a very different sort of Keeper in a desperate search for his missing sister.

So, um, I still have nothing more to tempt you with than the promise of another story in the same world with new characters and old, which I hope you love, if you take the chance.

A **review** is worth more to an author than the antidote to Rock Snake venom would have been to Alaric for…essentially this entire book.

Okay, maybe not *that* valuable but you get the idea.

If you enjoyed ***A Threat of Shadows*** and have the time to leave a review, you can do so on Amazon.

You can see a list of all my books on my website at jaandrews.com.

Thank you,

Janice

Tomkin and the Dragon

A bookish, unheroic hero, a maiden who's not remotely interested in being rescued, and a dragon who'd just like to eat them both.

"When they request a story from you,
tell *Tomkin and the Dragon*. I love that one."
~ Evangeline

If you'd like to read the story of Tomkin and the Dragon that came up several times in this book, it is published under the title ***A Keeper's Tale: The Story of Tomkin and the Dragon*** and you can find it for sale on Amazon.

Pursuit of Shadows - Keeper Chronicles Book 2
available September 2018

A vicious clan chief,
a suspicious ranger,
a swarm of frost goblins.
The list of things that could get Will killed keeps growing.

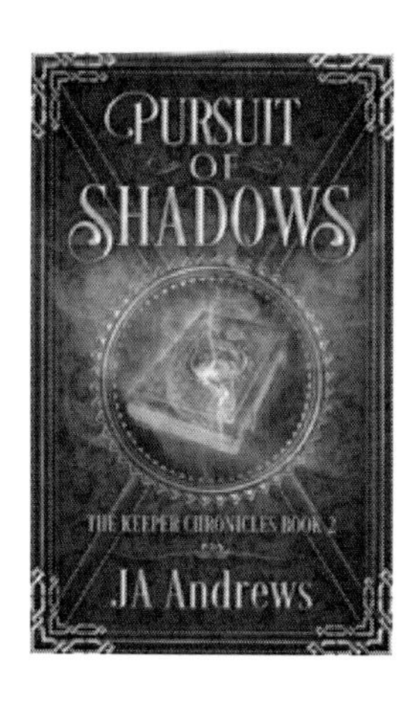

Keeper Will crossed the Scale Mountains to investigate rumors of a Shade Seeker gathering an army of nomads. But he should have been back by now.

Book 2 of The Keeper Chronicles follows Will on his journey through the Roven Sweep of the nomads. New characters and old friends meet up in the continuation of the Keepers' adventures.

To be notified when new books are published, you can sign up for JA Andrews' newsletter on her website, jaandrews.com.

Please enjoy this sneak peek at the prologue of ***Pursuit of Shadows.***

PURSUIT OF SHADOWS

THE KEEPER CHRONICLES BOOK 2

Prologue

THE AIR in the normally drab village square shivered with magic.

Will felt as though he'd stepped into a different world. More people than he'd ever seen were gathered together, the high-spirited crowd causing the weathered buildings around them to fade into the background. The nutty smell of roasted sorren seeds wafted out from the wayfarer's wagon, and Will's mother had bought him not one, but two sweet rolls.

Vahe of the Flames stood far back on the stage, surrounded by dark walls and an arched roof, his voice low as he told of three children trapped deep in the lair of a mountain troll. His fingers toyed slowly with a handful of fire, flickering just above his palm, seemingly burning nothing but air. Will couldn't pull his eyes away.

The wayfarer's black hair and pointed beard mixed with the shadows on the stage. His voice rolled out with dark menace as the trolls crept closer to the children. Will's fist clamped into the sticky dough of his sweet roll, and he leaned closer to his mother. When his arm brushed hers, a jab of disapproval flashed into his chest, off-center and too muted to be his own. His mother watched Vahe with the same sternness she turned on Will whenever he played too roughly with baby Ilsa.

Pulling his arm away from her, the feeling faded. He rubbed his skin as though he could erase the memory of it. It happened more and more often lately, these echoes of what other people were feeling when he touched them.

Vahe continued, his voice still low and foreboding but the spell had been broken. Will remembered that the stage was a wagon. Not a normal wagon—a wayfarer's wagon. Like a house with wheels. Except houses didn't come in dazzling colors, or have fronts that could lay open like a ramp, leading down to the village dirt. Vibrant ribbons fluttered from the edges of the roof, quivering brightly in the evening breeze, but inside, Vahe's dark orange flame lent a brooding feel to the shadows. It caught on unknown things, flashing back glints of burnished copper.

The tale ended with a quick escape by the children and Will's mother put her arm around his shoulder.

"Let's get home." Her disapproval rushed into him again, filling the left side of his chest and leaving a mildly sour taste in his mouth.

"But wayfarers never come here. And he might tell more stories."

"I've heard enough." Her tone made it clear the decision had been made. "Tussy needs milking. And that man takes entirely too much pleasure in frightening children."

Milking a goat was a terrible reason to leave. If only Tussy would run away one of the times she broke out of her pen. With a sigh he felt down to his toes, Will followed her, weaving through the crowd of villagers in the dusty square, hoping Vahe would start a story his mother would be interested in hearing.

Instead Vahe began to do tricks with the strange orange flame in his hand, making it appear and disappear, tossing it through the air, even dropping it onto a pile of dry grass without setting it aflame. He tossed it toward the crowd. It disappeared for a moment when it reached the sunlight, then Will caught a glimmer of it hovering over someone's head. It slid over another, and another, people's hands reaching up and passing through it unharmed. It came close and Will held his breath. When it shifted above Will, the top of his head tingled for a heartbeat. A jolt like lightning shot through him. Every bit of his skin stung like the prickles of a hundred tiny thorns, and the air around him shimmered with yellow light. The flame winked out and the sparkles disappeared

"The fire likes you, boy!" Vahe cried.

Will rubbed his hands across his arms, trying to brush away the last of the prickly feeling. The crowd oohed appreciatively, and Vahe started another trick. But Will's mother waited at the edge of the crowd, her mouth pressed into that thin line and her brow creased with worry.

The sun beat down on the dirt road leading out of the dingy village, and the whole way home through the low, winding hills, Will couldn't shake the tingly feeling that crawled across his skin.

At the edge of their yard the creak of the goat pen caught his attention. Tussy was shoving her little horns under the bar, pushing open the gate—again. The brand new shoots in the garden almost within her reach.

Will ran forward, stretching his hand out as though he could reach across the entire yard. Too far away to reach her, he could do nothing but hurl fury at the stupid goat for interrupting the storytelling, and for endlessly escaping her pen.

Except the fury *did* hurl out of his hand with a ripping pain and the gate slammed shut.

Agony stabbed up his arms and he dropped to his knees, his own cry of pain drowning out Tussy's insulted bleat. A new circle of winter-brown grass around him marred the summer yard, brittle and dry, like the old, worn out grass of fall.

Shiny blisters swelled on his palms and he curled forward, gasping and choking on the pain. Worry and pity washed over him like cool water even before his mother's arms wrapped around him.

"A Keeper," she whispered, looking from his hands to the withered grass. A fierce pride blazed up in Will and he sank against her, letting her emotions drown out his own fear and pain.

Hours later, he lay in the cool quiet of the cottage and the roiling turmoil in his chest was thankfully all his own. His parents and Ilsa slept in their curtained alcove, the barrage of emotions from them finally quiet. Since he'd closed the gate that had changed. He could feel everything they felt. No one had to touch him now, they only needed to be close.

He rubbed this thumb over the frayed edge of the cloth his mother had wrapped around his blistered hands, his mind spinning.

Magic. He'd done magic. He'd somehow sucked life out of the grass and used it to shut the gate.

The idea hung in the silent cottage both alien and obvious. Part of him was still shocked, but if he was honest, he knew something magical had been happening for months and months. Not with searing, hand-burning pain, but with mumbled, nudging hints. That empty, endless hollowness he'd felt when he shook hands with the butcher at his wife's funeral. Or the day they cheered as Ilsa took her first, wobbling steps—when Will's mother had grasped his shoulder, he thought his heart might burst into a million pieces.

But he couldn't really be a Keeper, could he?

He'd closed a gate from across the yard, and everyone knew the sign of new Keeper magic was burned hands. He stretched his fingers until shots of pain lanced across his palms. If he'd done magic, would the Keepers have to take him? His heart quickened. He'd get to go to the hidden Stronghold. He'd see the queen in her palace. He'd never have to weed the garden or milk Tussy. He'd be rich. He could buy his father a mule, and Ilsa a real doll instead of that ugly rag she carried everywhere.

Will pulled the thin blanket up to his chin, trying not to get too excited. He wasn't the sort of boy who became a Keeper. He was the sort of boy who could never get the goat pen to stay closed.

A foreign terror crashed into him, stronger and darker than anything he'd ever felt and he shrank down into his bed. He strained to hear any sound, but his father's snoring continued, low and steady, and nothing else stirred in the cottage.

He squeezed his eyes shut. *Please don't let me feel their dreams.*

The sensation swelled until he couldn't stay still any longer. He rolled out of bed and tiptoed toward the curtain. The sensation grew stronger. His breath grew shallow and his heart thrummed in his ears as though he stood atop a cliff—or being chased by something monstrous.

Will pulled the curtain back, desperate to wake them from such a nightmare.

Bright moonlight poured in the window, landing on the bed where his parents lay sleeping. Ilsa and her rag doll curled between them and the wall in a tangle of dark curls. All three were still.

But in the window above them perched a man with a black pointed beard.

Vahe.

Will froze, his hand clutching the curtain. Vahe's gaze snapped up, and Will's gut clenched, whether from his own fear or the wayfarer's, it was impossible to tell. A silver knife appeared in the man's hand, glinting in the moonlight. Slowly, the man raised a finger to his lips.

Will's breath caught in his throat. He needed to yell, scream, something. But his body refused to move.

Vahe shifted his grip on the knife until it pointed down at Tell's chest.

"Come with me, boy," he whispered, the words barely more than a rustle of wind.

The muscles of Vahe's arm rippled as he shifted the knife over the thin form of Will's parents. Even if Will woke them, they were no match for this man.

A fierce anger stirred in his gut, an anger all his own at this man for threatening them, for daring to come into their house. For being stronger than his parents.

Will stepped forward and let the curtain fall behind him.

He flexed his hands slightly. It had worked on the gate. He just needed to push Vahe out the window. Then he could lock the shutters and yell until the neighbors woke.

The desire to push the wayfarer grew stronger and stronger until it filled him, shoving out Vahe's storm of emotions. Every bit of Will wanted that wicked face, that silver knife, and that dreadful excitement out of his home. And out of himself. Will lifted one hand and pointed it toward the wayfarer. Pain shot across his palm as he focused all his fury at the man.

Vahe's eyes widened and he grabbed at the window, bracing himself. "Come," he ordered between clenched teeth. "No one needs to get hurt."

Will pushed harder until his palm burned and the wayfarer threw all his weight against the force of it. Vahe's black hair and beard blended into the night. Will could see only pale cheeks and glittering eyes.

A stray thought wandered across Will's mind, a memory of the withered grass this afternoon. Was the garden outside withering now, fueling whatever he was doing?

He didn't care.

Slowly, a finger's breadth at a time, Vahe slipped backwards.

A small gasp yanked Will's attention down. His mother lay on the bed in front of him, white as moonlight, gasping for breath, her fingers scrabbling against Will's other hand where he clutched her arm. Will snatched his hand back, and the fire racing through him stopped. His fury turned to horror.

It wasn't from the garden. He'd been pulling all that power out of her body.

Everything moved at once.

His mother took a deep, shuddering breath.

His father stirred.

Released from Will's fury, the wayfarer toppled forward, falling into the room, the knife slamming into Will's father's chest. His mother screamed and Ilsa woke, adding her small cries to the chaos. Terror and fury filled Will and he didn't know if it was his or theirs. Pain and panic and desire rushed in, threatening to tear him apart.

Vahe looked up from the knife, his face shocked. He reached toward Will again. "Come here, boy!" he hissed.

Will backed away from Vahe's anger, his mother's terror, and his father's too-still form.

A shout and pounding on the cottage door behind Will made the wayfarer's anger flare hotter. Vahe's eyes bored into Will, his fury thrumming in Will's chest.

Will's mother screamed for help. Vahe hurled a last glare at Will, then snatched up Ilsa. She cried, reaching out toward her mother, her dark curls pressed against Vahe's neck.

"Stop," Will pleaded, taking a step closer.

The door to the cottage splintered and flew open. Neighbors rushed into the small cottage, bringing in a frenzy of emotion.

The wayfarer yanked his bloody knife from Will's father's chest with a snarl. Still clutching Ilsa, Vahe plunged out the window, his anger tearing out of Will, leaving him hollow of everything but his mother's screams.

You can continue reading Will's story in **Pursuit of Shadows,** available on Amazon.

ACKNOWLEDGMENTS

Thank you to Cheryl Schuetze for your unending patience with my questions, rants, insecurities, and updates through phone calls, emails, texts, and any other form of communication I could think of to bother you with. Your help has been invaluable.

To the Fantasy Faction, thank you for the excellent critiques and the camaraderie. Special thanks to GL Burke, Caroline Sciriha, Sherry Bessette, Joey Harpel, Sam Taylor, Morgyn Star, and Rod Santos for all your input. Without the group, this book would still be a random collection of chapters that don't quite work together.

To Shelley "Sherlock" Holloway, thank you for your amazing editing, your eye for detail, your patience with my semi-scatterbrained ways, and all the commas.

Thank you, Dane, at eBook Launch for the beautiful cover, which you made despite being given feedback that involved words like "froofy."

Thank you Ren for the beautiful map and Wojtek Depczynski for the amazing artwork.

And most of all, thank you to my husband. You've been unfailingly supportive and generous while I've tried to wrangle this book into shape. And you've been more than patient, waiting for almost a decade to actually read this story. I hope you enjoy reading it as much as I enjoyed writing it. I love you.

ABOUT THE AUTHOR

JA Andrews is a writer, wife, mother, and unemployed rocket scientist. She doesn't regret the rocket science degree, but finds it generally inapplicable in daily life. Except for the rare occurrence of her being able to definitively state, "That's not rocket science." She does, however, love the stars.

She spends an inordinate amount of time at home, with her family, who she adores, and lives deep in the Rocky Mountains of Montana, where she can see more stars than she ever imagined.

For more information:

www.jaandrews.com

jaandrews@jaandrews.com

facebook.com/JAAndrewsAuthor